A. Patchett Martin

Life and Letters of the Right Honourable Robert Lowe, Viscount

Sherbrooke

Volume I

A. Patchett Martin

Life and Letters of the Right Honourable Robert Lowe, Viscount Sherbrooke
Volume I

ISBN/EAN: 9783337017514

Printed in Europe, USA, Canada, Australia, Japan

Cover: Foto ©Raphael Reischuk / pixelio.de

More available books at **www.hansebooks.com**

LIFE AND LETTERS

OF THE

RIGHT HONOURABLE ROBERT LOWE

VISCOUNT SHERBROOKE, G.C.B., D.C.L.

ETC.

WITH A MEMOIR OF SIR JOHN COAPE SHERBROOKE, G.C.B.
SOMETIME GOVERNOR-GENERAL OF CANADA

BY

A. PATCHETT MARTIN

IN TWO VOLUMES—VOLUME I.

WITH PORTRAITS

LONDON
LONGMANS, GREEN, AND CO.
AND NEW YORK: 15 EAST 16th STREET
1893

TO

CAROLINE, VISCOUNTESS SHERBROOKE

IN THE HOPE THAT SOME MEASURE OF SUCCESS

MAY HAVE ATTENDED

MY EARNEST ENDEAVOUR

TO MAKE A GREAT ENGLISHMAN RIGHTLY UNDERSTOOD

BY HIS COUNTRYMEN

THIS WORK IS RESPECTFULLY DEDICATED

PREFACE

THE small amount of time and pains which Lord Sherbrooke bestowed on his Autobiography may be gathered from a perusal of the brief personal memoir which forms the Introduction to these volumes.

When, however, it was represented to him that his share in the formation of contemporary history would be of interest to the public, he readily assented to the preparation of this work, and rendered whatever assistance was in his power. It is true that the imperfect measure of sight, which he had once enjoyed, had entirely deserted him; but he retained his lifelong habit of attention to every subject presented to him, and his criticism on what was read was always valuable and suggestive of further sources of information.

It is superfluous to record the obligations I am under to the relations and intimate friends of Lord and Lady Sherbrooke. Their kindly aid has been invaluable; and without it, the accomplishment of my task would have been impossible. Those who knew Lord Sherbrooke well regarded him with a sincere affection which made their co-operation a labour of love. But on the part of a very large number of correspondents at home

and abroad, from whom I had little to expect, I have met with
an evident anxiety to further the work, which, though due to
their esteem for Lord Sherbrooke, leaves me under a heavy
debt of personal obligation.

Several of Lord Sherbrooke's old friends and contemporaries
have favoured me with written reminiscences, which I have
embodied in this work, while others have communicated their
information verbally. In the former category I must especially
mention Lord Sherbrooke's schoolfellow, Lord Selborne, who
has been good enough to contribute his narrative of an unbroken
friendship of over sixty years. Professor Jowett, the Master
of Balliol, has sent me a personal memoir of one who was to
him much more than a statesman—the fine scholar and close
friend, to whom he thought fit to dedicate his Thucydides.
With these should be linked the name of Canon Melville, with
whom Lord Sherbrooke enjoyed the happiness of an uninter-
rupted intercourse extending from Oxford days to the last
months of his life.

Among another group of friends whose intimacy commenced in the drier regions of official intercourse and ripened
into warm friendship, I would name Sir John Simon, K.C.B.,
author of *English Sanitary Institutions*, who was for many
years associated with Lord Sherbrooke in the initiation and
subsequent work of the Medical Department of the Privy
Council. I have left Sir John's clear and concise statement of
that relationship to stand, as he has written it—in my humble
judgment an invaluable record of a noble joint achievement.

From Sir Rivers Wilson, Sir Thomas Farrer, Lord Thring,
and other notable men who have been officially associated

with Lord Sherbrooke, I have received most valuable assistance. I am under special obligation to Sir Douglas Galton,
the friend and travelling companion of Lord Sherbrooke on
his American and Canadian tour of 1856. Acknowledgment
must also be made to Mr. Cotterell Tupp, formerly of the
Indian Civil Service; to the Hon. Lionel Tollemache for the
kind offer of his unpublished manuscript reminiscences; to
Mr. Topham Hough, for the very interesting Pedigrees to be
found at the close of the second volume; as well as to General
Sneyd for papers and notes concerning the Kidderminster
riots, kept by him at the time.

Of those who have courteously placed letters at my disposal,
letters of especial value in the case of one to whom correspondence was so difficult, I am greatly indebted to Lord
Sherbrooke's sisters and to Mrs. Sherbrooke of Oxton. Among
others whose kindness in this respect must be specially
acknowledged, I must mention the Duchess of St. Albans, the
Earl and Countess of Derby, Canon Melville, Mr. Gladstone,
the Marchioness of Lansdowne, the Countess Granville, the
Countess of Airlie, Sir F. B. Outram, Sir Archibald and Lady
Dunbar, Mrs. Michell, Archdeacon Boyd, the late Sir George
Macleay, Sir William Windeyer, and Mrs. Billyard of Sydney.

Among other correspondents to whom I am indebted for
aid and sympathy are—the Earl of Cranbrook, the Earl of
Wemyss, Mr. Goschen, the late Dr. Charles Wordsworth, the
Dean of Westminster, Rev. E. S. Ffoulkes, Sir William Smith,
Sir John Lubbock, Sir Richard Quain, Professor J. A. Froude,
Mr. Henry Reeve, Sir John Pender, Colonel Capel Coape,
Sir Juland Danvers, Lord Lingen, Sir Reginald Welby,

Rev. Wm. Rogers, Dr. Richard Congreve, Mr. R. A. Macfie, Mr. Edward Jenkins, Mr. T. B. Boulton, Rev. J. Pickford, Professor Goldwin Smith, and Mr. Moberly Bell.

The kindness of Mrs. Chaworth Musters in sending her correspondence with her uncle, has been supplemented by her personal recollections of Lord Sherbrooke, and by much valuable incidental information with regard to the family history of the Lowes and Sherbrookes.

Following the *Life and Letters of Robert Lowe, Viscount Sherbrooke*, will be found a brief memoir of Sir John Coape Sherbrooke, G.C.B. For the papers and documents on which this narrative is mainly based, I am indebted to Mrs. Sherbrooke of Oxton. It is here necessary that I should acknowledge the courtesy of the present Duke of Wellington in giving permission, through the late Lord Sherbrooke, for the publication in this memoir of two unpublished letters, written by his illustrious grandfather to Sir John Sherbrooke during the Peninsular War.

I have only to add that my task has been greatly facilitated by the fact that all documents, family and private letters and papers connected with the late Viscount Sherbrooke, have been placed unreservedly in my hands.

A. PATCHETT MARTIN.

London: *March* 1893.

CONTENTS

OF

THE FIRST VOLUME

CHAPTER XXVII

THE CLOSING YEAR IN AUSTRALIA

ILLUSTRATIONS

ERRATUM

Page 64, *line* 15, *for* July 28, *read* July 27.

LIFE

OF

THE RIGHT HON. ROBERT LOWE

VISCOUNT SHERBROOKE

——◆——

INTRODUCTION

THE life of Robert Lowe, Viscount Sherbrooke, falls naturally into three epochs—Oxford, Sydney and London were, in turn, the scenes of his active life, and no higher testimony is needed to the greatness and versatility of his powers than the fact that in fields so dissimilar he reaped the highest distinction. Differing, however, as they did in other respects, these epochs of his life had one point in common : they were periods of incessant labour. Such a life, even under ordinary circumstances, leaves little leisure for retrospect, but, handicapped as he was by semi-blindness, the accomplishment of each day's task was sufficient without the toil of recording it.

Lord Sherbrooke had, moreover, a positive repugnance to autobiography. It savoured to him of egotism ; and it is solely due to the intervention of friends that he left even the brief and incomplete memoir which is here appended. Written in the interval of comparative rest which followed his resignation of office in 1876, it is marked by his habitual directness.

With characteristic energy, this memoir was 'type-written' by his own hand. Even towards the close of life, and with his all but total want of sight, Lord Sherbrooke took a certain delight in mastering our latter-day mechanical contrivances.

This chapter of autobiography, it will be seen, is a rapid retrospect of his entire life. At first it seemed the better plan to begin this work in the usual way, with a full account of his birth, parentage, education, and public career, weaving in from his own memoir the 'purple patches' of his vigorous phrases and apt allusions. By this means a certain order and continuity in the narrative might have been preserved. But after careful reflection, it was felt to be unfair to such a man as Lord Sherbrooke to break up, or in any way remodel his all too brief personal reminiscences. Here, in these few pages, we have at least his own account of those events and incidents in his life which he most vividly recalled in old age—the rough schooldays at Winchester, the studious years at Oxford, the chance meetings with Wordsworth and Darwin, the call to the Bar, the threatened total blindness, the long voyage to Australia. Here, too, he pays his pathetic tribute of affection to his wife, the faithful companion and constant helpmate in his darkest as in his happiest hours; and here he passes a singularly unbiassed judgment on his remarkable and in a sense unprecedented career, in which he gives his own explanation of his one striking failure—the failure to win the passing plaudits of the multitude in a democratic age.

A CHAPTER OF AUTOBIOGRAPHY

If, as is generally and not without good reason assumed, the success of an undertaking is proportionate to the care and labour employed in preparing for it, I confess I do not enter on the task of autobiography under very favourable conditions. During the course of an active and laborious life it never occurred to me that there was anything in it which was worth handing down to posterity. I never was able to understand the use of keeping accounts or keeping a journal. Accounts are, of course, indispensable to those who are entrusted with other people's money, but why a man should keep accounts against himself, I never could understand. It never occurred to me that anyone else would want to know what I said or what I did, and as for myself it always appeared to me that every one is inclined to talk and think a great deal too much about him or herself. Egotism, in fact, appeared to me just one of those tendencies of human nature which least of all require to be encouraged.

I have kept no correspondence. I must also confess that my defect of sight is no slight disqualification; of its greatness those who have had no experience can form little idea. It is one of those subjects about which it is impossible to deceive oneself. Besides, I have never found my chief pleasure in society; why then should I undertake a task for which I profess no particular vocation, and for which I have neglected to store up much information which was once in my power? I have two reasons: I have been pressed by many friends to

leave behind me some account of a life which they are good
enough to say they believe is sufficiently out of the common
track to be worth recording ; I also am vain enough to believe
that a narrative of the very great difficulties with which I have
had to contend and which I have contrived to surmount, may
possibly be useful to some who are inclined to throw up the
cards before the game is lost, and to impute to adverse fortune
the result of their own want of steadiness and enterprise.

I was born at Bingham, a small town in the south of
Nottinghamshire, of which my father was the Rector, on
December 4th, 1811. I was a younger son, one of six children.
The living was a good one, and my father had some property
of his own. My mother was the daughter of the Rev.
Reginald Pyndar, rector of Madresfield, near Malvern.

I had the misfortune (which I share with a sister older
than myself) to be what is called an albino. I presume
there is no one so entirely free from personal vanity as to be
able, without some feeling of reluctance, to discourse on his
physical defects and infirmities. But happily, not having been
endowed by Nature with a poetical temperament or having a
special gift for self-torture, I have contrived to bear this infliction with tolerable equanimity. My poor sister was not
so fortunate ; she was, I think, the gentlest and the best person
I ever knew, but was very keenly alive to this misfortune.
Had I felt my peculiarities as she did, anything like public or
even active life would have been to me an impossibility ; but,
putting sentiment aside, the misfortune was serious enough.

The peculiarity of my eyes consists in the total absence of
colouring matter ; this occasions, of course, especially in a
man, a very marked peculiarity of complexion, amounting in
early youth to something of effeminacy. For this evil, however, I have found age a sovereign cure ; but as the absence
of colouring matter extends to the eye, it necessarily occasions
a great impatience of light. The eyelids must always be
nearly closed, and so I never have been able to enjoy the

luxury of staring anyone full in the face. Of course this intolerance of light must be attended with something very closely approaching to pain. I cannot even conceive the state of a person to whom sight is a function free from all pain and distress, but as I have no standard to measure by I may perhaps exaggerate my own misfortune. The cause of this annoyance is the total absence of what is called the *pigmentum nigrum*, the dark rim which surrounds the pupil of the eye and absorbs the rays of light which are not needed for the act of vision, and only confuse and disturb it. But, in addition to this defect, I had to contend with a malformation of the eye; one eye has never been available to me for reading, and the other was hypermetropic—that is, the refracting power was so slight that the focus must be very near the back of my head. I began life, in fact, very much in the state of persons who have been couched for cataract, with the two additional disqualifications that I had only one eye to rely upon, and that had no *pigmentum nigrum* to protect it.

So hopeless did my visual prospects appear that I was six years old before any attempt was made to teach me my letters. Of course, the natural remedy for my sight would have been to use strong magnifying spectacles such as are recommended to persons who have been couched for a cataract. I do not know if such an idea was ever entertained, but I have every reason to be glad that it was not acted on, for experience has proved that the eye was quite unable to bear it.

As it was, my progress was so slow that I was eight years old before I began the great business of life—in other words, entered on the study of the Latin Grammar. So great was the difficulty I found in the beginning of my career that my mother was of opinion I was quite unfit to be sent to school, and that there was no chance for me in the open arena of life. Happily for me, my father formed a truer estimate of the case, and it was decided that the experiment should be tried. I, at least, was never troubled with any misgivings. Nature had given me as some compensation for many deficiencies excellent health, good spirits, an easy temper, and a heart which has never failed me in all my trials and difficulties.

The first public event which I remember was the death of the Princess Charlotte, and my surprise at the extreme grief felt by everyone around me for a person whom they had never seen, and I had never heard of. I remember, also, being much affected by the death of Napoleon, though, as I derived my first knowledge of his career from Sir Walter Scott's *Biography*, I do not know whence I derived my sentiment. I enjoyed the privilege and delight of reading all the writings of the author of *Waverley* after the *Heart of Mid-Lothian* as they came out, a literary pleasure which nothing since has ever equalled. I may mention to my credit that I never doubted that Scott was the author: the ground of my belief was a quotation which is to be found in *The Bride of Lammermoor* and in the notes to *The Lady of the Lake.*

> If thou be hurt with horn of hart
> It brings thee to thy bier,
> But barbers' hand boar's tusk can cure,
> Therefore thou need not fear.

I argued that if the poem and the novel had been written by different hands, the quotation would have been acknowledged by the writer of the novel who might well forget that he had inserted it in a note. I was always very positive as to Scott's authorship of the novels, and received some not unmerited rebukes from my elders and betters for presuming to set my opinion against persons who must know so much better than I. I hope I bore my victory with becoming moderation, but am by no means clear on the point. Our life was a very secluded one. Our nearest, and indeed almost our only, neighbour was the family of Mr. Musters, the husband of Byron's Mary. A visit to my grandfather in Herefordshire in summer, and to Mr. Sherbrooke of Oxton, whose estate has now passed into the hands of my eldest brother, were almost

the only breaks in the monotony of our existence. I did not
shine as a playfellow, and so reading, which had been my
great difficulty, became my great pleasure.

In 1822 I went to school at Southwell, where my father's
family once lived and where many of them are buried. There
is one of them, one Gervase Lee, in whom I always took a particular interest because he was fined 500*l.* by Archbishop
Laud in the Star Chamber for writing a scurrilous ballad on
the Canons of the Cathedral church of Southwell. I used to
fancy that some shreds of his mantle had descended on me,
though candour obliges me to confess that his performance
was utterly without literary merit, and according to the rule
of Horace—' *si mala condiderit in quem quis carmina jus est
judiciumque* '—the poet richly deserved all he got.

I spent two years at Southwell, and one year at a school
at Risley in Derbyshire, and in September 1825 I went to
Winchester as a commoner. This was a most important
epoch of my life ; anybody can get on somehow at a private
school, but a public school to a person labouring under such
disabilities as I did was a crucial test under any circumstances,
and Winchester, such as it was in my time, was an ordeal
which a boy so singular in appearance, and so helpless in
some respects as I was, might well have trembled to encounter.
Since my time the buildings which we occupied have been
pulled down, the hours have been altered, and what I write
now has no application to the Winchester of the present day,
but such as it was in my time I will describe it for the benefit
of boys who think they are badly treated.

The school consisted of 200 boys ; 70 collegers and 130
commoners. The collegers were well lodged and fed, had an
excellent playground, and the run of the schoolroom when the
masters were out of it. In commoners things were very different ; the bedrooms were shamefully crowded, there was a very
small court—reference being had to the number of boys who
were shut up in it—there was a hall of very moderate dimen-

sions, considering that in it we lived, studied, and had our
meals, there was generally a game of cricket going on, and as
my cupboard happened to be what is technically called 'middle
on,' the pursuit of the Muses was attended with some difficulty.
I have often said to myself—'*I nunc et rersus tecum meditare
canoros.*'

In these miserable quarters much of the time which was
not spent in school was passed. We were expected to be
down at six in summer and a quarter to seven in winter; we
went into school at half-past seven and stayed there till ten,
then we had breakfast—bread as much as we could eat, a pat
of butter each, and one pail of milk among 130 boys, for this
we made a *queue*, every fag with his jug. Occasionally, when
the competition was more than ordinarily severe, the pail was
upset, and the school went milkless to breakfast. Tea and
sugar we might find for ourselves if we had the money, they
were sold to us at the buttery hatch on account of whom it
might concern. We went into school from eleven till twelve,
from twelve to one was our play hour; the field was half a
mile off, so that to make the most of it we usually ran there
and back and came in streaming with perspiration. At one
we dined! At two we went into school, where we remained
till six, then supper— bread and cheese and beer, then work
in the hall till half-past eight, then to bed. Twice a week we
had what was called a 'remedy'—I suppose because it was
worse than the disease, applying that name to the ordinary
school days,—we were marched two and two to the hill a
mile off, and in consideration of this airing were shut up in
the hall for four hours. Sunday was a particularly miserable
day; two hours in chapel, nearly three in the cathedral, one
hour to walk, and the rest shut up in our court and hall.

It will be seen from this statement that we fasted from
seven o'clock in the evening till half-past ten in the morning;
that four hours and a half were interposed between rising and
breakfast; that we had no food for breakfast but bread; that

we dined three hours after breakfast and immediately after an hour of violent exercise. The result may be easily imagined —we were ravenous at breakfast and there was nothing but bread to eat unless we had pocket money to buy food; out of breath and reeking with perspiration we loathed our dinner, and it was only when in school that we felt hunger which there was no means of appeasing for hours, and then with the (to gentlemen's children) uncongenial fare of bread and cheese. Our pocket money, as long as it lasted, went in buying the food with which we ought to have been supplied, and when that was gone we bore our loss as best we could, only too happy if we could coax a colleger to impart to us something from his comparatively liberal dietary.

We were, it will be observed, never alone by day or by night, so that the power that one boy possessed to annoy another was almost boundless. We were, besides, debarred of our natural liberty, and the high spirits of youth, missing their natural vent, found employment in mutual torment. Into this place such as I have described it, I was introduced at the rather advanced age of thirteen. I was placed in the second class in the school, and thus escaped fagging. I was strong and healthy, and did not greatly care for our meagre fare : nor, I must say for myself, did I ever make any complaint of anything or anybody ; but the ordeal I had to go through was nevertheless really terrible. For the purposes of relieving the weary hours of enforced society I was invaluable. No one was so dull as to be unable to say something rather smart on my peculiarities, and my short sight offered almost complete immunity to my tormenters. This went on, as well as I can remember, for about a year and a half, and then, as even the most delightful amusements pall by repetition, it died out.

Two things I may mention as rather remarkable ; one, that though I believe never accused of a want of physical courage, I never fought a battle ; the other, that though I suffered so severely from torments of all kinds, I never felt at the time or afterwards any ill-will towards my persecutors. I never deceived myself as to my personal peculiarities, and I think I had sense enough to see that, situated as we were under conditions which made us all more or less miserable, I could have nothing better to expect; ill-fed, shut up, or forced as it were upon each other, I have no doubt that much of what happened was inevitable. At any rate, I had effectually solved the problem as to whether I was able to hold my own in life, and proved by a most crucial experiment that I was not too sensitive nor too soft for the business.

The present Lord Selborne was next to me in the class, and as there was no taking of places, he continued there. I do not think this would have been the case otherwise, as he was a very clever boy, much more industrious than I, and had a father who made him work during vacations. In my fourth half-year, though I was only half-way up in my class, I gained the second prize, and was in consequence promoted to the first class a year before my time.

Latin and Greek had now become easy to me, and I contented myself with my lessons and spent the rest of my time in reading English, which I thought at the time a great piece of idleness, but have since learnt to consider some of the best spent hours of my life, for it was thus I learnt the art of speaking and writing correctly, to which I owe almost everything.

In the fourth year of my residence at Winchester, I became a prefect. As this institution still exists, and has drawn upon itself no little public notice, I will say a few words about it, and should be very glad if anything I can say shall draw renewed attention to the subject. It will be gathered from what I have already said that the school was conducted with a view to make the expenses to the Master as small as possible. We had only two men-servants to wait on 130 boys; of course it followed that in a similar spirit there were not enough masters to do the work, and one reason why we were so unmercifully long in school was the want of more masters, and the consequent impossibility of a subdivision of classes.

The result was that a good deal of the discipline of the school was entrusted to the prefects; they had to keep order, and as a reward for thus doing the duty of under-masters, were invested with personal inviolability, besides the power of fagging the other boys as before mentioned. Thus I found myself at the mature age of sixteen invested with infinitely more power, with infinitely less control, than I have ever had since. A stick was put into my hand, and I had to walk up and down the hall and keep silence by applying the said stick to the back of any boy whose voice or conduct disturbed the silence of 130 boys. I had besides the power of tunding, a punishment far more severe than that of flogging, which was in fact little better than a farce. I do not think that at first, at any rate, I abused my new power. I had no great zeal for the discipline of the school, which I not unreasonably considered was no affair of mine. But an event happened which entirely changed this state of affairs.

The senior prefect had made himself unpopular with the boys, and on one occasion when he was about to inflict a tunding the boys rescued his intended victim from his grasp. Of course we, his colleagues, thought the world was coming to an end, and in truth we had some sort of ground for our indignation, for it was obviously impossible for us to maintain the discipline of the school, which most improperly, as I think, was confided to us, if we were not invested with the inviolability of the Roman tribunes. So we made our complaint to the head master, and he very injudiciously expelled the poor boy, who had been guilty of the offence of causing a rescue. I cannot help thinking that a much lighter punishment would have been quite enough for an offence which had in it no really serious delinquency, and that it would have been wise to consider a little more seriously the results of such a measure. The boys (though I really think that under the provocation

they behaved at least as well as could be expected) were not
unnaturally very angry.   They made us feel this in every way
they safely could ; we on our side were not slow to retaliate,
and thus, as Hume says of the days of the Popish plot, the
two parties within the narrow limits of the law vented against
each other their mutual animosity.

At last things grew so serious that my colleagues became
frightened, and gradually more and more indulgent, till at
last the boys were allowed to do pretty much as they pleased.
I am not aware that any very bad results followed, and looking
at the matter from this distance of time, I am not at all sure
that I should not have done better to have followed their
example.

If I could have persuaded myself that there was any
generosity in it I might have yielded, but I was perfectly aware
that any relaxation of the reins would be imputed to fear, and
to that I could not bring myself to consent.   The half year
ended without any change, and on the re-assembling of the
school after Christmas holidays, the headmaster communicated
to us his wish that the discipline of the school should be
relaxed.   To this I most joyfully acceded, and content that it
should be known to the school that I acted not under fear
but under the express directions of the headmaster, I for a
half year let them do just as they pleased.   I cannot help
thinking that however economical or convenient it may be to
put a stick into the hand of a boy of sixteen and allow him to
use it upon his schoolfellows, it is neither fair on the tunder
nor the tunded.   If servants are wanted they ought to be
supplied from some other source than the junior scholars, and
if more masters are wanted they ought to be supplied from
some other source than the senior boys.

I left Winchester after four years' residence, and in October
1829 went up to reside at University College, Oxford.   It
would be ungrateful of me to part from Winchester without
recording my gratitude to my tutor, Mr. Wickham.   He was,

as far as I may presume to judge, an excellent scholar, and, what to a boy of my temperament, smarting under much undeserved ill-usage, was more important, he really took an interest in me and spurred me on to exertion. I never shall forget the pleasure in the midst of all that I had to endure to find that there was some one, and that, a person placed so high above me, who did not despise me for being unlike other people, and who took a hearty interest in my success. I had a great wish for knowledge of all kinds. I learnt from my mother and aunts a little French and Italian, and I had a great desire to learn mathematics. But this failed because the mathematical master at Winchester had never pursued his studies beyond the Fourth Book of Euclid. I do not think that such knowledge as I obtained of Latin and Greek was of the kind best suited to make a figure in examinations. I had very little acquaintance with the writers on the niceties of the learned languages, and consequently was at a great disadvantage at examinations as they were then conducted. It was also an intolerable labour to me to look out words in a dictionary. My plan, which was almost unconsciously forced on me by necessity, was to make myself, as far as I could, thoroughly master of what I read by every means in my power. If there was a question of the meaning of a word, I could always tell the passage where it occurred in any author that I had read. I was within the limits of my reading a complete dictionary of parallel passages. Thus what I knew was all my own, and was exactly proportioned to the amount of my reading : there was no cram in it, and, if not very showy, it was solid, resting upon a genuine basis—the very words of the author— and their comparison with and correction by other passages. I suppose the truth is that this plan, which necessity forced upon me, was good as far as it went, but would never have led to any real eminence as a scholar, though it satisfied my aspirations as a student, and was sufficient for my requirements as a teacher.

The change from Winchester to Oxford was delightful. It was a change from perpetual noise and worry to quiet, from imprisonment to freedom, from an odious pre-eminence to a fair and just equality. I was delighted with the kindness of my companions, and for the first year I did very little more than thoroughly enjoy the change. Mine was not in those days a reading college, and the tutors told me very fairly and very truly that the greatest kindness they could show me was to dispense with my attendance at their lectures. That year is the only period in my life during which I can tax myself with idleness, and though I look back with regret at the thoughtlessness which could so waste my opportunities, I cannot greatly wonder that I yielded to the temptation. I came up at the commencement of my second year full of good resolutions, to which, on the whole, I very fairly adhered. I determined to take a double first-class and set to work accordingly. This was a great mistake. A first-class in classics was easily within my reach with moderate industry, but a first-class in mathematics was to me a very difficult, and on looking back I might almost say an impossible, undertaking. The pursuit of this *ignis fatuus* occupied by far the largest part of my time at Oxford, and the labour of two long vacations, and probably prevented my obtaining any of the minor University distinctions. It was not, I think, that I had any especial difficulty in understanding mathematics, though I must confess to rather an awkward symptom, a desire like that of Macaulay, to argue the point and to contend that what I was told was conclusive reasoning, was not conclusive at all. I still believe that many of the conclusions of mathematics are more certain than the premisses ; when we know that a conclusion is true and that all the steps of the demonstration except one are also true, we know the excepted position must be true whether the reason we give for its truth be true or not. Thus I imagine that most persons are much more certain that two *minus* quantities multiplied together produce a *plus* than they are of the cogency of the argument by which this position is sought to be proved. At any rate, I had no decided aptitude for mathematics, and I could not have selected any study in which my defective sight told so heavily against me. Small diagrams and figures were to me a species of torture; they absorbed in the effort to see them the attention that was needed to understand them. When I came to write them out matters were still worse. It was a great triumph if I could make my writing intelligible to myself and very improbable that I should make it intelligible to others. I had a most excellent tutor in Mr. Walker; indeed, the only fault I have to find with him is that he thought much too well of his pupil and fully believed that I should have triumphed over difficulties with which I really was quite unable to cope. I believe that what Horace says of drunkenness is true of physical defects, and that the faculties corresponding to defective organs become themselves enfeebled. *Corpus onustum naturæ ritiis animam quoque prægravat una atque affigit humi divinæ particulum auræ.*

Thus I apprehend bad sight impairs the power of observation, and bad hearing of attention. I must console myself with the reflection that though a mistake as regards university distinction, the study of mathematics was probably the soundest and most sensible part of my education, as being the key to the study of physics.

On looking back on this part of my life I am much struck with the utter absence of anyone within my reach to whom I could apply for advice in these and similar questions. It is mortifying to think how much waste of time and, what is still more valuable, eyesight, I might have been saved if I had had the good luck to meet with some one who possessed the experience that I so much needed to advise me how to turn my very slender, and, as it then seemed, precarious means of acquiring information to the best account. My cotemporaries were mostly country gentlemen or embryo clergymen whose ambition was centred on the not very difficult object of obtaining a degree as a necessary preliminary to taking orders. My object should have been to have found for myself pursuits which depended more on the mind than the eye, but I never thought of such things, and it would have been a good fortune which I had no right to expect had I found anyone capable of looking so far beyond the narrow routine of a University as to think of them for me.

The first thing that brought me into notice at Oxford was a burlesque poem on a visit paid by the Duchess of Kent and the Princess Victoria to the University in 1833. I had been reading the macaronic poems of Dr. Geddes, and was seized with a desire to emulate him. The best I can say of my performance is that it succeeded, having gone through seven editions; that it contained a true prophecy, that Her Majesty would reign thirty years, and that having succeeded so far beyond my expectations and deserts, I had the good sense not to try my fortune again in a vein which owes so much to mere novelty and eccentricity, and of which the public ear would so soon tire. As it has been long out of print, I subjoin a copy.[1]

Another source for me if not of fame at least of notoriety, was the Union Debating Society. At that time it was peculiarly fortunate in its leading members; Gladstone, Sidney Herbert, Lord Lincoln, Gaskell, Tait, Palmer, Cardwell, Rickards, Anstice, Massie, Trevor and others, whose names I do not recall at the moment, formed a brilliant assemblage of talent and eloquence whose early promise has since been amply fulfilled.

We were in what appeared to wiser and more experienced heads than ours to be the full tide of revolution. Many speeches were made which would not have disgraced, and some that would have adorned, a Parliamentary debate. I well remember the first time I heard Gladstone speak. It was on the

[1] See pp. 88–90.

emancipation of the slaves in the West Indies. As far as mere elocution went he spoke just as well as he does now in 1876. He had taken just as much pains with the details of his subject as he would have if he had been Secretary of State for the Colonies. He did not launch into commonplaces about the rights of man, but he proposed a well-considered and carefully prepared scheme of gradual emancipation. It is not too much to say that even then he gave full promise of all which he has since achieved. I remember that I proposed that the King ought to make new Peers in order to pass the Reform Bill, and that I could only get four people to vote with me. Subsequently I had a good deal to do with the memorable schism of the Rambler. The Union Society had elected a president against whom there was no serious objection, but who was not a *persona grata* to some of its principal members. This was after most of the stars I have mentioned had set. The dissentients, instead of taking their defeat in good humour after the manner of Englishmen, resolved to set up an opposition society which was to be called the Rambler, at the same time retaining their position in the old society. The obnoxious president sought my help. I thought, as I still think (and forty years have not obliterated the impression), that he was very ill used. I am not so sure about the measure we took. We proposed that the members of the new society should elect between the new society and the old. We had a furious debate and failed to carry our motion. People cooled down —they saw that the thing had a ludicrous as well as a tragic side, and the matter is now principally remembered by a mock Homeric poem, by several authors, in which the present most learned Dean of Rochester, Scott, bore a distinguished part —a wit before he was a lexicographer. *Debita Trojanis exercet spicula fatis.*

But how shall I relate my own share in the transaction ? It was my task to open the debate, which I do not doubt that I did with quite as much bitterness as the occasion required.

Afterwards the president, the Helen who had made this war, rose to speak, and I, as a librarian, took the chair. The speaker met with considerable interruption, and among others from Mr. Tait of Balliol, the future Archbishop of Canterbury, and I, not being, it is to be feared, in a very judicial mood, fined the future Head of the Church 1*l*. for disorderly conduct. The rule was that at the end of the year an appeal lay against this decision, at which Tait and I fought it out, and my ruling was maintained by a very small majority. So I hope I was right, but am by no means confident.

Nature gave me a strong, almost childish, taste for all sorts of sports and games, but she in a great measure cancelled the gift by denying me the power of taking part in them. Water, that is, swimming, furnished me with my only amusement at Winchester, and the same element provided me with my principal amusement at Oxford in the more agreeable and athletic exercise of rowing. Even now I am conscious of some childish vanity in recording that I was chosen one of the crew of the University in a match which we were to row against Cambridge. I was entrusted with the important place of 'seven,' and as the match never came off, I may assume that I should have distinguished myself highly, without the possibility of contradiction. At any rate, though our boats were of very primitive construction, we should have rowed our match at Henley instead of Hammersmith, in the presence of the inhabitants of the little country town and the gentlemen and ladies of the neighbourhood, instead of in a whirlpool of steamers and the roar of thousands of spectators. We should have escaped the comments of newspapers on our skill and strength, and no money would have changed hands on the event.

I remember when I was at Oxford I was a great advocate for all athletic sports, but I am bound to say my wishes have been more than gratified. The facility of transport has made these matches public instead of private affairs, the public schools, always on the look-out to find some excuse to lighten the labours of teaching, have placed cricket at least on a level with the ordinary studies of the place, and the little that is taught is made less in order to indulge the silly vanity of parents, and to open to dulness also its road to fame.

A dunce at Euclid, and a dab at taw.

I spent the long vacation of 1831 reading mathematics with a tutor at Barmouth, a singularly beautiful place. This expedition was memorable to me for several reasons. In going there we, that is my elder brother and myself, passed over the Liverpool and Manchester Railway a few months after it was opened. People who have been brought up to railways cannot conceive the wonder, delight, and astonishment that such a journey occasioned ; it was as if the Arabian Nights had suddenly become true. I can never forget the delight of the passage or the agony of thinking how soon it would be over ; then there was the sight of the Menai Bridge, then, and perhaps still, one of the wonders of the world, and as beautiful as wonderful ; then the drive under Snowdon with Gray's Ode in my mind, and the glorious sail from Tremadoc to Barmouth across the Bay of Carnarvon. It was Nature and Art opening on us all at once for the first time. Here also, though last, not least, I met with the lady who afterwards became my wife, and who has now for forty years been the faithful companion of my chequered destiny, and to whose zeal, industry, and energy I owe in no small degree such success as I have obtained.

Here I met for the first time the illustrious Darwin. He was making a geological tour in Wales, and carried with him, in addition to his other burdens, a hammer of 14 lbs. weight. I remember he was full of modesty, and was always lamenting his bad memory for languages and inability to quote. I am proud to remember that though quite ignorant of physical science, I saw a something in him which marked him out as superior to anyone I had ever met : the proof which I gave

of this was somewhat canine in its nature, I followed him.
I walked twenty-two miles with him when he went away, a
thing which I never did for anyone else before or since.

My next vacation I spent in a little farmhouse, about a
mile and a half away from Gosport, reading mathematics with
Mr. Walker. There were very few steamers on the Solent in
those days, so I bought a little boat with a sprit-sail, and
amused myself with sailing about, often quite alone. I was
often out by myself all night, and cannot imagine how I escaped
being drowned, as I had no special knowledge of the management of a boat, and troubled myself very little whether the
weather were fine or stormy.

In the spring of 1833 I went up for my degree, and took a
first class in classics and a second class in mathematics. This
was a disappointment to me, for I was sure that I knew enough
to entitle me to a first class, though I felt perfectly conscious
that I had not brought my knowledge properly out. There
were thirteen of us in the first class in classics. Among them
stand the names of Liddell and Scott, the present Bishop of
London, and Lord Canning. My examination in Divinity
was very amusing. It will be remembered that I had made
myself rather conspicuous by my speeches in the debating
society, and I suppose it is to that that I must attribute the
very singular examination to which I was subjected by Mr.
Lancaster, one of the classical examiners. It was to the
following effect : —

Examiner : ' Which gave the better counsel to Rehoboam, the
old men or the young ? '

I : ' The old men. It was quite right to lighten the taxation.'

Examiner : ' Did not Solomon obtain large revenues by commerce ? '

I : ' I don't think so. Princes have, as Adam Smith tells us,
always been bad traders ; we do not know what he exported to
Ophir, but he brought back gold and silver, mere articles of luxury,
and monkeys and peacocks, not, I apprehend, a very profitable con-
signment.' (A laugh.)

Examiner : ' Still, the country is described as being very

prosperous under his government, and the revenue is described as
being large.'

I: 'Yes, but then only see how it was squandered: there was
the Temple, the Golden Throne, and the Sea of Gold, and the lions,
and the cherubim, and the mercy seat.'

Examiner: 'Still, that hardly bears out the opinion of the old
men.'

I: 'No, sir. There was besides the support of 300 wives and
700 concubines. We often see a man ruined by one wife: surely
a thousand women were enough to ruin a whole country.' (A general
roar of laughter.)

Examiner: 'Thank you, sir. Your examination has been very
pleasing.'

I was examined in *The Knights* of Aristophanes in the
well-known passage where the rather striking defects of the
sausage seller are proved to be so many recommendations for
the trade of a demagogue; and, finally, a pro-proctor, who had
caught me out in some small delinquency a few months before,
selected from Juvenal the passage :—'*Ebrius et petulans qui
nullum forte cecidit.*'

I was very well pleased with all this, because I felt sure
that unless they had intended to give me a first class, they
would not have introduced this scene of high jinks mixed up
with party politics into the schools, and thus given me the
opportunity of saying that my speeches at the Union had
lost me my class. This was about six months after the
passing of the Reform Bill, and it is only fair to acknowledge
the good humour with which the whole affair was treated. It
gave, perhaps, rather a false *éclat* to my performance, and
was doubtless the means of obtaining for me the further
questionable advantage of a large number of private pupils,
which, as will be seen, had a considerable influence on my
future destiny, and by no means altogether for good.

I ought to have mentioned that Mr. Woods, a member of
University College, took a first class at the same time. The
College ought to have been much obliged to us, for they had
not had a first class for nine years, and we had not the slightest

assistance from the tutors, whom I, at least, paid for tuition
I had never received, and to be exempt from which my tutor
justly considered a great boon. I was entitled by the usage
of the college to books to the value of 17l. 10s. I chose the
Attic orators, and Bekker's *Plato*. My tutor tried hard to
dissuade me from my choice, on the ground that these were
books which it was quite certain I should never open. I am
very happy to think that in this he was entirely mistaken.
Almost all the Fellowships at University were clerical, so that
I had nothing to hope in that quarter. The only other notice
which I received from my college was that a prize was offered
for the best essay by any member of the college under the
degree of a Master of Arts. The Master sent for me, and requested me not to compete, and to make the fact known, for
fear, as he said, I should discourage competition.

In the summer of this year, my brother and I made a
walking tour through Scotland. It was the year after the
death of Sir Walter Scott, and we were full of his writings.
The interest of such a tour at such a time can hardly be
imagined. But we had the good fortune to travel with a great
living poet—no less a person than Wordsworth. I am afraid
I was not then as well acquainted with his poems as I ought
to have been or as I have become since. My principal amusement, I am ashamed to say, was to watch his demeanour under
the torture which the indiscriminate and by no means over-
refined praise of Scott inflicted upon a poet justly conscious
of higher merits than the coarse taste of the age was disposed
to allow him. He absolutely writhed under the perpetual
references to Fitz James and Roderick Dhu with which he
was regaled by the passengers of the *Loch Lomond* steamboat,
and at last in despair began to a very unsympathetic audience
a criticism on Scott's English; the only point I can recollect
is that in the line—

> Loch Katrine lay before him rolled,

he said it should have been ' unrolled.'

I also remember that he recited his own sonnet on the Mill of Inversnaid.

I met with him again on the steamer going to Staffa, when we had an adventure to which he partly alludes in his sonnet on this his second visit to Staffa. His son, my brother, and I, climbed up to the summit of the island where there is a very fine view, and he became extremely poetical. As the sea was rough the steamer was moored at some distance from the island, and we were transferred to a coble which landed us and was to bring us back. At the end of one of Wordsworth's finest periods one of us happened to look round and observed that the coble had left Staffa and was very near the steamer which was rolling heavily. Staffa is uninhabited, and the prospect of remaining there for a week without food or shelter was by no means inviting. We made signals of distress and had the satisfaction of seeing the coble, after having put its passengers on board the steamer which was rolling heavily, return for us. We had no reason to expect a pleasant reception; a delay of three-quarters of an hour is sufficiently irritating even without the addition of sea-sickness. As we approached the steamer we could see the passengers drawn up in an ominous semicircle with the captain in the arc, red and lowering like a comet. We were all seized with the utmost reverence for Wordsworth, whom we insisted on sending up the ladder first. What passed I do not know, for, happy in my insignificance, I mingled with the crowd and left the poet to his fate.

In October I returned to Oxford, having made up my mind as to the course of life I meant to pursue. I was but poorly fitted for the solution of a problem which involved questions which might have puzzled a wiser head than mine. Prudence would have counselled me to take orders, get a Fellowship, and work my way through Oxford to whatever haven Fortune might open for me; but as I had a decided objection to the Church, I determined to go to the Bar. This was a very unwise resolution, and one I am sure I should never have formed if I had possessed a friend who could have laid the whole case before me. If I had been asked such questions as these :— 'Can you see the face of a witness?' 'Can you watch the countenances of a jury so as to judge whether what you say finds acceptance with them or no?' 'Can you in a crowded Court take full and accurate notes of evidence and cases?' 'Can you read through a long affidavit in a fog or by candle-light?' 'Can you find your place readily in a long brief or report?'—all these and many more such questions I must have answered in the negative. However, it was on this impossibility that I had set my heart, and, the matter being resolved upon, I had next to consider the way to get called to the Bar. For this two things were necessary; one to get a lay Fellowship, the other to support myself and bear the expenses incident to the study and the entrance into the legal profession.

I happened to know that a lay Fellowship at Magdalen confined to Nottinghamshire would be vacant in two years, which solved the first difficulty, and for the second I had to rely on finding a sufficient number of pupils. And now I began a labour compared with which everything else which I have had to do in my life has been mere play and recreation. The business of a private tutor at Oxford may be described to be to give an hour a day to each pupil. Had I meant to make teaching my profession I should have gone to work with more moderation, but I thought, and justly, according to the plan I had laid down for myself, that I was bound to work as hard as I could in order to carry out my ideal. For seven years I took as many pupils as I could do justice to. My number very often amounted to ten, and in addition to this, for five years out of the seven I took pupils during the long vacation. I do not think I could have gone on with it much longer. It has at any rate had this good effect, that all other work has seemed to me trifling after it. To dismiss this subject at once I may say that I was very popular as a tutor and retained my number up to the last, and finished in November with four pupils of mine in a first class of six. I have lost the list of my pupils, but I am proud to mention amongst them Lord Justice Mellish, Mr. Gathorne-Hardy, Mr. Charles Reade the novelist, Mr. Clough the poet, Mr. Congreve, and the late Father Dalgairns. I had not the honour to be known either to Mr. Newman or to Dr. Arnold, but so many pupils came to me from those two distinguished men that I flattered myself, perhaps too readily, that it was not wholly fortuitous.

In 1834 I spent the long vacation with some pupils in Wales. The latter part of the time we spent at Festiniog, where I had a most extraordinary escape. About half a mile from the village there is a fine mountain stream which has worn itself an exceedingly deep channel, and makes a series of cataracts. There is also in the stream a very remarkable rock called 'Hugh Lloyd's Pulpit.' I walked down to the brook after my work was over to look at one of these cascades which was called 'The Black Pools.' The rock projected over it so that the fall seemed directly under my feet. I laid hold of the branch of a tree to steady myself while I looked over, my foot slipped on the mossy bank, the branch that I held broke, I fell on my side, rolled over and over three or four times, and then shot clear over the precipice. People are described in such situations as having their whole life pass before them, as losing their breath, as dead before they reach the ground. None of these things happened to me. I seemed a long time to be rolling over and over in the air. I remember hoping that I should be killed outright, and then the relief of finding myself in water. I rose to the surface like a duck and on looking round found myself in a deep basin with the waterfall facing me, high rocks all round, and one very close to the place where I had fallen in. After a futile attempt to get out by the way that I came in, which showed that I had not quite recovered my senses, I swam down the stream and crawled

out at the first point where the bank began to slope. I
sprained my ankle and my hand, was only able to crawl on
all fours most of the way home, and ended by fainting with
the pain. They said the height of the fall was 120 feet. On
this I can give no opinion, for my experience has proved to
me that the worst possible way of measuring a height is to
fall down it. My kind old friend, Martha Owen the landlady,
whose name, if there is gratitude in man, ought to be green
in the valleys of Wales, and who bore no inconsiderable
resemblance to Scott's Meg Dodds, took excellent care of me,
and I felt no permanent bad effects from my accident.

The next year was a memorable one. The Fellowship at
Magdalen fell vacant and I was elected without a competitor.
I took a party of pupils to read at Beaumaris, and three
months after I had obtained the Fellowship which had formed
so prominent a part of my scheme for being called to the Bar,
I effectually cancelled that part of my programme by engaging
myself to the lady whom I had met at Barmouth. It was a
matter that might have waited a little while, but I had a
motive which induced us to rather precipitate matters. If I
vacated my Fellowship during that year, my younger brother
would be sure to get it. I had taught him at Oxford, he had
obtained a second class, and as he intended to take orders
would thus be provided for for life. So we arranged matters
accordingly, and were married in March 1836. As I never
was a full Fellow, all that I received from the munificence of
William of Wainfleet was 10l.

The summer of this auspicious year we spent in a tour in
Switzerland ; we left England in the beginning of June and
did not return till the middle of October. We walked, I may
literally say all over Switzerland, for not only did we visit the
Oberland and Chamouni, but Appenzell, St. Gallen, and the
Grisons. My wife was an excellent walker, and thus our
slender resources, being relieved of the charges of transport,
held out till the end of our long campaign. We walked 700

miles in two months; my wife, who drew extremely well, carrying her sketch-book and drawing materials, and I our wardrobe and the money, which, being silver, was the heaviest of all. We returned to Oxford, bought a small house between Christchurch and Folly Bridge, and set to work at the business of life in good earnest. This lasted for four years, during which I underwent an enormous amount of drudgery.

The Oxford of to-day, owing to changes in which I have been so fortunate as to bear a part, is very different from the Oxford of forty years ago. At that time we were governed academically and socially by what I can only describe as a clerical gerontocracy. Almost all power was vested in the heads of colleges, an office to which men seldom succeed when young, and in which there is no superannuation. Bacon says that a university should be like a beehive, '*quo neque sit reutis aditus*,' and certainly the institution was well qualified to secure that its government should not be of a too revolutionary or innovating character. It might perhaps have occurred to some people that I, who was able to obtain in the open field of competition more pupils than I required, might have been a useful auxiliary to the not very powerful tutorial staff of the college to which I belonged. I do not believe such an idea was ever rejected, because I do not believe that it ever occurred to anyone.

Magdalen was less of a reading college than University, and, as the Duke of Wellington once told the authorities, had been notorious for idleness ever since the time of Gibbon. Our president was a scholar and a gentleman, but his reign began in the reign of Louis the Sixteenth. If such a plan as that of utilising me had ever been broached, I am sure it would have been overruled. I was popular with the Fellows but I was a decided Liberal, and worse than all was known to entertain very strong opinions in favour of the repeal of the Corn Laws, a most distasteful heresy in academical eyes, as having a tendency to diminish the value of Fellowships. The heads of houses had the usual quality of a narrow and factitious aristocracy—they were socially exclusive. Not that this would have been any great loss in itself, but the evil was that Oxford was too small to support two societies, and so those who had not university or collegiate rank enough to place them in what was somewhat irreverently called 'the cod's head and shoulders' set, ran some risk of having no society at all.

As for us, we found an ample indemnity for general society in youth, health, constant employment, and in the kindness of many of my old college friends. In 1837 I was appointed a Master of the Schools, or in other better understood words a 'little-go' examiner. This I owed, if I remember right, to my connection with Magdalen College. One of our Fellows was Proctor and he gave me the appointment. Among my colleagues were Dr. Dyne and Dr. Kynaston, who have since been remarkably successful as schoolmasters; Dyne at Highgate, and Kynaston at St. Paul's. I held the office for two years. Our duties were laid down for us by statute and there was no difficulty in performing them, except that to do so was extremely unpopular and quite contrary to the spirit of the place. Our duty was to see that the students of so many terms' standing were not wholly wasting their time and might with propriety be allowed to continue their studies at Oxford. One would have supposed that the wish of all parties would be that this duty should be strictly and creditably performed; sometimes, indeed, I have been thanked by a tutor for cutting short the career of an idle and dissipated young man whose bad example was doing injury to the college, but much more frequently the matter was received with a growl and visible annoyance. We were, in fact, to compare small things with great, judges residing among a small society greatly interested in the manner in which we administered justice—all whose sympathies were, so to say, with the criminals.

As people talk very much and understand very little about what they call University teaching, I will try to explain the subject, though I sincerely hope that long before these pages see the light, the explanation may have become unnecessary.

The University teaching of which these persons speak is the teaching of Oxford and Cambridge—now, the word University as used at Oxford and Cambridge has two distinct meanings. Its proper meaning is the body incorporated by the Crown, which has by virtue of that incorporation the privilege of conferring that particular title of honour which is called a degree. In this sense the Universities are not teaching bodies at all. There is, however, another sense in which the term University is used : it is used to include all the colleges of which the members of the University are also members, and it is in that sense that University teaching is used. Now, is this union of teaching and conferring degrees in the same hands a good or an evil ? The colleges of Oxford and Cambridge must be regarded not only as places for giving instruction ; the honour and credit of the University are kept up by those who take high honours, and public opinion in the Universities is in favour of keeping up this, the show part of the system. Examiners may be as strict as they please in the amount they require, and no objection is made. But it is quite different with regard to the ordinary pass degree and the ' little go.'

Those persons who desire a degree, either as a title to orders or as a social distinction, are the great bulk of the University, and the whole weight of opinion in the University is in favour of treating them very leniently. Instead of a competition which of the two shall give a degree that implies the greatest amount of attainment, and as therefore the most honourable to giver and receiver, the competition between Oxford and Cambridge has hitherto been which can offer a degree on the easiest terms. There is no other way of explaining the ad-mitted fact that at both Oxford and Cambridge the degree is discreditably low. It thus appears that University teaching carries with it as a necessary result a degradation of learning, because those who teach, instead of working up to a fixed

standard can fix the standard for themselves. Nothing would
improve the Universities as teaching bodies so much as to take
out of their hands the power of conferring the ordinary pass
degree, and conversely nothing would tend so much to enhance
the value of a degree as placing it in the hands of persons
who have no pecuniary interest in reducing it below a fair and
honourable standard. It was this tendency to keep down the
standard of examinations in order to fill the colleges that I felt
and resisted as far as my humble position admitted. I find
exactly the same evil still existing, only people have been
somehow persuaded to consider that evil as a merit.

Another trouble seems to me to impend over the new plan
of University teaching. When the system is once firmly
established in any great town, the request is sure to be made
that the standard of knowledge should be raised to the level of
a University degree. This can hardly be refused, and indeed,
as the outside public become more and more aware of the
nakedness of the land, it will be strange if a demand for more
than the University standard should not be heard. At any
rate, if Nottingham shall obtain an equality of examination
with Oxford and Cambridge, the demand is sure to follow in
no long time that, as the proficiency is equal, the degree shall
be the same. Then we shall have reached the graves of the
Scythians—the equality will never be granted, because to grant
it would be to strike a fatal blow at the college system and the
very comfortable maintenance which a great number of very
worthy persons derive from compulsory charges for tuition,
besides room rent, and some other little matters. The result
will be a quarrel and a separation.

I return to my biography with this observation, that in my
judgment the Civil Service Commission might very easily be
enlarged so as to perform the office of a University and an
examiner of schools for the whole country. Examining is a
judicial function and would be well placed in such hands as a
commission responsible to Parliament.

In 1837 I took a party of pupils to Dinan, in Brittany, having been, as I believe, the first private tutor who ventured to carry his pupils beyond the sacred precincts of the United Kingdom. I have often regretted that I did not try Ireland.

The next year, 1838, seemed likely at one time to have entirely altered my course of life. Sir Daniel Sandford, the Professor of Greek in the University of Glasgow, died. There was a great competition for the Professorship, a most eligible situation, for the emoluments were said to be 2,000l. a year, and the session only lasted six months. The election was in the hands of the *Senatus Academicus*, that is, thirteen professors. I never dreamt of aspiring to such a prize. However, it came to pass that for some reason which I do not know, the electors declared themselves discontented with the candidates and invited others to come forward. I had a relation who had married Mr. Findlay, of Easterhill, who lived about three miles from Glasgow. My testimonials were, as I believe testimonials always are, a splendid instance of what Bentham calls the fallacy of indiscriminate laudation. I know not whether I had begun to entertain any doubts as to my grand plan of going to the Bar. I certainly had a warning, which I will mention presently, which ought to have influenced my mind in this direction. I went to Glasgow and spent a month there, with the assistance and under the advice of my kind friend Mr. Findlay, and at the end of that time had every reason to believe that my exertions had been crowned with success.

My antagonist was Mr. Lushington, one of the original candidates; at the end of my canvass the numbers stood three for Lushington and the rest for me. It was with indescribable pleasure that I saw apparently within my reach an honourable competence to be earned by moderate labour in a field in which I felt confident I could discharge the duties required of me without any impediment from those physical infirmities which I had at last begun to estimate a little more

justly. But my prospect was soon overclouded. Mr. Lushington had only three adherents, but they were true and
staunch. It was in the power of the *Senatus Academicus* to
translate one professor to another and more highly paid chair
in case of death. Now, as my evil star would have it, Dr.
Milne, the Professor of Moral Philosophy, was at this moment
dying. Equally unfortunate, my principal supporter, the
Professor of Ecclesiastical History, was a candidate for the
expected vacancy. The three professors who supported Mr.
Lushington pointed out to the Professor of Ecclesiastical History that they certainly could not prevent him from electing
me for the Greek Professorship, but that if he carried that it
was in their power by throwing their votes into the adverse
scale to prevent him from obtaining the Chair of Moral Philosophy. The menace had its effect. The professor threw his
weight into the opposite scale, Mr. Lushington was elected to
the Greek Chair, and my quondam supporter to the Chair of
Moral Philosophy.

This was to me a very bitter disappointment. I was weary
of the monotonous drudgery of teaching ; I had every reason
to suppose that I had succeeded, and the election after all of
one who had been among the first list of candidates looked
something like a breach of faith. These feelings were not
much soothed by the reflection that I had been sacrificed
simply to the interests of a third person without the slightest
regard to the merits of the case, but I soon took a cooler and,
I honestly believe, a juster view. The main fault lay in the
miserable system of translation. After all it was perhaps too
much to expect that my supporter should prefer my interest
to his own, especially as he had given me no personal pledge.
I must also admit that I believe Mr. Lushington to have been
a better scholar than myself, and am happy to record that
after thirty-two years of most excellent service he has retired,
carrying with him the respect and regard of the whole University.

About this time my eyes gave me very distinct notice that I must give up all idea of reading by candlelight. This was a very great distress to me, as it cut me off from what has always been my greatest pleasure. The decline having manifested itself so early, gave me much reason to fear that this was only the first step towards a still greater failure of sight, and ought, I think, to have made me give up my scheme of the Bar altogether. But the dogged resolution which sticks to its purpose in the face of almost insuperable obstacles is in itself an element of prosperity, and answered in the long run, though in a very different way from anything I had imagined. From that time till now, some forty years, I have never been able to read by candlelight, and when I think of all the things that I might have known if I had not had this misfortune, I am astonished how persons who have all their winter evenings to themselves contrive to know so little.

Some sacrifice I resolved to make to this new misfortune. I do not think I chose my victim well. We had the great honour and privilege to have as Professor of Sanscrit at Oxford Mr. Wilson, a man of profound erudition and the author of the great English and Sanscrit Dictionary. He was not over-burdened with pupils, and he took, or seemed to take, pleasure in teaching me. Under the guidance of this most admirable scholar and most charming companion, I gained a very fair knowledge of the grammar of this complicated and difficult language. I read through the Laws of Menu, and a good deal of the *Ramayana*. The language is beautiful, and easily read. I really had conquered the main difficulties, and had I gone to Glasgow should, I do not doubt, have mastered it thoroughly. I can even now repeat many verses from the *Mahabharata*. It is a great pity that so noble a language should not have been the vehicle of a more interesting and instructive literature.

In 1839, I took a party of pupils to Ambleside. The expedition was remarkable mainly for the fact that during the whole three months we had only three days of fine weather. In 1840 I took a party a second time to Dinan, and in this year my residence of eleven years at Oxford, and my seven years labour as a private tutor, came to an end. As the time drew nearer I became more timid as to making the plunge. A small office worth, if I remember rightly, less than 300*l.* a year, a Pre-lectorship of Logic, had just been created, and I really think if I had obtained it, I should very probably have shrunk from the plunge into the great world which I was about to make. Happily I did not get it, and so the plunge was made.

It is usual for novelists and moralists to represent youth as the season of overweening confidence and self-estimation : that is not my experience. Some of the ablest men I have known have thrown themselves away for want of a manly confidence in themselves, from a sickly over-refinement, or from indolence concealing itself under the mask of humility. As far as I have been able to observe, the first step in life is greatly crowded with competitors, but this once passed, the scene entirely changes, and instead of a struggle for existence, the difficulty is to find men equal in any tolerable degree to the duties required of them.

I did not start from Oxford wholly ignorant of law, for I had carefully read over twice, I think, Cruise's *Digest,* a most excellent work on Real Property, the most abstruse, but also the most systematic, part of the Law, and, therefore, the part most easily acquired by private study. We sold our house in Oxford for something more than we gave for it, and established ourselves in London, in Burton Crescent. In both my legal teachers I was very fortunate ; they were Mr. Coulson, afterwards counsel to the Government, and the present Sir Barnes Peacock.

It was rather late to begin, and I had to give my mind a serious wrench before I could get it to look at things from the dry legal point of view, that is to discard all facts and all thoughts except those which were necessary for the decision of the case. After a much longer time and harder struggle than my conceit told me was necessary, I completely conquered this difficulty at least. But when I came to the mysteries of special pleading, I stood aghast at its mingled iniquity and absurdity. It will probably escape the reprobation which it so signally merits from posterity because no human being will be found willing to learn it for the purpose merely of knowing to what monstrous folly and iniquity, custom, tradition, and the pride of knowing something extremely difficult will reconcile really able and honest men.

The very name of this false and mischievous science is utterly misunderstood. Every one not a lawyer believes special pleading to mean an over-refined and sophistical argumentation. Nothing of the kind. It means in fact stating your case, telling your adversary what you undertake, or require him to prove. As each party is well aware of what the matter in dispute is, such a proceeding has always appeared to me quite superfluous; but so far from this being the case, the difficulty was not to find out what the law was, but, given the law, how to state your case without being tripped by some miserable technicality. At the time when I began my studies, this system was in all its glory. I think about eight of the sixteen volumes of Meeson and Welsby, in which this wonderful system is developed, were published. I cannot express my disgust at finding that the principal difficulty I had to overcome was not the rules of evidence, nor the vast and complicated common and statute law of England, but the art of stating my case so that my future client might not be ruined because I made some slip in stating what I was prepared or wished him to prove. And yet so powerful is habit that the only thing that I can reproach myself with as a barrister is having on one or two occasions availed myself of some of the tricks of this wretched trade in order to obtain a success to which on the merits I was not entitled.

It is only fair to record that at last the good sense of the Bar itself rose up against this iniquity, and has swept it away, though I hold the opinion that there is still far too much of it left. In written statement of the case and defence of this view I am supported by very high authority.

I was called to the Bar in, I think, January, 1842. The question was, what should I do next? I had no hope of immediate business, and might think myself very fortunate if, at the end of seven years, I could pick up a few briefs at sessions. I resolved to do that which, if it was to be of any use, I ought to have done long before, to take the best advice I could get as to the probability that if business came, I should be able to do it. I consulted Lawrence, Travers, and Alexander. They said that I should become blind in seven years, recommended out-of-doors employment, and spoke of Australia or New Zealand as suitable places for the purpose. This strange advice, as I may now by the light of experience presume to call it, entirely subverted and demolished the whole plan of my life. It is not very difficult to imagine the bitterness of such a revelation: to be told at eight-and-twenty that I had only seven more years of sight, and to think of the long night that lay beyond it was bad enough; but the reflection that the object which I had struggled through a thousand difficulties with such intense labour to attain was lost to me, was almost as bitter.

However, fortunately neither my wife nor myself were of a disposition to sit down and lament over the inevitable. That such great authorities could possibly be entirely wrong in a matter on which they spoke with such confidence and so much precision never entered our minds. Taking this opinion as our guide we sat down calmly to consider what was the best course that was open to us under the new conditions that were thus started upon us. It was impossible to give worse advice than that which I had received from my three learned advisors. They chose to fix the exact term of seven years for the time during which I was to enjoy the blessing of sight, and for this, as subsequently appeared, they had no grounds whatever. This they must have known, for there was no incipient disease of the eye, as has been abundantly proved by the fact that from that time to this—some forty years—I had been quite free from any ocular disease. But, condoning this most unpardonable mistake, and supposing that I had some disease, the advice was the very worst that could be given. My eyes, being unprotected by a *pigmentum nigrum* and having nothing but white lashes to screen them, were peculiarly subject to injury from the blazing sky of Australia, which is one of the brightest and most trying in the world. Had I followed their advice literally and betaken myself to outdoor employment, I cannot doubt that blindness must in no long time have been the result.

It seemed quite clear that it was vain to think of the English Bar, for I could not, as above remarked, hope to do anything worth speaking of here, before the night that was to come in which no man can work. Equally clear was it that I had neither capital nor knowledge, nor sight, which would enable me to become a settler in a new country. Thus it was impossible for me, on the supposition which I never thought of disputing, that the opinion was correct, either to follow my own plans or those that were suggested for me. But it occurred to me that I might unite the two. The Bar at Sydney was said to be very lucrative, and at any rate in a new country I was sure of having a speedy trial and making something before the fatal seven years expired, so we decided to go to Sydney, and on June 8th, not six months after I was called to the Bar, we sailed in the good ship *Aden* for New South Wales. A few weeks after we had sailed, a letter was sent to me, which, had it reached me in time, would most probably have altered my destination, and with it my whole career in life. It was an invitation to become a contributor to the *Times*, but at that time I was in the tropics.

Of all the descriptions of a long voyage, the best I ever read (anyone who refers to it will see why) is that given in Washington Irving's *Astoria*. There were a great many passengers ; the first occupation was sea-sickness. This took from about a week to a fortnight according to the constitution of the patient. My wife was an exception, for she never really got over it during the whole voyage. When this was over the second stage was gluttony ; people talked of nothing but what they had eaten, were eating, or were going to eat. The fare of a ship is necessarily rather monotonous, and so this subject after a while lost its charms. After the coarser passion of greediness was exhausted came the gentler influence of love ; as we approached the tropics, the disposition to flirt increased ; it was very hot and there was nothing else to do. This also had its season and ended in a copious crop of jealousies and quarrels. Factions were formed, and the most dreadful threats uttered as to what should happen when we reached the shore. But Time, as Sophocles says, is a good-natured god, and the heat of the quarrels died away for want of fresh fuel to feed them. The fifth act of the drama, for it divided itself with true scenic propriety, was a general combination against the captain. He was by no means exempt from errors of judgment, and, strange to say, his manners were by no means perfect. He had not candles to last till the end of the voyage, so he seized ours for the binnacle, and, worst of all, the voyage lasted four months. At last, even this amusement, the only thing in which we all agreed, palled upon us, and we sank into a state of absolute vacuity.

Two events only broke the monotony of the voyage ; the first was a call at St. Jago, a Portuguese convict settlement, one of the Cape de Verde islands—I presume the name was ironical, for of green there was none, and nothing could exceed the drought and barrenness of its bare and rugged mountains. There are few sights more beautiful than a sunset among the Canary Islands, with Fogo, an active volcano 7,000 feet high, in the foreground, and the green and crimson clouds of the tropics behind.

The other incident was of a less agreeable nature. Our captain was very careless, especially about fire ; we had been in the habit of constantly remonstrating with him as to the danger of allowing candles to be taken into the hold without protecting them. At last we had the satisfaction of saying, ' I told you so,' though we seemed very likely to pay dear for the pleasure. What we had predicted came to pass : the candle was dropped and the straw in the spirit room took fire just as we said it would.

When the Antiquary saw the *phoca* overthrow Hector, and scuttle off with his walking-stick, his first emotion was pleasure. ' I am glad of it,' he said, ' I'm glad of it with all my heart.' But this did not last, and we began to reflect that the ship was to the north of her usual course, and that we might before long have to choose between burning and drowning. It is strange that even at such supreme moments, as it is the fashion to call them, the mind is still open to ludicrous impressions. The ship was rolling heavily when a little boy came staggering along the deck with a cracked pie-dish in his hand which might have held a half-pint of water, and emptied it into the hold. I thought of Huss, the faggot, and the old woman, and could not help laughing. The fire was extinguished and we were quit for the fright.

We had another narrow escape. In the long stretch from the Cape to Australia we overran our dead reckoning, so that, when we believed ourselves to be three hundred miles from land, we found ourselves one morning at daybreak within two miles of Cape Otway, then a desolate promontory in the colony of Port Phillip. The addition of another half-hour to our miscalculation would have made all the difference. I had the satisfaction, as a member of council, of voting for placing a lighthouse on this very spot.

At last, after a voyage of nearly four months, we found

ourselves, not in Sydney but in Melbourne; that is to say, with still five hundred miles to go. The state of Melbourne was at this time very peculiar. It was in the by no means enviable position of being a dependency of a dependency, governed by a colony which was not permitted to govern itself. A good deal had been done in the way of building, but some cause, to us unknown, had arrested its progress in mid-career. The place seemed stricken with paralysis, everything was at a standstill, everybody wanted to sell and nobody wanted to buy. No purchaser would look at a house unless it was at the corner of a street. In the middle of the main street were two considerable rivers facetiously named by the inhabitants after their rulers and governors, the *Williams* and the *Latrobe*. We were told that someone had been drowned in one of these urban streams not long ago.

To regret that I have no money has been to me during the whole of my life no uncommon sensation, but I never remember experiencing it so poignantly as on this occasion. It required no very strong foresight to be aware that here was an opportunity such as no man could expect to see twice. For a very few thousand pounds a man might have possessed himself of property which in a few years would repay him much more than tenfold, and why, oh why had I not got it?

We arrived at Sydney about the middle of October 1842 and had our first experience of the climate in the shape of a dense fog which lasted for three days, during which the thermometer stood steadily at 115. We took a small house in Macquarie Street overlooking the Domain and the beautiful saltwater lake, as we should call it in England, which forms the peerless harbour which will, I believe, place Sydney at the head of the Australian colonies.

I was not long in obtaining a fair amount of business at a rate of remuneration which, to one who had been working ten hours a day at seven shillings an hour, seemed very ample. But here a new misfortune beset me. The prophecies of my three Job's comforters had made me very nervous about my eyes ; I suffered somewhat from the glare of an Australian summer, Sydney being one of the most dazzling places in the world, and in an evil hour I consulted a doctor. He cupped me and advised me that it was absolutely necessary that I should discontinue my practice which was rapidly increasing. I doubt if I should have been so docile to my Sydney Æsculapius if his opinion had not tallied with the opinions of the London doctors. The time has come, I said to myself, sooner than I thought, and if I do not wish to be wholly blind I must give up my business. This was the lowest ebb of my fortunes ; it really seemed as if I was destined to sink into a situation in which I should look back with regret on the position which it had cost me so much trouble to quit. To make the thing complete I was forbidden to read, so that all that remained to me was to forget what I had learnt, enlivened by the joyless dignity to starve.

However, in this the lowest ebb of my fortunes, I found several alleviations. The principal was the extraordinary good fortune which gave me the acquaintance, and I am proud to say the friendship, of Mr. William Macleay. He had been secretary at Paris for claims of English subjects, and afterwards had been a commissioner for the extinction of the slave trade at Cuba. He was an excellent classical scholar, he knew more of modern history and biography than anyone with whom I was ever acquainted, and in addition to all this he was a profoundly scientific man, thoroughly conversant with zoology and entomology. An excellent companion, with a store of caustic wit, he reminded me continually of the best part of Scott's *Antiquary*. It fell to my lot to do him some service for which he never knew how to be sufficiently grateful. It would have been a good find to meet with such a person anywhere, but in a remote colony it was a good fortune for which one could not be sufficiently grateful. I have not seen and shall not see his like again.

Another alleviation of my condition during this most trying period of my life was the opportunity which my compulsory idleness afforded of making ourselves well acquainted
with the beautiful scenery of the colony. New South Wales
is rich in fine coast and river scenery, and in peculiarly fine
waterfalls. There is a district fifty miles south of Sydney
called Illawarra, which seemed to me to be the nearest
approach to a terrestrial paradise. The glorious sea coast,
with caverns which flung up their spray far inland, the
enormous trees on the top of which the bellbird fluted its notes
into the air, the lovely flowers and the profusion of animals in
all their strange varieties, made of this delicious district a
fairyland, the very place where a man might pass his time
with no other regret than that of being totally useless.

Among all the difficulties with which it has been my lot to
contend in a long and not uneventful life, the greatest, and
the least appreciated by the public, was the defect of sight.
It was not merely that for forty years I have been obliged to
abstain from reading by candlelight, nor that I was threatened, by the ignorance of my medical advisers, with the
almost certainty of blindness ; the real evils were of a nature
which, if I had understood and anticipated, I should never
have had the courage to face. So long as it was only a business of teaching pupils I did not feel it ; they wanted to learn
and were quite ready to take anything I told them either for
truth or for what would be as good as truth for their purpose.
But it was a very different thing when I came to deal with an
auditor who was either hostile or indifferent. I could not see
the face of the witness whom I was examining, I could not
see the faces of the jury whom I was addressing, and worst of
all I could not see the impression I was making on the House
of Commons, and have often for want of this faculty fallen
into mistakes which I could gladly and easily have avoided.
Nor was this all. Those impressions which we receive imper-

fectly, we remember badly. I have never been able to recognise the faces of persons whom I do not see frequently, and the consequence is that I spend a great deal of my time in fencing with persons whom I do not know but who know me very well. This has deprived me of numberless friendships and intimacies which I should have been glad to cultivate, and the loss of which I sincerely lament.

But the worst of all was when I came to hold really high and important office as Chancellor of the Exchequer. He who has to refuse many things to many men has need to exert some counteracting power to neutralise the offence, which if he does his duty he is pretty sure to give. Nature, though in many respects a hard stepmother, had, I may say without vanity, bestowed on me some power of conversation. My dear and lamented friend, Sir George Lewis, used to say that, if he were to be cast away on a desert island, I was the associate whom he would choose. And I have been told that Sir Alexander Cockburn said that I was the companion he would choose on a wet day in a country house. I might say with Shakespeare : ' Wherefore are these things hid ? ' Why did not you employ whatever conversational power you possessed in making yourself popular ? The answer is given in what I said before. I could not conciliate my victims or my antagonists because I could not find them. Thus, with a quiet temper and a real wish to please, I have been obliged to submit all my life to an amount of unpopularity which I really did not deserve, and to feel myself condemned for what, after all allowance has been made for numerous faults and follies, were really rather physical than moral deficiencies. The fact also that I had contrived to raise myself to so prominent a position prevented people from making allowance for physical deficiencies which, if better known, would doubtless have been more generally allowed for.

[Here the memoir ends abruptly. It is indicative of the slight importance which Lord Sherbrooke himself attached to it, and of the labour it had cost him to ' type ' it, that he never attempted to reproduce the concluding portion, which, by an unhappy fatality, was lost in its transmission through the post.]

Rev. Robert Lowe. Jr
1806.

CHAPTER I

PARENTAGE AND DESCENT

ROBERT LOWE, Viscount Sherbrooke, was, as will be seen from his own account, of clerical descent on both sides. His father was the Rev. Robert Lowe, Rector of Bingham and Prebendary of Southwell, Notts, and his mother was the daughter of the Rev. Reginald Pyndar, Rector of Madresfield, Worcester. The mere fact that clerical celibacy is the law of the great Latin Church is proof positive that much may be said for it, from a purely sacerdotal standpoint. But England, as a State and as a nation, has assuredly been the gainer by the legalising of the marriage of her priesthood at the Reformation. It would astonish most persons, were the facts fairly placed before them, to find how much of the greatness and stability of our Empire is plainly due to the worth and patriotism of the ' sons of the clergy.' To go back only a hundred years, it may be doubted if there would now be an independent England at all, save for the little sickly offspring of a Norfolk parsonage, who fell at Trafalgar—but not before he had secured the inviolability of his native shores. In quite other ways, who, in our own day, has done so much by his individual genius to show that England and England's language should ever be foremost in the world, as that gifted and patriotic son of the Lincolnshire rectory—the late deeply lamented poet laureate?

These are merely two conspicuous instances. But the number of eminent Englishmen who first saw the light in a quiet parsonage, and received their early and indelible impressions of the world from its inmates and through the medium of its associations, is legion.   One of the most notable is the subject of this biography, although it must be admitted that Lord Sherbrooke was among the least ecclesiastical of English statesmen.

The so-called law of heredity clearly contains a great truth, Like produces like; and a man of genius or of great talent is, as a rule, the child, or at least the descendant, of gifted and remarkable people.   The Rev. Robert Lowe, Rector of Bingham, was a man of distinct ability and of great individuality—qualities which only needed a wider stage for their display, to have made him famous.   He was of the old-fashioned type of squire-parson it is the custom to revile now-a-days in the cheap prints, but which Mr. Froude, with the illustration of his own father, the Archdeacon of Totnes, before his eyes, so finely commemorates.

The Rev. Robert Lowe was some years older than Lord Byron, and had known him intimately at Southwell in his early youth.   The Miss Pigot who was a literary friend of Byron, was a cousin of Mr. Lowe, as was also the Rev. J. T. Becher of Southwell, to whom the poet addressed the verses beginning, 'Dear Becher, you tell me to mix with mankind.' Mrs. Chaworth Musters, who kindly sends the following letter, adds that her grandfather was naturally excessively annoyed at having been made the mouthpiece of an untruth; and that the coolness which arose in consequence lasted up to the end of Byron's life.

Lord Byron to the Rev. R. Lowe.

8 St. James Street : May 15, 1809.

My dear Sir, I have just been informed that a report is circulating in Notts of an intention on my part to sell Newstead, which is rather unfortunate, as I have just tied the property up in such a manner as to prevent the practicability, even if my inclination led me to dispose of it.   But as such a report may render my tenants uncomfortable, I will feel very much obliged if you will be good enough to contradict the rumour, should it come to your ears, on

Mme Lèvre
(1806)

my authority. I rather conjecture it has arisen from the sale of some copyholds of mine in Norfolk. I sail for Gibraltar in June, and thence to Malta when, of course, you shall have the promised detail. I saw your friend Thornhill last night, who spoke of you as a friend ought to do. Excuse this trouble, and believe me to be, with great sincerity,

Yours affectionately,
BYRON.

One wonders, in reading his letter, whether the noble bard remembered two of the lines in the verses he had sent to Mr. Lowe's kinsman :—

> Deceit is a stranger as yet to my soul,
> I still am unpractised to varnish the truth.

It should be added that the poet actually sold Newstead in 1811.

The rector of Bingham, it will be seen, was a leading country gentleman as well as the priest and pastor of a rural flock. He was a keen sportsman and above all a mighty hunter. The eldest son Henry, afterwards Mr. Sherbrooke of Oxton, would often ride to cover with his father ; and sometimes the younger son, Robert, notwithstanding his semi-blindness, would be permitted to do the same. So strong, indeed, was his inherited love of sport that he would, in his father's absence, take one of the hunters from the stables on the sly and scour the country on his own account--a grave offence, and, if discovered, visited with condign punishment.

The following rhymes, still remembered in the county, give us a glimpse of the rector's reputation as a local Nimrod :—

> Next little Bob Lowe, on his little brown mare,
> Comes nicking across with all possible care.
> On her he rides steady; but when he rides Stella,
> No man in the hunt can be his playfellow.

(And of his cousin, Mr. Sherbrooke) :—

> Who is it that rides at that hedge there full slap ?
> 'Tis Sherbrooke, I see, by the cut of his cap.
> Sir Calidore clears it, top binding and all,
> And ne'er puts his rider in mind of a fall.
> (Notts Hunting Song. By the Hon. Philip Pierrepoint.)

Anti-pauper System, established at Southwell in 1821, is essentially different from that established at Bingham in 1818.   I see no difference in the principle at all. One definition will include both. It is a system by which able-bodied paupers are forced to depend upon their own exertions by the agency of a workhouse, the same as that adopted at Uley, with which you claim affinity; and it is mentioned by Captain Nichols as based upon the same principle as that introduced by him at Southwell, where it is now flourishing under your able management. The only difference I see upon reading your pamphlet is in the details, some of which if I were acting on a greater scale I should adopt, but I am so fond of simplicity and of acting by general rules in imitation of Divine Wisdom, that I hate exceptions, or anything which throws the principle upon which I stand into obscurity; and minute detail would be quite impracticable in a single parish managing its own poor. We are both, however, acting upon precisely the same principle; and if you were to divert the system of my principle, you must strike out the word 'anti' from the name you have given it, and then what remains of the name would exactly describe what would remain of the system.

I am quite ashamed to write so much on the subject of self; it is an odious subject, but I am driven into a corner. I cannot but avow what I said to Mr. Cowell, and I cannot but justify myself in saying it. Whilst, however, I claim priority in point of time, I by no means claim priority in point of merit. Yours is the palm of having extended the system over an immense tract of country, and of having published it to the world in the most convincing form, and I willingly resign it ; whether you came in at the first, second, or third watch, you have watched well and deserve the thanks of your country.

I am very sincerely yours,
ROBERT LOWE.

It will be seen from this letter that the rector of Bingham distinctly laid claim to the paternity of the principle on which the new Poor Law of 1834 was based. Lord Sherbrooke always asserted that his father was the author of that measure which was really founded on the workhouse experiments made by himself in the first instance, and afterwards by Mr. Becher and others, in the county of Nottingham. We have perhaps advanced in the matter of social economics since the time of the Rev. Robert Lowe; and, also, we live in a time of

loose socialistic theories propagated by sentimental literature.
It would be easy enough to ridicule the notions of the rector
that the paupers of Southwell were doing harm by practising
the gentle art of Izaak Walton in the local stream. Let us
turn to the pages of that Liberal but thoroughly sober-minded
historian Dr. S. R. Gardiner, and we shall then see what the
evils were which Mr. Lowe strove to remedy, not without a
certain measure of success.

The Poor Law as it existed (i.e. before 1834) was a direct
encouragement to thriftlessness. Relief was given to the poor at
random, even when they were earning wages, so that employers of
labour preferred to be served by paupers, because part of the wages
would then be paid out of the rates. The more children a poor man
had the more he received out of the rates, and in this and in other
ways labourers were taught that they would be better off by being
dependent on the parish than by striving to make their own way in
the world . . . By the new Poor Law passed in 1834, workhouses
were built and no person was to receive relief who did not consent
to live in one of them. The object of this rule was that no one
might claim to be supported by others, who was capable of supporting
himself, and residence in the workhouse, where work would be
required was considered as the best test of real poverty.[1]

In even stronger words, the evil of the old Poor Law and
the benefits that followed on the Act of 1834, with regard to
national as well as individual thrift, is shown by Mr. Frome
Wilkinson, one of the latest and best authorities, in his work
previously cited.

Doubtless, like all human devices, the 'Workhouse system'
was liable to abuse; and some relaxation in the matter of outdoor relief was found necessary. But the principle—despite
Lord Beaconsfield's sentimental dislike of it—was essentially
sound.

It was but natural that the Rev. Robert Lowe should, after
1834, have a great deal of correspondence with the new Poor
Law Commissioners. One of the most interesting of these
letters was written from Ireland by Mr. Edward Gulson, in 1839.

---

[1] *A Student's History of England*, p. 911. S. R. Gardiner.

This gentleman had previously acted as assistant Poor Law Commissioner in Notts and Lincolnshire, and was regarded at head-quarters as one of the ablest of officials. Mr. Gulson was, in fact, specially selected to go to Ireland to divide that country into 'Unions,' under the Poor Law Act; and in writing to Bingham he gives a graphic picture of the condition of the country, and winds up by cordially inviting Mr. and Mrs. Lowe and the young ladies to the romantic shores of Rostrevor. Ireland, like the poor, is always with us, and Mr. Gulson's letter will be read all these years after it was written with considerable interest by serious-minded public men (see Appendix).

The perusal of such letters shows plainly that the rector of Bingham was looked upon, not only as a very intelligent correspondent, to whom it was a pleasure to dilate on public matters, but as a leading social reformer in his county. The following brief letter is hardly likely to find favour with some of the moving personages of our day ; but it is informed with the true Lowe spirit, and might have been written by Lord Sherbrooke himself. It is from the rector to a lodge of Oddfellows with which he had been associated :—

Rev. R. Lowe to the Oddfellows.

October, 1832.

Gentlemen,—I became a member of your lodge upon the oft-times repeated assurance that you were associated solely for the purposes of benevolence and that you had no concern with politicks in any way whatever, either directly or indirectly. Circumstances have now arisen which evidently show that I have been misled, and I beg you not to consider me any longer a member of your Union. I understand that you espouse my own political opinions, but I deem all Unions of every kind upon such subjects fraught with so much danger to the State, so much inconvenience to the public, and so much mischief to the members themselves, that I can never consent, ardently as I am attached to my own principles of liberty, to further them by such means.

I am, Gentlemen,
Your obedient Servant,
ROBERT LOWE.

The rector of Bingham had yet another gift over and above his active, well-knit physical frame and his clear and powerful intellect. He had the artistic sense, and would quote and linger over the lines of the poets whom he loved in a way never forgotten by those who heard him. Almost to his dying day Lord Sherbrooke would recall the impressive manner in which his father read the Lessons in the village church, and many friends will remember how he would reproduce the tones of the voice. Above all, he never forgot his father's manner and intonation in pronouncing the Blessing. 'It was beautiful,' he would say, ' simply beautiful.'

Such, briefly, was the Rev. Robert Lowe of Bingham ; by no means, it is to be feared, an ideal clergyman to this generation. To the devoted followers of Dr. Pusey belongs the distinction of removing the huntsman's coat from the back of the higher-class English rural clergy. With the diffusion of the sacerdotal doctrine, it was felt that a body of men, so specially set apart for sacred duties, should not join in the ordinary sports and recreations of the laity, especially if a distinctive dress was *de rigueur*. It may be admitted that, with keen and enthusiastic natures, there must always be a danger of a favourite pastime becoming a passion ; and doubtless the clergy can find nobler work to do than hunting, shooting, and fishing. But under the new dispensation there has also disappeared too often the wise and intelligent interest in social problems, the rare and exact scholarship, the old-world courtesy and good breeding. It is the loss of the first of these that is most to be deplored in an age of rash experiment and confident ignorance. There is no doubt that the English clergy now-a-days, especially in the cities and towns, take a stronger personal interest in the well-being of their poorer fellow-creatures than ever before ; but the interest is too largely either professional or sentimental. It needs the application of broad and general principles, and the patient investigation of cause and effect, to solve our complex social problems :

mere sentiment, however charming and touching, can never go far. It may be a minor point, but the utterly incomprehensible way in which the magnificent language of the Liturgy is too often, now-a-days, gabbled through cannot but make us regret the fine reading of an earlier and a more sturdy race of men.

To go back to the preceding generation. Lord Sherbrooke's grandfather, Robert Lowe of Oxton, High Sheriff of Notts (1802), was likewise a man of light and leading in the county. In the marvellous archives of the British Museum may be found a thickish pamphlet entitled ' *General View of the Agriculture of Nottingham. By Robert Lowe (of Oxton).*' This was originally published in 1794, but, unlike the majority of pamphlets—not on party politics or partisan theology—it ran into a second edition, and was re-issued in 1798. No one can glance at its pages and the accompanying map, showing the soils, &c., of the county, without recognising that its author was a man of knowledge and capacity. A large silver salver is still preserved in the family, which was presented to Robert Lowe of Oxton by the bank at Newark ' for an obligation not to be surpassed ': he had guaranteed them 120,000*l.* during a financial panic in 1803.

The Lowe family, who came originally from Cheshire, had been for some generations settled in Nottinghamshire and seem always to have been people of standing and substance. In the reign of Queen Anne, the first instance of ' bounty' was a present of as much timber to the chapter of Southwell by Samuel Lowe (Lord Sherbrooke's great-great-grandfather) as was necessary for the building of a vicarage house. The only other which appears on record is a contribution of 500*l.* by the Duchess of Newcastle. It was this Samuel Lowe's son who married Elizabeth Sherbrooke, one of whose sons was the father of the rector of Bingham.

It is commonly held—perhaps erroneously—that distinguished men owe more to the mother than to the father.

We have seen that Lord Sherbrooke's father, though he was no doubt far from popular with the evil-doers and the wastrels of Bingham, was a notable man, with aims and energies far beyond the reach of ordinary persons. His mother was a woman of singular refinement, grace and charm. She was a good and affectionate mother as well as a beautiful and attractive lady of the rectory; and beloved by all.

A writer gives the following picture of *Prebendary Lowe and his Family at Southwell* :—

'Long ago we remember, in the old vicarage drawing-room after a dinner-party, examining the face of a tall boy on the verge of manhood, who sat in a corner, with his face towards the wall, in a room which, though lighted up for company, was dim then in comparison with the lights of the present, and saw with wonder that in the almost darkness, the object of our curiosity was deeply engaged in a book he was reading. That boy was the present Lord Sherbrooke; his father was then in Residence, and his beautiful dark-eyed mother made it even more strange that two of her children should be albinos. The Prebendary himself and all the other members were a remarkably handsome family.'

The present rectory of Bingham is much altered from what it was in Lord Sherbrooke's childhood; but the old mulberry-tree on the lawn is still standing, round which he and his brothers and sisters used to play the parts of the heroes and heroines of the Waverley Novels.

Fifty years afterwards, when one of these children of the rectory was Chancellor of the Exchequer, he made the following reference to the favourite author of his boyhood, in a speech delivered at Glasgow when he was presented with the freedom of that city :—'Long before I had the privilege which this honour confers, I belonged to that generation whose youth was fed with the Waverley Novels. I had the pleasure and privilege of reading most of those novels as they issued from the press, causing a literary excitement and delight that nothing which has been given since has in any way equalled, and nothing, I venture to say, is ever likely to surpass. To us, the youth of that far-away time, Scotland was a fairyland—the Arcadia of our dreams ; and our aspirations were to visit and see the spots that the Wizard had made his own and our own. From that time, whenever I had the opportunity, I always spent my holidays in Scotland. My affection has been a disinterested one, for I have neither the power nor the will to make war on your deer, your fowl, or your fishes.'

There is a picture of the garden and orchard at Bingham by the late Alfred Miles, the well-known artist, whose father succeeded Lord Sherbrooke's as rector. Among the earlier rectors was the father of Sir Christopher Wren, and also Archbishop Abbott, Laud's predecessor at Canterbury.

As already stated, Mrs. Lowe was the daughter of the Rev. Reginald Pyndar, who was of the family of Pyndar of Duffield in the county of Derby. The name of this family occurs in the list of gentry in the time of Henry VI. Reginald Pyndar of Duffield was sheriff of the county in 1684.

Either he, or his son, removed to Kimpley in Gloucestershire. Reginald, the representative of this family, who died in 1788, had taken the name of Lygon on succeeding to the estate of Madresfield in Worcestershire. His son William was in 1816 created Lord Beauchamp of Powick, and in 1815 Earl Beauchamp and Viscount Elmley. He died in 1816 and was succeeded by the late Earl.

We have here an explanation of the oft-quoted remark of the late Earl Beauchamp, who at the time of Robert Lowe's great anti-reform speeches, when his name was on every tongue, used to refer to him as ' My distinguished kinsman.' The Irish branch of the Bechers were also kinsmen of the Lowes (see Pedigree). The Rev. Reginald Pyndar, Lord Sherbrooke's maternal grandfather, seems to have been of the same type of vigorous parson-magistrate as was the rector of Bingham. The Pyndars are of the same family also as Sir Paul Pindar.

Few men of good birth ever took less personal interest in questions of lineage and the intricacies of pedigrees than did the late Viscount Sherbrooke. Not one single particular of his family history here set forth was obtained directly from himself. The only ancestor to whom he refers in the preceding memoir is the feeble lampooner of Archbishop Laud.

Strange to say, the most complete family tree hitherto published of the Lowes and Sherbrookes will be found in a huge tome compiled by that sturdy and uncompromising Radical, the late Mr. Peter Taylor, for years Member of Parliament for Leicester. The work, which was ‘ printed for private circulation,’ is entitled *Some Account of the Taylor Family* ; and in it he has traced the pedigree of every family directly or indirectly connected with his own.

It is stated that when Mr. Taylor offered to present Lord Sherbrooke in the Lobby of the House of Commons with his handsome but bulky book, he was amazed to be met with a blank refusal. Had the work-harassed statesman been able with his dim eyes to recognise that his refusal caused pain and mortification to a very worthy if inconsistent man, he would have been the last to decline or disdain this ponderous gift. Who knows but that he may have suspected the unsolicited volume would be followed by a deputation desirous of dipping its hand in the public purse ?

For the series of Pedigrees to be found at the end of the second volume I am indebted to Mr. Topham Hough, himself a kinsman of the late Lord Sherbrooke. Apart altogether from the interest of these pedigrees to students of genealogy, those of the Dabridgecourt and Becher families disclose two remarkable facts concerning the kin and ancestry of Lord Sherbrooke of which he was not, I think, himself aware. Robert Lowe was the thirteenth in lineal descent from John Hampden, of

Great Hampden, Bucks, the progenitor of the ever memorable John Hampden and John Pym.

The literary reader will surely be interested to learn that William Makepeace Thackeray and Robert Lowe were of the same kindred; while to the historian and the politician it will be even more attractive to find that John Pym, the great Parliamentarian, who curiously enough represented Calne in the House of Commons in the time of the ill-fated Charles I., was a kinsman of the most distinguished representative of that borough in the more tranquil and happier reign of Queen Victoria.

It is a curious and interesting fact that the ancient family of Dabridgecourt, which came into England with Philippa of Hainault and established itself at Strathfieldsaye in Hampshire, with branches in Warwickshire and Nottinghamshire, and which is now, so far as can be ascertained, extinct in the male line, produced in the seventeenth century John Pym, and in the nineteenth century William Makepeace Thackeray and Robert Lowe. The Dabridgecourts, one of whom was a Knight Founder of the Order of the Garter, were lords of Strathfieldsaye for nearly three hundred years. From the Dabridgecourts the estate passed by purchase to the Pitts, from whom it was bought by the nation early in the present century for the great Duke of Wellington.

Two other distinguished kinsmen of Robert Lowe may here be mentioned. The one eminent as a statesman and man of affairs, making a great figure in Irish history; the other eminent in the world of science and thought, a sagacious seeker after knowledge, and philosopher. Through his descent from Richard Boyle, Archbishop of Tuam, Lord Sherbrooke was related at once to Richard Boyle, the ' great ' Earl of Cork, and to his not less famous son Robert Boyle, one of the Fathers of the Royal Society.

APPENDIX TO CHAPTER I

Ireland and the Poor Law.

Rostrevor : December 5, 1839.

My dear Sir,—I think you will perhaps like to know how we are going on this side the Channel, and I have great pleasure in thus reminding you that I have a lively remembrance of the kindness I have experienced at your hands, and of the pleasure I have had in my friendly intercourse with your family. I believe I may safely say we are getting on well and rapidly in organising the Unions into which Ireland will be divided. I have this week completed the district assigned to my charge, my last Union is finished, and I already begin to ask myself where I shall ever form or organise another, in Scotland or the West Indies ? We have, however, very much to attend to, and it will take us many years to work out the system to its intended results.

Ireland will be divided into 129 or 130 Unions. Of these 93 are already constituted. In nearly all, new Workhouses have to be erected, but as in this country the Commissioners (and not the Guardians) have this part of the business in their own hands, *we* purchase the ground, lay down the plan, employ our own architect to superintend the works when contracted for. We are getting on fast in this respect and already some of my houses begin to astonish the natives. I am more forward in this district, comprising the counties of Antrim, Down, Armagh, Louth, and Monaghan, than they are in any other, for I have new houses, each for 800 inmates, partly roofed in. The population is so dense in this part of Ireland that our houses are necessarily very large. I have scarcely any Unions, though of moderate size, say eight miles round the centre, with less than 60,000, and generally 70 or 80,000 inhabitants. In the Belfast, Armagh, and Newry Unions, I am building houses to contain 1,000 each, for the population in each is above 80,000. We build cheaply in Ireland. Very excellent substantial *stone* houses to hold 800 are built for 8,000*l*., including six acres of land, *fittings* and *furniture*. The houses for 1,000 will be completed for less than 10,000*l*. each, including every expense. All which I see convinces me that the Workhouse System, if *properly* applied, will prove quite as applicable and quite as beneficial to Ireland as to England.

It is true that the labouring population of this country live so wretchedly that it will be impossible to lay down any diet or rule for their food which will not be superior to that on which the poor subsist at their own homes. It is impossible for me to describe the wretched scenes I have witnessed as regards the food on which the independent poor of this country live. So also by their houses. A workhouse will be a palace compared to their cabins. But they riot in dirt and filth. Cleanliness will be unbearable, and, above all, the Irish are so impatient of restraint, they have so great a repugnance to everything approaching to regularity and control, that I have no fear of their willingness to enter the Workhouses. Already I hear the beggars and mendicants declare they will never go into them, and, as far as the North of Ireland (with which I am at present only acquainted) is concerned, in the fear which was expressed in Parliament that the Workhouses would be swamped, it is, I am sure, the last thing we have to apprehend. You are probably aware that in Ireland no valuation or assessment of property exists upon which a poor rate could be founded. We consequently have to value all property throughout Ireland and in each Union before any Rate can be made. This is an immense work, and engages very much of our time and attention, and will necessarily continue so to do for at least a year to come. Ireland is a blank in this respect. No valuation of occupations exists for any purpose whatever. If you had to value all the property in an English Union it would be a great work, but *you* would have officers in each parish, who would be entrusted with the duty, whilst here there are no officers of any description whatever, since there has been hitherto no local administration of any kind.

Again, in England there are competent valuers on all sides, whilst here, as no valuation has ever been wanted, we have no valuers. All is a blank as to matters of business or organisation, and we have to depend upon our own exertions and management entirely. There are advantages as well as disadvantages attending this state of things, but it only proves how little the state of Ireland is fully understood on your side the Channel. Again, the *vast* subdivision of land here, as compared to anything known in England, creates impediments to which, before coming here, I was a stranger. In one of your parishes the farms and occupations are well known and the list is short. Here the holdings are small and almost endless. I cannot better describe this state of matters than by giving you an instance, which I have just had under my eye, and the particulars of which I have taken from the landlord's books and on the spot. I do not give it as a singular instance : it is a fair example. I must quote some one instance in order to explain, and I only take this as a common one.

Mr. Shirley, M.P. for South Warwickshire, has a fine and *well-managed* property in the Co. Monaghan. It consists of an area of 31,000 acres, in a ring fence. Of this area, 3,000 acres are turf bog (for firing) and water, and 28,000 acres are *arable* land. Upon this 28,000 *acres*, 28,000 *inhabitants are located*, and there is not a town or village upon the estate. The people are all in cabins, or small houses, dotted in every direction over the land. They do not strike the eye in the distance when looking at a large surface, as an English eye might imagine, for most of the houses are made of turf and are covered with grass sods, or straw grown green, and, therefore, are so much the colour of the land that you scarcely see them.

But to go on with this estate. From the 28,000 acres, Mr. Shirley derives a *nett rental* of 24,000*l.* per annum, and the estate is not highly rented. He has no less than 4,000 *direct tenants* letting land and paying rent, and consequently, *on an average*, they only pay 6*l.* per annum each, and yet at the present moment there is not 150*l. arrear upon the whole estate.*

The 28,000 acres are, therefore, divided between 4,000 tenants, every holding has to be valued separately, and in Ireland *rent* is no criterion of value ; rent depends upon the kind of landlord under whom tenants live, upon the fact of whether the land is *sublet*, once again divided, and sublet twice, and so on till the nominal rent may be five times the real value, and the real rent just what can be extracted from the poor tenant beyond his own bare subsistence. Of the 28,000 persons located on Mr. Shirley's 28,000 acres, 26,000 are Roman Catholics and 2,000 are Protestants of all denominations, and I may add there is neither a policeman, a constable, a soldier, nor a magistrate upon the whole property. What think you of the picture ?

I wish, however, to tell you that, as far as my observation extends, I have found the principal landed proprietors of the North of Ireland a benevolent, kind, well-intentioned, and, in public opinion, a much injured class of gentlemen. It has been too much the custom by those who are strangers to the circumstances under which the landlords are placed to decry the landlords of Ireland as a hard-hearted class of men, who had little consideration for those around them. I assure you I think just the contrary ; for whatever my opinions might have been before I better understood the condition of the country, I certainly must give them as a body the credit of doing all in their power to better the condition of their tenantry. They are, however, the creatures of circumstances far beyond their control.

What can Mr. Shirley do with his 28,000 people ? To turn them off would be to turn them to starvation, and, by the bye, it is more than his or his agent's life is worth to turn a tenant out whilst he pays his rent.

There is a *combination*, the fruit of circumstances and years of mismanagement of former days, which is beyond the law as *regards the tenure of land*, but in *this respect only*, and if a man does not pay his rent, he forfeits the protection which would be otherwise afforded him.

The original error for which most of the landlords of Ireland are now paying so dearly, and as far as I can see without remedy, was created by the gross and abominable perversion of parliamentary influence to private purposes. That man who could make most 40s. freeholders, could best demand favours from the Ministers of the day, and time was when upon this very Shirley Estate, 2,500 freeholders were taken up to the poll like a flock of sheep. There they and their families now are, the day of reckoning has come, and though Mr. Shirley is one of the most benevolent of men, spending money without limit in educating the people—letting his land lower than any landlord about him, affording every possible assistance towards improvement—yet such is the picture which his estate affords.

You will be pleased to hear that a vast change has taken place in public opinion as regards the Poor Law for Ireland. When I first came to this part of the country I found the greatest possible mistrust, misconception and objection to exist against the measure.

I remember when I was last at your house and about coming to Ireland, that we expressed ourselves rather at a loss why I was directed to the North. I soon found out. Every man was opposed to the law; from the North the great opposition in Parliament had emanated. But I assure you I now do not know where to find an opponent. Without reference to party or religion, I am assisted cordially and heartily by all. Every gentleman lends a helping hand. There are no steady, business-like men as in England—there has been nothing hitherto for them to do in public matters—but from Lord Roden, who is one of my chairmen, and with whom and his Lady, Mrs. Gulson and myself have been staying at one of the most beautiful places which Nature can produce, Tullymore Park, to the Catholics amongst whom I have many esteemed friends, I now find but one opinion—that the measure will do great good and will in time work out great practical improvement in the state of society.

The amount of rate will, I feel confident, be light, as it always must be when the Workhouse system is strictly adhered to, and properly managed. It will not in Ireland amount to 1s. in the £., one-half of which the landlords, and the other half the occupiers, pay. In this part of Ireland it will not be so much—in the poorer districts perhaps rather more; though I doubt if anywhere it exceeds 1s., including all establishment and other charges. Every man now holding land gives away far more than this to the mendicants and others; they all now feel that the measure will be a great relief.

I wish you would come and see us; we live in a beautiful spot, Rostrevor near Newry. The sea is before our windows, bounded by mountains 2,000 and 3,000 feet high. At any rate we could show you much that is new, and variety without end. Excellent steam packets leave Liverpool three times a week for Warren Point, near Newry, within two miles of our house, where we would meet you.

We have plenty of room, and we much wish you would bring Mrs. and the Misses Lowe, in whose society I have spent many hours on which I look back with the greatest pleasure. I expect Lord Worsley over in the Spring salmon-fishing. We have to go to the extreme North and West of Ireland for it, and to rough it occasionally, but we catch great numbers there.

At Ballina, 2,000 fish, salmon and trout, are taken out of the river every morning. At the Giant's Causeway we saw them in shoals and caught some, but the weather was too fine.

I cannot conclude this long, straggling, and perhaps tiresome letter, without most sincerely thanking you for your great and continued kindness to my brother-in-law, Mr. Massey, who, I can assure you, is very grateful for your goodness to him. If Mr. Henry is with you, pray remember me kindly to him; tell him of the salmon and assure him I shall be very much delighted to see him here and to take him amongst 'the finest Pisintry in the world.'

I hope both he and yourself will try to contrive it. The passage is only fourteen hours from Liverpool, and the ladies must not be left behind. Pray give Mrs. Gulson's and my kind regards to them, and

Believe me, my dear Sir,
Yours most truly,
EDWARD GULSON.

Rev. Robert Lowe,
Bingham Rectory.

We hope to get a good Act this Session for England, and a good Vagrant Law for Ireland.

CHAPTER II

CHILDHOOD AND SCHOOL-DAYS

(1811-1829)

'The child,' Wordsworth tells us, 'is father of the man.'
Lord Sherbrooke, who was not even the eldest member of the
Lowe family, seems to have begun his law-making in the
nursery. The children of the Bingham rectory, in the order
of their ages, were :—

> Ellen Pyndar Lowe.
> Elizabeth Agnes Pyndar Lowe ; born, 1809 ; died, 1860.
> Henry Porter Lowe (afterwards assumed the name of Sher-
>   brooke on inheriting the estates) ; born, September 3, 1810 ;
>   died, June 12, 1887.
> Robert (afterwards Viscount Sherbrooke) ; born, December 4,
>   1811 ; died, July 28, 1892.
> Frederick Pyndar Lowe ; born, 1813 ; died, October 12, 1872.
> Margaret Anne Lowe.
> There was also Mary Anne Lowe, who died an infant in 1810.

It seems to have struck the future Chancellor of the
Exchequer and Home Secretary, that even this tiny community
needed the restraints of a legal code to keep them at peace
and in order. He accordingly formulated the following somewhat Cromwellian code :—

Code of Laws instituted by the Lowes in Defence of their Society,
    1819.   (Compiled by Robert Lowe, aged seven and a half years.)

(1) That no one may take a chair when there is another person's
clothes on it.

(2) If a King or Queen do anything unlawful they must be de-
throned, and another chosen by election of the people.

(3) That no person or persons may fight with a brick army for any affront except about the bricks.

(4) That whatever they say in a passion shall be considered as nothing.

(5) That when a law is passing and the votes are equal, the ages of both parties be added up, and those that have the most gain and the law is passed.

(6) That no person may laugh in Court, or fidget about, under pain of being turned out of the Society till that time next day ; and likewise that no one may have a sword at meals or make disagreeable noises at any time.

(7) That when we ask any of the younger class of the Society to give their opinion on any law, that they are not told who agrees to it and who does not.

(8) That no member of the Society may have a stick on Sunday.

(9) That nobody may bribe any person to give their vote about any law.

(10) That every law must be written on the day that it is made.

(11) That no law shall be proposed on Sunday.

(12) That no law shall be made after six in the evening.

(13) That no person may have a book at meals.

Lord Sherbrooke has told us himself that, owing to his deficient eyesight, he was eight years old before he 'began the great business of life—the study of the Latin grammar.' In these more indulgent days, many may think this age quite young enough, while others may hold that it were better never to enter on this study at all. It is somewhat singular that Robert Lowe should have begun the study of Latin precisely at the same age as his future most intellectual opponent on the floor of the House of Commons ; but John Stuart Mill had the advantage—or disadvantage—of having begun Greek when only three years old. In after years Lord Sherbrooke had more than one brilliant fling at the classics, and he even said irreverent things of the whole scheme of University training. But such chastisement was after all from the loving hand of a friend ; or, rather, it was the protest of a true son of *Alma Mater.* Despite his theories, to the end of life he was passionately fond of the classic writers, and was one of the last of the scholars among the ranks of our public men.

Yet the commencement of his studies seemed sadly unpropitious. His mother, he expressly tells us, was opposed even to his going to school, considering his eyesight a fatal barrier to all learning. His father, however, took a more hopeful view, and in any event thought it better that the boy who was so vigorous in mind and body—save for his unfortunate eyes—should take his chance with the others in the competition of the schoolroom, and the rough-and-tumble of the playground.

Accordingly Robert Lowe, in his tenth year, was sent as day scholar, while his father was in residence as Prebendary, to a private school at Southwell, and afterwards to an ancient grammar school at Risley in Derbyshire, where gentlemen's sons began their Latin education.

But his real education (and therefore his troubles) began when he was entered as a Commoner at Winchester. He was then fourteen years of age. Nothing can well exceed his own forbidding account of his life at this famous public school ; and reading it over one understands the fervour with which the boys on ' breaking up ' have sung from time immemorial ' Dulce Domum ' !

Lord Sherbrooke, in writing this description of the Winchester of his early youth, was careful to point out that it in no way applied to the Winchester of our day. The reform is generally said to have set in with Dr. Moberly and Dr. Charles Wordsworth, who were in charge of the school after Robert Lowe had left it for Oxford. Certain of Lord Sherbrooke's contemporaries at Winchester have given almost as gloomy a picture of their school experiences, notably Mr. T. Adolphus Trollope in his very interesting reminiscences, *What I Remember* ; and his younger brother, the late Anthony Trollope, who, however, is even more severe on the Harrow of Dr. Butler, to which school his erratic parents sent him after he had been three years at Winchester. Anthony Trollope's greatest enemy at Winchester was his own brother, who, I presume, occupied

that singular post of prefect, for he tells us that ' as part of his
daily exercise he thrashed me with a big stick.'

It is perhaps only fair to Winchester to bear in mind that
at that time the other great public schools were quite as bad.
It is amusing to compare the hard life of the young gentry of
England, forced to go to Eton, Harrow, or Winchester in those
years, with that of the petted ' gutter-child' in the Board
School of to-day, whose sacred person must by no means
receive chastisement, whatever his offence may be.[1] Anthony
Trollope's misery at Harrow was even more intense than at
Winchester. Then there is the story of the famous Dr. Keate of
Eton flogging a dozen innocent boys, who were sent up not
to be physically punished, but to be prepared for confirmation.

It was a Spartan time ; but in thinking with a shudder of
the brutalities of Winchester in 1825, let us not forget that
three of its boys rose in after life by sheer force of ability
to be Cabinet Ministers and peers of the realm—Robert
Lowe, Viscount Sherbrooke ; Edward Cardwell, Earl Cardwell ;
and Roundell Palmer, Earl Selborne. Another complaining
Wykehamite of that period—Tennyson's ' most generous of all
Ultramontanes,' William George Ward, passed through its
iron tyranny apparently unscathed ; for, at Oxford, he displayed such vivacity of mind and vigour of body, that he fairly
worried his nominal master, Newman, into the Church of Rome,
and his favourite pupil, Clough, into Infidelity. Nor can either
of the Trollopes be regarded as a broken reed—Who was more
constant at the desk or eager in the hunting field than the

---

[1] ' It is very satisfactory to find that a summons against a London Board
schoolmaster for whipping a boy has been dismissed. There was no suggestion
that the punishment was unreasonable or excessive, and the summons was
merely taken out because the boy had for absenting himself from school
received two canings on two different days. The boy said he did not like going
to school, and his mother supported his view. It is simply another effort to
enforce one law for the rich and another for the poor. If the headmaster of a
public school were to be summoned every time a young gentleman was
" swished," we should be told that the boys of the upper classes were becoming
effeminate.'—St. James's Gazette, October 1892.

author of *Barchester Towers*?   In the whole range of modern
men of letters, can we indeed point to a more typical, sturdy
Englishman than Anthony Trollope, unless it be his brother,
who, in his eighty-third year, is the most distinguished of Anglo-
Italian publicists, and still looks out on this fascinating world
with the intelligent, ever-inquiring eye of the scholar and the
thinker.[1]   Nor does this by any means exhaust the list of
eminent Winchester boys who passed through the school during
this dark hour of anarchy tempered by flagellation.   There was
also among the contemporaries of Lord Sherbrooke, Tindal,
afterwards Chief Justice of the Common Pleas; and shortly
before his time, in 1820, there entered a yet more distinguished scholar, Christopher Wordsworth, afterwards Bishop
of Lincoln, one of the great ornaments of the English Church
of the nineteenth century.

It is plain that neither the tyranny nor the mismanagement under either Dr. Gable or Dr. Williams, in any way
injured or weakened these illustrious Wykehamites.   In reading Lord Sherbrooke's account too, it is only fair to remember
that his physical infirmity would have made any form of
public school-life irksome and in a measure dangerous.   Mr.
Adolphus Trollope bears testimony to the fact that while his
old schoolfellow was 'respected, he was not liked,' simply because he could not take part in the rough games of the playground.   To a boy of Robert Lowe's great vigour of body as
well as of mind, with his consequent high health and good
spirits, this must have been no slight deprivation.   At Oxford,
where there was boating, at which his preternaturally short
sight was no great drawback, he became one of the strongest
of oarsmen.

In a letter of condolence on the death of his famous
schoolfellow, Mr. Adolphus Trollope writes to the present
Viscountess Sherbrooke—

[1] Thomas Adolphus Trollope died at Clifton, November 11, 1892, while these
pages were passing through the press.

My recollection of him after the sixty-five years—or thereabouts —that have passed is as perfect as on the day after I last saw him. I can recall every trick of his manner, his voice ; and could put my finger on the spot in the schoolroom where I last saw him standing. There are, of course, but few of our contemporaries remaining ! There is Lord Selborne ; the Warden of New Coll., by whose side I dined the other day, and perhaps half a dozen country parsons, sprinkled—as salt—over the country.

This brief reminiscence will form a prologue to the following tribute to the memory of his old schoolfellow and his oldest friend, which Lord Selborne has been good enough to write for this chapter. Not only are these reminiscences of Robert Lowe at Winchester interesting in themselves, but with regard to the school itself, they show, as it were, the other side of the shield. Lord Selborne writes :—

'My knowledge of Robert Lowe dates from November 1825, when I first went to school at Winchester, being then thirteen years old. He was a year older, and had come to the school only two months before. I was placed next to him at the bottom of the form (senior part of the fifth we called it), next to the highest. There was in that, and in the higher form into which we passed in due course of time, no change of places ; so Lowe and I continued, until he left in the summer of 1829, always to sit together at lessons. We also slept in the same room during great part of the first three years, and in these ways we were thrown very much into each other's company. This was a good thing for me, for we were both ambitious, and there was a useful and always friendly rivalry between us, especially in verse exercises ; Latin composition (and sometimes English also) being much cultivated in those days, and being an almost certain road to the honours both of the school and of the Universities.

'Each of us may have done something to sharpen the other's wits, but I think the balance of obligation, and of the risk of taking things too easily if there had not been such a stimulus, was on my side. Now and then we agreed to have special competitions with each other in particular exercises, and neither of us was unwilling when he thought the other had the superiority, to acknowledge it.

' Lowe was not a boy with whom successful rivalry was possible without a continual effort, and he certainly did much more to keep me up to a high standard of exertion than anybody else.

' He had the drawback of a nearness of sight so great that he could not read without bringing the book close to his face, so as almost, if not quite, to touch it, and he could not write with ease. I remember an epigram of his on " Sleep " (such epigrams, called " Vulguses," were among our tasks on several days in the week), in which he described his own experience of the consequences of lying in bed too long in the morning, as we both sometimes did. It ended :—

> Scribendum est, pigro scribendi ferre laborem,
> Et servanda meæ terga dolore manus.
> Talia si fuerint tua munera, perfide Morpheu,
> Lumina linque, oro, nostra—vel usque tene.

This difficulty of sight was not only against him in school work, but it disqualified him from entering into school games and athletics, in which he might otherwise have been likely to excel, as he learnt to do, notwithstanding it, in swimming ; and it might have stood in his way, if he had been obliged to repel by his own strength any rough usage from his schoolfellows. Boys are not apt to be considerate in their treatment of each other, and I have no doubt he had his share of trials at Winchester, but I think upon the whole he held his own as well as most of us, and was never very roughly handled.

' This may have been partly due to the impression made by his force of character, and partly to the feeling that, but for one disadvantage, no one would have been more capable of defending himself, or more prompt to do so ; for he had a very high spirit and courage, and was not wanting in strength for his age. But I am also willing to believe that most of his schoolfellows, of equal or greater age and strength, would have been ashamed of taking an unfair advantage of one who could not see as well as themselves, and such as were of a meaner spirit may perhaps have been restrained by the better feeling of others.

'Still, he must have felt the strain of contending with difficulties from which his competitors and companions were free, though his pluck and energy enabled him to surmount them ; and this may have sharpened his sense of what was bad in the life and moral atmosphere, and uncomfortable in the arrangements, of the school.

'Certain it is that Winchester never obtained that place in his affections which (in spite of everything which might have had an opposite tendency) it did in my own,[1] and in those of most other Wykehamists. Drawbacks enough upon our comfort there undoubtedly were, for Winchester in those days was as different as possible from what it is now. The commoners, 130 in number, to whose body he and I belonged, were inconveniently crowded together in a large brick building like a barrack, and on three days in the week we were confined to it and the schoolroom, except for one hour before dinner. The hours and meals were not at all well arranged, and in every part of the system there was a more than Spartan austerity.

'We had, however, in our Head Master, Dr. Williams, an excellent man and thorough gentleman, of a generous and kindly nature, who taught well, and had the faculty of interesting the more active-minded of his scholars in their work. The range of teaching may have been limited in comparison with that of the present day ; but it was effective

[1] See 'Lines projected and partly written, on the Four Hundred and Fiftieth Anniversary of the Opening of Winchester College,' March 25, 1843. By Roundell Palmer. *Annals of My Early Life*, Bishop Charles Wordsworth (Longmans), p. 396.

within that range, and Lowe was one of those who profited by it most.

'He became a very good verse-writer and a first-rate scholar, of the robust and tasteful, rather than the minute and technical, kind. When near the top of the school he displayed his poetical gift in a voluntary English exercise upon "The Music of the Spheres," which was recited by him at the public speeches then annually delivered at Easter, and which took high rank among other performances of the same kind by the ablest boys of our own and former generations.

'He was remarkable, even then, for a ready caustic wit, and for a capacity of saying sharp things, which, if they were not always pleasant (I came in for my share of them), left no sting behind. I do not remember any occasion on which we had a serious quarrel. The longer I knew him, the better I learnt to understand the generosity as well as the force of his character.

'He left Winchester a year before I did ; and I followed him in 1830 to Oxford.'

No one can read this narrative of schoolboy days, although written at an interval of some sixty-five years from the time and events it describes, without feeling its essential veracity. In it Lord Selborne has presented us with the brighter side of Winchester life, under the old Spartan *régime*.

Sir Thomas Farrer, of Abinger Hall, writes : 'Some time in the fifties, Lowe, Cardwell, Roundell Palmer, and Henry Halford Vaughan dined with me together. The talk fell on Winchester, and it was characteristic of the men that Roundell Palmer, with true *esprit de corps*, stood up stoutly for his old school ; while the others, and especially Lowe and Cardwell, abused it as a coarse, brutal, cruel school.'

Winchester is now, like all our great public schools, entirely changed ; in many respects, doubtless, for the better. Bishop

Charles Wordsworth, in his *Annals of my Early Life*, tells us in his own modest way of the work he himself did under Dr. Moberly, to soften, and, so to speak, Christianise the school. The ' discipline of the rod '—which, however, the wisest of men thought essential in the training of youth— was practically abolished by the Bishop of St. Andrews [1] while second master at Winchester.

It was the recognised method of dealing with boyish offences. And no doubt my predecessor Ridding was equally ' plagosus ' with his superior ' Orbilius,' Williams, who succeeded Gabell : for the second master equally with the head master had the power of the rod. It was not, I believe, unusual for him, after morning school, to castigate in that manner not less than four or five boys at a time who had been ' tardy chapel.' But I can remember when, in reply- ing to the toast of my health in the Wardens' Gallery at a Domum Festival, I had the satisfaction of stating that not a single boy had been flogged by me during the whole of the long half-year which was then ended. And certainly there had been no relaxation—but quite the contrary —in the needful discipline of the school (pp. 236– 237).

No one can presume to doubt the testimony of the good Bishop ; and all we can charitably hope is that, under its improved and more humane discipline and its wider and more enlightened curriculum, Winchester may some day again produce three such men as Lord Sherbrooke, Lord Selborne, and his own brother, Christopher Wordsworth.

Lord Selborne, with characteristic impartiality, sums up what his schoolfellow really gained at Winchester. It made him (he writes) ' a very good verse-writer and a first-class scholar of the robust and tasteful, rather than the minute and technical, kind.' Lord Sherbrooke himself supplements this testimony by his grateful tribute to his Winchester tutor, Mr. Wickham. But—*more suo*—he goes further, and states that Winchester settled for him an even graver question than

---

[1] Dr. Charles Wordsworth died on Monday, December 5, 1892, at St. Andrews. The *Times*, in a leading article on the death of the venerable pre- late, remarks : ' Among the many eminent men who have borne the name of Wordsworth, he will be remembered as by no means the least eminent.'

that of mere scholarship—' It solved the problem as to whether
I was able to hold my own in life, and proved by a most
crucial experiment that I was not too sensitive, nor too soft
for the business.'

As to his fitness for the battle of life, there will be much
to say later on. With regard to his verse-making there
can be no doubt that Winchester fostered and stimulated
the practice; but even as a child at Bingham, Robert Lowe
' lisped in numbers.' Many of his schoolboy effusions
have been preserved, and nearly all are very superior to
the average of juvenile verse. To his family and immediate friends these must possess a peculiar interest, in which
the ordinary reading public can hardly be expected to par-
ticipate.

There lies before me now a small bundle of such verse,
some written in childhood at Bingham, but most at Winchester. One of these youthful poems arrests the attention
more from the subject than the treatment. The lines are
headed, *The Fidelity of the Swiss Guards to Louis XVI.*;
and signed, *Robert Lowe, Junr., Winchester College*, 1828.
They show, as clearly as Wordsworth's later Toryism or Pitt's
abandonment of his policy of Peace and Reform, how profound
was the reaction in England against the excesses of the French
Revolution. For Robert Lowe was never a blind worshipper
of the ' divinity that doth hedge a king '; on the contrary, he
was opposed to any form of Conservatism which appeared to
him to be based on traditional ignorance or innate stupidity.
But his nature abhorred anarchy and lawlessness and the wild
frenzy that at times seizes on mobs, usurping and over-riding
reason and common-sense even in the most ancient and civilised communities—

Red ruin and the breaking up of laws.

In these schoolboy verses, in which he passionately calls
upon us to do honour to the Swiss mercenaries who so nobly

gave up their lives for the French King, he gives expression in four powerful lines to the prevailing political sentiment of his whole life :—

> Not theirs to wish to break the regal chain,
> To bid the many-headed Monster reign.
> To plunge the land in anarchy and blood
> For vain chimeras of ideal good.

CHAPTER III

OXFORD

(1829–1833)

The Undergraduate—' Union ' Debates and Classic Wit

As a supplement to Lord Sherbrooke's own graphic account of his career at Oxford, the following narratives by Lord Selborne and Canon Melville may fitly open this chapter. Having already told us that Lowe left Winchester a year before himself—that is in October 1829—Lord Selborne thus continues his reminiscences :—

' We were at different colleges not very near each other— he at University College, I at Trinity ; but we met frequently, both in the society of the place and at the " Union " Debating Club, in which we both for some time took a leading part, as did our schoolfellow, Cardwell, Tait (afterwards Archbishop of Canterbury), and others of our friends. Lowe was then, as since, a nervous, incisive speaker, always taking the Liberal side on the political questions which we discussed. There was a schism in the Union in 1833, arising out of the very inadequate cause that the set of men to which we belonged, having for some time had the predominance in the offices and business of the society, were outvoted in the election of a new president, and a clever Radical named Massie, not a favourite with us (though I know no good reason why he should not have been) was placed in the Chair. Lowe took his own line on that occasion, and supported Massie ; in which he was, I have no doubt, quite right. But the dissentients withdrew for a term or two and formed a new society, called the "Rambler," whose debates, for a short time, eclipsed those of the Union. This, the new Government of the Union thought high treason; and they made a motion to expel us, which Lowe supported, but which was defeated by a large majority, at a crowded special meeting, after a very lively debate. Lowe was one of the heroes of that fight; and his prowess in it, as well as that of the other principal speakers, was celebrated in mock Homeric strain—in a *jeu d'esprit* of doggerel Greek called *Uniomachia*, which obtained at the time some local celebrity.'

Canon Melville thus recounts the story of the early academic period of Lord Sherbrooke's career :—

'Robert Lowe left Winchester for Oxford in 1829. Unlike his schoolfellows—Roundell Palmer and Edward Cardwell—he never held a college scholarship. But though so far seemingly short of their successes, the first being a scholar of Trinity and the last of Balliol, this was due to the fact that the endowments of University College were at that time confined to localities with which Robert Lowe had no connection. Otherwise the three schoolfellows had careers very remarkable in their similarity and coincidence. Each attained the highest academic distinctions. Roundell Palmer gathered all the chief University prizes except the English essay. Edward Cardwell was a double first class man. Robert Lowe only lost his mathematical first class through his very defective sight interfering with the clear record of his work ; his nose, as was said at the time, obliterating much which his hand had written. His classical first was well understood in Oxford to be of a high standard. The late Bishop of London, Bishop Jackson ; the late Dean of Christchurch, Dr. Liddell ; Scott, late Dean of Rochester, and others who afterwards became eminent in their several spheres, were in the same class.

'Robert Lowe passed these examinations and took his B.A.

degree in Easter term 1833. The undergraduate life was
spent much as such life at that time generally was. University College, with its close foundation, was not then a literary
college ; and Lowe owed his own successes to his own mental
activity, not at all to collegiate aid. Indeed, so conscious was
the tutor of the time of his own inadequacy to train such a
pupil, that the college offered to excuse Lowe the college lectures, and supply him with a private tutor, if he pleased,
from among those distinguished at the time as trainers for the
final examination. But it was the inherent energy of his
own mind that induced study and led to its results. The
three friends on one occasion started the question among
themselves—what caused them to work ? Cardwell said he
did not really know why he worked—he fell into the way of it
—so far as he did work. Roundell Palmer admitted that he
worked to obtain the prize to which it led. Lowe said he
worked from the love of the pursuit.'

Mr. Francis W. Newman, the well-known surviving brother
of Cardinal Newman, supplies the following quaint reminiscence
of Robert Lowe as an undergraduate :—

'When I was a young Fellow in Balliol College, Oxford, a
young boy, perhaps aged sixteen, not yet of full height,
appeared before us Fellows, as candidate for a vacant scholarship, in the close of November, probably 1830. He had white
eyelashes, &c., as an albino, and his name was Robert Lowe. He
wrote a huge text like a child learning to write. His examination was not such as to gain the honour sought ; that is, he had
elders who surpassed him. But among others of his judges,
I warmly applauded him and augured future success for him.'

Canon Melville gives the following account of Lord Sherbrooke's connection with the famous University Debating
Club—the Union :—

'The Union Debating Society was an early scene of those

powers which in the future were to raise Robert Lowe to Parliamentary success. He was elected February 16, 1831—after a memorable debate on a motion condemnatory of the Catholic Relief Bill—on which Mr. Gladstone spoke and carried an amendment by a majority of sixteen. Robert Lowe's first speech was in March following, on a motion in favour of the then system of popular education. Lowe opposed this, and was joined in the debate by the late Cardinal Manning in an amendment which was carried by twenty-six. After this he was a constant speaker—notably in June of the same year—for " the gradual emancipation of West Indian slavery through the promotion of personal and civil rights and Christian education."

' May 10, 1832.—R. Lowe moved, "That all taxes on knowledge should be done away ; " which with scarce any debate was rejected. Of the many public questions in which he took part it might seem singular that only twice did he plead for any motion—all the rest being in opposition. The decidedly Tory and anti-Liberal cast of the society at that time furnishes the explanation, as the one or two examples given above will illustrate.'

After 1834 heavy tutorial work precluded all but very occasional presence at the Union, of which Lord Sherbrooke always preserved the liveliest recollections ; and, like a distinguished contemporary and fellow-member of this far-famed debating club, he regarded it as one of the best institutions at Oxford.

It has been thought advisable to add some further particulars of these debates at the Union. For this famous debating society has played no small part in training our future statesmen and Parliamentary gladiators, from Mr. Gladstone himself to his latest Home Secretary, Mr. Asquith. Lowe ranked among the most brilliant of these Oxford debaters; and no one who knows human nature will smile in disbelief

or in derision when it is said that many of these debates at
the Union equalled, and perhaps surpassed, the efforts of the
same men in after years on the floor of either House of
Parliament. For they were then in the full flush and pride
of their strength and powers; eager to investigate and solve
the great problems of humanity, eager also to cross swords
with every foe, and only too glad to illumine the path of all
whom they judged to be misguided or in darkness. No mere
paltry considerations of expediency occurred to these fresh,
ingenuous minds; no sad premonition that the world would go
on much the same whatever their eloquent tongues might
utter.

What better proof and illustration of this can we have than
the case of Mr. Gladstone himself. 'Gladstone,' writes Mr.
Brinsley Richards, 'was elected Secretary to the Union in
1830 and President in the following year. It was soon after
this that he attacked the Reform Bill; and he spoke with
such trenchant force, such overflowing conviction, that Lord
Lincoln [afterwards Duke of Newcastle], transported with
enthusiasm, at once wrote to his father, to say that "a man
had uprisen in Israel."' Dr. Charles Wordsworth says of this
speech that it was 'better than any I heard in the House of
Lords, though I followed the five days' debate in that House,
and the Lords' debate was acknowledged to have been better
than that in the Commons.' The result of the speech was
that Gladstone was invited to stay at Clumber during the Long
Vacation, and the further result was that three years later
he got inducted into the Duke of Newcastle's pocket borough
of Newark.[1]

Mr. Gladstone was then, and for some years afterwards, the
'rising hope' of the 'unbending Tories'; while his future Chancellor of the Exchequer was one of the leaders of the small but
active Liberal and anti-clerical party at Oxford. Everybody
has read Sir Francis H. Doyle's graphic and amusing account,

[1] 'Mr. Gladstone's Oxford Days,' *Temple Bar*, May 1883.

in his delightful *Reminiscences and Opinions*, of his meeting with Lowe at the Union. How Thursday after Thursday he had watched ' affectionately and respectfully ' an ' old gentleman with snow-white hair, who seemed to have become a regular attendant,' and how he kept saying to himself : ' There is that dear old boy again. How nice of him to come and investigate what we are worth.' Sir Francis is careful to explain that he was himself ' as blind as a bat ' ; but having noticed the nice old gentleman he longed to know his name.

The information was soon to be vouchsafed to me. Whilst the Reform debate was going on, some earnest young Tory had denounced Lord Grey and his colleagues as a vile *crew* of traitors. He had hardly finished, when up jumped my patriarch (it was summer term, with the boat races in full force), and in a loud and vigorous tone of voice took him to task thus : ' The hon. gentleman has called her Majesty's Ministers a crew. We accept the omen, a crew they are ; and with Lord Grey for stroke, Lord Brougham for steerer, and the whole people of England hallooing on the banks, I can tell the hon. gentleman they are pretty sure of winning their race.'

Then it was Sir Francis Doyle found he had been ' revering as an old man the famous white-haired boy Bob Lowe.'

This story down to his latest years used to afford Lord Sherbrooke great amusement. I have more than once heard him exclaim, ' Those are the very words I used.'

One of the most memorable debates of this time was that of May 16, 1831, on the motion of Mr. Knatchbull :—

' That the present Ministry is incompetent to carry on the government of the country.'

To which Mr. Gladstone moved as a rider :—

' That the Ministry has unwisely introduced and most unscrupulously forwarded a measure which threatens not only to change the form of our government, but ultimately to break up the very foundations of social order, as well as materially to forward the views of those who are pursuing this project throughout the civilised world.'

The debate was prolonged for three days, and, on a division, the Ayes were 94—the Noes 38.

Among those who took part in this debate, and honorary members of this period (to some of whom reference is made in these pages), we find the names of Palmer, Lowe, Hicks Beach, Ackland, Sneyd, Anstice, Wilberforce, Wordsworth, Doyle,. Massie, Tait, Rickards, and Ward.

The late Dean Church—and there could be no more competent judge—declared that in his time Ward and Robert Lowe were the first speakers at the Oxford Union: ' Cardwell was equally fluent, but the effect of his speeches was injured by a touch of affectation.'

With both Ward and Lowe, according to the Dean's account, there was a strong sense of the seriousness of the matters in debate ; and they raised the atmosphere of discussion above that of a mimic parliament—playing at ministers as boys may play at soldiers—to that of serious men discussing views known and felt in all the importance of their bearing. If the palm must be given to either, Lowe carried it off in the directly political debates.[1]

Lord Cranbrook—then Mr. Gathorne Hardy—recalls the fierce warfare that was waged rather later at the Union between various members and Mr. (afterwards Canon) Trevor, who led the committee an uneasy life, and was so redoubtable a foe that ' once he put Ward into hysterics.' Lord Cranbrook writes : ' No doubt some of those more active in the Union than I was will have told you of Lowe's being more than once brought back, after taking leave of its debates, that he might encounter Trevor. I remember Lowe was much struck by his ability and his clear and forcible style of speaking. On one occasion when Lowe had returned Trevor quoted the lines :—

> Now fitted the halter, now traversed the cart,
> And often took leave, but was loath to depart.

' The next day when I went to Lowe, he was trying to find

---

[1] *W. G. Ward and the Oxford Movement*, p. 22.

the author. He found it to be Prior; and we then went on with our work. Lowe was much taken with the appositeness of the quotation.'

Sir John Mowbray, the present worthy member for the University of Oxford, recalls vividly the Homeric battle between the Union and the Rambler in the October term of 1833; nor does he forget the great incidents of the fining of the future Archbishop of Canterbury a pound, the recollection of which was a source of humorous delight to Lord Sherbrooke to the very last: 'It was indeed,' writes Sir John Mowbray, 'a battle of giants; is it not recorded in Greek verse in the *Uniomachia*, and in other lays in English?' So irate were certain leading members of the Union at the election of Massie, the 'Radical,' as President (with Lowe as Treasurer), that they seceded—among them Tait, Roundell Palmer, and Ward —and formed the Rambler. They boycotted the Union, the debates languished, and the benches were empty. Massie and his cabinet, determined not to be outdone by their antagonists, brought forward a motion to turn the Ramblers out of the Union. An extraordinary meeting was held at the larger room at the Star (now the Clarendon) Hotel, and there was a fierce debate. When the President was speaking, Lowe, as the next principal officer, occupied the chair. In the midst of the President's speech, Tait rose in great excitement—

Tait shook his tasselled cap and sprang to ground.

Lowe enforced silence and fined the future Archbishop one pound. The debate ended in the defeat of the motion; the Ramblers carried the day.

The next term (January 1834) a ministry of conciliation was installed and the feud was at an end. One remarkable fact, however, occurred. Tait appealed, after the new Ministry came in, against the fine imposed by Lowe; but the Union confirmed the fine.

In the summer term of 1835 there was again a party

We now come to the still more famous macaronic poem which Lowe himself composed on the visit of Queen Victoria— then the Princess Victoria—and her mother, the Duchess of Kent, to Oxford, in 1833. One very wet day in that year (writes Canon Melville) the Duchess of Kent and the Princess Victoria excited Oxford from heads to tails by a visit. Robert Lowe memorialised the event by a very witty macaronic poem. Even yet *rainy dies aderat*, and the hexameter verse which worked in the then leading hostelries :—

Angelus aut Mitre vicinave Stella Gazellæ—

are not forgotten. Spite of the doggerel element of such compositions, there was in Lowe's example such true classic ring that friends said he ought to write for the annual Latin verse Chancellor's prize. It was late in his undergraduate career, and he had never previously competed. He did, however, in that year : and though desuetude told against him, he only lost the victory from want of that finish which practice alone secures, running second to his friend Roundell Palmer.

Mr. Pycroft, in his *Oxford Memories*, states that ' copies were sent to every part of the world where Oxford men were to be found.'

Judging by the following letter, it would seem that Lord Sherbrooke, contrary to his custom, sent at least two copies of the poem himself to the sister University of Cambridge :—

Robert Lowe to H. P. Lowe, Esq., Trinity Hall, Cambridge.

University College (no date).

Dear Henry,—Many thanks for your letter, which amused me much, especially the part devoted to the malediction you are pleased to pronounce upon the Mathematical and Physical Sciences. You will be surprised to see the parcel that accompanies this note –it is a burlesque Latin poem, which is led by unavoidable circumstances to consider me as its author. Having been deemed worthy of the favour of the Oxford public, it is now about to make its appearance in the Sister University. You and Whitley will find copies for yourselves and be able to appreciate its merits at your leisure. . . . With regard to the various philosophical treatises you propose to my acceptance, sore doth it grieve me to say that I have caused a bookseller to suffer for the amount of the above-mentioned publications, with the single exception of Miller's Hydrostatics, for which I shall be grateful by the first opportunity that offers, as I am in no immediate want of it.

Tell Whitley if he has any regard for me he will write me a detailed account of his campaign in the long vacation, and how I stand in certain people's good graces. . . .

Your affectionate brother,
R. Lowe.

Few topical skits have enjoyed so long a life. The venerable Dr. Charles Wordsworth, late Bishop of St. Andrews, who was the tutor both of Mr. Gladstone and of the late Cardinal Manning, wrote just before his death: 'Not long ago I could have quoted several of the lines, which were clever and amusing; and I fancy a good specimen of his gift in humorous satire. Now, I can only recall the beginning of one, *Rainy dies aderat!* '

Sir John Mowbray declares that he was so delighted with Lowe's verses, that he learnt them when they first appeared, and that now, after nearly three-score years, he can quote almost the whole poem from memory.

Many other distinguished Oxford men, including Mr. J. A. Froude, who calls it 'a brilliant Latin poem,' have written to remind me of it, and several have specially urged on the score of its extreme rarity, as well as cleverness, its republication in this 'Life.' Lord Sherbrooke had indeed lost his own copy; but, fortunately, the one which he had presented to his old Radical friend Edward Massie sixty years ago has come to hand.

It only remains to add that Lowe's burlesque Latin poem was published before the amusing Greek verses, *Unio-machia*, which have sometimes erroneously been accorded the priority :—

POEMA CANINO-ANGLICO-LATINUM SUPER ADVENTU RECENTI
SERENISSIMARUM PRINCIPUM

Dicite praeclaram, Musae, mihi dicite Kentae
Duchessam, Princessque simul Victoria nostro
Singatur versu, Conroianusque triumphus,
Et quàm shoutârunt Undergraduates atque Magistri,
Et quantum dederit Vice-Chancellor ipse refreshment.
Rainy dies aderat; decimam strikantibus horam
Jam clockis, portae panduntur, then what a rush was,
Musa, velim, memores: si possis, damna recounta,
Quae juvenum nimis audaces subiere catervae,
Quot periere capi, quot gownes ingemuere
Vulnera vae ? nimium loyalas testantia vires.
Fugerat all patience, cùm jam procedere troopum
Sensimus, et loudo Mavortia trumpeta cantu
Spiravére: venit, venit, Oh ! carissima conjux
Guelphiadae ; ad currus equites spatiantur anheli.
Versibus hic fortes liceat celebrare cohortes,
Norrisiasque manus, Abingdoniamque juventum,
Multa the rain, et multa lutum, permulta caballi
Damna tulere illis : necnon wiva cuique criebat
Absentem ob dominum, neque enim gens est ea, cui sit
Flectere ludus equos, et pistola tendere marko,
Ast assueta to plough, terramque invertere rastris.
Quid memorem quanto crepuit domus alta tumultu ?
Intremuere scholae ; celsâ suspecta cathedrâ
Intremuit Christchurch, tremuit Maudlenia turris,
Ratcliflique domus, geminisque University portis,
Doctorum stipata choro pokerisque tremendis
Royalty ubi ingressa est, super omnes scilicet illa
Guelphiadas felix, dextram Rhedycina benignam
Cui dedit, accepitque sinu, propriamque dicavit.
Consedére duces, et tum Vice-Chancellor infit,
' Si placeat vestrae, Celsissima, majestati,
Nos tuus hic populus, tuaque haec Universitas omnis
Supplicibus coelum manibus veneramur, ut adsit
Omne good et pulchrum tibi filiolaeque serenae,
Quae matris guided auspiciis, eductaque curis,
In modern literis, Graecis etiam atque Latinis,
Triginta magnos volvendis mensibus orbes
Imperio explebit, regnumque à sede Londini
Transferet, et nostram multâ vi muniet Oxford.'
Insequitur loud shout ; loud shoutis deinde quietis,
Kentea pauca refert, set non et pauca fuerunt
Clappea, nec paucis se gratified esse fatetur

Curtseis, tanto mage gens perversa fatigat
Plausibus assiduis non inflexibile collum.
  Qualis ubi ingentes, conchâ veniente, portmantos,
Greatcoatosque, bagosque humeros onerare ministri
Bendentis vidi, quem dura ad munia mittit
Angelus, aut Mitre, vicinave Stella Gazellae.
Illa refert, ' We thank you, kind sir, for the honour you've done us,
Nought's interested us more in the tour, which we just have been taking,
Than this our reception in Oxford. I beg to assure you that I shall
Always endeavour to teach my daughter whatever is useful,
That she may be fit to reign over a great and a glorious people.'
    Dixerat ; et strepitu prodis. Conroie, secundo,
Phillimori deducte manu tibi tegmen honoris
Obvolvit latos humeros subjectaque colla !
    Jamque silent cunei ; tum rhetor with paper in hand
Ore rotundato narrat fortissima facta
Herois, narrat fidum Princessis amorem,
Multaque dicta before, et quae race postera dicet,
Protulit—in totum fertur vox clara theatrum—
    Olli sedato respondet pectore Praeses—
' Admitto causâ te, Vir Fortissime, honoris
Doctoris gradui civili in jure Periti.'—
    Heu ! nimium felix, civilia condere jura
Nescius, aut tenues linguâ distingnere causas.
Non Lincoln's Inn illum, non Intima Templa tulerunt
Furnipulive aedes clarum boastavit alumnum ;
Nec tamen inde minùs juris consultus abibat
Suffragiis doctis, et serto templa forensi
Vinxit, et insigni laetus terga induit ostro
Ah ! nullas miserûm causas subitura reorum.
    Tum subito Praeses, all things jam rite peractis,
' Nos hunc concursum extemplo dissolvimus,' inquit—
Exoritur clamorque virûm, clangorque tubarum,
Effudit vacuis turbam domus alta cathedris,
Unâ eâdemque viâ Princessam effudit et ipsam.
Curritur ad Christchurch, de Christchurch curritur All Souls.
Alfredi tandem fessas domus alta recepit
Hospitio of the best, sed quod magis hearty voluntas
Commendat domini cum sedulitate feloûm.
Plurima quam nitidâ quae stant opsonia mensâ,
Scrubbatumve platum, kidglovative ministri.
    Quis cladem illius luncheon, quis dishia fando
Explicet ? haud equidem quanquam sint voices a hundred,
Cast iron all, omnes dapium comprendere formas,
Magnificaeque queam fastus evolvere coenae.
    Egressis (neque enim possunt eatare for ever)
Gens effraena ruens, nondum graduatia pubes,

CHAPTER IV

OXFORD (*continued*)

(1833–1840)

Graduate—Fellow of Magdalen—Private Tutor, and would-be Professor

LORD SELBORNE thus closes his narrative of Robert Lowe's career at Oxford :—

'In 1833 Lowe took his degree with great honour—a first class in classics and second in mathematics. He was not long afterwards elected to a Fellowship of Magdalen, of which College I had myself become a Fellow in 1834 on taking my degree ; but I left Oxford in 1835 for London ; and had from that time till he entered Parliament fewer opportunities of meeting him than before. He married in 1836, and remained for some years in Oxford taking pupils ; and was beyond question the ablest and most successful private tutor then in the University.'

Lord Sherbrooke in his brief autobiography states that his failure to secure the double-first was a disappointment to him ; for (he writes) ' I was sure that I knew enough to entitle me to a first class [in mathematics], though I felt perfectly conscious that I had not brought my knowledge properly out.' Mr. Pycroft, who, however, like most anecdote-mongers, is as often wrong as right, states in his *Oxford Memories* that ' Lord Sherbrooke was pronounced by his tutors certain of a first in mathematics and not certain in classics.' Although·

this remark appears in a book of anecdotal reminiscences, it looks, in the light of Lord Sherbrooke's own statement, as if it had some foundation in fact.

In 1835 Robert Lowe was elected Fellow of Magdalen on the foundation of which birth in the county of Notts was a qualification. Two years previous to this, as he tells us in the Chapter of Autobiography, he had embarked on his labours as a private tutor. We have his own word for it that, compared with these labours, everything else in his career ' has been mere play and recreation.' More than one old Oxford man has written to express his very natural doubt as to whether even Lord Sherbrooke's head could have long withstood the strain of this terrific time. He often had, he tells us, no less than ten pupils ; and for five years out of the seven during which he was a private tutor, he also took pupils during the long vacation.

' I do not think (he writes) I could have gone on with it much longer.' One does not wonder at this confession when it is recorded that so able a man as the late Bishop Jackson, who as a private tutor had fewer pupils than Lowe, owned that his head was giving way.

Canon Melville, however, referring to this tutorial period, relates a story concerning Lord Sherbrooke which, under the circumstances, can only fill us with amazement for his capacity for work and his love of learning for its own sake.

Lowe was a much-sought private tutor—a function which he fulfilled for some years after taking his own degree. At one time he had so many pupils that, between nine in the morning and ten at night, he had besides his dinner-hour but one spare hour—viz. that from four to five. A friend similarly occupied met Lowe at the time one day in Oxford with a book under his arm and said : ' Where are you going ? Come for a turn in the country, as I do for my hour.' ' No,' said Lowe, ' it's the only time I have for a Sanscrit lesson with Professor Wilson.'

In Mr. Pycroft's *Oxford Memories* we light on the following :—

'Mr. Lowe,' said my friend Rendall, ' was the cleverest man I have ever read with.   He was so near-sighted he seemed to depend very little on his sight, and to know all his books by heart.   He had the widest Oxford acquaintance of any man of my day.'

With pardonable pride, Lord Sherbrooke himself bears out the truth of such statements by declaring that he was ' popular as a tutor,' and that he retained his ' number up to the last, and finished in November 1840 with four pupils in a first class of six.'   It will be remembered that he then mentions some of his more successful pupils, and recalls, with evident satisfaction, that many came to him even from those 'distinguished men' Mr. Newman and Dr. Arnold.   In his later years Lord Sherbrooke was much pleased by the following passage in a private letter of Mr. J. A. Froude : ' I remember Lord Sherbrooke well at Oxford before I went out of residence.   Indeed, I was almost his pupil.   I asked him to take me when I was going into the schools.   To his regret, I believe, and certainly to mine, he had no room for me.'

There could hardly be stronger testimony to the high esteem in which Robert Lowe was held as a private tutor, than is afforded by the following extract from a letter written by an old pupil but life-long political opponent, the Right Hon. Gathorne Hardy. Earl of Cranbrook : ' I was his pupil and had a great regard and esteem for him, as he was a man of singular honesty and frankness.   He gave great attention to those who read with him, and it was wonderful that with ten or eleven men at one time he saw each separately and never flagged.   At the same time he was reading on his own account, and I remember his telling me that he was learning a modern language (I think), Spanish.

' A pupil who failed in attendance he would plainly tell that he would not take his money unless he came, and when he saw that anyone had really no chance of honours, he would frankly tell him so.'

Another of his pupils, Dr. Richard Congreve, the cultured disciple of Auguste Comte, evokes a more sombre recollection of this period of Lord Sherbrooke's Oxford career : 'I was for a short time the pupil of Robert Lowe, Lord Sherbrooke, and I preserve a very grateful sense of the benefits derived from his teaching. I remember his expression as he closed the last lecture. "There," he said, "that is the last lecture I shall give in this place, where I have been selling my life-blood at 7*s.* 6*d.* the hour." '

Dr. Congreve kindly reminds me that Charles Arnold, as well as Arthur Hugh Clough, read with Lord Sherbrooke during a long vacation at Ambleside.

Lord Sherbrooke, as his old Oxford friends testify, was never idle. He took pupils even through the vacation, and in addition to his all but incessant labours with them, he was often engaged on some difficult and independent branch of study on his own account. It was in the Long Vacation, spent with pupils at Festiniog in 1834, that Lowe fell headlong over 'Hugh Lloyd's Pulpit,' escaping by a miracle with his life, as he himself has so graphically narrated. It is surprising what a number of persons have written to inquire as to the truth of this story, which has, evidently, in various forms enjoyed a wide circulation.

The following letter, written on this memorable vacation, to one of his oldest and most cherished friends, the Rev. W. Boyd, now Archdeacon of Craven and Vicar of Arncliffe, Skipton, for which I am indebted to the courtesy of the Dean of West-minster, is eminently characteristic, and in my judgment well worthy of preservation. Archdeacon Boyd was Lowe's contemporary at University College. 'Greatly and deservedly respected by him then and always,' writes Dean Bradley. It is generally believed that Lord Sherbrooke once declined to compete for a Fellowship in order that his friend might get it ;

like other men who have been called cynics, he did such
acts of self-effacement for those who were dear to him.

Robert Lowe to the Rev. W. Boyd.

Festiniog, Merionethshire: August 17, 1834.

Dear Boyd,—The idleness which prevented my writing to you
in the first instance has long been succeeded by that shame and repugnance which invariably follows the neglect, though it does not
always secure the performance, of a duty. I have been living all the
vacation hitherto at a little cottage in the neighbourhood of Barmouth, in a more secluded situation than 1 ever remember to have
been in before. This I may truly say was a subject of no uneasiness
to me; the only effort being to leave it, as I was sometimes obliged
to do, to visit my family who were living five miles off *en masse.* I
am convinced practically that the mind, when not warped by habit
or prejudice, has the faculty of adapting itself to its situation, when
in the way of amusement of being as dissipated, and when in retirement as solitary, as possible.

My studies have been divided between learning the alphabet and
forms of noun and verb in the Sanskrit grammar, and pursuing
German, without altogether forgetting my Hebrew. The Sanskrit
alphabet consists of fifty simple characters, which, by means of
initial and final consonants and vowels, and a compound and often
anomalous character for every double consonant, are multiplied to
upwards of a hundred. Over these difficulties, I am happy to say, I
have *triumphed unassisted,* though I cannot but applaud the wise
dispensation which conceals the future from our eyes, since, had
I known their magnitude ἐξ ἀρχῆς, it is more than probable I might
never have attempted them. The German, in which I hope you
also have been making progress, I find very easy and beautiful,
and a pleasant relaxation after my Oriental studies.

I have just removed, as you will see by my date, to Festiniog
a beautiful village among the mountains in the north of Merionethshire, where I mean to renew my acquaintance with Snowdon and
Co. I am not yet fully settled, owing to the crusade which is being
carried on against the grouse, who, few and diminishing yearly,
still linger in scanty coveys over the hills which their ancestors once
held undisturbed.

Thus far of myself. Now learn what I expect to hear from you
in return. In the first place, in the grand Tory festival,[1] which I
am delighted not to have attended, what part did you and yours

[1] The Installation of the Duke of Wellington as Chancellor of the University
of Oxford.

enact ? How did the week pass off, and how did you manage the immense journey into the Hyperborean regions which you are pleased to inhabit ?

Were you not amused with the Hebrew ode ? It tickled my fancy much —particularly where it said, ' The seekers of new things hath he not loved,' to turn the language of the Patriarchs and Prophets to the purposes of ephemeral politics, and to tune the harp of Judah, before which the mighty trembled, to sound the notes of flattery, was an indecorous species of desecration—a sort of adulation which it well became Magdalen Hall to invent and Oxford to patronise.

Have you read *The Edinburgh Review* on the installation ? If not, do. Please to let me know how your parsonical duties go on. I shall be delighted and interested with any detail on the subject. I am almost ashamed on looking back to see into what a tirade I have been led, but you know how it is with me—*Cælum non animum mutant.*

An accurate account of your studies, thoughts, intentions, and imaginations, which must have been many in the interval which my idleness has suffered to elapse, is but a small portion of what I expect to hear from you.

I see Palmer of Trinity, and Richardson of Wadham, are elected Fellows of Magdalen ; so much the better for somebody else. I have written to congratulate the former on his success.

Pray present my compliments to your father and sister, who I hope enjoyed their Newnham excursion as much as I did. Do not suffer your mathematics to become obsolete, as I still look forward to your triumphant return to Oxford.

Believe me,
Yours very sincerely,
R. Lowe, Junr.

P.S.— I hope I have spelt the name of your village right. My ideas have been confused by reading an account of a battle in which it is spelt Ryetown.[1]

It was in the year 1835 that Robert Lowe obtained a lay Fellowship at Magdalen. This, in its way, was a provision for life, and made him independent as to money. But three months after this, he engaged himself to Miss Georgiana Orred, whom he had met at Barmouth. This may well have

[1] The above letter is addressed to ' The Rev. D. W. Boyd, Ryetown, Newcastle, Northumberland.'

seemed an unaccountable proceeding to his father, and gave rise to an estrangement which was a source of much pain to the son. His determination to marry carried with it the impossibility of retaining a Fellowship, and ultimately taking Holy Orders, which the rector of Bingham desired. Robert Lowe's resolve to abandon his Fellowship and read for the Bar appeared a most ill-judged proceeding and greatly increased the annoyance of his father who thus saw all his plans frustrated.

It was an additional mortification to Lord Sherbrooke to find that almost every member of his family coincided with his father's views. It is pleasant, however, to learn that the affection of his brother Henry remained unchanged through all the troubles which ensued, as the following letter will testify.

Robert Lowe to H. P. Lowe.

My dear Henry,—I never remember to have been more affected by anything in my life than by your letter; it has been so rarely of late that I have met with any show of friendly feeling from my relations that I had ceased to expect it, more especially from you, whose every constituted notion of prudence is controverted by my conduct on this occasion. I have found no one else who has deigned to communicate with me on the subject who could disapprove without condemning, no one who did not seem to forget their originally kind feelings towards me in the strength of prejudice and remonstrance. My aunts are, luckily for me, on my side. Aunt Sherbrooke is, I hope, wavering, and could I have an interview with her might, I think, be made completely my ally. What I write now for is to press you to come and see me at Magdalen. You will find your quarters excellent and a bed at your service as long as you like to stay. I can then talk this matter over with you at our leisure and tell you many things of which you are not aware.

Matters at present stand thus : my father has interdicted me the Law, and refused to assist me in the prosecution of it. He says he will not allow me to marry without 500*l.* a year of my own besides *her* fortune. He has now driven me to extremity, and I have offered to make, not five, but seven hundred a year by taking pupils here. To this I am now waiting his answer ; it is not the kind of life I should have preferred, but if I am not to go to the Law all other professions are indifferent to me.

. . . . . .

Your affectionate Brother,

ROBT. LOWE, Junr.

In later life, Lord Sherbrooke by no means regarded the Bar as the ideal profession for one who could not discern the faces of judge or jury. But at this period he could see no other opening, being resolutely determined not to enter any profession for which he felt no true vocation. Having thus decided on his own course in life, and being above all things a man of the highest resolution and independence of character, he sought no aid from his father or friends. But his marriage, as will be shown, was from the first a singularly happy one, and the constant companionship of his wife from this time until her death seemed to him more than compensation for all his subsequent trials.

The following letters, written to his brother Henry just before his marriage, brimming over with almost schoolboy spirits, give a lively account of his pursuits and aspirations at this period.

From Robert Lowe to Henry Porter Lowe.

Oxford : June 10, 1835.

Dear Henry,—As you seem to have appreciated my last letter fully, and withal express a wish for another, I see no objection to gratify you, provided always that I can find enough to say to fill a sheet. It gives me great pain to renounce the thoughts of a trip to Spain, notwithstanding the lice, Carlists, and other plagues wherewith that miserable country is afflicted. I seem, however, much more likely to conduct two or three men to Beaumaris to read and boat than to indulge in any such vagaries. I had thoughts of East Cowes, but the guardian of one of my griffins stood out so stoutly against the place that I was obliged to change my hand and check my pride, and propose Beaumaris as a kind of compromise.

. . . . . .

As touches the law, I believe that the smallest sum for which it is possible to exist at one of the Inns of Court is 150*l.* a year, but

I have too good an opinion of your and my own notions of comfort to believe that we could vegetate under 100*l.* a year more. My Magdalen Fellowship (when got) will be a great assistance to me, as it will put 170*l.* into my pocket towards defraying my expenses in town.

The way of life I should pursue is to read about seven hours a day, which I consider enough for a Chancellor, never to dine in hall, seeing the dinners are exquisitely beastly, but to get into some club or other—the Junior University, for instance—where one would meet old acquaintances, read the papers, and dine. If you are really in earnest in your intention of study, I should advise you to read, mark, learn, and inwardly digest the first two volumes of Blackstone, particularly the first part of the second, and to throw in the last chapter of the fourth, which is a history of the English Law drawn with a very masterly hand. I should also recommend to your notice Hume, and Smollett, and Hallam in his *Middle Ages* and *Constitutional History of England*, and Robertson's *Charles the Fifth*. Most of these books are written in a very attractive style, and all of them treat of subjects which ought to interest every English gentleman, so that you could not possibly bestow your time better than upon them, whether you go to the Bar or not.

Since I began this letter I have been to London to keep a term, and seen Herbert, who inquired very kindly after you. The weather was hotter than I could have supposed possible at Senaar, and I lost so much bodily from heat, and pecuniarily from cabs, that I am but the shadow of my former self in both respects. Went to see Malibran act the *Sonnambula*, which she did well.

Aunt Sherbrooke and Aunt Elizabeth are coming here to-night on their way to London. I came down by the Worcester mail; night being the only time when a gentleman can travel in this weather: you will be happy to hear that it is accelerated, arriving in Worcester at a quarter-past eight, and the Gloucester in that town at half-past seven.

The Municipal Corporation Bill seems to have satisfied all sides, which I rejoice at not a little, as it will give the Tories a decided minority in the next Parliament. If you happen to fall in with a little book called *Major Downing's Letters*, read it by all means; you will find it one of the most amusing collections of slang you ever saw. I have got a Cambridge man to oppose me at Magdalen, a certain Rickards of Trinity, a first-class man, but I do not think he has much chance. If you mean to read Law, you must not do it by halves, for it is a very repulsive study, and London offers so many temptations to one to be idle that nothing but dogged resolution can save one from it.

Write soon and give me your views of Beaumaris and reading places in general, and believe me your affectionate Brother,

ROBT. LOWE.

The second letter was written a couple of months afterwards, when he had gained the Magdalen Fellowship, and addressed to his brother at Bagnères de Luchon.

No. 1, Green, Beaumaris : August 6, 1835.

Dear Henry,—I have used you wretchedly, horridly, d—nably, in not writing to you before, particularly as I have plenty to say. I got the Fellowship without much trouble, cause why, there was no opposition, seeing that three other horses who were to start were drawn, and I had nothing to do but to show my paces in walking over. I was settled at Beaumaris, and went up to Oxford for a week, on the Saturday of which I was elected, left by the ' Union ' at half-past eleven that night, met the mail in Birmingham, and got to Beaumaris at nine in the evening. What would your dog Frenchman say to that? By-the-bye, the King of the French seems inclined to avail himself of the infernal machine as an engine to silence the Press, and thus tread out the few embers of liberty still left to that deluded nation ; if that be so, I should feel almost inclined to wish that the next twenty-five gun-barrels aimed at him may be pointed with more precision.

I like Beaumaris of all things ; for bathing and sailing it is almost perfect, and the mountain view is splendid. I miss the mountain walks we had at Barmouth, but it is impossible to combine them with the sea, and I am content with my part of the alternative.

Excellent dinners, spoilt by jolting and eaten on an uncomfortable rickety table, and dignified by the name of picnics, are the order of the day. I have made acquaintance with the Vicar, Dr. Howard, and his family—very pleasant people ; and with Sir Richard Buckley, who lends us a six-oar, against which Mr. Lowe cautions me thus : ' It is full of *danger* and *destruction* in salt water—*cave caveto !* '

We ordered a play last night of some wretched comedians, who acted in a barn, and collected an audience which must have rejoiced the cockles of their hearts. They want me very much to pull in the regatta, which I am very unwilling to do, but do not know very well how to get out of it without appearing ill-natured. I am very much amused with your whopping adventure, which put me in mind of the ferryman at Ballachulish, only that the result in your case was more serious. My mind is clouded with a gentle envy when I read your description of the Pyrenees; I fancy I shall prefer them to the Alps.

We have a party of Cambridge men here who were fighting the other night, first among themselves, and afterwards with some Welsh sailors, waking me out of my first sleep, and confirming my theory of Cantabs. There is one of them whose supernatural hideousness is as impossible to describe as the Pyrenees themselves; a kind of man who, if he meant to make love effectively, ought certainly to wear a mask. I like Beaumaris much better than Barmouth, and am sure it would have pleased my sisters far more if they had had the wit to know it.

I had to make a speech upon my election the other day, which I did with considerable effect. You have no idea what a gentleman-like arrangement it is to be the only candidate for a Fellowship; it does away so completely with all foolish doubts and difficulties. I shall be very glad to hear more of your Pyrenean ideas, and will promise to answer any questions you may ask in your next letter, as I have mislaid your former one, and, I fear, answered it very imperfectly.

Your affectionate Brother,

ROBT. LOWE.

In the March following (1836), Lord Sherbrooke married— but a matter of such supreme importance must be dealt with in a separate chapter. After their wedding tour, Robert Lowe, with his wife, returned to Oxford, bought a small house (16 St. Aldate's), and for four more years he continued his wearing drudgery as a private tutor. In the following year (1837) he was appointed a master of the schools, as a 'little-go' examiner. His pungent comments on the duties of this office will be found in the Chapter of Autobiography.

The year 1838, as Lord Sherbrooke himself declares, seemed likely at one time entirely to have altered his course of life. The Greek Professorship at Glasgow, with a salary of 1,500*l.*, a house, and only six months' work in the year, fell vacant on the death of Sir Daniel Sandford. One can imagine how tempting this must have seemed to the newly-married, over-worked Oxford private tutor. The following particulars may be added to his own graphic account of the contest, in which he was worsted by Mr. Lushington.

In the *Life of Archbishop Tait*, by the present Bishop of Rochester and Canon Benham, is given the correspondence between the Archbishop and his brother, Mr. John Tait, on the subject of this Glasgow Professorship. Tait himself was anxious at first to secure the appointment, and he had two very strong recommendations—he was a Scotsman, and he had been a student at Glasgow. But he was an Episcopalian in orders as an Anglican clergyman, and he declined to subscribe to the Confession of Faith. He accordingly withdrew his name from the applicants, and in doing so wrote to his brother, 'I shall be sorry if they appoint an indifferent successor to Sandford.' Subsequently the future Archbishop wrote to the Principal of the University of Glasgow, formally withdrawing from the contest, and enclosing a 'testimonial in favour of another candidate, Mr. Robert Lowe.' [1]

The Bishop of Rochester has kindly looked over the late Archbishop Tait's papers, but has not been able to lay his hand on this testimonial. The following, however, was forwarded to Glasgow by the Rev. R. Michell, Lowe's private tutor and intimate friend; and was probably signed by Mr. Tait of Balliol, as well as by other distinguished members of the Union :—

Apprehending that an objection may be raised to Mr. Lowe as incapable, from the shortness of his sight, of keeping order in a large class, we beg to state our conviction that such an idea is founded on an exaggerated view of his physical defect, a defect which is far more than compensated in him by a high and resolute spirit, and commanding, though conciliatory manners. In proof of this opinion we beg to refer to a fact of which we were eye-witnesses.

Several years ago, at a meeting of nearly 200 members of the Oxford Debating Society, the subject being one of local and personal interest, the greatest disorder prevailed, so great as to baffle every effort to repress it, and to threaten the dissolution of the meeting. At this period Mr. Lowe took the chair, and by his decision and vigour, by fining one member and threatening others by name with the same punishment, he completely restored order, which was not

---

[1] *Archibald Campbell Tait. Archbishop of Canterbury*, vol. i. p. 68.

again interrupted." We believe if he was found capable of repressing disorder at its utmost height, if his sight served him in this instance to detect and punish the disorderly, that in a class where his authority would be so much greater, and through the absence of excited feelings the obstacles to contend against so much less, he could not fail to command the respect and attention of his pupils in the highest degree.

If, indeed, Archbishop Tait signed this testimonial, it was a truly forgiving and Christian act ; for, as Lord Sherbrooke has told us, it was none other than the future Head of the Church whom, on the occasion referred to, he had fined 1l. for ' disorderly conduct.'

However that may be, Lowe was not successful.   He admits—and we may well believe him—that it was a very bitter disappointment.   He was thoroughly weary of the monotonous drudgery of his daily life at Oxford, and, as the following playful letter, written at the time to the Rev. R. Michell, will show, he was very sanguine of getting the Professorship.

Robert Lowe to the Rev. R. Michell.

Glasgow : July 6, 1838.

My dear Michell,—What have you done with that there certificate ?   I am afraid you must have forgot the direction, and therefore write to make sure.   It is

Robert Findlay, Esq.,
Glasgow Bank,
Glasgow.

I am getting on well here, the thing rests between Lushington and myself, and I do not think my chance the worst of the two.   He has got two or three votes certain, but they are from the least influential and respectable members of the Faculty; the better class having fought shy, and shown full as much attention to me as to him.   The Principal, MacFarlane, will determine the point by adding himself to one side or the other.   I have pretty good reason to suppose that he is not ill-disposed to me.   Mr. Findlay's influence is very great, and my testimonials have beaten Lushington's in a much greater degree than I had ventured to hope.   Pray send that letter, if not already sent, as in the present state of affairs it is of great consequence.   I am writing from a Dodson and Fogg shop, kept by one of the young Findlays in Glasgow, and two Scots are jabbering law within a yard of me, which must be my apology in case this scrawl is incoherent.

Yours very truly,
ROBERT LOWE.

In a second letter to Mr. Michell, written on his return to Oxford, Lowe explains to his friend that he was beaten purely by local faction.

Robert Lowe to Rev. R. Michell.

Oxford : August 8, 1838.

My dear Michell,—Georgiana tells me you are anxious to hear from me the circumstances which led to my defeat at Glasgow. I had succeeded beyond my hopes, and one of those who afterwards opposed me, said they had put off the election on purpose to get such a person as myself. This I knew from unquestionable authority was the state of things the day before the decision ; three electors had pledged themselves to Lushington before I came forward, but all the rest (seven) meant to vote for me. My supporters quarrelled among themselves on a point which I am not at liberty to mention, but which had no connection with Lushington or myself, but turned upon their own local factions which in a self-elected body, as you well know, lie pretty deep ; to spite the rest one part of them went over to Lushington, and brought him in. Thus, after having triumphed over the united Whig and Tory interest of Scotland, Sir G. Clerk and the Lord Advocate, after having distanced Lushington in public opinion as far as he did the rest of the candidates, the turn of a straw rendered all my efforts futile. I soon made up my mind to the matter and came back home on Monday, with a resolution to think no more about it, which I have kept.

Very truly Yours,
ROBERT LOWE.

Although Lord Sherbrooke bore his disappointment in a truly philosophic spirit, far different to that in which poor Mark Pattison tortured himself over the loss of the Rectorship of Lincoln, yet how freshly the incident came back to him when, as Chancellor of the Exchequer, he revisited Glasgow to be presented with the freedom of the city in 1872 ! In the brilliant speech of grateful thanks, which he delivered on that occasion, he remarked :—'Gentlemen, I am also particularly happy that this honour has been given to me by the city of Glasgow, because, long years ago, the dream of my life was to connect myself much more nearly than I am ever likely to do with this city. I had at one time some reason to suppose that I might have been elected to the honourable and distinguished office of Professor of Greek in your University. To fail in that object was the greatest disappointment that ever happened to me in my life, but years soften everything, and I now can only remember that the place, I doubt not, is much more worthily filled by a distinguished and elegant scholar.'

It is somewhat suggestive to reflect that had Robert Lowe succeeded in this quest he would never assuredly have gone to Australia, nor would he in all probability have entered the arena of the House of Commons. The duties of such a professorship would have been congenial—he was never really an ambitious man, and its emoluments would have been ample for his wants. It is therefore more than likely that for the rest of his life he would have been known as Professor Lowe, and the world would never have heard of Viscount Sherbrooke.

Georgiana Lowe?
dau. of George Orred Esq.
of Tranmere, Cheshire.
1836.

CHAPTER V

MARRIAGE AND CONTINENTAL TOUR

(MARCH—AUGUST, 1836)

ON March 29, 1836, Robert Lowe was married by Archdeacon Wrangham, at Holy Trinity Church, Chester, to Georgiana, daughter of Mr. George Orred, of Tranmere, Cheshire.

The wedding-day was marked by an adventure which was sufficiently serious to test the fortitude of the young couple. Scarcely had the carriage in which they started for Festiniog left the city, when it was overtaken by a terrific snow-storm. The horses, blinded by the fury of the gale, struggled along the road, which at every step grew more difficult. Meantime the occupants of the carriage, unable to open the windows, were half-suffocated by the thick mantle in which they were wrapped. Further progress was beginning to be impossible, when, to the relief of the travellers, they reached a way-side cottage. Here they were hospitably entertained till the storm had spent itself; and, in the morning, they continued their journey.

Lord Sherbrooke, in his autobiography, devotes only a few lines to this epoch of his life. But he takes occasion to testify to the admirable qualities of the lady he had chosen for his wife—and these were no mere conventional phrases. From the day of their marriage they passed through many wearing and anxious experiences, and often life seemed hopelessly dark to them. But Mrs. Lowe never for a moment despaired.

Her faith in the great gifts and lofty purpose of her husband
never faltered, and her loyal, courageous spirit triumphed
over every difficulty. Writing of this time, Lord Sherbrooke
calls it an 'auspicious year'—and speaks of the tour in
Switzerland which they made in the summer, part of which
was enlivened by the company of his tutor, Mr. Michell, and
of another Oxford friend.

Of this tour Lord Sherbrooke handed me a diary, and
a brief personal narrative, for the purposes of this work ;
from these I propose to make somewhat copious extracts, if
only to show the mixed multitudes of English folk who now
' do ' the Continent (with or without the assistance of Mr.
Thomas Cook) how very different were the conditions of
foreign travel half a century ago.

The Diary.

Monday, June 13, 1836.—Left Oxford at half-past eight and
reached London at two ; got down in Oxford Street, went to
Colonnade Hotel, called on the Biddulphs, drank tea with Mrs.
Howe, 16 Cadogan Terrace, Sloane Street, Chelsea.—Hot !

Tuesday, 14*th.*—Went to Fenchurch Street in a 'bus for our
passport. It cost 7*s.* 6*d.* ; got it endorsed by the Prussian Consul,
Hebeler, for 5*s.* more. Went to the Exhibition at Somerset House.[1]
Liked Turner's *Rome,* and *Juliet and her Nurse at Sunrise,* and
Cortez reading an account of his atrocities to Pizarro.—Cortez is
much injured by posterity in being coupled with his illiterate
and unscrupulous contemporary. Went to the British Institution ;
admired Guido's *Annunciation.*

At the Water-color exhibition which we saw on Monday, admired
Nesfield's *View in Arran* ; Evans's *Irish Highlands* ; Fielding's
Summit of Snowdon ; *View up Loch Leven,* Fielding ; *Lancaster
Sands,* Cox ; *View on the Downs,* Fielding ; *Mill on the Conway,*
De Wint.

---

[1] In a private letter, Mrs. Chaworth Musters writes : ' One point that
shows the many-sidedness of my uncle's gifts was his appreciation and dis-
crimination of works of art. It seemed like an intuition, for we could never
imagine how he saw them. I have often been with him at the British Museum,
of which he was a trustee, and he has walked about with Sir Charles Newton,
looking at statues and works of Greek art, talking about them and criticising
them so ably.'

Got 200*l.* in bills of exchange from Coutts ; dined in the Colon-nade with Michell on Aldermanic fare :—white bait and beef-steaks. Went to the Opera, Grisi *Desdemona* ; Rubini *Otello* ; Tamburini *Iago* ; La Blache *Elmira.* After all it was a heavy performance and the audience not particularly brilliant. I was very tired, but Georgiana insisted upon staying to see the ballet. It was dreadfully hot.

Wednesday, 15th.—Left the Colonnade at six and drove to the Custom House. Having been duly imposed on by coachmen, porters, watermen, and other scum of the earth who frequent that locality, we weighed anchor for Rotterdam.

In addition to his entries in this Diary, Lord Sherbrooke re-wrote the following brief account of the first half of his trip :—

Lord Sherbrooke's Account of his Trip to Rotterdam and Bonn.

It was on a beautiful morning, on June 15th, 1836, that my hackney coach, having conveyed me through the deserted Strand and uncrowded Fleet Street with a facility which, in the middle of the day, could have been accounted for by nothing less than a pestilence, or invasion, deposited me at the Custom House. The great city was quiet, but a restless activity swarmed on the banks of the river. The voluble and amphibious race who inhabit these regions left me no time to speculate on the architecture of the Custom House (which I had leisure enough to contemplate on my return) and I was glad when I found myself free from their importunity, and safely *landed*—if I may say so—on the deck of the 'Namona,' steamer to Rotterdam. The rows of lighters gradually became less dense, the water visibly clearer and the banks more distant ; I looked up, and behold ! the sky was cloudless. Nature had done her part and Man was no longer there to mar it. We had no awning, but the black pennant of smoke which floated above us flung its broad shadow on the deck, and the sun seen through it was as completely shorn of his beams as through a piece of smoked glass.

Some time after we had lost sight of land, we fell in with a fleet of butterflies, steering they did not seem exactly to know where. This was quite an event to the boys on board, who employed the remains of daylight in chasing them from one end of the vessel to the other.[1]

Before daylight we had crossed the Brill, and on coming on deck at four I saw land on each side; but two streaks so narrow compared with the bold rocks of the Foreland, or even the level banks of the Thames, that it seemed more through courtesy than necessity that we condescended to keep in the middle of the channel, and refrained from forcing our way over an obstacle apparently so insignificant. We anchored at Rotterdam at 5 A.M., after a very short passage of only twenty-two hours.

There is nothing in the appearance of Rotterdam from the water to announce to the traveller the presence of a great commercial city. A simple row of old houses, with a single row of trees before them, with a spire or two rising behind, and fields on each side, as green as plentiful moisture can make, are all that is to be seen.

At the Hôtel des Pays Bas, I was shown up the painted staircase into a bedroom large enough for a troop of cavalry to bivouack in; having established myself in a corner of this apartment, I proceeded to do all that ablution could to remove that unutterable feeling of dirt and degradation which every-one feels who has passed twenty-four hours on board a steamer. This, and a copious libation of Dutch tea, which is really excellent, sent me forth into the town tolerably well satisfied with myself.

The canals that intersect the streets in every direction, the rows of trees by their side, the splendid country houses of the

---

[1] In the *Diary* at this point he adds: 'Soon after I had tumbled into my berth, somebody tumbled out of his; loud laugh from a gentleman who is generally quite within the limits of becoming mirth, and from all the circum-jacent aspirants after repose. Last thing I heard was Michell quoting from Æschylus—

Σπαρνὰς παρήξεις καὶ κακοστρώτους —'

merchants, with their marble floors, and ornamental chimney-
pieces and ceilings, showed at a glance that the Dutch were far
beyond the English in the art of making the haunts of Commerce agreeable.[1] All was strange and striking, language not
only foreign but absolutely unintelligible; the gay and flaunt-
ing appearance of the shops; the ships unloading at the ware-
house doors; the women, pretty, but of so different a class of
beauty from our island belles; and the extraordinary architecture of the houses.

The beau-ideal of a Dutch house seems to be to put into it
as many windows and of as large a size as possible, to cross
and surround these with the greatest possible quantity of
heavy woodwork, and to cover this with the greatest possible
quantity of paint. The brush is never out of their hands; one
coat is hardly dry before another succeeds, and negligent indeed
must be that householder who has not at least one painter in
full employment.

Having hired a carriage for twelve guilders, I drove to the
Hague. It is the fashion to rail against the ugliness of
Holland, but to me it was full of interest. (1) In Rotterdam
I saw for the first time the little mirrors disposed at the
windows to afford the inhabitants a view of the passers-by,
an arrangement which generally rouses the indignation of
tourists against the idleness and curiosity of the Dutch. But
as I have seen the same thing in almost every large town in
Germany and Switzerland, I must ascribe this to the unfortunate situation of Holland, which brings her in contact with
the English traveller before he has rubbed off a single prejudice
or acquired an idea beyond the manners of his own island.
(2) The crops are luxuriant to a degree unknown in England,
and the very cows and sheep seem conscious of their happiness,
revelling in the abundance which surrounds them.

[1] 'Walked out in the town, presented a letter to Monsieur Labouchere, for
whom we had a letter of introduction; found him just setting out for Amster-
dam; his office was very splendid.'—*Diary*, Thursday, June 16, 1836.

The ride to the Hague was diversified by a few church steeples, tame storks, and summer houses projecting into the middle of green stagnant ditches, with their wide unmeaning windows open to the road. The Hague is a pretty town, with streets so wide that they have almost the appearance of squares; its gallery of pictures is beyond all praise, and our dinner at the old Doellen [1] gave us a very favourable idea of Continental cookery. The palace in the wood looks like one side of a street, the other of which has been knocked down.

Sailed from Rotterdam next morning for Nimeguen, but had not gone a mile before the engine was deranged, and we were obliged to wait an hour and a half while it was being repaired. Notwithstanding many gloomy prognostications, we arrived at seven in the evening. Lady Mary Montagu compares this place to Nottingham. The comparison may do well enough, but the ' smug and silver Trent ' is little honoured by a comparison with the sluggish and turbid Rhine; and Nimeguen does not cover one-tenth of the ground of its British prototype. But there is a river at Macedon and a river at Monmouth, an eminence at Nimeguen and at Nottingham, and that suffices.

The next day and night I look back to with unmitigated disgust. The banks of the river are totally without interest, the steamer small, crowded, and unprovided with berths, and the heat intense, notwithstanding which the rain fell in torrents all night and deprived us of the miserable satisfaction of sleeping on deck.[2] We did not emerge from this aquatic

[1] ' Dined at the old Doellen most sumptuously, with eighteen dishes at 2 florins a head. Met with a mad old Dutchman in the coffee-room, with whom, in an evil hour, I entered into conversation. The consequence was that he teased us all dinner-time with his remarks ; he said, among other *sottises*, that his ideas when he spoke English were devotional, French martial, and Dutch amorous.'—From the *Diary*.

[2] His *compagnon de voyage* seems to have preserved his cheerfulness even under these depressing circumstances if we may judge by this entry in the *Diary* : ' *Saturday, 18th.*—Breakfast on eggs as usual, which gave Michell occasion to say that though our journey was not a triumph, it might fairly be called an *ovation*.'

black hole till one o'clock on the following day, when Cologne,
its cathedral with the crane on the top, and the long bridge of
boats which connects it with Deutz, rose before our impatient
eyes. The revolving altar-piece of Rubens, the tomb of the
three kings, and the purlieus of this dirty, irregularly built
town were soon looked over; and it was with great pleasure
that I left it by the packet for Bonn. The voyage from
Cologne is uninteresting, though there are two or three pretty
views of the Seven Mountains. Bonn is the seat of one of
those moral and intellectual abominations—a German university, a fact of which it is impossible to remain in ignorance
for a single half-hour, so great is the anarchy and disturb-
ance.

Lord Sherbrooke's narrative ends here, so the Diary is
resumed from the entries at Bonn.

The Diary (continued).

Monday, June 20th.—Rainy morning, looked over the College,
and obtained a good view from the Telegraph. Went down to the
quay at half-past ten. The porters refused to let us have our luggage
unless we paid a thaler, ten groschen more than the tariff. This
we refused, and began to put the luggage into the boat ourselves.
Hereupon ensued a scrimmage, the porters pulling and blaspheming
in French and German while a number of students who were standing
by laughed immoderately. Michell and I were the principal actors in
the scuffle, which was carried on with varying success till it was
interrupted by a little vapouring peace-officer who, without entering
into the merits of the case, took part most violently against us;
finally settled by Morgan paying the sum demanded. Digesting our
wrath as well as we could, we started. The first part of the Rhine
disappointed my expectations, moderate as they were; but the latter
more open part, from Andernach to Coblenz, fully equalled them.
Arrived at the Belvue, Coblenz, at half-past six, and were so pleased
with this beautiful city that we determined to remain there a day.
Walked over the bridge on the Moselle.

Tuesday, 21st.—Georgiana and I went a mile down the Rhine in
a rowing boat, which cost us a thaler, to an island from whence she
made a sketch. Returned at nine, and went to a banker, from whom
we got a twenty-pound note changed; we received twenty-three

Fredericks d'Or, four Thalers, and ten Groschen, which sum, after much calculation, we found to be right. The Frederick is worth 17s., the thaler, 8s., the groschen 1¼d. Coblenz (corrupted from the Latin *confluentes*) has one good street, a bridge of boats over the Rhine and of stone over the Moselle, and two squares, in one of which are trees whose leaves were almost entirely devoured by caterpillars; and in the other rose trees, in full flower, which, much to the credit of the inhabitants, remain untouched. At one o'clock set off for Ems on foot, the ancient Embasis, missed our road, and meeting fortunately with a German labourer, were set right. The country rises to a considerable elevation and then descends into the valley of Ems which is watered by a largish river. We saw on our walk four varieties of campanula and many other beautiful flowers; dined at the Englischer Hof, and returned in a pouring rain which obliged us to take refuge in a Diligence, in which we found a young Scotchman, an engineer residing at Bonn, who had been on a tour to Wiesbaden. Drank tea in the speise-saal, where the smoking was intolerable.

Wednesday, 22nd.—Were called at five o'clock, and discovered to our sorrow that it was a rainy morning, so wet that we gave up all idea of reaching Mainz. Went to bed again, did not breakfast until ten o'clock; after dinner went to see the fortifications of Ehrenbreitstein. The view is chiefly worth seeing from the clear idea it gives of the course of the Moselle and of the Rhine, above and below the confluence; otherwise hardly worth the trouble of the ascent. Ehrenbreitstein is garrisoned by 1,200 men, or two battalions.

Thursday, 23rd.—Steam to Mayence—hot day—bad company—disappointed with scenery—dined on deck--Georgiana began to be ill. Mayence is garrisoned by Austrians and Prussians, the former have dark complexions and drab uniforms. The cathedral is handsome, but red. Sour claret for supper.

Friday, 24th.—Off at six. Reached Manheim at half-past twelve. Michell lost his trunk by taking his time too much, and I forgot my bandbox; made our reclamation at the Bureau. Went in voiture to Heidelberg and looked over the castle.

Saturday, 25th.—Georgiana, though very sick, made three sketches of the Castle; and I, though nearly as bad, went with her. We then took a walk on the other side of the river—very hot. Michell got up to the top of the hill.

Sunday, 26th.—Hotter. Voiture to Carlsruhe; time from 11 till 7, distance 36 miles. Fine town, regular streets, square with orange-trees in it.

Monday, 27th.—To Baden; pretty road. Town inferior to Carlsruhe. Dined at the *table d'hôte* at 4—plenty of English. Disappointed in the town ; very sick.

Tuesday, 28th.—Parted with Michell. Left Baden at 8 ; dined at Offenburg. Georgiana and I began to feel better. Slept at Kissingen, which we reached at 11.

Wednesday, 29th.—Left Kissingen at 8, reached Freybourg at half-past 11 : saw the Cathedral, and bought a poem on it from the commissioner at the inn. Left Freybourg at 1, and arrived at Basle at 9. The coachman pulled up under a tree and cut us off a large branch of cherries.

Thursday, 30th.—Georgiana sketched and I 'jewed' till 2, when we started with the same *cocher* for Berne. G. sketched the Château of Ankenstein. Slept at Courendelin. Both of us quite recovered from our indispositions.

Saturday, July 2nd.—Having arrived at Berne at 10 the previous night, and put up at the Falcon, shopped till 1 o'clock, got my passport signed (by the *Chargé d'Affaires*) for Italy. Looked at the Alps ; Georgiana sketched the town from the Zurich road.

Sunday, 3rd.—Packed up, and arranged to leave a trunk behind us. Dined on buns and cherries : started for Thun in the diligence, arrived before sunset.

Monday, 4th.—Set off 6.30, walked along the side of the Lake till we got a view of the end thereof. Very hungry and hot. Got some bread and cheese, wine and kirschen wasser, at a little public-house. Bathed in the Lake and swam out to look at a view, to Georgiana's horror. Got back at seven, hot and tired enough.

Tuesday, 5th.—Left Thun by the steamer at 10. G. drew at the end of the Lake and I bathed, devoured by flies whose stings draw blood. Walked to Interlaken, about two miles. Fine sketch of the Jungfrau ; and picked out a sketch for next day. Lost our way coming back.

Wednesday, 6th.—Went out to take the sketch at 7 ; I came back at 11 and wrote journal and letters. Made various excursions on the following days, among which was one to the Giesbach in a boat ; got behind the Fall.

. . . .

Tuesday, 12th.—Left Interlaken for Lauterbrunnen on foot, having sent our clothes to Meyringen. Blazing hot. Georgiana sketched the Bösenstein. Arrived at Lauterbrunnen, and were reposing after the fatigue of the walk when Michell, Tireman, and Lakin walked in. They dined, and went back to Interlaken in the evening. Michell would not let them go with us over the Wengern Alp. Walked to the Staubach, which is like a bottle of ale foaming over—none of the force or fury of a cascade.

Wednesday, 13th.—Georgiana went with intent to sketch the Fall, but was so dazzled by the sun as to give it up. Took heart of grace and walked up the valley to look at the Fall of Schmadribach, which we should have reached if it had not been for an avalanche, which arrested our course when near it. Georgiana sketched a fall which (so unjust is fame) is higher and fuller of water than the Staubach.

Thursday, 14th.—Set off at 6 and walked over the Wengern Alp to Grindelwald. Dined on the Little Scheideck. Fine view of the Eiger in a mist. Refused to pay anything to the proprietors of the glacier.

Friday, 15th.—Georgiana sketched till 1; then she started on horseback, and Mr. Scholey and I on foot, up the Faulhorn. Quarrelled with the man who led the horse because he would not go far enough. Scoused him of his *pourboire*; my guide seemed half inclined to take his part. Got to the top of the Faulhorn, and slept there. There were a Frenchman, a Pole, and a Russian, and a German school.

Saturday, 16th.—Saw the sunrise in our blankets—beautiful view. When a mist came on, we descended to Rosenlaui, where we were overtaken by the rain and forced to stay the night. The Frenchman (who had told us he had climbed the Faulhorn in 4 hours when he had really been 9) going down the mountain without a guide lost his way, and, as John Bunyan says, I saw him no more.

Sunday, 17th.—Pretty place—glacier—precipice. Dog bit me, whereupon I wrote the following :—

> Dog of ungentle, churlish mood,
> I will not shed thy felon blood,
>   Though smarting from thy bite ;
> For since I choose to trust thy free
> And fawning show of courtesy,
>   In faith, thou'st served me right.
>
> I did but come awhile to view
> Helvetia's hills of snowy hue,
>   And rocks by torrents rent ;
> And if it were a fault, in sooth
> It did not merit from thy tooth
>   So sharp a punishment.
>
> But when from England others come,
> Self-exiled traitors to their home,
>   Then up ! vindictive cur,
> And drain from out their vampire veins
> The latest life-drop that remains
>   Of all they sucked from her.

Walked on to Meyringen. Saw the Reichenbach, and made arrangements for sending our things to Stanz. I dismissed my guide at Rosenlaui, who had come with us from Lauterbrunnen--slept on a shakedown.

Monday, 18th.—Left Meyringen at 10; weather re-established. Dined at Guttenen ; slept at Handeck, in the chalet on beds of hay. Mr. Scholey walked about above, and nearly frightened Georgiana into a fit. Curds, cream, &c. in abundance.

Tuesday, 19th.—Saw this most splendid waterfall, with its iris in full beauty, whereupon I wrote these verses :—

FALLS OF THE AAR AT HANDECK.

Fanned by thy whirlwind's everlasting play,
Crowned by thy iris, vestured in thy spray,
Throned on the reeling rock and quivering pine,
What charms, what terrors, mighty stream, are thine !
Two rival floods, no more asunder pent,
Leap raging down, on mutual ruin bent,
Like foemen grappling with their latest breath,
Who meet in fight, but never part in death.

Breakfasted on chamois, walked to the Grimsel, dined there, and walked to the glacier of the Rhone, where we slept.

Wednesday, 20th.—Walked over to Realp, an inn kept by the Capuchins, with whom I talked Latin.

. . . .

Tuesday, 26th.—Walked from Stanz to Stadt, thence in boat to Lucerne—beautiful view. Bought *Atala* and à little drawing-book for Georgiana, who has become fond of drawing buildings.

Thursday, 28th.—I ascended the Rigi with Scholey, of whom I took my leave at the top ; returned to Kussnacht, and walked with Georgiana, whom I had left below, to Aar.

. . . .

Saturday, 30th.—Walked to the top of Mount Albis ; got into the mud in the dark. Old woman with whom Georgiana would not shake hands.

Sunday, 31st.—Walked to Zurich.

Monday, August 1st. --Got a letter from Fred announcing his election [to the Fellowship at Magdalen]. Went in the *coupé* of the diligence to Schaffhausen—saw the Fall. Walked to Dusenhofen in the dark.

Tuesday, 2nd.—Walked to Stein. Georgiana sketched. Miserable hole, full of old nuns. Fell in with a *retour*, who took us to Constance.

Church, Lowe held, as against Keble, Pusey, and Newman, that instead of being weak or oppressed, she was altogether too powerful and dominant, especially at the University. He was therefore opposed root and branch to the 'Oxford,' or 'Tractarian' movement,[1] the aim of which was to combat, and, if possible, overthrow the rising tide of Rationalism and Liberalism in England by the revival of mediæval theology, and the strenuous assertion of the power and authority of the Church.

It may well be imagined that, to an intellect so essentially masculine and positive as Lowe's, much of the Tractarian propaganda, with its theological casuistry and mere word-spinning (as he would regard it), seemed too utterly futile to call for serious attention. In this he was plainly mistaken ; for the mass of men are led much more by their emotions than by their reason, and the Tractarian party alone, in Oxford at this time, appealed to the deeper feelings and pious sentiments of the rising generation. On this very point Newman makes a most pregnant observation :—

The Roman Church stops the safety-valve of excitement of Reason ; we, that of the excitement of feeling. In consequence, Romanists turn infidels, and Anglicans turn Wesleyans.[2]

Meantime the leaven was working, and these earnest young religious reactionaries were drawing some strange fish into their net.

There was Lowe's late schoolfellow, the unfortunate 'senior prefect,' W. G. Ward, who left Winchester an admirer of Mill and Bentham, and, after he reached Oxford, was for a while a religious Liberal of the school of Dr. Arnold. One would have thought when this same Ward became an avowed

---

[1] 'This title is surely to be preferred to "Oxford Movement," which seems to destine that ancient seat of learning never to move, except backwards.'— *Cardinal Manning*, by A. W. Hutton, p. 252 *n.*

[2] From letter of the Rev. J. H. Newman to Rev. H. J. Rose, in *Letters and Correspondence of J. H. Newman*, edited by Anne Mozley, vol. ii. p. 187.

Newmanite, and began to play those fantastic tricks which at
length closed Oxford and opened Rome to him, that Robert
Lowe would have paused from his daily drudgery of ten hours'
tuition, and sprung into the fray. Probably he regarded his
old schoolfellow's transformations of faith as too constitutionally pantomimic to be amenable to rational criticism. Doubtless he heard of the 'movement' from his more intimate
friend, Roundell Palmer ('Catholicus,' as he playfully styles
him); but what he heard evidently did not flutter his pulse.
Lord Selborne expressly bears testimony that 'he held himself aloof from the theological controversies by which the
minds of many Oxford men, resident and non-resident, were
much occupied.'

But Newman's *Tract 90* was too much for Robert Lowe,
and he forthwith entered into the theological fray by publishing an anonymous pamphlet, entitled *The Articles Construed by Themselves.* Ward promptly took up the cudgels, and
of course made Newman's position (as he doubtless intended)
absolutely untenable. Lowe retorted with great vigour, and
with but little consideration for the feelings of his fellow-
Wykehamist; which, to do Ward justice, he never murmured
at, for he preferred a stout foe, who could hit out straight
and hard.

It is singular, when we consider the future eminence of
Lord Sherbrooke, no less than the marked ability displayed
in these short controversial pamphlets, that his share in the
fierce battle that raged round *Tract 90* should have been
almost completely ignored. So far as I know, no writer on
this subject seems to have called attention to them except the
late Dean Church and Mr. Wilfrid Ward in comparatively
recent publications. Cardinal Newman himself, in his well-
known *Apologia*, in which he has so much to say of his own
tract, omits all reference to what Lord Selborne describes as
'perhaps the most sensible' of all the replies which it evoked.
But this is not surprising, as Newman evidently desired to

minimise Ward's position in the movement ; [1] and it was
Ward who, without consulting him, had rushed into the fray,
and in his own peculiar fashion joyfully admitted all the
charges brought against Newman and the party by their new
antagonist.

Mr. J. A. Froude, who was himself for a while a Newmanite,
and whose brother, Hurrell, was one of the actual founders of
the Anglo-Catholic party, has written, as only he could, on the
Oxford Tracts ; but he, too, makes no mention of Lord Sherbrooke's trenchant criticism of *No. 90*. On calling Mr. Froude's
attention to this oversight, he frankly replied : ' I had forgotten, or I never knew, that Lowe had written about *Tract 90*.
But his mental eyes were always wide open in those days,
however it might have been with his material ones.' It is
still more remarkable that Dr. Abbott, who has been devoting
so much time to Newmanism of late, should have apparently
overlooked a writer who in two short pamphlets anticipates so
much of his own work.

. Newman's object in *Tract 90* was to prove—or rather suggest—that the Thirty-nine Articles may receive a ' Catholic '
interpretation ; and that anyone holding ' Catholic ' dogma
and doctrine may, without undue reservation, subscribe them.
The Tract was published on February 27, 1841, and on the 8th
of March following the four senior tutors (of whom Mr. Tait
of Balliol, afterwards Archbishop of Canterbury, was one) expressly accused its author, writes Dean Church, ' with suggesting
and opening a way by which men might, at least in the case of
Roman views, violate their solemn engagements to their
University.' [2] On the 15th of March the Heads of Houses condemned the teaching of the Tract—precipitately and unwisely,
thinks Newman's great Anglican advocate, Dean Church.
Newman replied with his accustomed subtlety, but hardly
with his customary success, by boldly stating that the

[1] See Dr. Abbott's *Cardinal Newman in the Anglican Church*.
[2] *Oxford Movement*, p. 291.

Articles were ' written before the Decrees of Trent,' and hence
' were not directed against those decrees,' but merely, he
maintained, against certain popular superstitions and vulgar
errors which had crept into the Roman system by the sixteenth century. War was now fairly declared, and everyone
in Oxford ranged himself on one side or the other.

Then it was that Robert Lowe entered the lists. His first
pamphlet, *The Articles Construed by Themselves*, is now extremely
rare. I believe there is not a copy even in the Library of the
British Museum. He chose two mottoes, which clearly enough
reveal the temper of mind he was in after reading Newman's
most famous pamphlet :—

For though I do verily believe the Church of England a true
member of the Church, that she wants nothing necessary to salvation, and holds nothing repugnant to it ; and had thought that to
think so had sufficiently qualified me for a subscription, yet now I
plainly see, *if I will not juggle with my conscience and play with
God Almighty*, I must forbear. . . . And I plainly perceive that if
I had swallowed this pill, however gilded over with glosses and
reservations, and wrapped up in conserves of good intentions and
purposes, yet it would never have agreed with me.—*Chillingworth
to Sheldon.*

This is the last remedy, but it is the worst. It hath in it something of craft but very little of ingenuity ; and if it can serve the
ends of peace, or of eternal charity, or of a fantastic concord, yet it
cannot serve the ends of truth and holiness and Christian simplicity.
—*Taylor's Ductor Dubitantium*, chap. iv. rule 23.

The Articles Construed by Themselves has little of that
epigrammatic point and brilliancy which characterise almost
all the later writings or utterances of its gifted author. But,
from its own standpoint, it is a singularly able and convincing
piece of criticism. Lowe's chief point is, that in dealing with
the Articles as a religious test we can apply to them only
two principles of interpretation : the ' internal ' principle, by
which we construe the ' Articles by themselves,' and the
' external,' by which they are construed (or more likely mis-
construed) according to the real or supposed opinions of the

framers, or the personal convictions of the *subscriber*. The former, he declares, is the only sound principle, and is his; the latter, which must lead to confusion and evasion, is Newman's.

In other words, he says, with regard to subscription to the Articles the question is, Do we bind ourselves by what their framers *wrote*, or by what we think they *meant to write*. ' Clearly by what they wrote, for it is to that we subscribe.' In the following passage he vigorously traverses Newman's favourite device of discussing the *intention* of the Reformers who drew up the Thirty-nine Articles :—

By admitting this kind of evidence to explain the Articles we shall replace clearness and distinctness by the utmost doubt and uncertainty. The opinions of every eminent man of that eventful period must be ransacked and laid open ; his private discourse, his confidential letters, his isolated sermons, and controversial works must be examined ; the danger must be incurred of ascribing to him opinions which his more mature reason disavowed ; and this in a period when the human mind, awaking from the lethargy of a thousand years, found a boundless field of investigation open before it, and was obliged, from the imperious necessity of deciding many things, to make some hasty decisions, which it afterwards recalled. It is also undeniable that the Reformers, as independent thinkers, were struck, according to the varieties of their characters and modes of thought, more forcibly with some abuses than others. The sale of indulgences to one, the infallibility of the Pope to another, transubstantiation to a third, might appear the crying sin of Romanism ; and who has not observed that it is the tendency of controversy to confine its view wholly to the point debated, while all except·that are thrown into the shade, and passed over as *pro hâc vice* of little consequence ?

Coming to closer quarters with his astute opponent, he next proceeds to demolish the basis of *Tract 90*, which he states to be, ' that it is the duty of everyone to put such a construction on the Articles as may bring them into accordance with his own opinions, if possible.'

Mr. Lowe writes :—

What the limits to this possibility *are* it is not easy to say, but an examination of the Tract will show what they *are not*. For instance, it is possible (right ?) for him who believes that *some*

General Councils are infallible to sign an Article which says that
General (clearly meaning that *all* General) Councils may err—that
is, it is possible (right ?) for him to subscribe one proposition and
believe its logical contradictory.

In this spirit he discusses each of the points specially raised
by Newman to show that the Articles by some ingenuity are
'patient' of a Catholic interpretation.   He then sums up with
severity in these words :—

The principle which would interpret the Articles by reference to
our own belief is radically immoral, the true principle being, as was
shown above, to interpret them by themselves.   Holding fast this
noble and honourable principle, I cannot condescend so far below
its dignity as to follow Mr. Newman through his exposition
of individual Articles.   In some he has been more, in others less,
successful and ingenious ; but wherever he is wrong it has been by
design, wherever right by accident.   The same stain which our
Articles tell us attaches to works done before faith (the want of a
right motive) vitiates every one of his comments, and renders the
elaborate work of this deep casuist and learned theologian absolutely
worthless as a practical guide to the conscience.   Adopt his interpretation if you can believe it to be the literal one—*that* will only
degrade your understanding and confuse your ideas ; but shun his
principles like a pestilence when he would induce you to dethrone
conscience from her tribunal, and set himself, strong in all the soul-
destroying arts of verbal subtlety and mental reservation, in her place.

This is, no doubt, very plain language, and will sound harsh
in the ears of many good and pious persons, to whom
Cardinal Newman, without any formal act of canonisation, is
already a saint.   No thoughtful person would willingly wound
the susceptibilities of others, especially of those who are of the
salt of the earth.   But if we are to understand the issues of
this great controversy, which has so profoundly affected the
present and the future of two religious communions in this
country, as well as the hopes, aspirations, and lives of thousands
of men and women, it is essential to keep the facts steadily
before our eyes, and to hold our personal sensibilities and
predilections somewhat in check.

No writer on the England of the nineteenth century who

aims to go below the mere surface of political parties and so-called social movements but must pay respect, and even a measure of reverence, to the name of Newman. However, as with all men of distinct genius, his aims, character, and aspirations have been most completely misunderstood and distorted by his own followers. Mr. Froude seems to me alone to hit the mark when he speaks of Newman as a born ruler of men, and even compares him to Cæsar. At the first blush, the comparison seems extravagant, if not meaningless; but this is simply because we do not sufficiently realise that there are rulers and warriors in the realm of mind and spirit, as well as in the more material regions of kingdoms and principalities. From the time that Newman, in his post of influence as Vicar of St. Mary's and Fellow of Oriel, found himself in harmony with the views and aims of Hurrell Froude and John Keble, he set his face like a flint to oppose and overthrow the hated hordes of modern Liberalism, which were then besieging fiercely both Church and University. To expect him, as Charles Kingsley did, and as Dr. Abbott apparently does, to be always strictly fair, and impartial, and above-board in his battle with the enemy is like expecting the Duke of Wellington (who was Newman's favourite hero) to unfold his plans to the marshals of Napoleon in the Peninsula. Being a born ruler of men, he fought the foe with any and every weapon he could lay hands on, the more deadly and swift the better for his purpose. With every desire to be frank and confidential to his intimates, he told them no more than was essential for them to know as soldiers and subalterns.

Newman, on one occasion, referred to Keble and Hurrell Froude as the thinkers, and to himself as the rhetorician of the party. This was a strange error for such a man to fall into about his own position and source of influence: he was, in reality, the great strategist of the Tractarians. He was always cool, and, in a sense, calculating; however the battle fared, and whatever was said of himself, he never lost his head.

Nothing can be more suggestive than the letter he wrote to the Rev. Sir William Cope on the death of Charles Kingsley :—

> I never from the first have felt any anger towards him. . . . A casual reader would think my language denoted anger, but it did not. I have ever felt from experience that no one would believe me in earnest if I spoke calmly. . . . Rightly or wrongly this was the reason why I felt it would not do to be tame, and not to show indignation at Mr. Kingsley's charges.

One who could thus, for controversial purposes, affect a righteous indignation against an opponent, while remaining quite calm and unmoved, was certainly an intellectual strategist of a high order. Indeed it amounted to genius, and quite raised Newman, as a party leader, above such good and exceptional men as Keble and Pusey, who, in culture and knowledge, in social position, nay, even in the Christian virtues, were his equals, and in some respects his superiors.

This, I may confidently assert, was the view of Newman which Lord Sherbrooke held from the time when he was brought into actual conflict with him as the leader of the Tractarian party at Oxford.

It is, on the surface, rather singular that the widespread feeling among pious persons of the innate wickedness of anyone who could venture to oppose Cardinal Newman is chiefly confined to members of the religious communion which he abandoned. This is only on the surface singular; for the Newman these persons revere is the Newman of St. Mary's, Oxford, and he must ever stand out as their leader and spokesman before a harsh and hostile world. Thus, Dean Church, the very flower of Anglican culture, whose well-balanced mind and temperament gave even to his controversial writings a fine tone of courtesy and an exquisite grace and lucidity, fairly frowns and darkens whenever anyone attacks or even criticises Newman. Painful as it is to say so, the Dean summarises this controversy over *Tract 90* quite in the ordinary partisan spirit, and altogether unfairly to Lord Sherbrooke :—

The more distinguished of the combatants were Mr. Ward and Mr. R. Lowe. Mr. Ward, with his usual dialectical skill, not only defended the Tract, but pushed its argument yet further in claiming tolerance for doctrine alleged to be Roman. Mr. Lowe, not troubling himself either with theological history or the relation of other parties in the Church to the formularies, threw his strength into the popular and plausible topic of dishonesty, and into a bitter and unqualified invective against the bad faith and immorality manifested in the teaching of which *No. 90* was the outcome.[1]

It is instructive to contrast with this judgment of Dean Church the opinion expressed concerning this Tract by no less a personage than the late Cardinal Manning :—

Manning (writes Mr. A. W. Hutton) never got over the dislike he entertained for *Tract 90*. It always seemed to him of doubtful honesty. When, in the autumn of 1845, after his return from his first visit to Döllinger at Munich, Mr. Gladstone, much perturbed by the grave series of secessions from the Church of England, asked Manning if any one principle could be found that would explain them, the latter said, after reflection, ' Yes ; *want of truth.*' At a much later time he said that he thought he must have had in his mind the impression of dishonesty produced by the shifty arguments of the last Tract.[2]

If this be so, it is a pleasure to be able to record that on one question, at least, Lord Sherbrooke and Cardinal Manning were in complete agreement. But many good and pious souls, who find the spiritual sustenance they most need in the beautiful passages of the *Parochial and Plain Sermons*, in the personal revelations of the *Apologia*, and in the hymn, 'Lead, kindly light,' will continue to brand anyone who seriously differs from Newman as either hopelessly wicked or helplessly benighted.

No sooner was Lowe's attack on *Tract 90* issued than Newman's most intelligent and active-minded disciple,[3] W. G.

[1] *The Oxford Movement*, p. 294.
[2] *Cardinal Manning*, by A. W. Hutton, pp. 252–3.
[3] Disciple is hardly the word. Ward, as Newman himself said, was ' never a Tractarian, never a Puseyite, never a Newmanite.' He chose to ally himself with Newman, but was then and always purely a ' Wardite,' acting always on his own initiative, and, as will be seen, to the undoing of the party or parties specified.

Ward, again rushed into the fray.   He issued a reply to Lowe's pamphlet, entitled *A Few More Words in Defence of Tract 90* (he had already published *A Few Words*).   Newman, who realised as no one else did the strength of the forces slowly gathering against him, must have trembled at such unsolicited and compromising support.   With regard to the Articles, said Ward, the thing to do is to subscribe them in a ' non-natural sense.'   This was precisely what Lowe had pointed out was the real purport and outcome of Newman's teaching in *Tract 90*.

Lowe replied to Ward with *Observations Suggested by ' A Few More Words in Support of No. 90.'*   He now placed his name on the title-page and acknowledged the authorship of *The Articles Construed by Themselves*.   The motto, from his favourite Sir Walter Scott, evidently passed over the head of Ward, and pointed to Newman himself :—

> *For he by spells of glamour bright*
> *Could make a Lady seem a Knight,*
> *The cobwebs on a dungeon-wall*
> *Seem tapestry in lordly hall,*
> *And youth seem age, and age seem youth—*
> *All was delusion, naught was truth.*

In the pamphlet itself, however, he promptly turns his attention to his immediate antagonist :—

The first thing that strikes us is, that a man may, according to this view, conscientiously sign the Articles *without ever having read them*; that if he can satisfy himself that he was not *intended to be excluded, he is not excluded*. The Catholics (I use this term in this and in my last pamphlet as opposed to and exclusive of Protestants, not in its generic sense, in which Protestants claim to be Catholics as well as they)—the Catholics prove this by Melanchthon, by the Homilies, and other contemporary authorities.   But the disciples of Owen and Irving [1] see opened to them by such reasoning a readier and shorter argument for admission into the Church of England, an argument which, if they were blest by the teaching of a

---

[1] Robert Owen, the Socialist, and Edward Irving, founder of the Catholic Apostolic Church.

moralist like Mr. Ward, they would not be slow to use. How
could they, two sects only founded in the present century, be
intended to be excluded by Articles drawn up nearly three centuries
ago?   And, if so, how, upon Mr. Ward's principle, *are* they
excluded?

As throwing some light on this controversy, and particularly
on the tone adopted towards both Ward and Newman by their
vigorous assailant, the strange story of a clergyman named
Sibthorp is worth recalling.   This gentleman, after a visit to
Dr. Wiseman at Oscott, suddenly joined the Church of Rome.
After a while he seems to have grown tired of it, and came
back to the English Church and to Oxford.   Ward thereupon
wrote to a Roman Catholic friend with whom he was in confidential correspondence, 'By this time you have doubtless
heard of Mr. Sibthorp's step.   How unspeakably dreadful! It
makes one sick to think of it.'
    And Ward himself was then an English clergyman! Little
wonder that Robert Lowe, whose 'mental eyes' were now
thoroughly wide open, should bluntly tell him that his own
proper place was the Church of Rome.

Mr. Ward has given no reason for his rejection of my theory;
nor am I aware that it is incompatible with his principles, as it is
drawn from grounds common to Protestant and Catholic : but it is
incompatible with his *remaining in the Church*.   What matters it,
then, what its intrinsic merits may be?

This may well close the account of this controversy.
W. G. Ward was indeed the *enfant terrible* of his party.   He was,
personally, the most ingenuous and kindly-natured of men, as
the beautiful testimony of his steadfast friend, the late Archbishop Tait, sufficiently proves ; but he was what politicians
call an ' impossible ' man.   No one could work with him, and
while he alternately annoyed and amused his opponents, he
utterly decimated his friends and destroyed their cause.
    Ward, more than any single person, brought about, or at
least precipitated, the collapse of the Tractarian movement,

and by increasing Newman's trials and difficulties, forced him
to quit Oxford and finally to join the Roman Communion. It
was after surveying the wreck of fondly cherished hopes and
the ruin of long and anxious labours that Dr. Pusey declared
of the seceders to Rome : ' All had deteriorated except Newman, who was too good to be spoilt, and Ward, who was too
bad to be made worse!' Like most clever sayings, this was
not altogether just ; but if Ward were a trial to Newman, he
was a veritable pestilence to Pusey.

After Mr. Lowe had left these shores and had taken up
the threads of his life again in Sydney, news came of his
quondam antagonist's marriage. Now W. G. Ward had been
a fanatical upholder of the sanctity of priestly celibacy, and
he was still in Holy Orders in the English Church, while his
wife was then a devoted follower of Dr. Pusey. This characteristic proceeding brought down every form of ridicule on
the devoted heads of the Tractarians. To their horror and
disgust, too, Ward must needs marry just at the time that he
was on his trial at Oxford for publishing his *Ideal of a Christian
Church*, which, following *Tract 90* and the controversy thereon,
had arrayed all the University authorities against the party.
The announcement of his approaching marriage turned a
tragedy into a farce; but we may well forgive the High Anglicans
for not joining in the laughter. Ward himself writes to his
fiancée : ' J. Keble is *much pained*, and Archdeacon Manning
extremely so. . . . None of the company wished me joy, and
Church's manner at entering was decidedly cool.'

The humour of the situation must have struck the brilliant
Oxford exile at the Antipodes. In a prominent column of the
Atlas, he inserted a notification of the marriage though his
Colonial readers must have been sorely puzzled to know the
reason, for it is hardly to be supposed that a single subscriber
had ever heard Mr. Ward's name. How true it is that ' one
touch of Nature makes the whole world kin.'

Tract 90 and the consequent controversy mark the collapse, or rather the temporary eclipse, of Anglo-Catholicism at Oxford. But certainly W. G. Ward, its stalwart defender, did much more to bring this about than Robert Lowe, who so vigorously assailed it. To use Newman's own phrase, 'the game was up.' But he alone of the three leaders recognised, or at least admitted, it. It is, however, open to the followers of Keble and Pusey to point to the present changed condition of the English Church, and to maintain that they, and not Newman, took the wiser course. The Tractarians as a party were scattered and broken, and the rushing tide of Liberalism swept in and carried everything, at least for the time, before it. The struggle was maintained for some years, until Newman sought refuge in the Church of Rome (1845).

Robert Lowe had left Oxford, and was in London, studying the intricacies of special pleading under the late Sir Barnes Peacock. The following letter written by him at this time to the Rev. R. Michell, of Lincoln, will show how thoroughly Newman's pamphlets had aroused him to action :—

Robert Lowe to Rev. R. Michell.

34 Burton Crescent (undated).

I have read Newman's last tract, which I think a fond thing enough, and from which I am half-inclined to think he has a hankering for Popery after all, and not merely a speculative predilection for Catholicism, as I used to think. Why, otherwise, he should encumber his creed with purgatory, saint and image worship, and similar gammon, I cannot imagine. I must go and talk to Catholicus (that is, Roundell Palmer) on the point. Rumours are rife that you are going to do something dreadful at Oxford in the way of an answer to Newman by Convocation. As a Hampdenite, I can only think of Acteon

ὃν ὠμόσιτοι σκύλακες οὓς ἐθρέψατο
διεσπάσαντο.

The hounds will gather at the huntsman's hollo,
And where he leads the obedient pack will follow.

But if he goes among them without his red coat he is very likely to be torn in pieces. I shall be glad if such a vote is proposed, as it will give me an excuse, to myself, for revisiting *Alma Mater*, and venting the concentrated venom of years in one vote.[1]

This is, of course, not to be taken altogether literally. In writing to Michell and other intimate friends, it was customary for Lowe to express himself at times in an unconventional or humorous way; but beneath the fun there was clearly a serious intent.

[1] Speaking on the 'Oxford University Bill' (May 1, 1854) then before the Committee of the House of Commons, Lowe said: 'In 1836, eight hundred persons were brought up to condemn a work of Dr. Hampden's, which not one-tenth part of them had ever read. That same Convocation afterwards turned on those of whom it was the obedient instrument in 1836, like Actæon's dogs, and came up with the same want of reflection, and the same heat and violence, to condemn their doctrines.'

CHAPTER VII

IN LONDON

(1841–1842)

Called to the Bar—Emigration to Australia

ROBERT LOWE had matters to think of more nearly affecting his immediate future and that of his wife than the Tractarian controversy. Not only did he fail to secure the Greek professorship at Glasgow, but also a much smaller appointment, the then newly-created Prælectorship of Logic at Oxford. ' I really think,' he remarks, ' if I had obtained it I should very probably have shrunk from the plunge into the great world which I was about to make.'

As he did not obtain it, he decided to take the plunge. The little house, 16 St. Aldate's, was sold, and Mr. and Mrs. Lowe removed to 34 Burton Crescent, Bloomsbury, a locality never by any means fashionable, and far less so now than then.

Throughout his period of hard work and estrangement from his father, his aunt, Mrs. Sherbrooke of Oxton Hall, to whose estate and name his elder brother afterwards succeeded, was truly a friendly counsellor, a circumstance that he ever remembered with gratitude. The following letter, written at this crisis, lays open his plans, and is written in the manly, hopeful, yet affectionate tone of a young man, about to embark on a new, and perhaps perilous, enterprise, who craves for sympathy and hearty good wishes, as well as for counsel and admonition :—

Robert Lowe to Mrs. Sherbrooke, of Oxton Hall.

Friday : 16 St. Aldate's, Oxford.

My dear Mrs. Sherbrooke,—I think you will be pleased to hear
that I have at length fixed upon a house in London. My choice is
34 Burton Crescent, a very good house, and at a very moderate rent
(for London). I have been greatly dismayed in looking out for a
house by the immense rents which are asked. I find it absolutely
impossible to obtain a house for less than 100*l.* a year, including
rates and taxes ; my present one is 85*l.*, which with rates and taxes
will be brought to about that sum.

Burton Crescent nearly touches Euston Square with one horn
and Tavistock with the other ; it is about three-quarters of a mile
from Lincoln's Inn, and its vicinity to the New Road [now Euston
Road] gives an easy approach to the more westerly and fashionable
parts of the town.

My residence at Dinan has been particularly agreeable this
summer ; my lodgings commanded a most beautiful prospect, and
the previous knowledge I had gained of the people and country
enabled me to enjoy the pleasures derived from both to the utmost.
As a specimen of the price of provisions, my wife, myself, and an
English maidservant lived very comfortably for three months for
24*l.* I have also made some very kind and agreeable friends this
summer—a Mr. Leake, his wife, and daughters ; he was private
secretary to Lord Grey and has now a situation in the Treasury.
During the five days we were in London searching for lodgings we
dined with them there. . . . As a set-off to all this (which, however
slight in itself, to one so little favoured by fortune as I really looks
like prosperity), I have lost the dearest and kindest of my friends,
Mrs. Weguelin. She was the niece of Lord Sydenham, the Governor-
General of Canada, and daughter of a Mr. Thompson, who was
drowned in the Thames last year. . . . There was no one living
whom I more entirely loved and esteemed, and to whose society, as
residing near London, I looked forward with more pleasure. Nevertheless, not as I will, but as God will. She was only twenty-five.
I have also made friends with another family, of the name of
Tyndall. I stayed in Guernsey ten days on my return from France,
and received from them during that time the greatest and most
unceasing kindness.

It is always difficult to form an opinion of what is going on
in France from the provinces ; but I believe from all I could hear
and learn there will be no war this time. I am now in Oxford,
finishing off my pupils. My wife is in Hampshire with her brother.
You have perhaps heard that my youngest sister-in-law is going to

marry a Mr. Dunbar, eldest son of a Sir Archibald Dunbar, a Scotch baronet. The wedding is fixed for November 5.

With duty and love to Colonel and Mrs. Coape, believe me always,
    Most sincerely and gratefully yours,
                                    ROBT. LOWE.

Writing again to Mrs. Sherbrooke to thank her for the present of a law dictionary, he remarks : ' I am now working eight hours a day, and shall have hard work of it, as the term is three weeks longer than usual, owing to the lateness of Easter.'

Nor was Mrs. Lowe slow to recognise the kindness and sympathy shown to her husband and herself by his aunt at this their period of ' storm and stress.' Some passages in her letter to Mrs. Sherbrooke are very suggestive, revealing her own character as well as his severe drudgery, borne so uncomplainingly. ' His spirits,' she writes, ' are quite raised to their old level again, and he is as joyous as he was some years ago. I was not aware to its full extent how much he disliked his present occupation, and how heavily it weighed upon his mind, until I witnessed the relief the anticipation of release from it is to him.'

The letter continues in that strain of splendid confidence in her husband's power to overcome all difficulties, and to rise to any eminence, however lofty, which characterises all Mrs. Lowe's correspondence. ' He is reading law from morning to night : it seems quite a delightful occupation. I am also glad he appears to find the law so easy ; from the constant cultivation to which he has subjected his mind, the difficulties of which others complain appear trivial to him. He has already, I assure you, from his memory been able to correct two old lawyers on some law points. I look forward with the greatest assurance to his some day becoming a great man, he unites such rare industry with his abilities.'

After the young couple had left Oxford, Mrs. Sherbrooke continued her good offices, and did all in her power to reconcile the rector of Bingham to his son. The following letter, written evidently under great emotion, and in reply to some overture of his aunt, reveals Lord Sherbrooke's character in a truly noble light; few have ever written at any time of life so fine and manly a defence of their conduct and convictions :—

Robert Lowe to Mrs. Sherbrooke.

Saturday : 34 Burton Crescent.

My dear Mrs. Sherbrooke,—We have had a visit from Henry and Miss Fane; she is certainly not a beauty, but seemed very lively and good-natured. I was very sorry that the unfinished state of our house, in which as yet there is only one room habitable, hindered our seeing more of her. Henry dined with me on Friday, and seemed to think that my father's feelings towards me had undergone considerable modification, and, in fact, that he would be glad to hear from me. I have paused for further and more precise information before I take a step so important, and one which, if taken rashly, may lead to such serious results. Unless my father can prevail upon himself to abstain from going over again past topics of difference, there would be but little profit in provoking a correspondence which can lead to no good result.

It is not now, after all that I have done and suffered, that I am inclined to be wanting in the resolution I have long taken never to let hope, or fear, or any other motive, induce me to subscribe to any statement derogatory to my character, never for the sake of an immediate advantage to do my honour a lasting mischief. I trust, whatever may be the result of the overtures that have been made to me, you will do me the justice to believe that I approach the subject with every wish to conciliate, and that the concessions I am willing to make are only limited by the duty I owe to my own character, which I would not willingly lower in the opinion of my friends, and, least of all, of myself.

Surely this resolute attitude redounds to Lord Sherbrooke's honour. A more compliant and less sincere man would have surrendered at discretion; a more commonplace and vindictive nature would have borne a lifelong grudge against those whom he felt were dealing so harshly and unjustly with him. It is given to few men, and those of the rarest and best of our kind, to maintain their own self-respect with such dignity and modesty, such absence of self-assertion and vindictiveness. .

He then goes on to tell his aunt of his troubles with workpeople at Burton Crescent, and of his final success with pupils at Oxford. 'You will be glad to hear that I only sent four pupils up for their examinations at Oxford, and that they all appeared in the first class—a thing which, as far as I know, never happened to anyone before. So my star has set in glory.'

In the Chapter of Autobiography, Lord Sherbrooke tells us of his legal studies under Mr. Coulson and the late Sir Barnes Peacock, and gives us, with his customary vigour of phrase, his views on the iniquities of 'special pleading.' During his residence at Burton Crescent he kept up an intermittent correspondence with the Rev. R. Michell, who was now Fellow of Lincoln and Logic Professor.

The friendship between Lowe and Michell seems not to have weakened by time or distance. Years afterwards Lowe regularly forwarded copies of his speeches delivered in the Legislative Council, Sydney, to his old tutor at Oxford. Mr. Michell was then Public Orator (1848), and Bampton Lecturer (1849); but, despite these academic greatnesses, he apparently took the keenest interest in his former pupil's onslaughts on colonial governors and grasping squatters. 'He used to show these speeches to me,' writes the Rev. E. S. Ffoulkes, ' and would return them to Lowe full of revisions and annotations.' From such circumstances one gets a rather different view of Richard Michell to the jaundiced portrait of him in Mark Pattison's *Memoirs*. But perhaps, like other able men, Michell was a good friend and a good hater; while he liked Lowe, he disliked Pattison, and so showed quite different sides of his character to each.

Of the many letters which Robert Lowe wrote to Mr. Michell from Burton Crescent and from Sydney, only a few have been preserved; but these are sufficient to show

how close was the intimacy. To his old tutor and friend he poured out, in a semi-humorous way, all his troubles, financial, legal, and domestic. Of the mere business matters on which he consulted Michell, and which were then of such vital importance, there is no need to say anything further than this : despite all his expenses and difficulties, and the loss of his income as a private tutor, Lowe steered himself clear of the shoals of debt. As Mrs. Lowe remarks, he seemed to find the law comparatively easy, though its useless technicalities and obsolete procedure were by no means congenial to his intellect. This allusion to the late eminent member of the Judicial Committee of the Privy Council, Sir Barnes Peacock, is amusing : 'I am studying the noble art of Special Pleading under the wings of a man named Peacock—who is, indeed, covered with silver wings, and his feathers with gold.'

Later on he writes to Michell joyfully, to tell him that the breach between his father and himself is healed :—

I have not yet told you of what has happened in our family. I have received from time to time different intimations from divers quarters that my father was open to overtures to me. At first I held back; but the thing was so often and from so many quarters repeated to me that I began to believe it, and wrote accordingly a letter, not particularly conciliatory, which, to my infinite surprise, was swallowed greedily, and we are now the best friends imaginable. I have been staying in Notts, where we have been uncommonly well received, and everybody has taken an immense fancy to my wife ; so that they mean to compensate χρονον by ποσον. . . . My father has sent me 100*l.*, and Mrs. Sherbrooke the same, so that I am richer than ever I was before. . . . I leave my conveyancer in May to go to Mylne, of Balliol, an equity draughtsman, for a year, to pay whom one of my 100*l.* will come in very handy.

Thus practically closed the unfortunate misunderstanding between father and son ; but it by no means closed the latter's troubles and anxieties.

Robert Lowe was duly called to the Bar by the Honourable Society of Lincoln's Inn in January 1842. But the dark

clouds had not yet passed. The years of hard work told
their tale on his unfortunate eyes, now rendered most acutely
painful. Driven to despair, he consulted those wonderful
oculists, who examined his eyes and prophesied that he
would be completely blind in the space of seven years. It
may assist the narrative to repeat his own reflections on
receiving this dread intimation :—

> It is not very difficult to imagine the bitterness of such a reve-
> lation. To be told at eight-and-twenty that I had only seven
> more years of sight, and to think of the long night that lay beyond
> me was bad enough ; but the reflection that the object which I had
> struggled through a thousand difficulties with such intense labour
> to attain was lost to me—was almost as bitter !

He then proceeds to tell us that the impossibility of
doing anything at the English Bar before the night came
determined him, acting on medical advice, to emigrate to
Sydney ; and at the Bar of New South Wales try to make a
modest fortune in the allotted seven years. Truly, as he himself says, ' strange advice ' ; for, of all climes in the world,
that of Australia has the most dazzling atmosphere. To such
eyes as Lord Sherbrooke's, which instinctively shunned the
light as being so intensely painful, one would have thought
that a single summer in Sydney must mean total blindness.
However, as the sequel shows, he managed to avert that dire
catastrophe.

In the midst of this fresh trouble he writes as cheerfully
as ever to Michell :—

> It has been decided, with the consent of my father and friends, that
> I am to go to Sydney, in Australia, to try my luck as a conveyancer,
> an animal much needed in the Antipodes. It is rather a startling
> resolve ; but my wife does not dislike it, and I see little prospect of
> doing good here to decline a possible opening from any quarter.
> I want you to find me some introductions to the people at
> Sydney, as I know you have connections out there ; also to inquire
> at Oxford, so as to get me as many as possible. The Bishop I should
> like to know, and Dr. Lang, the head of the College.

It is strange that Lord Sherbrooke, then knowing nothing of Sydney, should have singled out those two eminent but mutually antagonistic Australian colonists. The Bishop was Dr. Broughton, an estimable and, in a sense, almost great, prelate, who owed his connection with Australia (originally as Archdeacon of New South Wales) to the Duke of Wellington. There is on record the Bishop's account of the decisive interview with the great Duke, for the full apprehension of which it is necessary to bear in mind that it took place in 1829, when Australia was indeed a *terra incognita* : ' He told me that in his opinion it was impossible to foresee the extent and importance of the Colonies; and added, "There must be a Church." I replied that I felt it my duty to accept the office. . . . He said to me, "I don't desire so speedy a determination. If in *my* profession, indeed, a man is desired to go to-morrow morning to the other side of the world, it is better he should go to-morrow or not at all." ' Dr. Broughton sent his reply within a week, which was submitted to the Archbishop and the King; and hence he became the first Bishop of Australia. Lord Sherbrooke always recognised Bishop Broughton's ability and sincerity, but as he was a follower of Lord Eldon politically, as well as a disciple of Dr. Pusey, they were destined to be in opposition. Dr. Lang was the most energetic and public-spirited of Scottish colonists, but often so wrong-headed and always so dogmatic that, though he became one of Lowe's followers and a genuine admirer (your true Scot hath ever a respect for character and ability), he too, at times, was made to feel the lash, and to writhe under that Socratic irony, the exercise of which in after years made its possessor famous in the House of Commons.

Mrs. Lowe bore this last heavy blow of fate with equal cheerfulness. She writes in the most sanguine and hopeful strain to her aunt, Mrs. Whitley, widow of Mr. George Whitley of Norley Hall :—

CHAPTER VIII

THE VOYAGE OUT

Letters for ' Home '—Fire at Sea—All but wrecked off Cape Otway—
Melbourne in 1842

THE Antipodean tourist of the present day who journeys to
Melbourne or Sydney on board one of those superbly fitted,
steam-propelled floating palaces which land him at his distant
destination in something over a calendar month, can form
only a very imperfect picture of the voyage which Mr. and
Mrs. Robert Lowe had resolved to undertake.

To a man or woman fond of the sea, and with the gregari-
ous instinct, a trip to Australia in a P. and O. or Orient liner
is a by no means unpleasant experience. There is plenty to
see ; all kinds of people to converse, dine, and quarrel with ; an
infinite supply of ozone ; and, perhaps, less danger to life and
limb than besets the denizen of a crowded city every day of
his life. As a consequence of these manifold advantages, a
quasi-amphibious race is springing up amongst us, who spend
a great portion of their lives in what is known as ' globe-trot-
ting.' But it was a very different matter fifty years ago, when
a long voyage in a slow sailing-vessel often made the passenger
realise the truth of Dr. Johnson's famous dictum, that a man
in a ship was worse off than a man in jail ; for, said he, ' the
man in jail has more room, better food, and, commonly,
better company, and is in safety.' Fifty years ago a voyage
to the Antipodes made an epoch in a lifetime.

The fast-disappearing band of grey-headed colonists who

can still vividly recall the feelings with which they left their
native land for the remote *terra incognita*, realising that in all
human probability they would never return, can alone enter
into the feelings of the young English barrister and his wife
bound for Australia in the early ' forties.' It was on June 8,
1842, about seven o'clock in the evening, that they embarked
at Gravesend on board the *Aden*, accompanied by their English
servant, Martha. The beginning of the voyage was propitious :
a fair wind blew them out of the Channel, while in the
dreaded Bay of Biscay the weather was calm ; later, the wind
rose and drove them close under the rock of Lisbon, so that
they could see the houses on the beach and the grand entrance
of the Tagus, where Sir John Sherbrooke had found himself
under quite different auspices some thirty years before.
Thence they sailed for Sant Jago, passing Madeira at a
distance of some miles, sailing close by the Desertas rocks,
which Mrs. Lowe, who had an artistic eye, noted as ' forming
beautiful pictures.' She had also an artistic hand, and took
sketches of them and of the coast of Portugal to send ' home,'
as she subsequently did in the case of many an Australian
scene.

From these islands Robert Lowe himself sent the following letter, addressed to his mother :—

Robert Lowe to Mrs. Lowe, Bingham Rectory.

Sant Jago : July 6th, 1842.

My dear Mother,—Our voyage has been slow, but hitherto very
prosperous and smooth. Georgiana has suffered much from sickness,
and still continues to do so, but I do not think she is otherwise ill.
We got out of the Channel on the second day, were becalmed in the
Bay of Biscay, and obliged by foul winds to pass close under the
rock of Lisbon, which is a very fine sight, covered with vineyards
and mulberries. From thence to Madeira we had fair but light
winds. Madeira we left so far to the right that we could only see
the outline, which is a noble one, higher and bolder than I expected.
There we caught the north-east trades, which carried us to 18° north
latitude, from which we have made a shift to steal on here, princi-

pally by availing ourselves of the alternate land and sea breezes.
Ladies cannot land here, the only option being between jumping on
a sharp rock, through the surf, and riding astride on the shoulders
of a naked negro.   I nearly had a serious accident in attempting the
former way, but escaped with a good ducking and some sharp bruises.
The best idea I can give you of the town is that it is like a large
farmyard ; the grass is not dried up—it does not exist. The buildings
are low and mean and perfectly uniform—white walls and red tiles,
square doors and windows.   The population sport every variety of
undress, from the full-dressed officer who is drilling the awkward
squad to the naked negro boys dabbling in the surf. We have
bought two goats, a quantity of oranges, pine-apples, bananas,
monkeys, turkeys, parrots, &c.   Our party is, upon the whole, a
pleasant one. I have made good play with the attorneys, and am
in a fair way of not languishing long for want of practice. . . . My
eyes are improved, in spite of the heat and the glare of the sea, and
of pretty diligent application to my studies. With best love to all
our dear friends in England, believe me, your dutiful son,

ROBERT LOWE.

A subsequent compact seems to have been entered into
between the young couple to give their English friends a fuller
account of their experiences of the voyage at its termination.
The letter of Mrs. Lowe, it will be noticed, solves a question
which has been often asked, as to whether Robert Lowe on his
voyage out saw anything of the small township founded by a
humble Tasmanian, one John Pascoe Fawkner, on the banks
of the river Yarra, destined to become the metropolis of the
colony of Victoria, in the political creation of which Lord
Sherbrooke, as the sequel will show, had no inconsiderable
share.

Before giving any extracts from this letter, it may be as
well to insert the following eminently characteristic epistle
from the pen of Robert Lowe himself—the first letter sent to
his friends in England after his arrival in New South Wales.
It was written from Paramatta, to which 'large village,' as he
describes it, the pair of young colonists had gone as the guests
of the Governor, Sir George Gipps, and Lady Gipps. Paramatta, or, as it was originally called, Rose-hill, was a favourite

place of residence of the earlier governors of New South
Wales.

Robert Lowe's Account of the Voyage.

Oct. 11th, 1842.

I have undertaken to give an account of our passengers, leaving
the beauties of Nature and art to the eloquent pen of my wife. The
captain (to begin at the beginning) was vain, obstinate, conceited,
perverse, and profane ; told lies to that extent that he became a by-
word in the ship ; clean and neat in his own person, but dirty,
disorderly, and unsystematic to a degree in everything relating to
his ship ; liberal as far as the griping avarice of his owners permitted,
and good-natured enough when vanity and obstinacy were not concerned ; a good navigator and bold seaman, who always carried on as
much canvas as the winds allowed, and sometimes more. . . . A
purser pensioned off by the East India Company, and a daughter who
was the very pink of vulgarity, but a good-natured, well-behaved
girl, require no further notice, except to mention that they had a
violent prejudice against the Americans, and were seriously alarmed
for fear they should kiss the ladies all round. Mr. C., a good-hearted,
good-natured, honest Irishman ; his wife uppish and snappish, but
obliging withal. I sat next to her, and she used to disgust me by
eating pig's fry, curry, and fat salted pork all together for breakfast.
Mr. Y., indolent, selfish, avaricious, ill-educated, good-natured, and
good-looking ; his wife having many virtues and three faults—rouge,
gum, and pearl powder. Mr. W., a landowner in Van Diemen's
Land, a very good, gentlemanlike, and well-informed man, though
his religion was tainted with enthusiasm and illiberality. . . . The
rest were a set of young men, boisterous, good-humoured, and
ignorant, who smoked and drank, and played at cards and draughts
and singlestick, and swarmed up the rigging. One was a nephew
of Lord Bute's ; two others, sons of a wealthy proprietor in Van
Diemen's Land, had been to England to be educated, an operation
which had been imperfectly performed. My employment during the
voyage was principally reading, but I am sorry to say that my eyes
latterly became so weak that I was obliged to give it up, as the
irritation of the nerves became so painful and incessant that I was
afraid if I persevered I should render them quite useless. Time will
show whether this is a temporary or permanent affection ; if the
latter, I have very little chance of doing anything good in the law
or any other profession. . . .

Judge Willis, whom I saw at Melbourne, once lived at Edwinstowe,
and knew all our Oxton friends quite well.

We had only two gales of wind on our voyage out, one off Tristan d'Acunha, between Rio and the Cape, the other in Bass's Straits, after leaving Port Phillip. The latter was really formidable, as it came from the south-west, and blew so hard as to render it difficult for us to carry any sail, which it was absolutely necessary to do to prevent our running on a lee shore. I will write again by the next ship.

Very truly yours,

ROBERT LOWE.

Owing to the infirmity of his eyesight, not only did Lowe write few letters during this eventful period, but from the same cause, as he himself frankly confessed, mere descriptions of places and scenes were not his *forte*. These were left to the facile pen of Mrs. Lowe, whose descriptive powers were quite equal to the task, and who, it will be seen, gives some particulars of the Melbourne of 1842 which may still be read with interest, especially by the descendants of the early colonists.

Her letter, giving a full description of the voyage out, written from Paramatta, and therefore just after their arrival in Australia, fully supplies her husband's descriptive omissions.

Mrs. Lowe's Account of the Voyage.

The island of St. Jago is very mountainous, and at times, in passing, the forms are splendid; but they are not more, I should think, than 2,000 feet high. We ran into a bay; here all was arid, not a green leaf to be seen, with a tremendous surf roaring night and day on the beach. I was most anxious to land—I had never ceased to be ill, and felt quite exhausted; to my regret, I found it could not be. Robert went on shore with a large party of passengers; they had to clamber on the shoulders of naked black men, and hold fast by their woolly heads. Robert got a bad fall on the rocks, but did not suffer from it afterwards. The island, they say, has fine valleys some miles in the interior, but Robert, from his hurt and the intense heat, did not venture into the island. The natives, who are a very handsome tribe of blacks, mulattos, and Portuguese, came on board the *Aden* laden with oranges, pine-apples, bananas, cocoa-nuts, tamarinds, pumpkins, monkeys, turkeys, guinea-fowl, parrots, &c. Great was the rush, as you may fancy, for them. On entering the bay we saw a ship at anchor called the *Dandalia*. The captain and surgeon of this sloop paid the *Aden* a morning call, and invited as many of the passengers as might wish to go on board the next day. We all liked the idea much, and accepted the invitation with the greatest pleasure. In the evening, as the moon rose, we heard a plashing of oars and the notes of a guitar, accompanied by a very fine voice : we found the officers from the American sloop were serenading us. After singing several songs, amongst the number ' Allan-a-Dale ' (all the songs English composition), they boarded the *Aden* and joined the gentlemen in the cuddy ; afterwards several came on the poop to join the ladies. I was astonished to find them so agreeable, and really like gentlemen ; but I must say the most agreeable were the captain, a Scotchman, and the purser, an Irishman, naturalised Americans. The next day they sent their boat for us, capitally manned, and we boarded. The sloop was in excellent order, carried 26 guns ; all things so clean and neat, with an excellently fitted-up cabin like a drawing-room, also a large dining-room. We walked all over the sloop, and then had cake and wine. Robert was quite pleased with the officers, and they appeared just as much pleased with him. They talked about America and England, and much political economy. They were quite American in one particular—much inclined to run down England and exalt America. Some of the officers returned with the party to the *Aden* to dinner. Robert and Mr. C. went back with them again, and returned by moonlight. I thought they would never have made a parting. During the evening we had a scene of the greatest confusion on board : the captain was detained on shore ; many of the sailors, steerage passengers, and intermediate passengers got drunk ; the boats with the supplies were nearly swamped, bringing bundles of turkeys and fowls, dead and living, tied together, the boats so full of water it was impossible to endeavour to save them ; oranges and all the fruits afloat, loaves of sugar melting ; pigs, grunting and squeaking, hauled up the side of the vessel, two beautiful goats and their kids half dead ; the ship a Babel of tongues, blacks, whites, and mulattos, all mingled, quarrelling and bargaining ; the steward of the vessel drunk, and our good-natured first mate in despair. At length the captain arrived in a dreadful ill-humour ; then came the English Consul, who was to supply the ship with several boatsful of fruit and poultry, &c. ; he and the captain quarrelled about prices, the captain declaring the Consul had cheated him. After sundry very forcible execrations on each side, the English Consul was ordered to descend to his boat or his departure was to be hastened by summary means ; accordingly, he and his blacks went, but, alas ! they took all the good things with them, and away went, to our great disgust, the delicious pine-apples, oranges, &c.

I have a sketch of St. Jago coloured. I assure you I deserve no small credit for my sketches, for I took them in spite of my horrid sickness. I was ill for six weeks, and became so weak I could scarcely move. We sailed during the night; I think we left on July 8. We were now to make all speed, but the winds soon left us, and we floated upon a sea as smooth as a lake. Here I began to grow better. I sat on deck all day, and took my meals there; I was not able to sit for a moment in the cuddy. I had two companions in the same state, but we began to get well together. The flying fish, dolphins, and now and then a whale, began to appear; the heat great, but under the awning I never found it too much. We had fine sunsets, but made no progress; we had to run to South America, and lay becalmed several days only two hundred miles from Rio Janeiro. We began to fear a scarcity of fresh provisions, having ninety-seven persons on board. All wished the captain to put into Rio; he would not, but talked in a vague manner of the Cape. We were thirteen weeks from the time we left London before we passed the latitude of the Cape. Here again a strong remonstrance was made to the captain about the provisions; but our next destination being Port Phillip, where we were to land half our passengers for Van Diemen's Land and Port Phillip, he would go on; greatly we apprehended the winds failing us again, but they proved fair, and we reached Port Phillip having provisions left for two days more.

One of the steerage passengers died of a low fever off Rio, and one of the sailors had the fever also. The passenger died on a Saturday evening from exhaustion, and on the Sunday he was consigned to the deep; he was laid on a plank, wrapped up in a sailcloth. One of our passengers read the Funeral Service over him. All were assembled. It was a painful scene; his poor brother, who was with him, was in deep affliction; all felt it much. A little boy of five years old was quite melancholy all day after, and asked me most anxiously and repeatedly if I really thought the man was gone to God. He said they told him his body would lie in the sea, but his soul would go to heaven; he sat with me during the service, and cried when they put the body overboard. I am quite fond of the little boy.

We had a most awful alarm when about six hundred miles from the Cape. Much had been said on the subject of the fearful carelessness on board about fire: the boys and men were allowed to go down into the hold with candles in lanterns not locked; they were in the constant habit of taking these candles out of the lanterns; the captain would attend to no remonstrance on the subject. About eleven o'clock on August 30 one of the children Martha took care of came pale as death into the cuddy, where I was sitting alone; the child could not speak, but pulled me on deck; there I heard a subdued whisper of ' Fire ! ' afterwards a sudden cry, ' The hold is on fire ! '

All rushed forward. The deck was prepared to be flooded, and leathern pipes were thrown overboard and buckets filled. It was truly awful, a heavy sea running ; no boat could have lived an hour, even had our boats been tolerable (we had but two small and one large, none seaworthy). Most providentially the fire had no time to spread, and was at once got under, the alarm having been given the moment the fire took place. I was glad to see the captain was so much frightened himself he could scarcely speak, and he afterwards sent a message into the cuddy to say we might rely upon it that in future the lanterns should be locked. The sailmaker and a boy caused the fire by dropping the candle into a bundle of straw whilst looking for stores, which, by the way, were never to be found when wanted, so much carelessness prevailing in every quarter. Could I have smiled at such a moment, I should have done so when I saw several of the boys balancing themselves with the greatest care, the vessel pitching, carrying water in pie-dishes, soup-plates, and coffee-pots, &c., losing most of the water by the way, endeavouring to add to the flood pouring through the great pipe. Shortly after this event the steward drank so dreadfully that he became mad, and was obliged to have a strait-jacket put on ; this proved to be *delirium tremens*, and he partially recovered. We were dreadfully crowded all the voyage, having at least ten too many cabin passengers, which, perhaps, may in some measure account for this catastrophe.

Many years afterwards Lord Sherbrooke jotted down in his autobiographical sketch that lively description of his voyage in the *Aden* in which, it will be remembered, he relates, as well as this incident, another of an almost equally alarming character.

It is somewhat amusing to compare his terse and epigram- matic account, beginning, ' Of all the descriptions of a long voyage,' with Mrs. Lowe's more flowing and discursive narra- tive. After relating the incident of the fire, with the amusing account of the ' little Jew-boy with the cracked pie-dish,' Lord Sherbrooke, it will be remembered, tells the story of the narrow escape the *Aden* had of going ashore at Cape Otway, adding, ' I had afterwards the satisfaction of giving a vote in the Council at Sydney for erecting a lighthouse on this dangerous headland.'

Let us turn again to Mrs. Lowe's letter. Her account of primitive Melbourne as it appeared to the eyes of the voyagers in 1842 will in all probability interest the dwellers in that city in 1892.

We reached Williamstown on Friday, October 1, having passed the longitude of the Cape on September 27. The harbour is quite an inland sea with low banks. We went up the river Yarra to Melbourne in a small steam-vessel, the river narrowing by degrees and very deep. On each side were native woods, now and then opening, and long, low rises of ground seen through these openings of a dull green, dotted over with dark-coloured trees like old stunted thorns; cattle grazing in large herds, and here and there settlers' cottages, with immense dogs sleeping at the doors. The huts, as I should call them, built of wood, with a little window on each side of the door. The banks of the river sloped in many places to the water, and large stones were on the banks; now and then dense wood on swamps, the trees with heavy green tops, covered with white flowers, but not high. Nearer Melbourne the hills rise high; blue mountains are seen, with heavy native forests between them and Melbourne; but I hear when on the spot you only find it dotted with trees like a park. There are also immense open plains; the scenery is much varied.

The town of Melbourne is built on a rising ground, of red brick, the streets wide and well laid-out, and some of the buildings substantial and handsome; the streets unpaved with deep ruts, no footpath by the sides. The Inn was tolerable, with a ginshop opening on the one side. We walked to Mr. Latrobe's, the Superintendent, to deliver a letter; there was a front gate, a drive, and an attempt at an English garden, the land before the house sloping to the river, and lightly covered with the native trees, with lovely wild flowers blooming beneath them, the scarlet geraniums growing magnificently. The land is valued at enormous prices in and close to the town; rent absurdly high. We went into a baker's shop during a shower, and entered into a long discourse with the people—Irish emigrants; they paid 100*l.* per annum for their miserable shop; it had but a bakehouse, one bedroom, sitting-room, and shop. I could see through the rafters. Bread, 11*d.* for 4 lb.; 12 eggs, 1*s.* 9*d.*; sheep, 6*s.* each; fowls, 12*s.* a pair; milk, 6*d.* a quart. Manufactured goods an immense price. I have sketches, which I will send. We left Melbourne at nine o'clock the next morning, and sailed away in the evening.

Although in his own correspondence of this period he entered into no particulars about early Melbourne, Lord Sherbrooke recorded in later years his impressions of this flying visit, which, for the convenience of the reader, are here repeated from the Chapter of Autobiography :—

'At last, after a voyage of nearly four months, we found ourselves, not in Sydney, but in Melbourne—that is to say, with still 500 miles to go. The state of Melbourne was at this time very peculiar : it was in the by no means enviable position of being a dependency of a dependency, governed by a colony which was not permitted to govern itself. A good deal had been done in the way of building, but some cause, to us unknown, had arrested its progress in mid-career. The place seemed stricken with paralysis. Everything was at a stand-still. Everybody wanted to sell, and nobody wanted to buy. No purchaser would look at a house unless it was at the corner of a street. In the middle of the main street were two considerable rivers, facetiously named by the inhabitants, after their rulers and governors, the Williams and the Latrobe. We were told that someone had been drowned in one of these urban streams not long ago.

'To regret that I have no money has been to me during the whole of my life a by no means uncommon sensation. But I never remember experiencing it so poignantly as on this occasion. It required no very strong foresight to be aware that here was an opportunity such as no one could expect to see twice. For a very few thousand pounds a man might have possessed himself of property which in a few years would repay him much more than tenfold ; and why, oh why had I not got it ? '

These reflections on the inevitable rise and progress of Melbourne, as they passed through his mind at the time, certainly redound to the sagacity of Lord Sherbrooke. But those who are acquainted with the early colonial annals know how desponding many of the old settlers were wont to be at those periods of depression which, no less than periods of inflation, mark the career of all such communities. When the Californian gold fever broke out, many were glad to sacrifice their holdings in Melbourne—which it was currently believed was then going to the dogs—and get away as fast as they could out of the colony. I remember in after years walking round one of these city blocks in Melbourne, on which Lord Sherbrooke appears to have cast longing eyes, with a gentleman who said : ' This all belonged to my father, but he thought the place was ruined, and sold it for a few pounds to get away. It is now worth several hundred pounds a foot.' He was of Semitic extraction, and the recital of the story evidently affected him deeply.

Mr. David Syme, the well-known Australian economist, in an article in the *Melbourne Review* some years ago on ' The Unearned Increment of Land in Melbourne,' gave a number of striking instances of the enormously enhanced values of city freeholds. These enhanced values mark the material progress of a community. But clearly those early proprietors who sold out must have feared something in the shape of an unearned *decrement* ; or there would be no such cases of miscalculation, which are almost as common in transactions in land as in any other kind of commercial speculation.

CHAPTER IX

IN SYDNEY

Port Jackson—Sir George Gipps at Paramatta—W. S. Macleay at Elizabeth
Bay—Condition of Sydney

IN opening the narrative of Lord Sherbrooke's career as an
Australian colonist, it may be as well to make a few preliminary
remarks as to the plan of this portion of the book.   It is true
that the period of time embraced in this section covers little
over seven years, but those years were the golden years of his
prime.   He arrived in Sydney on October 8, 1842, and was
therefore in his thirty-second year.

In making his home in New South Wales from 1842 to
1850, Lowe found himself a member of a strange, chaotic
colonial community, then in the very act of emerging from an
Imperial penal settlement into a free, self-governing British
State.   During almost the whole of this time he was an active,
indefatigable, public man, desirous above all things to assist in
this beneficent social and political revolution.   In other words,
as I shall hope to show, he helped most materially to lay the
foundation of what is destined to be a great and ever-expanding
English-speaking nation, spread over an entire island-continent
almost the size of Europe.

It is a trite remark that Englishmen, as a rule, cannot be
brought to feel an interest in colonial questions; but I am
fortunate in having for my central figure an Englishman whose
name is sure to secure me a hearing on these themes in the
mother-country.   My difficulty is rather with the colonial

public. Australians, it must be confessed, take only a languid
interest in the brief annals of their own community. Promising young communities, like promising young men, rarely
indulge in retrospect, and heed, for the most part, only the
present or the immediate future.

> With smoking axle hot with speed, with steeds of fire and steam,
> Wide-waked To-day leaves Yesterday behind him like a dream.
> Still from the hurrying train of life fly backward, far and fast,
> The milestones of the fathers, the landmarks of the past.

Despite this colonial habit of mind, it will be the purpose
of the succeeding chapters to show what a dominant part the
late Lord Sherbrooke took in bringing about—(1) the system
of self-government which now obtains throughout Australia,
Tasmania, and New Zealand; (2) the cessation of criminal
transportation to New South Wales; (3) the creation of the
colony of Victoria; (4) the establishment of the prevailing
system of national unsectarian education; (5) the settlement
of the people on the public lands and the growth of a genuine
yeoman class.

But before plunging into the vortex of early colonial
politics, it is only proper to give Mrs. Lowe's description of
the far-famed harbour of Port Jackson, on the shores of which
she was now about to make her home. Sydney Harbour, as
it is popularly called, seems to arouse the enthusiasm of the
most critical travellers; both Mr. Froude and Mr. Anthony
Trollope were excited by it to the highest flights of their
respective prose styles. The only exception known to me is
the Hon. Harold Finch-Hatton, who declares in his *Advance
Australia!* that he 'never saw anything more forlornly ugly in
the way of scenery.' The people of Sydney, it is said, never
forgive a slight offered to their harbour; in which regard they
can have no possible ground of grievance against Mrs. Lowe.

We reached the Heads of Port Jackson on Saturday, at two
o'clock. These Heads are quite barren, of golden-coloured rock, here
and there marked with deep brown, 365 feet high; the water rolls

against them, the lighthouse on the highest point. The vessel lay-
to a short time for the pilot, and a wild-looking boat with New
Zealanders rowing brought him. The vessel, every sail spread,
suddenly wheeled round an immense barren rock, and there was
Port Jackson, lying in beauty not to be described or imagined, before
us. We were close to land —I could almost have dropped a stone upon
it. Bays, promontories, almost in fantastic confusion, on every side ;
rocks, trees, thrown in every exquisite form together ; houses, cottages
of white stone, some half-hid in trees, others on rocks in every bay
and on every promontory, were here. The bay is immense, like a
large lake bounded on every side by rocks, which look as if they
had been formed for beauty alone ; and Nature has adorned them,
with the most exquisite taste, with trees, some of strange leaf and
form, but wonderful in beauty ; here and there trees of golden-yellow ;
the rock white stone, stained with rich red and brown, strange and
fantastic species of (I suppose) cypress-trees and lignum vitæ, and
bright and lovely flowers. We tacked first to one side of this
wonderful spot, then to the other, until my rapture rose almost into
a delirium of delight. Again we turned a spot with a sudden whirl,
and there was Sydney, and fine shipping before it—Sydney, built on
a rocky promontory of white stone, the new Government House,
superb, of stone, one side, and through a deep vista formed by promontories fading into distance the Paramatta river opens. I must
describe with my pencil if I can ; I cannot with my pen.

To Robert Lowe himself, from his unfortunate infirmity,
the glories of Sydney Harbour, under what to him must have
been a blinding glare of light, could not have been so entrancing. Not that he was insensible to the superb position of the
city which was about to become his home, for a little later
on he records : 'We took a small house in Macquarie Street,
overlooking the Domain and the beautiful salt-water lake, as
we should call it in England, which forms the peerless harbour,
which will, I believe, always place Sydney at the head of the
Australian colonies.'

He also notes a strange atmospherical phenomenon which
occurred shortly after their arrival, in the shape of a dense
fog which lasted for three days, during which the thermometer
stood steadily at 115°.

Mrs. Lowe continues her narrative of the first incidents

to row it at my disposal, to go on board the ship and about the harbour. Rent is a little fallen, owing to the bad times ; and horses are very cheap, which I rejoice to hear, as they are almost a necessary of life in this hot country. I never was so tired as yesterday, walking about Sydney from ten to five. I am quite at sea about a house at present, but hope to hear something soon. The weather is becoming hot, but the mosquitos have not yet attacked us.'

Paramatta, which the Lowes were now visiting preparatory to settling down as active denizens of the metropolis, is chiefly known to the modern tourist for its luxuriant orange-groves. It is really situated at the end of an elongated arm of Port Jackson, which received the native name of the Paramatta River. A great deal of the early history of the original penal settlement misnamed Botany Bay was centred at Paramatta. Hence the existence of the reformatory establishment for female convicts, which Mrs. Lowe depicts somewhat *couleur de rose*, I fear, in the next letter she wrote to her English friends :—

Sydney: Nov. 5, 1842.

I will endeavour to give you an idea of all we have been doing since my last letter, which I shall find difficult, as so many new sights and objects present themselves daily. Before we left Paramatta Lady Gipps took me with her to see the factory where the women who have been transported are confined ; they are principally hopeless characters, many being returned assigned servants. It is an enormous prison, with large yards, beautifully clean and airy ; I never saw any Union poorhouse or prison of any description so well arranged. The women are classed according to their abilities, and employed in washing and needlework, which are both surprisingly well done, considering that it is forced employment. There is also a large school, where the children are employed and taught. These poor unfortunates are children born in the factory, the mothers being returned assigned servants who have misconducted themselves. Poor things ! they are indeed truly the children born in sin. I could fancy their countenances bespeak their origin. The women when refractory are placed in solitary cells, partially dark, but extremely well aired. Sir George Gipps has done more than any governor for these prisons ; his management appears most judicious. From the factory we went to the Orphan School. I was extremely interested on seeing two aboriginal children, one about ten years old, the other eighteen months. The elder, the matron told me, is quite as clever, if not more so, than the generality of the children, and reads, and sews, and speaks English. We enjoyed ourselves much whilst at Paramatta. Sir George and Lady Gipps, when we had been there a fortnight, were to make an excursion up the country, and were so kind as to invite us to remain until their return; but Robert thought he ought to be in Sydney, as the Courts were open, so we tore ourselves away the day they set off.

So ended their first brief holiday in the New World. Returning to Sydney, they occupied lodgings until the house they had decided on taking in Horbury Terrace, Macquarie Street, was ready for them. In the meantime Mrs. Lowe records, with affectionate pride, that 'Robert has already had several briefs, and made 14l., which I think a great deal.'

The chief citizens, instigated no doubt by the example of His Excellency the Governor, now began to call upon the new arrivals, who in quick succession made the acquaintance of the judges, the Bishop (Dr. Broughton), the Colonial Secretary (Mr., afterwards Sir Edward, Deas Thomson), Mr. John Hubert Plunkett, Mr., afterwards Sir Roger, Therry, and other leading lights, nearly all of whom, it must be confessed, subsequently found themselves in anything but amicable relations with the brilliant and independent-minded man who had come amongst them, but who was not framed by nature to be a member of any coterie. Mrs. Lowe assures her friends in England that they would be astonished to see what splendid houses some of these people live in, 'built of white stone, and well furnished.' After referring to dinner-parties with these great ones of the little colonial world, it is amusing to notice that she is 'glad to say all the respectable attorneys have called!' Altogether, Mrs. Lowe seems to have been very favourably impressed at first with all classes of people in Sydney, and even mentions that the shopkeepers are not only agreeable in manner, but full of information. She was probably right in attributing this immediate social recognition in Sydney to the Governor's previous hospitality at Paramatta. But if, among these local notabilities, there were any capable of entering into and enjoying the social intercourse of a man whose brilliant scholarship and wit afterwards gained for him an almost unique position in London, then Robert Lowe hardly needed even a Viceregal recommendation.

There was at least one such colonist worthy to be Lord Sherbrooke's intellectual companion, with whom from the outset he established a firm and lifelong friendship. Probably there were others; but for no one in Australia did he entertain such warm feelings of personal regard and affection as for Mr. William Sharpe Macleay. He was certainly, as Lord Sherbrooke often said, a remarkable man to discover in such a remote community. Of an old Scottish family, educated at Westminster and Trinity College, Cambridge, William Macleay's devotion to science had earned for him the friendship of Cuvier before he followed his father, the Hon. Alexander Macleay (the old Colonial Secretary, and Speaker of the first Legislative Council), to Sydney. The Macleays were a most distinguished as well as most worthy family. No less than four of them have left their mark on the history of New South Wales. Assuredly they should find a place in such a work as Mr. Francis Galton's *Hereditary Genius*; for we note in all these Macleays alike the highest mental and moral qualities, coupled with great capacity for public affairs, and each with an inborn love of scientific research, which made them a family of naturalists. The brother of W. S. Macleay was also a lifelong friend of Lord Sherbrooke. I allude to Sir George Macleay, one of the heroes of Australian exploration, who accompanied the undaunted Captain Sturt in his memorable expedition to discover the course of the Murrumbidgee and Murray rivers in 1830.

In one of her letters Mrs. Lowe gives a charming picture of the Australian naturalist's home, near Sydney, which must have greatly astonished her English correspondents at the time, and may be still read with pleasure, if only as a proof that the much-despised 'Botany Bay' was not wholly, even in those days, a land given over to convicts and savages.[1]

Mrs. Lowe's Description of W. S. Macleay's Home.

A few days ago I saw one of the most perfect places I ever saw in my life, belonging to Mr. Macleay. How I longed that Mrs. Sherbrooke could but see this splendid sight. The drive to the house is cut through rocks covered with the splendid wild shrubs and flowers of this country, and here and there an immense primeval tree; the house is built of white stone, and looks like a nobleman's place. Mr. Macleay took us through the grounds; they were along the side of the water. In this garden are the plants of every climate—flowers and trees from Rio, the West Indies, the East Indies, China, and even England. The bulbs from the Cape are splendid, and, unless you could see them, you would not believe how beautiful the roses are here. The orange-trees, lemons, citrons, guavas, are immense, and the pomegranate is now in full flower. Mr. Macleay has also an immense collection of plants from New Zealand. I must not omit some drawbacks to this lovely garden : it is too dry, and the plants grow out of a white, sandy soil. I must admit a few English showers would improve it. As we went along the wild walks, cut through the woods, the native trees, covered with flowers, the views of rock, trees, and water were enchanting. The bays are innumerable, and resemble the Scotch salt-water lochs.

Mrs. Lowe's letter is full of her earliest Australian impressions, ranging from descriptions of native moths and butterflies to the speculations then rife in Sydney as to the new colony of New Zealand. She seems to have gathered that the latter would end in failure, but she had not then acquired sufficient

[1] The beautifully situated home of the scholar and naturalist is now no more, and on the site of its grounds stand the villas and houses of a 'genteel' suburb. Sir George Macleay, when showing me a picture of the house and grounds, said: 'My brother would never have consented to its demolition ; but Sir Henry Parkes thought fit to tax the land exorbitantly, with the view of "busting up" such estates near Sydney, and I at length was forced to subdivide it, and let it out on lease. But my brother,' he added, 'however much it might have added to his income, would never have allowed a tree or shrub to be removed.'

colonial experience to know that the well-to-do residents of an old colony are always prone to indulge in evil prognostications with regard to new and possibly rival settlements. Having themselves passed through the pioneering stage, and at last achieved something like Old-World comfort and a fixed abode, they are the first to proclaim that the newly-acquired territory is either too barren for cultivation, or that it is so fertile that the land can never be profitably cleared. So we may pass all this over without further comment.

It is more to the purpose that New South Wales itself, about the time of the arrival of the Lowes, was passing through one of its very worst periods of commercial depression. In the history of all colonies these periods constantly recur; and when they pass, and what are called ' the good old times '— that is, periods of reckless speculation and exorbitant prices— come again, the colonists forget them like a dream. On account of the direct effect this protracted commercial depression, which set in about 1841, exercised on the fortunes of Robert Lowe, I have taken some pains to inquire into its causes and extent. First as to its extent. From February 1842 to the end of 1844 there were 1,356 cases of sequestration under the new insolvent law in Sydney, and 282 in Melbourne, which was then merely the chief town in a district of the same colony. This gives a total of financial wrecks for the colony of New South Wales, within a period of less than three years, of 1,638. These sequestrated estates represented a total of indebtedness amounting to $3\frac{1}{2}$ millions sterling.[1] If we bear in mind that the entire population was then only 162,000, these figures will give a most vivid picture of what are colloquially called the bad times, during which the young English barrister arrived in Sydney with a view of making an independence for himself and his wife before the alloted seven years of eyesight had run out. The major portion of litigation on which lawyers thrive, it must be admitted, is a luxury, not

<hr>

[1] Westgarth's *Australia Felix*, p. 186.

a necessity, of social existence. When money is rolling in, or, what is practically the same thing, when credit is good, men will dispute over any fancied right or wrong; and the Law Courts become a very Babel of bustle and business. But when, as a consequence of this extravagant living and reckless speculation, comes the Nemesis in the shape of a peremptory note from the banker that outstanding bills must be met—which always happens at the time when there is nothing to meet them with—then men no longer are so eager to fight out their battles before a judge and jury. They become mean of spirit, and absolute Uriah Heeps in the way of bearing indignities, and the attorneys and barristers languish accordingly.

The commercial depression in Sydney between the years named seems to have been more like a thorough catastrophe than any event of the kind in the annals of the colony. As a rule, these so-called bad times, as the late Mr. Westgarth used to point out, should in reality be termed good times, for they are the periods when reckless expenditure and rash speculation receive a salutary check, and when people suddenly wake up to the necessity of living within their means. But the disease in the body politic which culminated in the crisis of 1841–44 in New South Wales, was deep-seated, and the colony sustained a check from which it did not completely recover until the era of the goldfields.

In the meantime, many of the leading merchants and squatters were irretrievably ruined. So general was the collapse, and to such an extent did the mere commercial gamblers and spendthrifts drag down the more solid and reputable colonists that, as Mr. Westgarth—who was then a settler in Port Phillip—truly remarks, 'we find many names intimately associated with the early history and recent splendour of the colony' in this appalling and indiscriminate herd of bankrupts. Thus, as he sadly observes: 'Many years of labour and care terminated in ruin, and a perceptible gloom overspread the population on the occasion of so general a distress and so melancholy a revolution of fortunes.'

Under such a state of things we are not astonished to learn that most of the private carriages in Sydney were given up by their owners, 'either from necessity or a sense of propriety.' As there were few or no private purchasers many of these once well-appointed equipages descended in the social scale, like their owners, and became common public conveyances.

In the very midst of all this gloom and wreckage Robert Lowe settled down in Sydney to what he elsewhere calls 'the wretched trade of an advocate.' I do not find that he was unduly depressed by this deplorable condition of things ; nor was he, like so many of the older settlers, haunted by the apprehension that the colony was irretrievably ruined.

It, of course, materially affected his practice and profits at the Bar, but, looking at the matter in a general light, he no doubt fully concurred with Sir George Gipps, who in a letter to Lord Stanley about this time shrewdly pointed out that ' the debts were those merely of one individual to another, and not of the colony collectively.'

From the time that he first caught sight of early Melbourne, then likewise in a state of lamentable depression, Robert Lowe seems to have been firmly impressed with the idea that Australia was inevitably destined to be the permanent home of a great and prosperous community. The following letter from his own pen, one of the very few which he wrote 'home' during his Australian exile, as well as giving an account of his prospects and position at that time, will also, from the general observations it contains, help to complete the sketch of Sydney in the early 'forties' :—

Robert Lowe's Impressions of Australia.

January 17, 1843.

We have now been some months in this colony, and though the vividness of first impressions may in some degree be impaired, I am able to give you a more complete and coherent account of everything than was possible at first. We are at last settled in a home after most herculean labour in arguing and bargaining. It is a very cheap one for this country, only 130l. a year. It is all front, with a very pretty view of Port Jackson, the Heads and the lighthouse. The air is excellent, and the mosquitos not nearly so bad as in lower situations. They are not really as tormenting as the midges were in Scotland. Our establishment consists of Martha, who is every day improving in health from this most excellent climate, a man-servant and a kitchen-maid. The man-servant we would gladly have dispensed with, but in this town where there are no water-pipes, the carrying water ourselves is a great economy, and a man is wanted to clean out and take care of my chambers. Our furniture is all unpacked and arranged ; it has come, upon the whole, exceedingly well, and had it not been for the *abominable* carelessness of the *abominable* man who packed it, we should have had no losses : the *Aden* was so extremely dry in the hold. The drawings are quite safe and all my books. In this country, where the rooms are not papered, but the walls and ceilings are left in stucco, a few pictures framed are something more than ornamental.

The weather has been on the whole very pleasant ; during the first two months no rain fell, and very considerable injury was done to the crops and fruit, although more rain fell during the year than in England ; yet from the peculiarity of the country, the absence of river drainage, and the presence of immense masses of sandstone rock which reflect the heat of almost a tropical sun, one day of fine weather does more to dry than two or three of rain do to moisten it. At Sydney, also, from its proximity to the sea, a very strong land or sea breeze is continually blowing, which assists the drying influence of the sun. The heat is seldom or never overpowering, and the mornings and nights are uniformly cool. On Sunday, January 8, the thermometer was 118° in the shade and 142° in the sun, yet we bore this perfectly well, and have often been more uncomfortable on a summer's day in England. We spent a few days at Government House, Paramatta, last week, the pears in some parts of the garden had literally been baked on one side on the trees by the hot wind, presenting not only the appearance, but the taste of the oven. A standard nectarine tree laden with fruit is a beautiful sight ; we are just in the height of the peach and nectarine season, and enjoy ourselves accordingly. A bushel of delicious nectarines is to be bought for 3s., as fine in flavour as any I ever ate in England. The peaches are as good as the general run of this fruit in England.

I am sorry to say that my eyes have grown so much worse, indeed so nearly useless to me, that I have been obliged most unwillingly to place myself under medical advice, and to debar myself from reading and writing altogether. Mr. Bland,[1] who is my doctor, attributes my inability to read, not to weakness of the eyes, but to an incipient tic douloureux which has been coming on for several years and which threatens, if not corrected, to be of a most severe description, menacing not only my sight, but eventually life. He entertains great hopes of being able to subdue this disorder, and has taken tolerably stringent measures for that purpose, by cupping, calomel, belladonna, &c., and a very strict regimen and low diet. I think he has done me some good and trust he may do more. I have got a very good clerk, who does literally all my reading and writing. I pay him 2l. a week.

This visitation is the more difficult to bear as, professionally speaking, I have been getting on exceedingly well, having made at least 100l. since my arrival in the colony. Times are extremely bad here; there have been upwards of 600 insolvencies in ten months, and law business has much diminished even since my arrival, but if my health will only permit, I do not fear getting my share. I am the junior barrister at this Bar, which is an advantage, and have already been concerned in one case for the defendant in which the plaintiff received a verdict for 1,200l. I have as yet had no opportunity of making a speech. We have now had more chance of seeing what the society here is. Upon the whole I think it very good, people are so much more liberal, so much less bigoted and narrow-minded than in England.[2] The ladies are not handsome, and those educated in the colony stupid, but of the rest everybody has seen something beyond the common routine of daily life in England and is rendered more agreeable accordingly.

The rest of the letter is concerned with the political outlook of the colony, and is exceedingly characteristic, as are the views expressed of the social condition of the people.

We have just received our new Constitution, and everybody is very busy about the contested elections. The franchise is 20l. per annum, a qualification in this country of high rents far lower than that of England, amounting, indeed, to universal suffrage, and that in an ignorant, lazy, vicious, and degraded community, the very last in the world who ought to enjoy it. . . . The result might have been very different had a better class of emigrants been sent out, for the free

[1] The political colleague of Wentworth, afterwards defeated by Lord Sherbrooke for the representation of Sydney.

[2] Lord Sherbrooke lived to modify this opinion. Doubtless he did not find the peculiar bigotry and narrow-mindedness of the Oxford clericals, but these human weaknesses cropped up in a different guise.

population is to the convict in the proportion of 25 to 3. But the majority of the persons sent out here have been selected for their uselessness in their mother country, as if there were any inherent virtue in the Southern Hemisphere which could turn incorrigible rogues into industrious labourers. Anyone with the wish and power to work may, even in these bad times, soon rise to independence. Stone-masons earn 9s. per day, very indifferent carpenters 7s., so there is no lack of inducement to emigration, but these people all seem to consider that to work was the only thing for which they were not sent out, and they are uniformly dissatisfied with their lot, and wish themselves back in England, although they allow they live in plenty and independence here, and would be starved or go into a workhouse there.

My total inability to write with my own hand, and the constant occupation which getting into our house has necessarily afforded to my wife, must be my excuse for not writing sooner. I trust it is not an excuse I shall have to offer again, but I have no idea how long a time may elapse before I am permitted to use my eyes again.

With best wishes to all my kind and dear friends in England,

Believe me theirs very truly,

ROBERT LOWE.

This was written, as he says, three months after his arrival, and so forms a fitting introduction to his future active life and public career in the colony. But we now come to a very sad interlude, which is, indeed, foreshadowed in the close of this letter.

CHAPTER X

A PERIOD OF GLOOM

Threatened Blindness—Bush Wanderings—Tribute to W. S. Macleay—
Return to the Bar

IN writing the concluding lines of the foregoing letter, Robert
Lowe little dreamt that within less than a month all his
bright hopes of professional success would have flown, and he
would be warned by his colonial doctors that unless he entirely
ceased to use his eyes he would almost immediately become
stone-blind. It is difficult to imagine a harder fate for a man
conscious of such great mental powers, and with so much
intellectual activity. He had been driven from England by
the warnings of eminent medical authorities, who had declared
that he might preserve his partial and painful eyesight as a
colonist in Australia ; now, within a few months of his arrival,
he was told that unless he abandoned his profession he must
inevitably become blind at once. Considering the mental
torture that these fallacious and equally dogmatic verdicts
must have caused the patient, it is not to be wondered at that
in after-years he should have recorded a severe condemnation
of such empiricism ; for, despite these prognostications, as all
the world knows, Lord Sherbrooke contrived to achieve success
in his profession, and eminence as a statesman, without any
material injury to his dim eyesight. In later years, reviewing
this frightful experience in Sydney, it will be remembered, he
made these comments :—

'The prophecies of my three Job's comforters [his London

doctors] had made me very nervous about my eyes. I suffered somewhat from the glare of an Australian summer, Sydney being one of the most dazzling places in the world, and in an evil hour I consulted a doctor. He cupped me and advised me that it was absolutely necessary that I should discontinue my practice, which was rapidly increasing. I doubt if I should have been so docile to my Sydney Æsculapius if his opinion had not tallied with the opinions of the London doctors. The time is come, I said to myself, sooner than I thought, and if I do not wish to be wholly blind I must give up my business. This was the lowest ebb of my fortunes. It really seemed as if I was destined to sink into a situation in which I should look back with regret on the position it had cost me so much trouble to quit. To make the thing complete I was forbidden to read, so that all that remained to me was to forget what I had learnt, enlivened by the joyless dignity to starve.'

This enforced idleness accounts for the apparent failure in the early part of his career in Sydney, which astonished Mr. David Blair, the compiler of *The Cyclopædia of Australasia.* But the fact that for the next six or eight months the name of Robert Lowe did not appear in the Law Reports does not mean, as Mr. Blair supposes, that the colonial attorneys were slow to recognise Lord Sherbrooke's abilities; but that he had been compelled by mistaken medical advice to abandon the pursuit of his profession altogether. How he contrived to exist during these succeeding months of compulsory and anxious inactivity is related very fully in the affectionate letters which Mrs. Lowe sent 'home' regularly. Some of these are very interesting, giving, as they do, descriptions of the various places to which she accompanied him with a view of whiling away the time that would otherwise have lagged so heavily. From the first of these letters we see that the colonial doctors were very peremptory in their injunctions, and left the patient no choice unless he had elected utterly to ignore their advice and to take the consequences.

Sydney: February 9, 1843.

My dearest Mother,—I cannot say with how much pain I write to tell you that Robert cannot go on with his profession. Dr. Bland and Mr. à Beckett say if he persists he will lose his sight. Besides tic douloureux there is inflammation of the iris; he has been cupped four times, has had leeches applied, and is now decidedly better. We must console ourselves as well as we can with the hope held out that if he refrain from reading and all study, in about twelve months he may be able to use his eyes again, but they say he can never pursue his profession. This disappointment is perhaps the greatest he has ever experienced; he had made a splendid beginning and was making about 1,000*l.* a year. We had looked forward with so much pleasure to the idea of being able to say how well we were doing. At present we have scarcely formed a plan for the future and are most unwilling to return home until we find nothing more can be done. I have some hopes that Sir George Gipps will give Robert something; he is most kindly disposed to us, but there is little to give—all preferment is so jealously guarded in England. I cannot tell you how kind everyone is to us, and how high an opinion they entertain of Robert. There are some Oxford men here who have talked much about him, indeed he never goes into any society without the people being at once impressed with the highest opinion of his abilities. Poor Robert! I fear he is doomed to disappointment, I know not how it is, but every effort seems to fail, and now, when all promised so well, it is indeed bitter.

After a few remarks upon the beauty of the country, and the healthfulness of the climate, Mrs. Lowe continues:—

My greatest difficulty at present is to find amusement for Robert. You may imagine the privations he endures with his love of reading and the constant habit of employing every spare moment over a book, now to be forbidden ever to read a line—I mean this literally. He does not read even the most trifling note. At times my spirits almost fail me, but Robert's good temper and happy disposition support us both. He bears this last trial much better than I do. We mean to see all we can of this country, but the times are very bad, though people hope the conclusion of the war with China will relieve them by opening a new trade.

Then with messages to Lady Sherbrooke, the widow of Sir John Coape Sherbrooke, and other friends, the writer sadly closes by remarking that she is 'not in spirits to write any description of persons or things.'

By the next outgoing ship she wrote to her mother-in-law in the same solicitous and affectionate strain.

Sydney: February 19, 1843.

I write again as soon as possible that I may tell you we think Robert's eyes better, but his cure can only be a work of time. Mr. Arthur à Beckett [1] thinks rather more favourably of his case than Dr. Bland, and says he may be capable of making some mental exertions in a year or two. Robert has asked Sir George Gipps to give him some appointment that will not require much eyesight, a Police Magistracy, or something of that nature; this will be worth about 500*l.* a year. We have also some other things in view, but they are too remote and indefinite to write about, our plans change daily, and I might write page on page were I to tell all we hope, fear and think. I fear it would be but an annoyance at this distance. Before we resolve upon returning home, we intend to be quite sure that we can do nothing here. Sir George and Lady Gipps are kind beyond measure, and I think we may hope that if Sir George can help us, he will.

Mrs. Lowe goes on to relate that Captain Bell, of the *Hazard*, a twenty-gun sloop then stationed in the harbour, had promised to take them to Hobart Town on his return from Norfolk Island, where he was about to convey Sir George Gipps, who had received orders from Lord Stanley to examine and report upon the system there pursued with the convicts. Though Mrs. Lowe appeared to be most anxious for this trip, it does not seem to have taken place, nor did Lord Sherbrooke ever set foot in Tasmania.

The letter continues sadly :—

I cannot bear to see him sitting hour after hour doing nothing, and change of air and scene are particularly recommended. We are also thinking of making an excursion to Illawarra; a most splendid district; we passed it on the coast, about a hundred miles before we reached Sydney. But this will in a great measure depend upon the possibility of letting our house whilst we are away. Lady Gipps has promised to mount us, and we are to go with her to Botany Bay; we are also to have

---

[1] Arthur Martin à Beckett, F.R.C.S., Staff Surgeon to the British Legion in Spain, arrived in Sydney 1838; afterwards member of the Legislative Council; died in Sydney, 1871.

the barge and take long excursions about the harbour.   This we are
to do whilst Sir George is absent; when he is at home, Lady Gipps
does not like to be away during the very few hours in the day she
can be with him—he has so much to do.

Mrs. Lowe carried out her plan of accompanying her
husband to various places up country with a view of occupying his time and thoughts.   They went to Illawarra and
stayed in a cottage at Wollongong, the chief town of the district.
There the clergyman took them in hand, providing them with
horses, and escorted them to a cattle station in the kangaroo
grounds where they were most hospitably welcomed by a Scotch
squatter and his sisters.   Mrs. Lowe was very enthusiastic
about the beauties of Illawarra, which she compares to
Westmoreland.   From Wollongong they were in the habit of
taking daily walks into the bush and conversing with the
small settlers, which I fancy the disabled barrister found more
congenial than much of the society small talk of Sydney.   As
a rule, these settlers at this time, unlike the bulk of the
emigrants who remained in Sydney, appear to have been
thoroughly happy and contented with their lot.   But in
Illawarra, as in the metropolis, the presumably wealthier class
of colonists (i.e. those who were wealthy ' on paper ') were suffer-
ing from the great commercial depression to which I have before
alluded.   These had been existing on borrowed money, for
which they were paying in some cases 15 per cent., and as a
consequence, when the crash came, their properties had to be
sacrificed.   One landowner near Wollongong, who had refused
14,000*l.* for his land only three years before, was glad enough to
get 4,000*l.* for it.   Such was the story they heard on every side.
Among these more or less unsuccessful squatters they came
across a nephew of Professor Wilson (Christopher North), who
was off to try his fortunes in China.

Meantime Mrs. Lowe writes:—

I think Robert is really better—he never reads ; being in the
open air is of great service to his nerves.   The palpitation is much

reduced about the temples. I flatter myself that at the expiration of a year he will again be able to read moderately. Our plans for the future are quite unformed, we do not mean to make a hasty decision. To employ Robert's mind without fatigue is the first great object. You cannot believe how patient and cheerful he is under all he has undergone, he never repines or gives way to low spirits. I read to him as much as I possibly can.

However bad the times may have been with these Australian country gentlemen, they displayed no lack of kindly hospitality towards the travellers. Pressing invitations came from all sides; and this, one is glad to say, has always been a feature of the squatter class.

Perhaps enough has already been said concerning the deplorable financial state of the country, but Australians, and particularly Victorians of the present day, will peruse with some astonishment such an account as the following description of their territories in the year 1843; and yet, as their current history shows, the old tale is ever being retold :—

You will hear no doubt of the crash of the Bank of Australia, the directors have been discounting bills to an enormous extent. What the consequence will be to this country no one can tell. The securities are in land, and it is said that at least 300,000*l.* worth of land will be at once thrown into the market and make land unsaleable. At Port Phillip, even land of the best quality will not now sell at all, though it has been under cultivation. This district (Illawarra) is the only part of the country where land is of any value.

These observations on men and things, in which Mrs. Lowe indulged in her correspondence, are, during this period, frequently interrupted by painful comments on the subject that was ever present to her mind :—

'We should enjoy ourselves so much if Robert were well. I am never free from apprehension about him, and it pains me beyond measure to see him unable to read.'

Towards the end of the month they were back again in Sydney, staying at Government House as the guests of Sir George and Lady Gipps, who had kindly invited them to remain until they could regain possession of their own house in Macquarie Street, which they had let. Mrs. Lowe, even after the subsequent rupture between her husband and the Governor, always recognised the kindness shown them during this trying time, especially by Lady Gipps. They were now again in the midst of such fashionable society as Sydney could then boast. The Viceregal party used to cross over to the North Shore, and ride into the country—the party numbering generally Sir George and Lady Gipps, Sir Maurice O'Connell (Commander of the Forces), Captain O'Connell, Mr. Parker,[1] and Mr. and Mrs. Robert Lowe.

This was alternated with trips to Paramatta, where they accompanied the Viceregal party to the races. However pleasant this kind of life might be to a fashionable *flâneur*, it must have been torture to such a man as Robert Lowe. He was again in the hands of his Sydney doctors, who were trying their nostrums upon him.

The Lowes next went to Bathurst, in a somewhat adventurous fashion, for they drove there in their own little carriage with one horse. After they passed Penrith and crossed the Emu Plains, they had to face the ascent of the Blue Mountains.

Here (writes Mrs. Lowe) all appearance of cultivation ceases. The road was surveyed and executed under Sir Thomas Mitchell's directions. The mountains are composed principally of sand rock, and form the most tremendous precipices I ever saw. The gum-tree covers the mountains in endless forests, and a more absolute scene of desolation imagination cannot conceive; I can scarcely term it beauty. The valleys are silent, no water to be seen or heard, and very few birds; now and then parrots of brilliant plumage fly across the road with a wild scream. We traversed scenery such as this I have attempted to describe for four days, and then reached Macquarie Plains.

[1] Private secretary to Sir George Gipps, afterwards Sir Henry Watson Parker, third Prime Minister of New South Wales; married in 1840 the youngest daughter of Captain John Macarthur of Camden Park, the introducer of the merino sheep into Australia.

Here they stayed with Mr. Lawson, who bears an honoured name in conjunction with Wentworth and Blaxland in the annals of pioneering exploits in New South Wales, and then pushed on to the station of General Stewart, some three miles from Bathurst. Mrs. Lowe, after a while, from an artistic point of view, disparaged these vast bush solitudes, whose monotony invariably strikes the traveller from other lands. On their journey back an adventure befell them, which I had perhaps better give in her own words.

In returning to Sydney we endeavoured to cross Mount Lambie. Here we found the road fearfully bad. About half-past four o'clock we stuck fast hopelessly in an immense pool of water. I remained with the carriage whilst Robert proceeded on foot to an inn about two miles and a half distant in search of help. I scrambled to the bank and there waited Robert's return. A heavy rain began to fall and night came on. In about two hours I heard steps and Robert appeared with three men and a horse. With great difficulty they extricated the carriage, and I had to mount the horse without a saddle to reach it, the roads were so deep in mud. We slept at a little inn and returned next day to Macquarie Plains, remained the night at Mr. Lawson's and returned by the old Sydney road, which was surveyed and laid down by Major Lockyer, which I think a much better line than Sir Thomas Mitchell's. We regained the high road at Solitary Creek, went on to the foot of Mount Victoria, and then turned off the road to Megalong to stay a few days with Dr. Palmer.

This hospitable squatter organised a kangaroo hunt for their amusement, and they were further greatly entertained by the blacks of the district, who climbed the trees in native fashion and pulled out opossums and squirrels by their tails, which caused them some diversion. They stayed several days at Dr. Palmer's, who, at parting, presented Mrs. Lowe with two pretty little parrots, and in due course they reached Paramatta ' with only *one* broken spring.'

This expedition certainly seems, in the recital, rough and somewhat dangerous for a lady; and one might think accompanied also with some peril to her companion with his deficient eyesight. But Mrs. Lowe expressly states that ' Robert

enjoys himself beyond measure in these expeditions, and he
gains much benefit; his eyes are decidedly better and his
general health good.'

Back again in their own house in Sydney, they were still
quite undecided as to what they should do. The doctors persisted in their opinion that the least exertion would bring
back at any moment the affection of the nerves of the eye.
Reading and writing of any kind were still absolutely forbidden. It was indeed a period of anxiety as well as of
gloom. The older colonists, with pleasant country residences,
were pressing in their kindly invitations ; and amongst other
noted homesteads where Mr. and Mrs. Lowe stayed during
this interval was Camden, the home of the Macarthurs, perhaps the most historic country house in all Australia.

They accepted Mr. James Macarthur's invitation, and he
met them at Paramatta with his carriage and drove them to
Camden. Here they were most hospitably entertained, and
saw all that could be done by art towards making an Australian
homestead in the bush present the appearance of an English
nobleman's country seat.

By this time it may be surmised that these wanderings
had begun rather to pall ; at any rate, mention of them in
Mrs. Lowe's letters is less frequent and less enthusiastic.
She now often writes as one full of forebodings of the ruin
that seemed to be impending over the entire colony. Perhaps
their own melancholy situation caused her unconsciously to
deepen the shadows of the picture.

There was, however, yet another of these ' up-country '
excursions on which Robert Lowe was unaccompanied by his
energetic and devoted helpmate ; and of this, at her express
request, he dictated a brief account which was slipped into
one of her letters and forwarded to friends in England. On
this occasion he was visiting his friend, Mr. Barker, a squatter
in the county of Argyle, which he himself subsequently represented in the Legislative Council.

This is his own account of his experiences and reflections on this occasion :—

September 8, 1843.

Having agreed to accompany my friend, Mr. Barker, to his establishment near Goulburn, in the County of Argyle, about 150 miles S.W. of Sydney, I am now to give an account of my expedition. We travelled in a very light carriage with large wheels drawn by two thoroughbred horses, so that the journey was neither so slow nor so laborious as that to Bathurst. Barker is a very agreeable companion, possessing great power of observation and a very complete knowledge of the country, its pursuits, and its inhabitants. The first day we travelled to Camden, a village built on the land of the Macarthurs and to which they have presented a new church with a very ambitious spire. It is situated on the banks of the Nepean river. The surrounding country is very rich and fertile, and requires nothing but the subdivision into small farms to become extremely productive. The road from thence to Goulburn has carefully avoided every fertile and improvable spot, a peculiarity observable in all Sir Thomas Mitchell's roads. About two miles from Goulburn you emerge from the eternal forest of white gum-trees, the ugliest and the most useless of the class, upon Goulburn Plains, which really do deserve the name, for they stretch without an intervening eminence to the Australian Alps on the one side, and the rivers which empty themselves into Lake Alexandrina on the other. These plains or table-lands, lying 2,000 feet above the level of the sea, are situated near the point where the eastern and western waters divide, and possess consequently a much more temperate climate than the neighbourhood of Sydney.

Here you no longer see the orange-tree, the banana, or Indian corn, but their place is supplied by European fruits and productions. The mornings and evenings are agreeably cool even in the height of summer, whereas in Sydney the hours between sunrise and ten o'clock, when the sea breeze generally begins to blow, are the most oppressive in the day. Mr. Barker's station is situated on the banks of the Wollondilly, which runs through a long, narrow valley formed by hills of volcanic origin, whose undulating slopes, thinly dotted with trees, sometimes advancing and sometimes retiring, have forced the river into an undulating channel, and form, when covered with cattle, a very pleasing pastoral landscape. We found everything going wrong, the sheep dying of catarrh induced by the neglect of the overseer in folding them on marshy ground, and everything conducted in the most wasteful and irregular manner. This is too often the case in Australia, where the evils of absenteeism are quite as great as in Ireland, or perhaps more felt, as everything

N 2

here depends upon the personal care and intelligence of the proprietor. We returned to Sydney in about three weeks. During
my stay I acquired some insight into sheep-farming, and am quite
certain that, if conducted with proper care and economy, it is a very
lucrative business at the present prices; but neither this, nor the
many other resources of this country, will save the greater number
of the proprietors of land and stock from that ruin which their
reckless speculation and grasping ambition have brought upon
them.

It was during these enforced wanderings in the bush that
the Lowes fell in with an old Oxford friend, Henry Denison,
the younger brother of the Bishop of Salisbury, whom Sir
Francis Doyle describes as being ' in his first youth a sort of
Admirable Crichton.' The race is not always to the swift.
Denison all but broke his neck by a fall from his horse in
Australia, and the brilliant Oxonian became a paralysed
wreck. Mrs. Lowe writes : ' Mr. Denison's health is so bad
that the medical men here advise him to return home. He
has promised the first time he is in Notts to call on Mrs.
Sherbrooke.'

Throughout all this trying time, in which he had so much
leisure to brood upon his great misfortune, Robert Lowe
never seems to have uttered a word of complaint or repining.
Almost any other man in the course of a narration like the
foregoing would have expatiated on the terrible deprivation
which thus sent him a broken and beaten man wandering
aimlessly in a strange land. It was, however, no part of his
manly philosophy ever to make others miserable by the recital
of his own woes. This, like every other high virtue, had its
own reward ; making him, at any rate, despite his affliction,
a thoroughly companionable man. To some extent this
enforced leisure, in which he saw much of the country and its
remote and isolated settlers, must have influenced for good
his subsequent career in New South Wales.

These bush wanderings must have brought him into
social contact with many persons who would not have had

opportunities of conversing with him, and discovering his remarkable gifts, if he had continued in the active exercise of his profession in Sydney. It may be safely said that he never passed a night under a squatter's roof without impressing and delighting his host by his wonderful knowledge and acumen, and his brilliant powers of conversation. In these early days, many of the pioneer squatters were themselves men of remarkable individuality, and in some cases by no means deficient in mental culture. Years afterwards, in an address delivered in London, Lowe spoke of them as 'gentlemen who formed the real aristocracy of the Australian colonies, men whose boast it is that there runs in their veins some of the best blood in England.'[1]

Robert Lowe, as already recorded, had greatly impressed the governor, Sir George Gipps, with his ability and capacity for public affairs; this fact, and his personal acquaintance with the squatters and isolated settlers, had a direct bearing on his career in the colony. It is with evident pleasure that Mrs. Lowe records the high opinion which Sir George Gipps had at this time formed of her husband's abilities.

Sir George (she writes) is constantly asking his opinion on all sorts of subjects, particularly questions of difficulty arising from the working of this new Legislative Council. This is a very high compliment from Sir George Gipps, who is notorious for never asking or caring for other people's opinions. He will scarcely listen, even so much as politeness requires, to those of his Government officials.

But for all this the days began to hang heavily, and it is plain that Lowe had practically abandoned all hopes of a colonial career. Mrs. Lowe sorrowfully admits that he is not likely to do much good in Sydney; and adds that they are greatly tempted to throw it all up and return to England.

[1] Speech on the Australian Colonies Bill, at the rooms of the Society for the Reform of Colonial Government, June 1, 1850. By Robert Lowe, Esquire, late Member of the Legislative Council of New South Wales.

This mournful epistle was written on October 8, 1843, but on the 30th of the same month another was sent, which revealed the silver lining of the cloud. Robert Lowe had been absolutely idle for eight months and a half, and during that time he had neither read nor written a line. He now decided to resume, with great precautions, the practice of his profession. It is not stated whether this was done with the approval of the two Sydney doctors, but it may shrewdly be suspected that the patient had decided on this course without further consulting them. He therefore procured the assistance of a clerk for his chambers, who was also to live at his house, so that he might be always at hand. He gave a distinct promise to his wife that if he felt the slightest symptoms of a relapse, either in regard to his eyes or his general health, he would then and there give up all idea of ever again practising at the Bar. With this she contented herself, reflecting that, 'if he does little, this will be an amusement.' With the increasing badness of the times, and the fact that he had to make a fresh start as a junior, there was very little likelihood of any distressing amount of legal business coming in his way.

Mrs. Lowe seems to have cherished the hope that Sir George Gipps would yet find some suitable post for the man of whose capacity he entertained so high an opinion. Lady Gipps had told her that Sir George declared that 'Mr. Lowe was the cleverest man in the country.' This raised her hopes to the altitude of a temporary judgeship in Norfolk Island or a police-magistracy somewhere in the back blocks of New South Wales. But the revenue of the colony was falling wofully, so that retrenchment was the order of the day; and under these circumstances Sir George Gipps was the very last man in the world to make a post for any friend, however deserving and capable he might be.

These weary months recurred to Lord Sherbrooke's

memory with vivid intensity when, some years ago, he sat
down to record the events of his past life.

Then it was that he paid the fine tribute to the memory
of W. S. Macleay: 'However, in this the lowest ebb of my
fortunes, I found several alleviations. The principal was the
extraordinary good fortune which gave me the acquaintance
and, I am proud to say, the friendship of Mr. William
Macleay. He had been Secretary at Paris for claims of
English subjects and afterwards had been a Commissioner
for the Extinction of the Slave Trade at Cuba. He was an
excellent classical scholar, he knew more of modern history
and biography than any one with whom I was ever acquainted,
and in addition to all this he was a profoundly scientific man;
thoroughly conversant with zoology, botany, and entomology.
He was an excellent companion, with a store of caustic wit
which reminded me continually of the best part of Scott's
Antiquary. It fell to my lot to do him some slight service
for which he never knew how to be sufficiently grateful. It
would have been a good find to meet with such a person
anywhere, but in a remote colony it was a good fortune for
which one could not be too thankful. I have not seen, and
shall not see, his like again.'

Such is Lord Sherbrooke's tribute to William Sharpe
Macleay, his most cherished Australian friend, who fully returned his affection, and whose admiration for his great
abilities, indomitable courage, and personal worth was unbounded. At his death in Sydney in 1865, William Macleay
bequeathed 1,000*l.* to Lord Sherbrooke and a like sum to his
wife as a mark of his friendship and esteem. It is not difficult
to imagine what a solace the conversation of so cultivated a
man must have been to one who felt that, despite his own
great powers and grasp of mind, his career, from impending
blindness, was about to close before it had well begun. Lord
Sherbrooke, it will be remembered, goes on to refer to the
bush wanderings of this gloomy period, and, with regard to

the loveliness of Illawarra, pathetically describes it as a place ' where a man might pass his time with no other regret than that of being totally useless.' But now, in defiance of doctors and specialists, he determined to go back to his law-books . and to active life in Sydney, be the consequences what they might.

CHAPTER XI

THE CROWN NOMINEE

(1843–1844)

Lord Stanley's ' New Constitution '—Richard Windeyer, the ' Popular Member '
—W. C. Wentworth, the ' Australian Patriot '—Lowe's Maiden Speech in
the Council—His Stand for Free-Trade—Becomes a Personage in Sydney

UNDER the new Constitution, which the late Earl of Derby, then
Lord Stanley, the Colonial Secretary of State, had bestowed
upon New South Wales in the year 1842, the old Legislative
Council, which had heretofore consisted entirely of officials
and Crown nominees, became largely a representative body.
It consisted of thirty-six members, of whom two-thirds were
elective, on a franchise of a 20*l.* rental or a freehold of 200*l.* in
value ; furthermore, there was a property qualification for
members of 2,000*l.* or a yearly value of 100*l.*

In addition to these twenty-four ' popular ' representatives
there were six salaried government officials, who might be
regarded as a kind of Cabinet, and six Crown nominees. The
Governor no longer presided, nor had he any direct voice
or vote in the Council. In the Viceregal speech which
inaugurated this, the first Parliament in Australia (August 3,
1843), Sir George Gipps thus explained the constituent
elements of his new Council : ' The Legislative Council,' he
said, ' is composed of three elements, or three different classes
of persons : the representatives of the people, the official
servants of Her Majesty,' and of ' gentlemen of independence
—the unofficial nominees of the Crown.'

Unfortunately Sir George Gipps, who was a soldier rather than a politician, too quickly forgot his own distinctions between the salaried Government officials and the Crown nominees. It would seem that Sir George, having nominated these latter ' gentlemen of independence ' to their seats in the Council, fully expected them to vote on all occasions with his salaried officials and to assist them in every way to thwart the ' representatives of the people,' who under this hybrid scheme formed a permanent but ineffective Opposition, as, despite their overwhelming majority, the Governor could always veto any measure which he considered inopportune or undesirable.

Some three months after the opening of the Legislative Council, the Speaker (the Hon. Alexander Macleay, elected in his 77th year) announced that he had received a letter from ' Richard Jones, Esq.,' resigning his seat; and further that His Excellency the Governor 'had been pleased to appoint Robert Lowe, Esq., Barrister-at-Law,' in his stead.   Mr. Lowe, having been introduced to the Speaker by the Colonial Secretary (Edward Deas Thomson) and the Attorney-General (John Hubert Plunkett) took the oaths and his seat.

The *Sydney Morning Herald*—then the only daily newspaper in Australia—seemed perturbed at this intrusion of a mere nonentity into the sacred precincts of this infant Parliament. In its issue of November 10, 1843, appears the following serious little article, which, in the light of subsequent events, it is difficult to read without a smile :—

Who is Mr. Lowe, the new member of Council ? is a question that has been asked pretty often within the last forty-eight hours, and it does not say much for the Governor's choice that it should have to be asked. All that is known of Mr. Lowe in the colony is that he is a junior barrister, who arrived here about fourteen months ago, and that, in consequence partly of ill-health and partly of want of success, it was understood some six months since he had determined upon retiring from the profession. He is a gentleman of very superior scholastic attainments, and was, until very shortly before he left England, a Fellow and tutor of one of the Oxford colleges. We are at a loss to conceive what claims Mr. Lowe had to be made a Councillor; he has had no colonial experience, he has no stake in the colony, and we must express our surprise that the Governor should have passed over all the old colonists to confer the office on a gentleman who is almost a stranger.

The *Herald* had not long to wait before its queries were answered. Although it was then the month of November, the year had not run out before the voice of the new nominee was very familiar in the ears of the older members of the Legislative Council; and when he thought fit, in the following year, to resign his seat, Robert Lowe had undoubtedly established his position as one of the leading public men in the colony of New South Wales.

After the weary months of gloom and disappointment described in the preceding chapter, this unforeseen introduction into public life was naturally highly gratifying to Mrs. Lowe.

In a letter to her mother-in-law, written the day before her husband actually took his seat in the Council, she thus refers to the event in her usual frankly unreserved and therefore interesting style.

Sydney: November 7, 1843.

My dear Mother, I write to you with so much pleasure in being able to tell you that Sir George Gipps has appointed Robert a nominee member of the Legislative Council. I assure you this is a high honour, and delights him greatly, it also inspires me with an additional overflow of vanity (which pray forgive) regarding Robert's abilities.

Sir George has placed him in the Legislative Council, he expressly says, to strengthen the Government, and looks forward to his being of great use. This appointment will give Robert an opportunity of bringing himself before the public, and will be of great use to him as a barrister. I shall have so much pleasure in sending the Sydney papers, as I know with what great interest and delight you will read his speeches. Now, my dearest mother, does not Robert overcome every obstacle and impediment? Even with the disadvantage of having had to retire from the Bar for a time, in a new place, amongst new friends, and with no real opportunity of displaying his talents, he has been able to impress everyone with the highest opinion of them and of his character. Sir James Dowling [the Chief Justice], Judge Stephen,[1] all whose opinions

[1] The present veteran, Sir Alfred Stephen, now in his ninety-first year—

are worth caring for, speak of him in the highest terms. He has
been in Sydney but twelve months and Sir George has conferred on
him the highest honour in his power to bestow, nor has there been
the least private friendship in this. Sir G. G. is notoriously a man
who has never even stretched a point for a private friend. This
appointment has no remuneration attending it, but much honour.
Robert's speeches will be printed and sent home with the Proceedings
of the Legislative Council; his name will thus be often before the
Home Government, and may thus prove of immense advantage.
There have been already very many fiery debates in the Legislative
Council, and are likely to be more.

How true it is that hope fulfilled is disappointment. In
less than a year from the evening when he made his first bow
to the Speaker, Robert Lowe felt compelled to send in his
resignation, simply because he could see no ' honour ' in being
the nominee of a man with whom he gravely differed on
almost every question of public policy, though, of course, this
divergence was not apparent either to Sir George Gipps or
himself when the seat was conferred upon and accepted by
him.

Then, although it was doubtless true, as Mrs. Lowe pro-
gnosticated, that her husband's brilliant speeches were ' printed
and sent home,' it may be doubted whether the Ministers
at St. Stephen's or the chief officials in Whitehall were able
to peruse those outspoken and often vehement diatribes with
pleasure or even equanimity. Their unlooked-for result, however, was to make the erstwhile nominee of the Governor
one of the foremost, and for a time the most popular man
in the community—but this is anticipating the chapter of
events.

Sir George Gipps, in selecting Robert Lowe as one of the
Crown nominees, did so simply to strengthen himself in the
Council. The Governor was a shrewd and able man ; though
it will be admitted on all hands that if he expected Lowe to
become either a lackey or a tool, he could hardly have made

formerly Chief Justice and late Lieutenant-Governor of New South Wales —
a near kinsman of Sir James Fitzjames Stephen and of Mr. Leslie Stephen.

a worse selection. But the Government officials in the Council were now confronted by a number of popular representatives, each of whom has left his mark in the annals of Australia. Dr. Lang, in his *History of New South Wales*, expresses astonishment at the 'great superiority of the first Legislative Council to those that have succeeded it;' and questions whether 'it has ever been surpassed by any legislature out of England in the British Empire.' To support his assertion he mentions the names of Lowe, Wentworth, Windeyer, and Cowper : to which in fairness should be added his own.

If from this list we omit Lord Sherbrooke's name altogether as that of a man quite apart, and in no sense a normal colonial member, and substitute for it that of Sir Edward Deas Thomson, then the principal Crown official, it may be safely declared that no subsequent Australian Legislature can present such a galaxy of really able parliamentarians.

It would seem from a letter of Mrs. Lowe's, written at this time, that the 'popular' representative whom Sir George Gipps most feared was Richard Windeyer, 'the Joseph Hume of the House,' as Dr. Lang styled him.

Richard Windeyer was an English barrister who had been on the staff of the *Times* and the *Morning Chronicle*.[1] He originated Todd's *Parliamentary Companion*, and as a friend of Colonel Perronet Thompson took part in the Anti-Corn-law agitation. He emigrated to Sydney in 1835, and became leader of the Australian bar. As a public man, his inflexible honesty and ability made him alike respected and feared.

'There is a barrister,' writes Mrs. Lowe, ' a Mr. Windeyer, an undoubtedly clever man, who has a strong party opposed to the Government—and the Home Government also ; this man

---

[1] Disraeli, when starting the *Representative*, informed Murray that he had engaged S. C. Hall 'and a Mr. Windyer, sen., both of whom we shall find excellent reporters and men of business. The latter has been on the *Times*.' (*Memoir of John Murray*, vol. ii. p. 206.)

is a popular member—to oppose him, and to conquer if possible, is to be Robert's main point.'

Again, how little it was foreseen that the popular member and the Crown nominee would, after a very short time, discover that they were meant to be allies rather than enemies!

Whatever the local press may have thought of the new nominee member, Sir George Gipps, as we have seen, had enjoyed special facilities for forming an independent judgment. In his despatch to Lord Stanley (November 10, 1843), Sir George, after announcing Mr. Lowe's appointment, describes him as 'a barrister of England and of New South Wales . . . . Mr. Lowe has been but a short time in the colony, but he was for many years a distinguished member of the University of Oxford, where he was a Fellow of Magdalen College and for some time one of the examining masters. He is a man of first-rate abilities and a fluent speaker.'

On these points the new member did not suffer either the Legislative Council or the colony to be long in doubt. At the time that he took his seat, the leaders of the Opposition were very busy with a Bill which some of them, and notably Mr. Windeyer, seemed to think a panacea for the terrible commercial depression under which New South Wales still continued to languish. Having acquired through Lord Stanley a certain measure of autonomy, such men as Wentworth and Windeyer would naturally want to exercise to the utmost the self-governing powers placed in their hands as popular representatives of the Council. It is highly significant of the general state of financial collapse that these ingenious pioneer legislators of the colony should, in this second session of their first Parliament, have devoted their energies almost entirely to monetary measures.

Robert Lowe's first speech was in opposition to a measure introduced by Richard Windeyer, called the Monetary Confidence Bill, which was designed to relieve the general bankruptcy by the creation of a State bank together with a system

of land debentures. A select committee of the House had
been appointed, and such financial and banking experts as the
colony could then boast had been examined by it. The report
of this select committee is of itself a most interesting document, but unfortunately far too lengthy to reproduce on the
present occasion. Like all experts, these early colonial
bankers gave diametrically contradictory opinions with regard
to Mr. Windeyer's proposed measure. That gentleman, who
was then admittedly the most brilliant advocate at the Sydney
Bar, introduced his Bill in a speech of great length and of
marked ability. If anyone out of mere curiosity cares to
turn to the reports of this prolonged debate on the Monetary
Confidence Bill, they will, I am sure, be amazed at the general
breadth of knowledge and superior dialectical skill displayed
by the chief speakers. It used to be a favourite line of argument, with those who are of opinion that the British Empire
would be welded together in a firmer and more satisfactory way
if the Colonies were directly represented at Westminster, that,
by becoming members of such an Imperial Parliament, the
colonial representatives would learn to take large and imperial
views and would cease to be engrossed in mere petty and
parochial debates. Let anyone who cherishes such a delusion
turn from a report of an average night in the House of
Commons to this discussion in the first, and only partially
representative, Parliament of New South Wales. Why,
Windeyer's speech alone would be sufficient to make the
reputation of many an aspirant to the Chancellorship of the
Exchequer.

The fact is, if you want resounding eloquence and far-
reaching and imperial views of men and things, you have only
to collect half-a-dozen needy geniuses bent on the reformation
of the world and the alleviation of their own pecuniary troubles.
Truly, Windeyer and his chief supporters used every argumentative art in support of their favourite panacea. They were
also in an evident majority, and it required some courage for

a new and untried man to rise and endeavour to disprove or
discount the five or six hours' eloquent oratory of the mover of
the Bill—backed up as he would inevitably be by the overwhelming Wentworth.

Robert Lowe, however, rose at once and delivered his
maiden speech in Parliament. He succeeded in enchaining
the attention of the Assembly, and sprang at a bound into
the front rank as a debater. It is not too much to say that
he met and fairly defeated Windeyer on every point. On
the third reading of the Bill, Lowe again spoke with the
same force and brilliancy; and besides that, his speech displayed a grasp of the whole subject of colonial finance, as
well as an intimate knowledge of the social and commercial
state of the colony, surprising in one who had been a resident
for so short a time.

William Charles Wentworth, I have been told by one who
witnessed the scene, looked up like a fighting cock who had
long been lord of the domain, but who finds himself unex-
pectedly confronted by a rival. Like all men of really great and
original mind he at once detected and appreciated ability in
another. Lowe's speech might have been perhaps somewhat
too academic in tone—fitted at times better for the Oxford
Union than for the Sydney Legislative Council—and he was
certainly not overburdened with colonial experience; he
had been, moreover, at too evident pains on this his first
appearance to prepare his case against Windeyer and his redoubtable supporter. But Wentworth, by the very manner of
his reply, showed that he recognised in the new-comer a foe-
man worthy of his steel. Like a skilful and practised debater
he began by smiting his opponent where his armour was
thinnest. Lowe, he said, had no doubt done his best in support of the authority which had given him his seat in the
Council. He had spoken eloquently at the dictation of his
constituent. He fully acknowledged that 'the efforts of the
hon. member from Horbury Terrace [Lowe's Sydney residence],

smelling of the lamp as they did and highly considered as they were, were nevertheless efforts of no small merit.'

Wentworth, whose great boast it was that he was a native of New South Wales—he was really born in Norfolk Island, which was then, however, under the rule of Sydney—was not likely to let his opponent off lightly for the crime of being what they call in Australia a 'new chum.' In his customary vigorous and antithetical way, he declared that 'all the opposition emanated from persons who were comparative strangers to the land, ignorant of its wants, ignorant of its history, ignorant, in short, of everything connected with it.' This was no doubt intended quite as much for Sir George Gipps as for his eloquent mouthpiece. Dr. Nicholson (now Sir Charles Nicholson, Bart.), a worthy pioneer settler, then one of the members for the district of Port Phillip, said that 'the peroration of the speech of the member from Horbury Terrace was very beautiful.' While the leading journal, which only a few days ago had wanted to know who Mr. Lowe was, remarked, the morning after the debate, that 'Mr. Lowe spoke in a strain of eloquence to which even the learned member for Sydney (Wentworth) was constrained to ascribe no small merit.'

On the division, Mr. Windeyer's Bill was carried against the Government by fourteen votes to seven; but Governors in those days were not what we English understand as Constitutional monarchs, for they held the powers of the Czar of Russia or the President of the United States. Accordingly Sir George Gipps promptly vetoed the measure, and that was the end of it.

In the next attempt to remedy the ills of the colony by legislation, the new nominee member assumed the initiative. A select committee had been appointed to inquire into the working of the Insolvency Act, then in force in New South Wales. The committee, which consisted of Dr. Nicholson (the mover), Mr. Charles Cowper (seconder), and Messrs. Lowe, Plunkett, Therry, and Wentworth, were indefatigable in the examination of witnesses and the collection of evidence. So serious was

the crisis that the most influential men in the community gave
evidence.

A report had been drawn up in which, among other things,
the abolition of imprisonment for debt under final process was
recommended. At the same time the Chief Commissioner of
Insolvency was to be invested with more extensive powers of
committal for acts of glaring dishonesty on the part of insol-
vents. Voluntary assignments in trust for creditors were also
advised. This class of legislation, which the Council felt itself
impelled to undertake with some degree of precipitancy, shows
how very serious the condition of the colony still was towards
the close of 1843. In the attempt to amend the Insolvency
Act, Robert Lowe, new as he was to the colony and the
Council, certainly took the principal part. ' In bringing up
the report of the committee,' writes Mr. David Blair, ' he
earnestly and eloquently urged the abolition of imprisonment
for debt ; a measure which subsequently became law, and was
the chief distinction of the first session of the Council.

A week after this triumph a very important debate took
place on the Tariff, in which Robert Lowe gave eloquent expression to his free-trade proclivities, which had already made him
feared and famous at Oxford. The debate in the Council which
took place on December 22 was on a motion of Wentworth's
to increase the duty on flour from 1s. 5d. to half-a-crown per
hundredweight. Mr. Lowe said he was altogether opposed to
the proposition. He also objected to the manner in which it
had been sprung on the Council. He had been told that all
his speeches smelt of the lamp ; but he wished that ' on this
occasion he could have had an opportunity of consulting that
lamp.' Not only had the hon. member for Sydney not given
any notice of this proposition, but he had endeavoured, and
had nearly succeeded, in lulling the vigilance of the committee
and carrying his measure unopposed ; for during the whole
of the session he (Wentworth) had declared his aversion to
all protective and to all prohibitory duties. It was true that,

even among the supporters of the proposal, there were differences of opinion as to whether it was protective, or merely for
the sake of the revenue. As a matter of fact, the effect would
be to tax the bread of the poor for the supposed advantage of
a class : already in this city there were hundreds who could
with difficulty procure a loaf, and the committee would now
take a slice from that loaf. The Legislature had been called
upon to relieve those people ; they had assisted them. But it
would be mockery now to adopt a measure which would render
all that they had before done of no avail. He would remind
the House of the fearful consequences of the Corn Laws in
England. 'Already civil war threatened the kingdom, class
had been raised up against class, discord and discontent uni-
versally prevailed, and matters were fast approaching to a
crisis which, if the fullest concessions were not made, would, he
feared, involve the Monarchy, the aristocracy, the British Constitution—all that an Englishman held dear, in one common
ruin. He would have the committee pause before they sowed
the seed of similar disasters for future generations. This
colony had been held up to the world as the refuge for all that
was disgraceful to humanity ; let not this Council be held up
as the receptacle for antiquated and foolish notions which had
been hunted out from every portion of the civilised globe.'

This speech thoroughly aroused Wentworth, who, from his
former easy ascendency in the Council, had grown somewhat
careless of his reputation as a parliamentary debater. To a
mind like his, essentially broad, and at the same time comba-
tive, the advent of such a speaker as Lowe, who never debated
even a local or parochial matter without referring to general
principles, was sure to act as a stimulant. It is curious also
to notice in this debate that Wentworth in his reply to Lowe
practically proclaimed himself a Protectionist. In this matter
the ' Australian patriot,' to give him his popular title, proved
himself the forerunner of the fiscal policy which has been

accepted by all the Australian colonies, with the exception of his own. No one could possibly read this debate without seeing that if, in after years, under responsible government, Wentworth had been called upon to shape a policy as Prime Minister of New South Wales, it would have been on Protectionist lines.

This was the first occasion on which Wentworth and Lowe were fairly matched in an exciting public debate. The older and more experienced man—Wentworth was twenty years Lowe's senior—was elaborately sarcastic in referring to the brilliant oratory of the hon. member from Horbury Terrace, which, although it was ' destitute of the lustre generally communicated by its previous preparation, was still an effort of much talent.'

The leading colonial journal, however, seemed to consider it of a higher order and, on the whole, more effective than Wentworth's own, ' with its usual mixture of elegance and vulgarity, of good sense and coarse abuse.' Lowe's, on the other hand, received unmixed laudation.

The session closed on December 28 ; and certainly, in the marvellously short interval from November 8, when he took his seat, the new nominee member had succeeded in making his presence felt in a very marked degree. His triumphs in the Council of course affected his status in the community. At the annual Christmas examination of the students of Sydney College, ' R. Lowe, Esq., M.C.' (writes a contemporary chronicler) ' examined the first Greek class, and selected a difficult chorus from the beautiful Greek play.' The other distinguished visitor who presided on the occasion was Judge (now Sir Alfred) Stephen. Among the pupils were younger branches of Wentworths and Stephens, and names such as Garrick—familiar enough to the Australians of the present day.

Robert Lowe had emerged from a mere person, and become a leading personage of Sydney. Mrs. Lowe, who watched his return to active pursuits with delight, and yet with trepidation, writes 'home' to friends : 'He scarcely ever reads a line, and I watch him with the most zealous care, for fear he should be tempted to use his eyes. He is so happy now it does me good to look at him.'

CHAPTER XII

Trial of Knatchbull—Lowe and Judge Burton—Dr. Elliotson of the *Zoist*—
' Mr. Lowe's Ethics '

LOWE's immediate success as a member of the Council naturally directed attention to him as a practising barrister.   He
had now actively resumed his practice ; but his income from
that source was not at first large, for the widespread ruin and
general depression had—to use his own happy phrase—
' effectually dried up the sources of litigation.'   Nor was
Robert Lowe ever at any time the actual leader of the Sydney
Bar.   In the first place, he never sought more business than he
could manage without risk to his eyesight, the imperfect nature
of which was in itself a terrible drawback.   Anyone who has
had experience of a law court may form an idea of the difficulty
he must have experienced in getting through the work of a
busy day before a judge and jury, with all kinds of papers and
documents to be referred to for the examination of witnesses
and the sifting of evidence.   Such a strain alone must have
been exhausting, both mentally and physically.   Still, despite
this almost insuperable difficulty, he managed to secure a fair
share of briefs, and his reputation as an advocate grew year by
year, until he certainly became, if not the leader, one of the
leading practising barristers in the colony.   Nor should it be
lightly assumed that his rivals were men of inferior calibre.
Wentworth, who was an intellectual giant in any field in
which he chose to exercise his powers, had, it is true, retired ;

but there were a number of other men then in active practice
in Sydney by no means to be despised, of whom Richard
Windeyer and the present Sir Archibald Michie, of Melbourne,
may be mentioned.

In the beginning of 1844 Robert Lowe was retained for the
defence in a famous murder trial, which I should have preferred to have passed over, as a matter better buried in oblivion,
but for the recent, and generally distorted, accounts of it which
have appeared both in England and Australia. I allude to
the trial of John Knatchbull for the murder of Mrs. Jamieson,
which took place in Sydney on January 6, 1844.

In that popular and entertaining work, *Oxford Memories*,
by the Rev. James Pycroft, there is, in conjunction with
various scattered reminiscences of Lord Sherbrooke, an account
of this trial, and of the miserable but well-born murderer,
which seems to have attracted some attention, especially in
Australia, where it has formed the basis of more than one
sensational narrative. Mr. Pycroft declares that Knatchbull
was a schoolfellow of Lord Sherbrooke's at Winchester, and that
his first offence was the embezzlement of a chronometer, of
which he accused a fellow-officer, he being then in the Navy.
The accused man managed eventually to bring home the charge
to the real culprit, who was tried and transported for the
offence.

In Australia, says Mr. Pycroft, ' he was at one time the
assigned servant of a friend of mine ; and before that, while
in barracks, another of my friends officially employed there
said he remembered that Knatchbull once came to him, and
volunteered for the office of flogger, to accompany him daily on
his rounds to administer lashes, as the poor wretches were
sentenced on daily complaints ; and a most savage flogger he
was.'

Mr. Pycroft goes on to relate that Knatchbull obtained a
ticket-of-leave, and that he was kindly treated by an old
woman, whom he poisoned to possess himself of her supposed

riches, but that all he obtained was 3s. 6d. Most of this story, despite its circumstantiality, is quite inaccurate.

It is, however, only too true that a seafaring man on a ticket-of-leave, known as John Fitch, but who was in reality John Knatchbull, murdered Ellen Jamieson in her own shop in Sydney by cleaving her skull with a tomahawk, and that he was most eloquently, though ineffectually, defended by Robert Lowe. The trial took place in the Supreme Court, Sydney, on January 25, 1844, before Mr. Justice (afterwards Sir William) Westbrooke Burton. The evidence against the accused was so clear that his counsel did not attempt to disprove the murder, but set up a plea of 'moral insanity.'

The evidence against Knatchbull at the coroner's inquest on the body of the murdered woman was indeed so overwhelming that the public verdict was given against him before the actual trial took place. The chief witness was a neighbour, who saw him prowling about the door and then enter the shop.

'I ran over,' he said, 'and found the door locked, and heard some strokes given, as of someone breaking a cocoa-nut with a hammer.'

He swore that he saw the prisoner inside at the window, and then gave an alarm to the 'old watchman,' and asked him for assistance; but he declined, saying, 'Well, what is that to me?'

Assistance, however, was procured, the back door was broken open, and the murderer was secured literally red-handed. Then the tomahawk was found under the bed, and the man with whom Knatchbull was lodging up to the night of his apprehension swore that the weapon was his property, and had been abstracted from his back yard, to which the accused had had access. Furthermore, there was found upon him the pocket of the deceased woman's dress, containing some seventeen pounds in silver and bank notes.

The prisoner, being called on for his defence, stated that he had particularly to request the jury not to be led away by

anything they had heard out of doors ; as a jury of free-born
Englishmen, he trusted they would give him a fair trial. The
coroner briefly summed up, and the jury, after a minute's
consultation, returned a verdict of Wilful Murder against John
Fitch *alias* Knatchbull, who was committed to take his trial.

The greatest of criminal lawyers might well have felt,
under the circumstances, that it was a hopeless case to defend.
It was here that the dialectical genius of Lowe came into
requisition ; and it may fairly be doubted if any counsel ever
set up a more ingenious or a more convincing plea for a man
whom he was compelled at the outset to admit was guilty of
the terrible crime with which he was charged. After solemnly
telling the jury that if, after all, ' the slightest doubt should
arise in their minds as to the prisoner's guilt they would be
bound to throw all the benefit of that doubt into the scale of
mercy,' he continued somewhat in this strain :—

It was not his intention, he said, to enter into any circum-
stantial details, for the duty which devolved upon him that
day was of a very different kind, and he should endeavour to
show that, even supposing, for the sake of argument, that the
statements of all the preceding witnesses had been true, ' the
prisoner was still one of those persons for whom laws had not
been made, and who, although for the peace and welfare of
society he ought to be placed under the most severe restraint,
ought not to be held responsible for his actions.' It was not
for the good of society, continued counsel, that the life of any
man who could not be held legally responsible for his actions
should be taken ; and he must most earnestly impress it upon
the minds of the jury that ' they did not sit there merely as
the avengers of blood.' It was not, he went on, because a
murder had been committed, with the terrible particulars of
which the evidence for the Crown had rendered them so
familiar, that they necessarily were called upon to avenge
that murder by delivering a verdict which would deprive
another fellow-creature of life ; for if any circumstances should

morning, and it would be for the jury to determine whether
any sane man would prepare to clasp the hand of the bride at
the altar by imbruing his own in the blood of another woman ;
and whether, if a want of money was supposed to be the motive
which actuated him, he had not a much readier mode of supplying that want by discounting some of the bills which were
found upon his person. . . . He regretted that he was not in a
position to call witnesses to testify to the state of the prisoner's
mind. It was no great boon that he asked for this unfortunate man, for even if acquitted upon the ground of
insanity, he must be confined for life in a lunatic asylum, as
a rightful protection to society against one with so dangerous
a disposition. He (Mr. Lowe) was aware of the narrow imagination of our forefathers, which would limit the attention of a
jury to the simple fact whether a person charged did or did
not commit the crime of which he was accused ; but he could
only hope for the dawning of a brighter day, when their
attention might be extended also to a full inquiry into the
motives which led to that crime.'

In a most eloquent peroration he earnestly besought the
jury to temper justice with mercy ; and in that spirit he asked
whether they could believe that a man with the great advantages originally possessed by the prisoner could have fallen
step by step into the lowest depths of degradation unless urged
on by some resistless demon of insanity—by whom (if guilty
of the crime now laid to his charge) he had been incited to its
perpetration. If they found the prisoner guilty of the crime,
and yet believed him to have been driven by this insane and
irresistible impulse, the ends of justice would no more be
answered by making such an irresponsible being expiate his
offence on the scaffold than by the public execution of a savage
animal.

The judge before whom this case was tried—Mr. Justice
Burton—was an extremely conscientious man, of good ability
as well as high character, but an orthodox Churchman, not

given to metaphysical subtleties. In his summing-up he expressed the gravest dissent from the line of argument adopted by the brilliant advocate. It was the first time, he said, that he had ever heard the doctrine broached in a Court of Justice, that a man was not to be held accountable for crime because he had been impelled by an overpowering internal impulse. Mr. Justice Burton then summed-up very strongly against the prisoner, whom the jury declared guilty, and who was thereupon sentenced to death.

There is a very curious sequel to this sensational trial. The *Zoist*, a ' Quarterly Journal of Cerebral Physiology and Mesmerism,' had just been started in London under the auspices of Thackeray's friend, Dr. Elliotson, to whom the great novelist dedicated *Pendennis*. It was altogether a remarkable publication, on many subjects greatly in advance of the time; it seized upon the report of the Knatchbull trial and reproduced it verbatim, as showing the inefficiency and barbarism of capital punishment. In the original article with which the editor of the *Zoist* prefaced this report, he gave a picture of the criminal career of Knatchbull much fuller, and painted in much darker colours, than the more recent sketch by the Rev. James Pycroft. But for all that, Dr. Elliotson argued that Knatchbull's crime was so evidently the result of a debased cerebral organisation, that to hang him was a mere wild act of revenge on the part of society, which was itself responsible for the murder of the unfortunate Mrs. Jamieson. It is not feasible to reprint here the long train of argument by which this apparent paradox was sustained. But the writer was fairly in ecstasies with the line of defence taken by Knatchbull's counsel.

' We felt great pleasure while perusing the speech of Mr. Lowe. It is consolatory to find one voice held up upon the side of mercy in a colony where crime is so frequent and where there is a constant arrival of the worst characters from the mother country.'

The *Zoist* then went on to express its surprise and satisfaction that the brilliant barrister should have drawn his
arguments ' from our science ; ' adding that he 'laid down the
doctrine of philosophical necessity with clearness and precision.'
It quoted with marked approval several of the more telling
appeals from the speech ; and then it lashed with unmeasured
scorn the pious remark of Judge Burton in his summing-up,
that if ' wickedly-disposed men will yield step by step to the
approaches of the evil one, they must expect to be led at last
by the tempter to that precipice down which it was his desire
to cast them.'

It is not difficult to imagine what reply Dr. Elliotson made
to the Sydney judge. ' It appears to us,' retorted the editor,
' that if a being is seduced by a power which he did not call into
existence, and over which he has no control, then there is a
very urgent reason presented why he should be exonerated
from the consequences of his offence.'

By the time that the *Zoist* reached Sydney, Robert Lowe had
a paper of his own, the *Atlas*. He accordingly reproduced the
article from Dr. Elliotson's journal, which seems to have had
the same disquieting effect on the *Sydney Morning Herald* as the
Vestiges of Creation, and later on the *Origin of Species*, had on
the favourite family journals in England in the last generation.
But the *Herald* of that day had a political as well as a religious object in view, as Robert Lowe, who had in the meantime resigned his seat as a Crown nominee in the Council, was
then standing for the pastoral constituency of St. Vincent. He
was accordingly attacked as an impious person, who might
undermine the faith and morals of even its hardy squatters.
The *Herald* in effect revived the question, which Judge
Burton originally started, of the irreligious character of Mr.
Lowe's defence of Knatchbull. It was opposed, they declared,
to the ' first principles of Christianity.' This led to a correspondence, the essential portion of which is quite worth re-
producing. The correspondence was headed :—

The Ethics of Mr. Lowe.

To the Editors of the *Sydney Morning Herald*.

Gentlemen,—Will you oblige me by referring to the report of my speech on the trial of Knatchbull for murder, which, I believe, will be found in the *Herald* of January 25, 1844, and by pointing out what doctrines it contains opposed to the first principles of Christianity, and what those principles of Christianity are to which you consider those doctrines to be opposed?

I am, Gentlemen,

Your obedient servant,

ROBERT LOWE.

Horbury Terrace : March 24, 1845.

The editors, little suspecting the practice their antagonist had had in theological disputation at Oxford with Newman and Ward, promptly took up the challenge. They pointed out that Mr. Lowe had opposed the principle of man's free agency, which they considered to be the ' first principle of the Christian religion.' ' It is opposed likewise,' they added, ' to the whole tenour of that sacred history which is designed to exemplify and demonstrate the depths of human depravity, and to

assert Eternal Providence,

And justify the ways of God to man.'

The reply to this fresh attack has been described as a masterpiece of polemical discussion ; it is certainly a very characteristic rejoinder. With the omission of a few paragraphs not essential to the argument, it reads as follows :—

' You bite against a file ! Cease viper.'

Sir William Draper to Junius.

To the Editors of the *Sydney Morning Herald*.

Gentlemen,—When I asked you to point out the doctrine of Christianity to which my speech was opposed, I expected to be referred to something held by Christians in common, and not to the doctrine of the Wesleyan Sect ; for it may be, gentlemen, that I am not a Wesleyan Methodist, and, not to keep you in further suspense, the fact is that I am a member of the Church of England. You are not ignorant of this, but you probably *are* ignorant of the Articles of that Church. I therefore beg to subjoin a copy of her

tenth Article, and to refer you to the eleventh, twelfth and seventeenth, which will, I apprehend, show clearly that though *you* may
consider the foundation of the whole system of Divine Government
to be man's free agency and consequent responsibility, the Church
of England, whose Articles I have repeatedly subscribed, does not.

. . . . . .

Had I foreseen that, in defiance of all usage and all principle,
the arguments used to persuade a jury were to be fastened upon me
as my own opinions, and used against me for electioneering purposes, I would have reported the speech myself. There are many
things in that report I never said, but I am in the habit of attach-
ing so little weight to what falls from counsel in argument, that I
should have thought it ridiculous egotism to meddle with it.

This last touch is very characteristic. Nothing seems to
have aroused Lowe's contempt at any time more than when a
political opponent, or a newspaper, expected him to support,
on the hustings or in Parliament, the opinions which he may
have expressed as an advocate in a court of law. He was
never enamoured of those arts and artifices which are so
useful for the winning of verdicts, and spoke of them as ' the
tricks of this wretched trade.'

It was an aspiring wish of the Arian Milton [he adds in allusion
to the *Herald's* quotation] to ' justify the ways of God to man ; ' but
it is a wish which can never be accomplished ; the existence of evil
will meet the presumptuous speculator at every turn and fling him
back into the shallow nothingness of his nature. ' Dangerous it
were,' says the eloquent and judicious Hooker, ' for the feeble brain of
man to wade far into the doings of the Most High, whom, although
to know be life, and joy to make mention of His Name, yet our
soundest knowledge is to know that we know Him not as indeed He
is, neither can know Him, and our safest eloquence concerning Him
is our silence, when we confess without confession, that His glory
is inexplicable, His greatness above our capacity and reach.'
' He is above and we upon earth, therefore it behoveth our words
to be wary and few.'
And now, gentlemen, I have done with you. I ask you for
principles, and you give me inferences. I ask you for Christianity,
and you give me Methodism. You are now at full liberty to inter
this slander by the side of his deceased brother of last week, and as
you seem rather at a loss for something to use against me at the

present time, I will take the liberty of suggesting a few topics myself.

I ride a very ugly horse, that clearly proves me an Atheist, for who else could be so insensible to the beauties of the noblest animal of the creation. I live in a very small house, which clearly shows I must have a contracted mind, and I am sometimes known to play at billiards, which shows a strong though, it may perhaps be expedient in candour to admit, not quite fully developed propensity for gambling.

I am, Gentlemen,

Your obedient servant,

ROBERT LOWE.

There was a yet more personal and pathetic sequel to this case. In the issue of March 9, 1844, the *Sydney Morning Herald* printed this brief report in its law notices :—

Before Sir James Dowling, Chief Justice.

IN THE MATTER OF THE ORPHANS JAMIESON.

In this case Mr. Lowe applied by petition to be appointed guardian of these infants, at the same time expressing his willingness to give such security as the Court might require. The application being unopposed was granted by the Court.

The two little orphans of the murdered woman—a boy and girl—were taken by Mr. and Mrs. Lowe and carefully brought up by them in their own home. Writing to Mrs. Sherbrooke of Oxton, at the close of 1845, when they were living in their own delightful house at Nelson Bay, some few miles out of Sydney, Mrs. Lowe makes this touching reference to the children: 'The little boy and girl, whose mother Knatchbull murdered, are still with us. The little girl is a great favourite with Robert; she reads for him if I am engaged, and is not only clever but an exceedingly good child. The boy, just four years old, is quick and can read a little. They give no trouble, and the servants are very fond of them. The little girl carries my notes and messages, the boy goes with her, and she is as steady and sensible as a grown-up person; her father died a year before her mother, to whom she seems

to have been much attached. The poor little thing is quite
premature in mind, which I have no doubt may be attributed
to her having known so much early sorrow. She talks to
the little boy and comforts him if he cries, as if she were his
mother.'

The sequel of the story is a sad one, and hardly encouraging
to philanthropists. Mr. and Mrs. Lowe brought them to
England, and they continued to live with them until the girl
died at the early age of thirteen. An excellent appointment
was obtained for the boy, but he abandoned it without reason,
and, after various vicissitudes, went out to New Zealand and
served for a while in the colonial forces against the Maoris.
Like the proverbial bad coin, he came back and was a source
of much trouble and anxiety to his benefactors. It was in
reference to him that Lord Sherbrooke made the remark :
' What evil that I have done has ever been visited upon me
like this one good action ? '

The story thus simply set forth may, perchance, sound
strange to a world which has proclaimed Lord Sherbrooke
to be a cynic, a hard man of logic, unemotional and without
human feeling. Talking over the matter with Sir John Simon
(who had often seen the young Jamiesons), I made some
such natural observation as this, when he went on to tell me
of many another ' nameless, unremembered act,' which to his
knowledge Lord Sherbrooke had performed. ' He was not
only,' he added impressively, ' the clearest-headed man I ever
knew, but the best-hearted.'

CHAPTER XIII

LAYING THE FOUNDATION OF PARLIAMENT

Chairman of Committees—The Chaplain—Dr. Lang and State Churches—
Breach of Privilege—Duelling in Sydney—Anti-Corn-Law Speech—Parallel
between Canada and Australia—Report on Education

The foundation of Parliamentary Government in Australia
was laid by the 'popular' or representative members of Lord
Stanley's Legislative Council, of whom Robert Lowe became
the virtual leader. Through their action the colonists were
taught not to be satisfied until they had achieved the rights
and privileges of self-governing Englishmen. But to us the
most singular side of the story is that the achievement should
have been won in great measure by the action of a young
English barrister, who, at the outset at least, was merely the
nominee of the Governor. If, however, we investigate the
proceedings of this single and only partially representative
Chamber during its earlier sessions, we shall find that
Robert Lowe did more to secure to colonists the civil and
political rights of Englishmen than any other member of
the Council.

As soon as the session of 1844 opened (May 28th) the
Colonial Secretary proposed a gentleman as Chairman of Committees without salary. Mr. Lowe promptly objected to the
election of a chairman unless a salary were placed on the
Estimates. In the clearest way he pointed out that by such
appointments they were laying, well or ill, the foundations of
their parliamentary system. It was essential that the chair-

P 2

man should always be in attendance, and the Council could not exact such attendance from an unpaid officer. He therefore moved an amendment that an address be presented to the Governor, recommending that an item be placed upon the Estimates to meet the salary of the Chairman of Committees. This amendment was duly seconded, but on being put to the vote was lost. Dr. Lang, who subsequently became one of the great champions of Australian autonomy, supported the Government.

Two nights afterwards a discussion took place which throws some light on a question which has often been asked as to why public prayers are dispensed with in opening the proceedings of Australian legislatures. It will be seen that the question was settled in what may be termed an agnostic spirit through the irreconcilable views of avowedly religious persons, each of whom would have his own form of prayer or none at all. The subject was introduced by Mr. (afterwards Sir Charles) Cowper, who moved ' That public prayers to Almighty God be offered up daily at the opening of this Council as soon as the Speaker shall have taken the chair ; and that a chaplain, who shall be a clergyman of the Church of England, be appointed by the Speaker to perform this duty.' The Anglicanism of this motion was regarded as an outrage by Dr. Lang, who, as well as being a legislator, was the leading Presbyterian minister in Sydney ; a man whose theology was of the old Covenanting type, to whom prelacy was almost as abhorrent as Popery. After him rose a Mr. Robinson, then member for Melbourne, who belonged to the Society of Friends ; he also objected to Mr. Cowper's motion, though he admitted that the prayers of the Church of England were very beautiful ; but he equally objected to Presbyterian prayers. After this Quaker gentleman had had his say, Robert Lowe got up and made an admirable and quite delightful speech. He said he had not had an opportunity of speaking on this subject last session, but having been brought up under the 'hallowed shade of the Church of England,' he should like to say a few words on the subject now. The speech of Mr. Robinson, he declared, showed how very easy it was to carry the principle contended for by Dr. Lang to an absurdity. The 'honourable and reverend member' thought he had gone far enough to avoid offence to all, yet he must now be convinced that it would be difficult indeed to stretch the resolution sufficiently to satisfy all the vagaries of the human mind. The Council should therefore adhere to the one principle, that the majority shall bind the rest. At the same time he (Mr. Lowe) objected to the system of the United States of clerical elections, and preferred that the appointment of chaplain should be vested in the Speaker. He thought the words 'clergyman of the Church of England' in Mr. Cowper's resolution might be omitted; although he did not anticipate a time when the members of that Church would be in a minority in that Council. Whatever their own particular views were, however, they could not do better than entrust the appointments to the hands of the Speaker.

Other leading members spoke, but despite the fact that two-thirds of the Council belonged, like Mr. Cowper, to the Anglican communion, his motion was lost; and no subsequent legislature in Australia, I believe, has ever appointed a chaplain or instituted a particular form of public prayer for the opening of its proceedings. It will be seen that Robert Lowe was in favour of such an appointment under certain conditions, but it may be gravely doubted whether it would much tend to edification while men's minds are so divided on the subject of religion. At the same time, had the two-thirds majority of the Council belonged to any other communion than that of the Church of England, they would no doubt have forced their own chaplain and their own form of prayer on the Council.

Lowe next took a prominent part in the debate on a motion of Dr. Lang, who had asked for a committee 'to con-

superiority in others; but they become the trusty clansmen of him who proves his chieftainship by the ordeal of personal combat.

Dr. Lang crossed swords no more with Robert Lowe. As he proudly records, he sat with him (one ought, perhaps, to say, in the language of the Conventicle, *under* him) on the Select Committee on Public Education. By his change of front on this subject, Lang acknowledged the presence of a mind far superior in grasp and culture, and quite equal in straight-forwardness and honesty, to his own.

At the close of this biting oration Lowe made an allusion to a quondam ally of Dr. Lang, a certain Alderman Macdermott, which led to the question of breach of privilege being raised for the first time in an Australian legislature. So irate was the alderman when he perused his morning newspaper that he sent a challenge to Mr. Lowe, who declined to meet him, chiefly on the ground that as a member of the Council he was responsible solely to that body for his words. He therefore refused either to apologise or to fight a duel. It may sound somewhat strange to hear of duelling in connection with the annals of such a colony as New South Wales. But in no British community was the practice more rife, and the curious in such matters would find much to interest them in the accounts of duels fought by prominent public men in the colony, from 1801, when Lieutenant-Colonel Patterson fought Captain Macarthur, down to the encounter between Mr. (afterwards Sir) Alexander Donaldson and Sir Thomas Mitchell in 1851.

There was probably no one on whom this practice could entail greater annoyance, not to say danger, than it did on Robert Lowe, who possessed one endowment and one defect which seem to have irresistibly impelled other men to challenge him—a sharp and witty tongue, and very imperfect eyesight.

I do not propose in this narrative to give details of all the

cases when he was called out. More than one kindly old
colonist has asked me gravely whether I believed that these
challenges came from persons who really meant, if they got an
opportunity, to murder an almost blind antagonist. I feel
no doubt on the point; and it affords one of the strongest
illustrations of the essentially immoral nature of duelling.
Such discreditable stories were best forgotten. This challenge
of Macdermott, however, really marks an epoch in the constitutional history of Australia, and the circumstances must
therefore be related.

Macdermott had been blackballed by the Committee of
Management of the Australian Library; a proceeding which
for some reason so disgusted Dr. Lang that he threatened to
bring the matter before the Legislative Council on the ground
that the Library was in the receipt of State aid, and should
therefore not have dared to blackball any *protégé* of his.
This struck Lowe as a characteristic instance of Dr. Lang's
arrogance; and so he referred to it in the debate on the
Church Temporalities Acts, without any feeling of malice
towards Macdermott, of whom, in fact, he had not the slightest
personal knowledge. But a night or two afterwards, a Dr.
Macfarlane called at his house stating that he was the bearer
of a letter from Macdermott, which ran as follows:—

8 George Street. Sydney:
Friday evening, June 28, 1844.

Sir,—My attention has been directed to a paragraph in the
Sydney Morning Herald of to-day, in which you are represented
as having alluded to me. I beg to inquire with what object such
allusion was made. My friend, Dr. Macfarlane, who will deliver you
this letter, will receive your reply.

I have the honour to be, Sir,
Your obedient servant,
H. MACDERMOTT.

To — Lowe, Esq..
Horbury Terrace, Sydney.

While his unwelcome guest waited, Mr. Lowe glanced at
the contents of the missive, and at once expressed his opinion

that in sending such a letter Macdermott had been guilty of
a breach of privilege ; and then, bowing Dr. Macfarlane out of
the door, he requested him to say that he declined to send any
answer whatever. The next day about noon, on returning to
his chambers in Elizabeth Street, he found his nocturnal visitor
and a gentleman, who turned out to be a Captain Moore,
awaiting him ; the latter stated that his instructions were
to demand an immediate apology or to propose ulterior
measures. Mr. Lowe declined either, but condescended to
give his explicit reasons for so acting. In the first place he
said that, as a member of the supreme Legislature of the
colony, he was entitled to full liberty of speech in that Legislature—a privilege he intended strenuously to maintain so
long as he had the honour to occupy a seat in the Council.
He went on to say that, even if this obstacle were removed, he
could not think of meeting Macdermott, as he was not his social
equal. Macdermott, I may say *en passant*, had been a private
or sergeant in a line regiment. But only those who have no
knowledge of the ethics of duelling will fail to see that, in
urging this objection, Mr. Lowe was using an argument that
would appeal to all duellists of the old school, who never for a
moment imagined that anyone but a gentleman had any
honour to avenge.

After gravely listening to these objections Captain Moore
again insisted on an apology, which Mr. Lowe again refused
to make. Then the captain waxed wroth, whereupon he and
his friend were desired to vacate the office. They, however,
said they were not going to be turned out, whereupon Mr.
Lowe said : ' If you will not go, you will not prevent me from
leaving,' and accordingly left his chambers, which they shortly
afterwards vacated. After this unpleasant scene he conferred
with one or two leading members of the House, and they
agreed with him that the only course was to obtain a warrant
and have these parties bound over to keep the peace. Macdermott and his two friends were therefore apprehended and

brought before the Mayor of Sydney. Mr. Lowe was himself summoned to attend at the Police Office to support his
case, and a very graphic account he gave of the proceedings
in his subsequent speech on the Breach of Privilege question
in the Legislative Council. There can be no doubt that
public sympathy, as it is loosely termed, was on the side of
Macdermott; however, the case was so clear that the Mayor
bound the parties over in 200*l.* personal security, and two
sureties of 100*l.* each.

Mr. Lowe, however, was wanting in neither moral nor
physical courage, and he determined at whatever cost to his
personal popularity to pursue the matter until he had placed
the whole question of the privileges of colonial members of
Parliament on a firm and satisfactory footing. In his admirable speech in the Legislative Council (July 8, 1844), in which
there is not a single trace of personal feeling, he placed the
subject before his fellow members with great force and
clearness. His argument, in brief, was that in a matter of
this kind, the Legislative Council possessed the same powers
as the House of Commons, and could therefore commit any
person for insulting a member. In support of this, he particularly referred to a decision of the Privy Council in 1836
relative to the Legislature of Jamaica, in which one Augustus
Hardin Beaumont was the appellant, and the Speaker of the
House of Assembly, the Provost Marshal, and a number of
constables and gaolers, were respondents. He went at length
into this case, quoting the entire speech of Mr. Baron Parke
in pronouncing the judgment of the Privy Council.

All the leading members of the Council took part in the
debate, and it was finally decided by a majority of fifteen to
thirteen that the Attorney General should prosecute Macdermott and his friends in the Law Courts. This subsequently
fell through, and as the proceedings were needlessly protracted,
public interest in the matter gradually died out.

At the request of a large number of citizens, the Mayor

called a public meeting, and resolutions were passed against
the appropriation of public money for the purpose of the
prosecution. For the time Lowe was the most unpopular
man in the colony; and the Council, for the action it had
taken, shared the opprobrium. But Robert Lowe cared
little for popularity at any time. It was ever the law of
his intellectual being to be guided and actuated by broad
general principles. As a member of the first Colonial Parliament, he conceived it to be all important that there should be
absolute freedom of debate. Those who cheered his opponent
and petitioned the Mayor cared for none of these things; but
his unpopularity was as shortlived as a passing cloud, and in
a year or two he became the veritable idol of the people of
Sydney.

I should certainly not have been tempted to dwell at any
greater length on these old and, happily, forgotten personal
quarrels, had not an Australian gentleman, Mr. Bloxsome, now
of Exmouth, kindly sent me the following interesting personal
narrative of the first duel in which Mr. Lowe was involved in
Sydney. These are Mr. Bloxsome's own words:—

'I had the pleasure of Mr. R. Lowe's acquaintance during
the whole of his career in N.S.W., though I was only a lad
at the time. One circumstance is indelibly impressed upon
my memory, namely, that I and a schoolfellow named Bell,
in company with my late father (whose guest Mr. Lowe was
at the time), pulled him across Sydney Harbour from the
North Shore to fight a duel one morning, either in the
year 1844 or '45. The duel was to have taken place with Mr.
E. Broadhurst, a barrister in Sydney, and I well remember
hearing my father say that Mr. Lowe said to him as we were
pulling them over in the boat: "They think because I can't
see that I can't fight; but they will find that they are mistaken." The duel did not take place, owing to the mismanagement of Mr. Broadhurst's second, Mr. Horace Flower. Mr.

Lowe's second was Captain O'Connell, eldest son of Sir Maurice O'Connell, Commander of the Forces in N.S.W. We landed Mr. Lowe and my father at Woolloomooloo Bay, close to "Tarmon's," the residence of Sir Maurice O'Connell. My father said to us lads : " Now, boys, go over to Robinson's Baths the other side of the Bay, and wait until we come." We, not knowing the errand they were on, waited and waited in the boat until ten o'clock at night, having had nothing to eat all day, and it was not until that hour that Mr. Lowe found it useless waiting any longer, so we all returned to my father's house on the North Shore.'

It may be added that Captain O'Connell shortly afterwards published in the newspapers an account of this affair, which in the main coincides with Mr. Bloxsome's recollections. On showing this letter at the writer's special request to Lord Sherbrooke some few years ago, he characteristically observed with a smile : ' My antagonist must have had a higher opinion of my prowess even than I had myself, as he never appeared on the scene.'

It need hardly be observed that such incidents must have been very alarming to Mrs. Lowe, who, in fact, grew more and more fearful lest some catastrophe should befall him.

Duelling remained in fashion in Sydney well on to 1850. Like all customs, good or bad, it died a lingering death. We may date its decline from the year 1847, when Mr. (afterwards Sir Charles) Cowper publicly declined to meet Mr. Boyd, a well-known squatter, who had challenged him. The *Sydney Morning Herald* devoted a leading article to the praise of Mr. Cowper, on the ground that he had made a stand against a senseless and often sanguinary custom.

Later on in the Session Mr. Lowe, still a Crown nominee, delivered a very important speech in support of his own motion 'that Petitions to Her Majesty and both Houses of Parliament be adopted by this Council humbly praying that they will be pleased to admit corn, the produce of the Australian colonies, on the same footing as Canadian corn.'

This takes us at a bound to the period of the Corn Laws in England; and it is curious to note the spectacle of Robert Lowe in a remote dependency waging war against the Protectionism of Sir Robert Peel, Lord Stanley, and Mr. Gladstone, then President of the Board of Trade. Mr. Lowe was exceedingly severe on these eminent English statesmen for making a difference, in this matter of the duty on corn, between one colony and another.

'In Australia there was a whole population of British origin; the greater part of the Canadian population was alien in language and in blood. We had not yet raised our hands against the mother country; Canada had been recently the scene of rebellion. Canada had never contributed to the welfare of the mother country. Canada had only created expense. This colony, on the other hand, produced an export every year increasing in quantity and becoming more valuable to the mother country by enabling her more successfully to compete in her woollen manufactures with the whole world. If England persisted in this Joseph-and-his-brethren sort of system, she would retain perhaps numerous dependencies, but she would never become the vast united empire which she ought.'

The conclusion of this speech can hardly fail to interest certain leading English statesmen even at the present day.

'Simple, however, as the question might appear to us here, and just, as we might imagine, was the claim we urged, that claim had been discussed in the House of Commons, and had been rejected. On looking over the debate as reported in the papers, he (Mr. Lowe) was surprised at the manner in which Mr. Gladstone had opposed it; he almost blushed at the amount of sacrifice which Mr. Gladstone, the liberality of whose views was so well known, had made to party feeling. . . .

· The interests of the colony were never considered, and the question itself was only discussed with a view to the amount of grain this colony was likely to export in proportion to the amount required by Great Britain. . . .

' One of the speakers in the House of Commons, suggested that, however small the effect at first, Australia might export largely after a time and then the interests of the landowners would be affected. This was in truth the only reason ; they forgot that we were Englishmen, and claimed to be placed on a general footing with themselves.'

Mr. Lowe was very much in earnest on this question of the duty on Australian corn ; and drew up with his own hand a petition to the House of Commons, which I transcribe not only as a curiosity of colonial political literature, but also as an interesting document for the future historians of Canada and Australia :—

Mr. Lowe's Parallel between Canada and New South Wales.

To the Honourable the Commons of the United Kingdom of Great Britain and Ireland in Parliament assembled : -

The humble petition of the Legislative Council of New South Wales in Council assembled,

Humbly showeth :

That your petitioners have learned with feelings of bitter disappointment that your Honourable House has recently refused to extend to them the privilege accorded to Canada of importing corn and flour at a nominal duty into England. The wool, the staple export of this colony, is exposed to the rivalry of the whole world, and by its competition has been the means of keeping down the price of the raw material of a most important English manufacture, whereas the heavy duty on Baltic timber, imposed for the protection of Canada, has been felt as a grievous tax on the British householders and shipowners.

That your petitioners have contributed nearly a million of money for the coercion of prisoners of the Crown, an object of a purely British character, and upwards of another million to introduce the starving poor of the British Isles into New South Wales as advantageous to the mother country as to the colony, while the

recent rebellion in Canada has cost vast sums to the British
Treasury, and been followed by the loan of 1,500,000*l*. for the
use of the colony under a Parliamentary guarantee.

That the Crown Revenue was surrendered to Canada in consideration of a civil list of 75,000*l*. in a population of a million and a
half, whereas a civil list of 81,000*l*. has been imposed on a
population of 170,000, and the revenues are not only not
surrendered, but are threatened to be increased, by a strain of
the royal prerogative, to treble the present amount.

That Canada enjoys the responsible government, while the Colonial
Office will not even suspend its decisions to give your petitioners
a hearing.

That the contiguity of Canada to the corn-growing States of
America affords great facility for smuggling grain, which the
isolated position of Australia renders impracticable.

That this is a settled, Canada a conquered colony. That the
population of one is British ; of the other, to a great extent,
French. That the laws and manners of England prevail in the
one, and those of France in a great part of the other ; and that
in none of these points are your petitioners conscious of any
inferiority to the Canadians.

That the quantity of corn which your petitioners would be likely
to import, though of immense consequence to them, would be
utterly insignificant to so large a market as that of the United
Kingdom. That if the agriculturists of England are sensitive
as to the admission of foreign corn, the constituents of your
petitioners also have their sensibilities, and great as is the loss
which they incur by exclusion from your markets, they feel yet
more keenly the ignominious badge of inferiority which the
decision of your Honourable House has affixed to them.

Your petitioners therefore humbly pray, that your Honourable House
will admit wheat, maize, and flour the produce of Australia,
into the United Kingdom on the same terms as wheat and flour
the produce of Canada.

Robert Lowe had already taken the first step towards
making practically his own the great question of public education in Australia. Still as a Crown nominee, but exercising,
as he did throughout, the greatest possible independence of
action, he moved for a select committee to inquire into and
report upon the state of education in the colony.

The select committee was duly appointed, and as its
labours have been productive of results of far-reaching and

historical importance, the names of its members should be given. As the question of education is so intimately mixed up with that of religion, it may be as well to show how the various religious denominations were represented on what was known as Mr. Robert Lowe's Select Committee. Of the ten members, five belonged to the Church of England, viz.— Robert Lowe, Charles Cowper, Richard Windeyer, Dr. Nicholson, and Deas Thomson ; two to the Church of Rome : J. H. Plunkett, the Attorney General, and Roger Therry ; two to the Church of Scotland : Sir Thomas Mitchell and Dr. Lang; and one to the Society of Friends : Joseph Phelps Robinson. Mr. Lowe himself acted as Chairman and was, in a very especial sense, the life and soul of the entire committee. The report of this committee, upon which the educational systems of the various colonies have in the main been based, is here given in the Appendix. We are now nearing the close of Robert Lowe's career as a Crown nominee in the Legislative Council of New South Wales.

APPENDIX TO CHAPTER XIII

REPORT OF ROBERT LOWE'S COMMITTEE ON PUBLIC EDUCATION

Extract from the Votes and Proceedings of the Legislative Council,
No. 17
(Friday, June 21, 1844)

6. Education :—Mr. Lowe, pursuant to notice, moved that a Select Committee be appointed to enquire into, and report upon, the State of Education in this Colony, and to devise the means of placing the education of youth upon a basis suited to the wants and wishes of this community.

Question put and passed, and the following Committee appointed accordingly :—

Mr. Lowe	Mr. Therry
Mr. Cowper	Mr. Windeyer
Dr. Lang	The Attorney General (Mr. Plunkett)
Sir T. L. Mitchell	
Dr. Nicholson	The Colonial Secretary (Mr. Deas Thomson)
Mr. Robinson	

List of Witnesses Examined

James Robert Wilshire, Esq.
George Allen, Esq.
Rev. Ralph Mansfield
Henry Macdermott, Esq.
William Augustine Duncan, Esq.
Rev. James Fullerton, LL.D.
Rev. Robert Allwood, B.A.
Mr. Edward M'Roberts
The Most Rev. John Bede Polding,
  D.D., Roman Catholic Arch-
  bishop
William Timothy Cape, Esq.

Mr. Peter Steel
Mr. James Cosgrove
Mr. Bartholomew Peter Scannell
Mr. John Hunter Baillie
The Lord Bishop of Australia
The Rev. John Saunders
The Rev. Robert Ross
Mr. Peter Robertson
The Rev. John M'Kenny
Charles Kemp, Esq.
William Macarthur, Esq.

The Select Committee of the Legislative Council appointed on the 21st June, 1844, *to enquire into and report upon the State of Education in this Colony, and to devise the means of placing the education of youth upon a basis suited to the wants and wishes of the community*, have agreed to the following report.

Your Committee have examined a number of witnesses embodying every shade of religious opinion, and have thus, they believe, brought the question of education, with all its attendant difficulties, fully and fairly before the Council. The present state of education in this colony your Committee consider extremely deficient. There are about 25,676 children between the ages of four and fourteen years; of these only 7,642 receive instruction in public schools, and 4,865 in private ones, leaving about 13,000 children, who, as far as your Committee know, are receiving no education at all. The expense of public education is about 1*l.* per head; an enormous rate after every allowance has been made for the necessary dispersion of the inhabitants of a pastoral country, and the consequent dearness of instruction. While your Committee admit that this deficient state of education is partly attributable to the ignorance, dissolute habits, and avarice of too many of the parents, and partly to the wants of good schoolmasters and school books, they feel bound to express their conviction that a far greater portion of the evil has arisen from the strictly denominational character of the public schools. Many of these schools have indeed attained a considerable degree of excellence under the management and inspection of the clergy, and it would be most unjust to charge upon them those defects in the state of public education which your Committee believe are the natural result of the plan by which that education has been regulated.

The first great objection to the denominational system is its expense; the number of schools in a given locality ought to depend on the number of children requiring instruction which that locality contains. To admit any other principle is to depart from those maxims of wholesome economy upon which public money should always be administered.

It appears to your Committee impossible not to see that the very essence of a denominational system is to leave the majority uneducated in order thoroughly to imbue the minority with peculiar tenets. It is a system always tending to excess or defect, the natural result of which is, that wherever one school is founded, two or three others will arise, not because they are wanted, but because it is feared that proselytes will be made; and thus a superfluous activity is produced in one place and a total stagnation in another. It is a system impossible to be carried out in a thinly inhabited country, as many of its firmest advocates have admitted to your Committee, and being exclusively in the hands of clergy, it places the State in an awkward dilemma of either supplying money whose expenditure it is not permitted to regulate, or of interfering between the clergy and their superiors to the manifest derangement of the whole ecclesiastical polity.

It has, indeed, been suggested to your Committee that a denominational system might be allowed to continue in Sydney and the larger towns, while a general one was adopted for the County Districts, but your Committee cannot yield to this suggestion; convinced as they are of the superiority of a general to a denominational system. and conceiving, for reasons to be stated hereafter, that the present denominational schools may place themselves under the Government Board of Education, and thus continue to derive support from the public funds, without the slightest surrender of principle, your Committee have thought it better to recommend that one uniform system shall be established for the whole of the Colony, and that an adherence to that system shall be made the indispensable condition under which alone public aid will be granted.

Your Committee have had under their consideration two General Systems of Education: the British and Foreign System, and Lord Stanley's system of National Education; the first of these appears to them to be surrounded with insurmountable difficulties. These difficulties are stated in Mr. Secretary Stanley's letter to the Duke of Leinster of October 1831. 'The determination to enforce in all their schools the reading of the Holy Scriptures, without note or comment, was undoubtedly taken with the purest motives; with the wish at once to combine religious with moral and literary education, and at the same time not to run the risk of wounding the peculiar feelings of any sect by catechetical instruction or comments which might tend to subjects of polemical controversy. But it seemed to have been overlooked that the principles of the Roman Catholic Church were totally at variance with this principle, and that the reading of the Holy Scriptures, without note or comment, by children must be peculiarly obnoxious to a Church which denies even to adults the right of unaided private interpretation of the sacred volume, in articles of religious belief. These views are borne out by the experience of this colony. When the British and Foreign System was proposed in 1839, it was not supposed the Roman Catholics could join in it, and it was intended that a separate system should be established for them. Your Committee are not prepared to recommend a renewal of this project, which would perpetuate that which they are most anxious to avoid—the denominational character of public education.

Your Committee have decided to recommend to the Council Lord Stanley's system of national education, the only plan sufficiently comprehensive to include both Protestant and Catholic. This system was devised to carry out the recommendation of a committee of the House of Commons in 1828, 'that a system should be adopted which should afford if possible a combined literary and a separate religious education. and should be capable of being so far adapted to the views of different religious persuasions as to render it in truth a system of National Education for the lower classes of the community.' The key-stone of the system is a Board composed of men of high personal character, professing different religious opinions. This Board exercises a complete control over the schools erected under its auspices, or which, having been already established, place themselves under its management and receive its assistance. The following are the conditions under which aid is granted :—

1. The ordinary school business—during which all the children of whatever denomination they be are required to attend, and which is expected to embrace a competent number of hours in each day—is to consist exclusively of instruction in those branches which belong to a literary and moral education. Such extracts from Scripture as are prepared under the sanction of the Board may be used, and are earnestly recommended by the Board to be used during those hours allotted to this ordinary school business.

2. One day at least in each week (independently of the Sunday) is to be set apart for the religious instruction of the children, on which day such pastors, or other persons as are approved of by the parents or guardians of the children, shall have access to them for that purpose, whether those pastors have signed the original application or not.

3. The managers of schools are also expected, should the parents of any of the children desire it, to afford convenient opportunity and facility for the same purpose, either before or after the ordinary school business (as the managers may determine). on other days of the week.

4. Any arrangement of this description that may be made is to be publicly notified in the schools, in order that those children, and those only, may be present at the religious instruction, whose parents and guardians approve of their being so.

5. The reading of the Scriptures, either in the Authorised or Douay Version, is regarded as a religious exercise, and as such is to be confined to those times which are set apart for religious instruction; the same regulation is also to be observed respecting prayer.

The following passage from the Eighth Report of the Commissioners of National Education in Ireland, being their report for the year 1841, will also tend to explain the nature of the religious instruction imparted under this system : ' It seems still to be supposed that we prescribe the studies to be pursued in all national schools, and that we exclude the Scriptures ; but the reverse is the fact; it belongs not to us, but to the local patrons of each to determine the course of instruction to be given therein, subject only to a power in us to prohibit the use of any books which we may deem improper, and so far are we from prohibiting the use of the Scriptures that we expressly recognise the right of all patrons to have them used for the purpose of religious instruction in whatever way they may think proper, provided that each school be open to poor children of all communions, that due regard be had to parental right and authority ; therefore that no child be *compelled* to attend, or be present at any religious instruction to which his parents or guardians object, and that the time for giving it be so fixed that no child be thereby in effect excluded, directly or indirectly, from the other advantages which the school affords. We may add that in very many of the national schools religious instruction is given day by day, as it may be in all if the patrons think proper, by means both of the Holy Scriptures and of the approved Catechisms of the Church to which both the children receiving it belong ; but the times for reading the Holy Scriptures and for Catechetical instruction are so arranged as not to interfere with or impede the scientific or secular business of the school ; and no child whose parents or guardians object is required to be present or take part in those exercises. Still further to show how unwarrantable it is to represent us as excluding instruction by means of the Holy Scriptures, we request your Excellency's attention to the following extracts from the preface to the Scripture lessons which we have published. These selections are offered not as a substitute for the sacred volume itself, but as an intro-duction to it, and they have been compiled in the hope of their leading to a more general and more profitable perusal of the Word of God.'

'The Board of Commissioners earnestly and unanimously recommend those lessons to be used in all schools receiving aid from them. And to the religious instructors of the children they cheerfully leave, in com-municating instruction, the use of the sacred volume itself, as containing those doctrines and precepts, a knowledge of which must be at the foundation of all true religion. The Law of the Lord is unspotted, con-verting souls ; the testimony of the Lord is faithful, giving wisdom to little ones.'

Your Committee would beg to lay before the Council one more passage extracted from a communication from Lord Stanley to the Synod of Ulster : ' His Majesty's Government fully recognises the right of all who choose it to read the Sacred Scriptures, but the exercise of this right in the case of infants must be subject to the control of their parents and natural guardians, and in point of time in the national, as in all other schools, it must be limited by the appropriation of certain hours to certain other branches of study.'

From these extracts your Committee think it will be manifest that the national system is not fairly open to the charge of neglecting religious instruction. It teaches in the ordinary school hours as much of the truths of religion as can be imparted, without entering on controverted subjects, and it offers every facility and encouragement in its power to induce the

teachers of the different denominations to fill up the outline by com-
municating to the children those peculiar doctrines which the nature of a
general system forbids it to teach. Your Committee cannot but hope that
religious teachers of all denominations will feel that this is the direction
in which their activity can be most profitably employed, and that they are
far more likely to contribute to the spread of true religion and the dis-
semination of their own opinions, by co-operating than by competing with
this system, which, as it teaches nothing hostile to any sect, and excludes
none from teaching their own doctrines, deserves the hostility of none.

It has been the good fortune of this system to disarm many opponents
and to convert them into its advocates. As an example of this your
Committee have much pleasure in referring to the evidence of the
Rev. Mr. Saunders (p. 95) who, with others, opposed this system in 1836,
and who now most earnestly recommends it. Of the secular instruction
communicated under this system, your Committee do not think it necessary to speak at large. The school books have been compiled with the
most admirable care and judgment, and will save much trouble to those
in whose hands the management of the system shall be placed.

Your Committee have appended to their report (see Appendix) several
documents with the view of giving the Council the amplest information in
their power, and they feel well convinced that the more the plan is
examined the more favourably will it be viewed.

Your Committee also trusts that that part of the Protestant community
which would have preferred the British and Foreign System will appreciate the spirit of fairness and impartiality to all parties which has
actuated them in their present recommendation, and will rather join in
promoting a scheme which falls somewhat short of their wishes, than
throw obstacles in the way of the only practicable scheme of general
instruction. Your Committee also trust that Christians of all denominations will feel that the adoption of this system will tend to soften down
sectarian feelings, and to the promotion of union, toleration, and charity.
' In order to carry out their recommendation, your Committee think that
a Board should be appointed by the Governor, of persons favourable to the
plan proposed, and possessing the confidence of the different denominations.
For the success of the undertaking must depend upon the character of the
individuals who compose the Board : and upon the security thereby afforded
to the country that while the interests of religion are not overlooked, the
most scrupulous care shall be taken not to interfere with the peculiar
tenets of any description of Christian pupils.'

To this Board it will probably be necessary to attach a salaried
secretary ; they should be invested with a very wide discretion as to the
arrangements necessary for carrying the system into effect, and all funds
to be henceforth applied for the purpose of education should be administered by them. When such a Board is once constituted, it will be easy
for them to select from the mass of valuable information and suggestion
contained in the evidence appended to this Report principles to guide
them in the execution of their duty.

Your Committee are unwilling to forestall the deliberations of this Board, but they venture to express a hope that, notwithstanding the evidence of many witnesses to the contrary, no compulsion will ever be employed to induce parents to send their children to school. Such a measure is hostile to the liberty of the subject and would infallibly rouse a spirit of determined opposition.

Your Committee are not prepared to recommend the establishment of local Boards of Education, conceiving that a central Board with an efficient system of inspection will produce results more uniform and satisfactory.

The foundation of a Normal or Model School in Sydney, for the training of schoolmasters, appears to your Committee to be an indispensable step; and the establishment of some general principle, or proportion, according to which the funds of the State are to be advanced, will merit their most serious attention.

Your Committee trusts that measures will be taken to counteract the spread of ignorance beyond the limits of location by the appointment of itinerant preachers, and by the distribution of books of a moral and religious tendency, free from sectarianism. They would also call attention to the suggestion made by several of the witnesses with regard to the establishment of Industrial schools, which, if practicable, would seem to be the fittest training that could be devised for an Australian settler.

Your Committee would also express their opinion, that if it is intended that education should be valued, it must not be gratuitous, at least to those who can pay for it.

Your Committee trusts that the liberality of the Legislature will not allow this important object to fail for want of the requisite pecuniary aid. This aid, they hope, will not exceed by a very large amount the sum now annually devoted to education, and they feel fully convinced that no money can be expended by a State to better advantage than that which is appropriated to such a purpose.

Your Committee think that this Board should be incorporated, in order that all property required for educational purposes may vest in them, by which the trouble and expense necessarily attending the vesting of property in trustees will be avoided.

ROBERT LOWE, *Chairman.*

Legislative Council Chambers, Sydney :
    August 28, 1844.

educated audience. Much of his speech was clearly beside the mark, and it was so interminably long and ill-arranged that, despite his vigorous delivery, it must have wearied the Council.

The seconder of the resolution was the Quaker member, Mr. Robinson, who stuck close to the financial aspects of the question, and showed how much Port Phillip contributed to the general revenue, and how little she got out of it in the way of public works. There was an ominous silence on the Government benches. It is true that the Colonial Secretary, Mr. Deas Thomson, from an unflinching sense of duty, rose and attempted something in the nature of a tentative reply to the Port Phillip separatists. Dr. Bland, one of the popular Opposition members for Sydney, also opposed the resolution as premature. Dr. Nicholson ably supported his colleagues, Lang and Robinson, and maintained the desirability of a much more extended subdivision of the Australian provinces. Then there was another ominous pause, when suddenly the far too independent Crown nominee rose, and made his breach with Sir George Gipps absolutely final by delivering a really memorable speech against the Government, and in favour of the separation of Port Phillip. After a few preliminary sentences, in which he disclaimed agreement with 'the theory of endless provincial subdivision' which Dr. Nicholson had mooted, Robert Lowe uttered the famous declaration :—

As a general rule, the interests of the Colonies are not consulted by frittering them away into minute particles, but by combining as large a territory into a single State as could be effectually controlled by a single Government. I cordially agree in the abstract truth of the motto prefixed to the article in the newspaper of this morning, that 'Union is strength,'[1] and I would extend that principle to the whole Colonial Empire of Great Britain. I hold and believe that the time is not remote when Great Britain will give up the idea

[1] The *Sydney Morning Herald*, which strongly opposed the separation of Port Phillip.

of treating the dependencies of the Crown as children, to be cast adrift by their parent as soon as they arrive at manhood, and substitute for it the far wiser and nobler policy of knitting herself and her Colonies into one mighty Confederacy, girdling the earth in its whole circumference, and confident against the world in arts and arms.

Nevertheless, he went on to argue, the separation of Port Phillip from New South Wales was inevitable, though he dreaded 'that the result might be a war of tariffs and restrictive duties, which he held in utter horror and aversion.' Delivered in a mere provincial assembly, this speech rose to truly Imperial heights. Unlike most eloquent speeches, it bore fruit, for in a very few years the new colony of Victoria—named by its own wish after the Queen—came into being.

On going to division, Dr. Lang's motion was lost by 19 votes to 6, the minority consisting of the five Port Phillip delegates and Mr. Lowe.

On the rejection of his motion, it occurred to the indefatigable Dr. Lang, that as the Port Phillip members were unanimous, a most effective petition on the subject might be sent to the Queen. This he accordingly drew up, and he and all his colleagues signed it. Lord Stanley sent back a favourable reply; but some subsequent delays ensued owing to a change in the English Ministry, and the transformation of the district of Port Phillip into the colony of Victoria was not proclaimed until July 1, 1851.

To the *Sydney Morning Herald* the speech and vote of Mr. Lowe on this occasion were quite unaccountable. That respectable journal could only attribute it to his intention of offering himself for a Port Phillip constituency. Of course, this motive had nothing whatever to do with his conduct; but every thoughtful Victorian must have a feeling of regret that this distinguished English statesman, who played so leading a part in obtaining the creation of the colony, did not, when he became a representative member, sit for one of the Port Phillip constituencies.

Referring to this subject of the separation of Port Phillip, Sir Charles Gavan Duffy, then a Victorian colonist, thus characterised Lord Sherbrooke's action :—

The motion was supported by the representatives of the district, but opposed by all the members for New South Wales, with a single exception, but a memorable one—that of Robert Lowe, who is now employing his great powers upon a more conspicuous stage.[1]

But in a more recent allusion to this circumstance Sir Charles, in an article in advocacy of Irish Home Rule, clearly insinuates that Lord Sherbrooke, as the former supporter of Port Phillip separation, was inconsistent in his opposition to Mr. Gladstone's present Irish policy :—

Robert Lowe, then a practising barrister in Sydney, who was not a political pedant in colonial affairs, considered the union between Port Phillip and New South Wales an injustice and a grievance, and voted for its immediate repeal.[2]

This seems to imply that it is political pedantry to decline to support Irish Home Rule if one has strongly upheld the policy of dividing a colony into two. But from his valuable Victorian and Irish experiences Sir Charles, of all men, should recognise that there is no analogy between the two cases. Port Phillip demanded, with complete unanimity, through her six delegates, not merely Home Rule, but absolute separation from New South Wales. Robert Lowe, though a New South Wales member and a Crown nominee, swayed by the justice of the claim, supported it, as his speech shows, on the broadest of Imperial lines. Will Sir Charles Duffy tell us, as he quotes this colonial illustration of the benefits of Home Rule to Victoria—Does Ireland, or does she not, demand complete separation from England as Port Phillip did from New South

[1] *Melbourne Review*, October 1876.
[2] 'An Australian Example,' by Sir C. Gavan Duffy, K.C.M.G. (*Contemporary Review*, January 1888).

Wales ? If not, then there is no analogy at all between her case and that of Port Phillip. Robert Lowe was clearly of opinion in 1844 that the 20,000 inhabitants of that district should be altogether severed politically from New South Wales ; and it is needless to say that since 1851 Victoria has been as independent of New South Wales as Canada is of France, or the United States of England. It is doubtless because Lord Sherbrooke believed that the logical if not inevitable outcome of the Home Rule policy is the total separation of Ireland from Great Britain that he declined, not from political pedantry, but from a profound feeling of patriotism, to follow his former leader down the steep declivity.

A week after the delivery of his speech in favour of the separation of Port Phillip, Robert Lowe presented the Report of the Select Committee on Education (see Appendix, Chapter XIII.), and moved that it be printed, and taken into consideration on the Tuesday week following. He then made this brief announcement of the resignation of his seat as a nominee member of the Legislative Council :—

It will not be in my power to take charge of the Report on that day, because, having performed the task of preparing it which the Council had done me the honour of delegating to me, it is my intention immediately to resign my seat as a nominee of the Crown in Council. I regret this the less, however, as I am convinced from the zeal and earnestness with which the inquiry has been prosecuted by the other members of the committee that these measures could not be in better hands than theirs. As to the reasons which have induced me to take this step, it is unnecessary here to state them. I would simply repeat my former assertion, that I entered the House unfettered and unpledged, and I would add that I now leave it without any communication on the subject, direct or indirect, with His Excellency the Governor.

The question that the Report be printed was put and carried. Thus ended for the time being Lowe's connection with the Legislative Council of New South Wales. His resignation of his seat as a Crown nominee took place on

August 30, 1844—less than two years after his arrival in the
colony, and less than one from the time of his nomination by
Sir George Gipps. Yet what a mark he had made in the
political history of Australia during that brief period !
In addition to the independence of his action in the
Council, where he found himself compelled on most questions
to support the Opposition against the Government officials,
there was also a private misunderstanding between Mr. Lowe
and Sir George Gipps. It is an old story, which has been
often told, but generally with gross inaccuracy. Shortly after
Mr. and Mrs. Lowe had taken up their residence in Sydney,
and were still constant visitors at Government House, certain
damaging reports were spread about some persons who also
enjoyed the *entrée*. These reports were believed by the
Lowes but ignored by Sir George Gipps, who continued to
invite the discredited persons; whereupon Mr. and Mrs.
Lowe ceased to accept further Viceregal invitations. Accordingly, those who could not otherwise understand Mr. Lowe's
opposition to Sir George Gipps's officials in the Council
attributed it to this private misunderstanding. Such persons
realised that for a Crown nominee to act with independence
was not the way to achieve a salaried post in the Council—
and for what other reason Mr. Lowe had entered the Council
they were at a loss to see.

Mr. Roger Therry, the chief courtier of Sir Richard Bourke,
who at first found some difficulty in winning his way into the
good graces of his more rugged successor, Sir George Gipps,
seized the opportunity to make an attack on Lowe for his independent action as a Crown nominee, purely as a means of
ingratiating himself with the Governor. It was, he said, like
the adder which stung its benefactor to death. Wentworth
gave this taunt currency at the Sydney election of 1848, when
Lowe opposed him. He even said that this absurd attack
drove Lowe out of the Council. The facts are plain enough :
Lowe resigned his onerous nominee membership, finding his

views quite irreconcilable with those of Sir George Gipps, who had appointed him. The remark of a pliant Irish lawyer, eager for fresh, highly-paid employment, which the Governor alone could bestow, had no effect whatever in determining Lowe's resignation. He may have well felt some amazement at such a speech coming from such a quarter. Imagine Bishop Ken, or some other stout old Nonjuror, accused of venality by the veritable Vicar of Bray! Yet this story of Thorry has been given over and over again as the reason of Lowe's resignation.

Years afterwards, on his return to England, Lowe described the anomalous position of a Crown nominee in his terse and most felicitous manner : ' If I voted with the Government I was in danger of being reproached as a mere tool ; and if I voted with the Opposition, as I did on most questions, I was reproached by the officials as a traitor to the Government. In fact I was in this position—if I voted with the Government I was taunted with being a slave ; and if I voted against them I was taunted with being a traitor.'

When, in the year 1845, Mr. Lowe sought to represent the constituency of St. Vincent and Auckland, the *Sydney Morning Herald*, which for some reason opposed his election, declared that he was a mere place-hunter, and that he had resigned his seat as a Crown nominee simply because he differed from the Governor ' on a question of etiquette.' Such a man, actuated by mere pique, would (the *Herald* feared), if it suited him, rush into the Governor's arms, and forget his pledges to the people. To this newspaper attack Lowe, contrary to his custom, replied, and at some length :—

Place-hunters, men of no fixed principle, and sycophants do not usually quarrel with governors on points of etiquette, or make their support conditional upon being allowed to exclude whomsoever they please from their houses. I may be servile, or I may be dictatorial, but I cannot be both.

He then reviews his conduct while sitting in the Council

as a Crown nominee in words that must remain his best defence, if, indeed, any defence be necessary :—

> I never was a thick-and-thin supporter of the Governor, nor yet in Council was I his bitterest opponent. I entered the Council sincerely anxious to do my duty to the country, and voted against the Government on the Water Police Bill, my vote turning the scale against them, almost immediately after I was appointed nominee ; this is at the very time when, according to you, I was qualifying for the office of Groom of the Stole. When I found the Governor and Council brought into direct collision with each other, I resigned my seat, feeling a repugnance to vote systematically against the person to whom I owed it, and being firmly determined not to injure the country for whom I held it. Those who, like you, habitually seek for the most paltry and miserable motives for the conduct of public men, will of course attach no credit to my assertion ; but there are spirits more honourable and generous than you, who will believe me when I say that my conduct in Council would have been precisely the same had no private difference existed between the Governor and myself.

Nothing can possibly be added to this statement ; it may be accepted as an absolutely truthful summary of his motives and public conduct during the brief time that he sat as a Crown nominee in the first Australian Parliament.

The rupture between Mr. Lowe and Sir George Gipps grew wider after the former re-entered the Legislative Council as a ' popular,' or elected, member. In a very short time Lowe became the leader of that dangerous Opposition which Sir George had at one time hoped he would have been the means of overthrowing. This of course gave point and piquancy to the oft-repeated tale that it was on a mere question of etiquette that Robert Lowe had quarrelled with the Governor.

It is now quite five-and-forty years since Sir George Gipps was laid to rest in the cloisters of Canterbury, followed a few years afterwards by his friend, Bishop Broughton, who died at the house of Lady Gipps, and is also buried in that great cathedral. Of the Governor's political opponents, Wentworth, Windeyer, Cowper, Lang, all have long since passed away ; and to these we must now add Lord Sherbrooke himself. Under the circumstances, one touches as lightly as possible on the private feuds and personal quarrels of that old fierce time in Sydney. Lord Sherbrooke himself said to me some few years ago : 'It was always a great regret to me that I had been compelled to oppose Sir George Gipps so strongly, as he had always been personally most kind.'[1]

APPENDIX

Speech delivered by Robert Lowe in the Debate on the Separation of Port Phillip. Legislative Council, Sydney, August 20, 1844.

Mr. Lowe said that far different from his friend, Dr. Nicholson, was his theory with regard to the prosperity of the Colonies. As a general rule, the interests of the Colonies were not consulted by frittering them away into minute particles, but by combining as large a territory into a single State as could be effectually controlled by a single Government. He cordially agreed in the abstract truth of the motto prefixed to the article in the newspaper of this morning, that ' Union is strength,' and he would extend that principle to the whole Colonial Empire of Great Britain. He held and believed that the time was not remote when Great Britain would give up the idea of treating the dependencies of the Crown as children, to be cast adrift by their parent as soon as they arrive at manhood, and substitute for it the far wiser and nobler policy of knitting herself and her Colonies into one mighty Confederacy, girdling the earth in its whole circumference, and confident against the world in arts and arms. Neither could he agree that the separation would be otherwise than injurious, in some extent, at least, to New South Wales. It implied the loss of a fertile and wealthy province, already paying much more into the Treasury than it drew out of it ; and he was also fearful that a separation might be attended with that animosity and ill-feeling which were so apt to prevail between neighbouring States, and that the result might be a war of tariffs and restrictive duties, which he held in utter horror and aversion; but still, compelled by the force of truth and justice, he was bound to say that these considerations came too late.

When the district was first settled, it became the duty of Government to consider, and they doubtless did consider, what was to be its future destiny, and he firmly believed that that destiny was separation. He could not agree in the wisdom of the decision, but it was too late to object now. The district had been placed out of the jurisdiction of the Sydney courts ; its boundaries had been defined, its accounts kept separate from the first ; it was provided with officers presiding over every department of the Service ; the machinery was ready—all that was needed was independence.[a] It was

[1] See *Australia and the Empire*, chap. i., ' Robert Lowe in Sydney.'

not natural, it was not reasonable, that any community of Englishmen
should remain content with such a state of things—they would be despicable
if they did so. It was the essence of a good Executive Government that it
should be well acquainted with the concerns of its subjects, and they with
it ; that it should act upon public opinion, and be reacted upon in its turn.
How were these conditions of good government realised for Port Phillip ?
The Executive knew little of the province, the province less of the Executive. The very arrangements of the post, which only gave a few hours for
answering a letter, rendered it impossible that due consideration should
be given to matters of urgency. The system might now be able to be
improved, but it had prevailed for years. The representation assigned to
Port Phillip in that Council was a still greater evil. If Lord Chatham
was right in saying that the idea of virtual representation was contemptible ; how much more contemptible was the actual representation of Port
Phillip. He did not scruple to say it was no representation at all ; he
granted the ability of these gentlemen, but what was their local knowledge :
they did not profess to possess it. Representation in his opinion meant
something more than the sending persons to vote and speak in a popular
assembly ; it meant the power and opportunity of sending persons well
acquainted with the wants and wishes of the community, of which they
formed a part, and able to turn that knowledge to the best account in
every emergency that arose. That power, that opportunity, was denied
to Port Phillip. Suppose that Port Phillip were separated from this colony
and annexed to Canada, with the right of sending six representatives to
its Assembly. They might, no doubt, find six Canadians who would take
the office on themselves, but was that representation ? And if not, what
was the practical difference between Canada and Sydney ?

The last and most intolerable evil he would mention was that Port
Phillip was the dependent of a dependency ; was governed by a viceroy's
vicegerent ; was saddled with a double evil of two absentee governments.
Did the Council adopt his language, they would say to Port Phillip : ' We
have eaten too long the bitter bread of dependence to wish to have de-
pendents of our own ; we have felt too long the evil of having our money
spent on British objects, to wish to spend the money of others ; we have
felt too long the evil of being governed by strangers from England, to wish
to intrude strangers upon you.'

If they hold this language, they would be indeed applying the golden
rule of Christianity, which is true in politics as in morals. He believed
with the Colonial Secretary that Separation would be eventually carried,
and he did not believe that any vote of that House would either accelerate
or retard it ; but they also had justice to ask, they also had grievances to
redress. And if they failed in their petition, they would have the bitter
reflection that they were only receiving back in their bosom the same
measure which they had meted to their brethren.

CHAPTER XV

THE EDUCATION QUESTION

Sir Richard Bourke and Lord Stanley's Irish National System—Attitude of Dr. Ullathorne—Robert Lowe becomes its chief advocate—First Speech to the people of Sydney—Roger Therry and M. Guizot—Mr. Lowe and the Council checkmated

On the base of the statue of Sir Richard Bourke in Sydney may be read these words :—

He established religious equality on a just and firm basis, and sought to provide for all, without distinction of sect, a sound and adequate system of national education.

It is true enough that he 'sought,' but through no fault of his own he failed to ' provide ' such an unsectarian system of national education, which was avowedly based on Lord Stanley's Irish scheme. Sir Richard was Governor-General of New South Wales and its dependencies from 1831–1837, when he was succeeded by Sir George Gipps.

It is not a little astonishing to find that the chief supporter of this plan of unsectarian education, which Sir Richard Bourke first tried to introduce into Australia, should have been the Roman Catholic Vicar-General, Dr. Ullathorne, afterwards Bishop of Birmingham. It was also supported then, and afterwards in the time of Sir George Gipps, by the two leading Roman Catholic laymen in the colony, Mr. Roger Therry and Mr. John Hubert Plunkett, both of whom were originally sent out to Australia as high officials by the English Whig Government, then in alliance with Daniel O'Connell. Plunkett was a high-minded gentleman of strong religious convictions; so that his unwavering support of a system of education now denounced as 'godless' is almost as noteworthy as that of Dr. Ullathorne himself. It was doubtless the co-operation of these three leading Roman Catholics [1] which aroused the suspicious ire of Dr. Lang, and other influential Protestant public men in the colony, who contrived to defeat the well-laid plan of Sir Richard Bourke.

It was inevitable that such a body as the newly constituted Legislative Council, under Sir George Gipps, should revive the subject of public education. All that was wanted was a popular leader, who had now turned up in the person of Robert Lowe. Unfortunately, after procuring the select committee and presenting its report (which was, in a very special sense, his own), Lowe felt himself compelled to resign his seat. This was a severe loss to the cause of which he was the champion. After Lowe's retirement from the Council, Mr. Robinson, the Quaker member for Port Phillip, moved a series of resolutions, based on the report of the select committee, in favour of establishing a national unsectarian system of education to be controlled by a Board whose members should represent the various religious bodies. It was on the occasion of this debate that Dr. Lang, who had been converted from sectarianism, spoke, he tells us, for three hours, ' during the whole of which time Mr. Lowe was present in the House.'

But if Robert Lowe's voice was silent within the walls of the Council, it was raised for the first time, and most effec-

[1] Mr. Rusden's more subtle explanation of this compact is, that Sir Richard Bourke was actuated by the policy of his Whig masters in Lord Melbourne's Cabinet: ' In his speech to the Council in 1833, he (Sir Richard) was able to say that he had it " in command from the Secretary of State to represent their wants "; and to promise the co-operation of that functionary in giving assistance to Roman Catholic schools, and appointing additional Roman Catholic chaplains. Thus early did the Whigs bid for support in Ireland by offers of colonial patronage. . . . Between January 1832 and December 1835, they paid " outfit and passage " for nine Roman Catholic priests and catechists. In the same period, they paid outfit and passage for one clergyman of the Church of England.'—*History of Australia*, vol. ii. pp. 144-5.

tively, on this education question, at public meetings in the city of Sydney. The first of these meetings was convened by the Mayor, Mr. J. W. Wilshire, at the request of a number of citizens, and took place on September 2, 1844, at the Sydney theatre. Lowe's experiences on his first attempt to address a mass meeting in the colony were by no means pleasant. In fact, he and most of the speakers were refused a hearing. The following attempt to report him on this occasion will convey some notion of his rowdy audience :—

Mr. Lowe came forward to move the first Resolution [hisses]. As Chairman of the Select Committee of the Legislative Council [cries of *privilege ! privilege !*] appointed to inquire into and report upon the subject of education, he had thought that it was only right to come forward and to propose a Resolution which was one step towards the carrying out of the recommendations of that Committee, which had been submitted to the public in various ways, and which he had no doubt that those present were prepared to discuss with him. [Uproar.]

After several other persistent attempts to obtain a hearing, he was completely howled down.

One or two Roman Catholic priests and a journalist of that persuasion here mounted the platform, and secured some degree of tranquillity for a time. Mr. Lowe, despairing, however, of a hearing, concluded by simply moving the resolution :—

That it is the duty of the State in every Christian community to provide the means of a good Common Education to be conducted agreeably to the principles of the Christian religion.

The only speaker who succeeded that evening in getting a hearing was the Rev. J. M'Encroe, a well-known Roman Catholic priest, who denounced at great length the judge and packed jury who had tried Daniel O'Connell—which, as the Mayor mildly pointed out, had no very direct bearing on the subject in hand.

The inevitable result of this disgraceful proceeding was to enlist on the side of Mr. Lowe the sympathies of that

large but undemonstrative body of people who happily exist
in every British community, but who do not turn up at
public meetings, nor under excitement revert to the harsh
noises of primeval man. Several letters in the press, written
evidently by this better type of citizen, attest the general indignation that was felt at the ungracious reception accorded
to Mr. Lowe and his friends. But the Mayor of Sydney—to
the end of the chapter a strong supporter—was not the man
to rest content with this abortive effort, and accordingly he
convened a second meeting, which was held on the following
Saturday afternoon at three o'clock in the theatre of the
School of Arts. The chief speaker was again Mr. Lowe, and
on this occasion he experienced an enthusiastic welcome and
was accorded a most respectful hearing. This speech may
therefore be considered as his first public address to the
people of Sydney. It was in every sense worthy of himself
and of the occasion. The following synopsis furnishes the
best commentary on the report of the select committee, and
will show the great difficulties which he and his colleagues
were contending against in a sparsely populated pastoral
country like New South Wales—' sown,' as it had been, with
the ' rotten seed ' of convictism—in their efforts to preserve
the rising generation from lapsing into unadulterated savagery.
After explaining at some length the object and practical working of Lord Stanley's system, Mr. Lowe thus proceeded :—

Such a system was especially adapted to a community like that
of New South Wales, not only from its fairness to all, but on account
of its ductility and plasticity, which would enable it to adapt itself
to the great variety of religious denominations into which the people
were divided. The system which was now proposed required no
compromise, unless, indeed, it should be argued by any that religious
instruction alone should occupy all the hours of every day which
were passed in the school by the child. He had himself been at
school in former years, and he knew well that if he had attempted
to devote the whole of his time, day after day, to reading the Bible
instead of attending to his other studies, he should have been well
flogged—and well he would have deserved it, and the only objection

which anyone could urge against the system was that the Bible was
not the subject of everyday study. He thought it an advantage that
the schools should be under the control of a Board rather than
under that of isolated and antagonistic clergymen. Twenty-one
witnesses have been examined by the Select Committee, seven of
whom were in favour of a Denominational System, while fourteen
advocated a general system of education. Among these seven, too,
it must be recollected, there were those who had been called, not so
much to ascertain what system might best be introduced, but what
terms they were willing to accede to ; such were the Lord Bishop of
Australia (Dr. Broughton), Archbishop Polding and Mr. M'Kenny,
the head of the Wesleyan Connexion. The Committee did not
expect that these witnesses would assent to any proposition of a
general system ; they wished only to ascertain their opinions as to
the state of education in the colony—to hear from them the means
they would suggest to remedy evils the existence of which all
acknowledged, so that they might lay the matter before the Council,
fully and fairly, exhibiting all the dangers and all the difficulties
against which we have to contend. But the evidence of the two
most important witnesses in favour of Denominational education
did not militate much against the general unsectarian system which
the committee proposed.

Mr. Lowe then proceeded to read from the official records
of the Legislative Council the report of the evidence of Dr.
Broughton, the English Bishop, and—what was more to the
point—that of the Roman Catholic Archbishop, Dr. Polding.
When we bear in mind that Dr. Polding, unlike the former
Vicar-General, Dr. Ullathorne, was an avowed enemy of the
general, or unsectarian, system, his admissions in favour of
Lord Stanley's Irish scheme are well deserving of reproduction.
Dr. Nicholson, a member of the special committee, asked if
the Archbishop were acquainted with the Irish system of education. The Archbishop replied that he was ; and he was then
requested to state his views of that system.

‘ I think,’ he said, ‘ it is a system well devised for the circumstances under which Ireland is placed. It is not, I acknowledge, the
system I would adopt, nor do I believe that any person in my situation would adopt it voluntarily. Still, there are advantages
attending it. The bringing up of the children together—the exclusion of books which misrepresent religious tenets ; which teach

children to hate, and to hold others in contempt by reason of such
misrepresentation; which teach them practically that a lie loses the
odiousness of its character in such matters, and perjury its dreadful
wickedness; and the abstraction of the food of religious prejudices,
which tend so much to sour society and to alienate men from each
other.   These are advantages which cannot be estimated too highly.'

On the platform, supporting the Mayor and Mr. Lowe, was
a remarkable and motley group, including Dr. Lang, Mr.
Roger Therry (still staunch to the cause of unsectarianism), and
Mr. Lowe's old duelling antagonist, Alderman Macdermott.
By far the most important speech after Lowe's was that of
Roger Therry.   He was a somewhat subtle and obsequious
person, a man as fond of office as a cat is of the fire.   During his
varied career he had seen much of men and things, had written
a 'Life' of Canning, and was a kinsman as well as an early friend
of Daniel O'Connell.   As was always said of him in the colony,
Therry was a legal Vicar of Bray in the skill and tenacity with
which he stuck to lucrative office.   It is therefore greatly to his
credit that he remained staunch to his convictions on the education question, though the head of the State to whom he looked
for promotion, as well as the head of his Church, was opposed
to the policy of Sir Richard Bourke.   Rising after Mr. Lowe at
this great public meeting, Mr. Therry read an extract from a
private letter which he had received in 1836 from Sir Richard
Bourke, which showed how determined that able Governor had
been to introduce into the colony Lord Stanley's Irish system.

In that letter Sir Richard observed: ' The principal
feature in the Irish plan, namely, the separation of literary
and moral from religious instruction, will suit the mixed creeds
of our population.   The subject of general education in this
increasing colony is that upon which *I am most anxious.   I
have set my heart on laying a good foundation whilst I am in
office.*   I dread much, even in this reforming age, the blighting
influence of religious intolerance.'

Mr. Therry then became autobiographical, and told the
meeting that in 1822 he was the Secretary of the National

Society of Education in Ireland, and that from that time he had become convinced ' that in a community of mixed creeds the only system that could succeed was one that adopted as its leading principle the affording the same facilities for education to all classes of professing Christians, without any attempt to interfere with the peculiar religious opinions of any or to countenance proselytism.'

Mr. Therry then went on to prove that many of the Irish Bishops, such as his friend the well-known Dr. Doyle, were strongly in favour of Lord Stanley's plan.

In the course of his really excellent speech, Mr. Therry gave what he truly regarded as a striking instance of the spread of toleration, an instance which I venture to think very few modern readers have ever met with, and which therefore I quote in his own words :—

Look to India, and see how the spirit of toleration and Christian charity has advanced there. An officer of the name of Martin, who had risen from the position of a private soldier to the rank of a Major-General in the British Army, left on his death the whole of his property (which was very considerable) towards the endowment of a public school. It was the wish of the Bishop of Calcutta, Dr. Wilson, to found this school on the express doctrines and discipline of the Church of England ; but finding such was not the design of the founder, that truly excellent and Christian bishop applied himself, in the spirit of that charity which hopeth all things and believeth all things, to ordain the establishment, so that while it afforded sound practical education to all sects of Christians, it should offer no offence to the opinions of any.

Mr. Therry brought his speech to a conclusion by the following words of a great French politician, which were loudly cheered by the whole meeting :—

It is desirable (says M. Guizot, with his usual wisdom), it is desirable that children whose parents do not profess the same religious opinions, should early contract, by frequenting the same school, those habits of natural good-will and tolerance which grow into sentiments of justice and union when they become fellow-citizens. The strife and struggle of the world, do what we will, must always give rise to differences and dissensions enough. Let us not promote

would it not be equally yielding in New South Wales, and thus become moulded and fashioned by that very Church of which its advocates are already so jealous.'

That Bishop Broughton took the decided stand he did against the introduction of Lord Stanley's Irish system into New South Wales is, I take it, proof positive that he considered it would not give his Church any such ascendency in education matters. As well as being a very upright and excellent man, he was not wanting in political shrewdness. His policy has been followed by all the Anglican bishops in Australia, even including Dr. Moorhouse.

CHAPTER XVI

THE next act in the Australian career of Lord Sherbrooke reveals him in the *rôle* of a journalist. He resigned his seat in the Council in August 1844, and all through September was very prominent at the great public meetings held in Sydney on the education question. Politically, the colony was in what is termed a state of transition, and the minds of men were much agitated on public questions.

Financially, New South Wales was still in a deplorable state; but the Governor was resolved that he, and not the Council, should provide the much needed remedy. Sir George Gipps, like many leading English statesmen of the day, was a disciple of that eccentric genius, Edward Gibbon Wakefield, the most gifted but most misleading theorist who ever bent his mind to the solution of colonial problems. It was in obedience to the teachings of Wakefield that the Imperial Parliament in 1841 (when Australia, as we have seen, was in a state of general insolvency) passed an Act fixing the minimum price of land at 1*l.* an acre. This caused interminable disputes between the Governor and the Legislative Council. Sir George's subsequent land policy led to the establishment of the 'Pastoral Association of New South Wales.' Robert Lowe had joined this body just before he

resigned his seat in the Council. He had devoted a great
deal of time to the study of the land question, and was
accounted the most active member of Mr. Charles Cowper's
Select Committee appointed to report upon all grievances
connected with the lands of the territory. He had, indeed,
made himself as familiar with the agrarian as he was with
the education question in the colony.

But what was the use of all this knowledge, as he had no
longer a seat in the Council? It was this consideration,
doubtless, which led him, then a busy barrister in excellent practice, to assist in founding the *Atlas*, a ' Sydney
Weekly Journal of Politics, Commerce, and Literature.' The
first number appeared on Saturday, November 30, 1844, and
opened with an exhaustive essay, entitled ' The Present
Condition and Future Prospects of New South Wales.' This
article, which was probably a joint production, was in effect
the manifesto of the pastoral tenants and settlers, who
were quite at the mercy of the Sydney executive—or, in
other words, of Sir George Gipps. But the *Atlas* was by no
means devoted merely to the advocacy of land reform. Not a
question bearing on the prosperity or future greatness of Australia but was treated in its attractive columns, sometimes in
weighty and eloquent prose, often in light and pungent verse.

I have before me as I write the late Lord Sherbrooke's
bound volumes of ' marked,' or ' office ' copies of the *Atlas*,
which reveal to those who are acquainted with the initials the
names of all the chief contributors to this remarkable journal.
In the earlier issues a very large proportion of the leading
articles were from that powerful pen which, in after years, in
the columns of the *Times*, appealed often with irresistible
force to the statesmen and reading public of Europe. Most
of these *Atlas* ' leaders ' were devoted to local and ephemeral
topics, which would no longer interest even the immediate
descendants of the old pioneer squatters of New South Wales,
who so keenly relished them when they first issued from the

press. But by its treatment of what might be called Anglo-colonial problems the *Atlas* may fairly claim to have been second only in importance to the Legislative Council itself in achieving self-government for Australia.

The prevailing 'note' of the *Atlas* during the short period that the late Lord Sherbrooke directed its style and policy was its outspoken common-sense. He never allowed it to rave, and though he freely used both invective and ridicule, the journal was never hysterical. Take the following plea for Australian self-government, and observe how fairly the balance is held between the mother-country and the colony :—

The grand object to be attained, then, is legislative power commensurate with our knowledge and our wants. We can only ensure it by steadily and temperately showing that we understand and shall not abuse it. It is galling, no doubt, to be treated as an infant after the period of infancy has passed away ; but it is not a pleasant display to see a child kicking itself out of its mother's arms merely because it is conscious of legs and convinced that it can run alone. Let us show that we have that high qualification for civil liberty which consists in putting moral chains on our own passions. Let our representatives have patience, while they steadily and respectfully press in the direction of the great object ; the granting of which by the mother-country will be the surest means of strengthening and continuing those amicable arrangements which both parent and child must be anxious to retain.

These are wise words ; and it may not be out of place to remind the rising generation of Australians, who have merely reaped the reward of the labours of their forefathers, that the great men who really won for them their civil and political rights were patriotic Englishmen, profoundly stirred by the noble traditions of our common race ; and that, however much they may have quarrelled with Governors and Downing Street officials, their loyalty to England and to English institutions was the mainspring of all their actions.

The number of leading articles written by Mr. Lowe for the *Atlas* during the time of his virtual editorship—that is, from its foundation up to May or June 1845—is simply to make a speech to an inattentive assembly a shade more ignorant than himself; that the Under-Secretary knows just enough of us to adopt some crude and impracticable theory, like the one-pound-an-acre scheme, or the civilisation of the aborigines, to which he adheres with the desperate tenacity of ignorance and presumption; and that the clerk, our real governor, who is utterly unknown and irresponsible—who will not be praised if we are governed well, nor blamed if we are governed ill—should take it as easy as possible, and content himself with echoing back the despatches he receives, *sometimes enlivening the matter by an occasional abuse of the Governor for something perfectly right, just to show he has an opinion of his own.*

This subject of the government of remote colonies by means of despatches from Downing Street seems at times to have struck Mr. Lowe in such a ludicrous light that he could no longer argue the matter in pungent leading articles, but was compelled to fly for relief to parody and metrical skits. His old schoolfellow, Edward Cardwell, who, in after years, held the seals of the Colonial Office, figures amusingly in one of these parodies.

LAW FOR A DEPENDENCY

*Referre sermones Deorum et
Magna modis iterare parvis.*

Scene : Downing Street. *Time: noon.* Lord Stanley *discovered reading the advertisements in the* Times. *To him enters* Mr. Cardwell.

    Lord Stanley. Oh! Mr. Cardwell, I have sent for thee
Because they tell me that thou art a man
Quick in debate, and prodigal of words,
And one to help thy party at a pinch.
Sit down, I pray.
    Mr. Cardwell. I humbly thank your Lordship,
And, as you do desire me, take my seat.
    Lord Stanley. Fain would we have thy services, young man,
But at this time there is no office vacant,
Nor dare we make a new one, lest Young England
Should say we are corrupt.
    Mr. Cardwell (rising).   Then, my Lord,
I think I have no further business here;
And so I take my leave.

Lord Stanley.   Stop, Mr. Cardwell.
We cannot make a vacancy, 'tis true,
Nor a new office, but we can revise one,
And will, for you.   Know, then, the Colonies
Say they'll no more be governed without law.
Justice they shall not have—but law they must.
And so we want a lawyer sage and subtle,
By whose advice to act; but ere I give you
This high appointment, you must let me try
Whether you understand the law or *no*;
For ignorance I hate ; and Mr. Stephen
With the first lawyers in the land is even.
Here, take an instance.   You have doubtless heard
That New South Wales has got a Constitution :
Such an Assembly, I should think, was never
Seen since the time of Romulus—all thieves—
Several who have not yet received their pardons ;
And Stephen says they voted it a breach
Of privilege to pick a Member's pocket
While in debate engaged.   'Tis sad to think
The spurious Liberalism of the age
Should give such rascals power.
      Mr. Cardwell.   Sad indeed !
      Lord Stanley.   Well, sir, these rascals have presumed to make
A law about their filthy sheep and cattle,
For which we've written them a sharp Despatch,
Whereon I would interrogate you briefly.
      Mr. Cardwell.   My Lord, according to my utmost knowledge
I ready am to answer.
      Lord Stanley.   Tell me, then,
If any difference exist in law
Betwixt the pledge of personal estate and alienation ?
      Mr. Cardwell.   Very great, my Lord.
If personal estate or goods be sold,
Possession ought to follow the transaction ;
Or if the seller still do keep the goods
It is, so Twyne's case says—a badge of fraud :
But if the property be only pledged,
Possession in the pawner does not give
The slighest badge of fraud !   'Tis true, if bankrupt
The mortgagor become, his assignees
Will have a preference o'er the mortgagee,
Because the property does still remain
Within the order and disposing power
Of him they represent.
      Lord Stanley (rising sternly).   Sir! I intended
To have promoted you to mighty honour,

But, finding you so grossly ignorant
Of the first axioms of the legal science,
I do repent me of my former purpose.
Sir, had you been a lawyer, you'd have known
That mortgages of personal estate
Are held by English law in perfect hate.
For law, indeed, we do not greatly care,
Save that injustice must not be too bare.
Away, young man! and seek your special pleader;
If you talk thus you'll never be a leader.

At times the Colonial Office is let alone, and theology takes the place of politics in the pillory. On these occasions the devoted followers of Dr. Pusey and Dr. Newman were often handled in unceremonious fashion. Now and then a little sweet is mixed with the bitter. There is an article on 'Early Closing of Shops in the City' (*Atlas*, January 4, 1845), in which the present Duke of Rutland is very handsomely dealt with. The article strongly advocates the early closing movement, and commends to the attention of the wealthier classes of Sydney 'the example of Lord John Manners and his friends, who have, indeed, on this occasion nobly vindicated a humanity above their rank.'

The *Atlas* boasted a 'Poets' Corner.' Sometimes this little nook was filled by one of those 'Swiss Sketches' written on the honeymoon tour; but just as often a set of satirical verses would appear dealing with Sir George Gipps and his *entourage*. These skits were often composed by others, but unless signed they were invariably attributed by the Sydney public to Mr. Lowe. He was, indeed, popularly credited with writing the whole of the paper every week; so that, an announcement appeared one morning over the leading article stating that the 'entire contents of the journal are *not* by one hand.'

However, it is quite true that the *Atlas* owed its vogue and popularity chiefly to Lowe's satirical epigrams and skits in verse. It is not that these verses were always so very witty or clever, but they were invariably so *apt*. For instance, when Mr. Roger Therry, who had basked in the smiles and favour of Sir Richard Bourke, had at length succeeded in getting into the good graces of Sir George Gipps to the extent of securing the judgeship in Port Phillip, Mr. Lowe made very merry in the ' Poets' Corner ' of the *Atlas*. Therry, like Mrs. Gilpin, had a frugal mind, and prior to starting for Melbourne advertised the sale of his furniture and effects, including the portrait of his former patron, Sir Richard Bourke. The subject, it must be admitted, was a tempting one, and in its next issue the *Atlas* suggested the following

INSCRIPTION FOR THE PORTRAIT OF SIR RICHARD BOURKE.

Here goes the Portrait of Sir Richard Bourke,
For whom I long did all the dirty work ;
His way of ruling was a perfect see-saw—
The voice of Jacob, and the hand of Esau.
Unlike our dear Sir George, whose accents sweet
With his mild deeds in dulcet concert meet.

He's got a Statue and a long Inscription—
Here goes his phiz to pay for my subscription !
But, sainted Gipps ! should limner e'er incline
To trace on steel those lineaments divine,
I'd never sell that superhuman face—
Never !—till someone else had got your place !

Roger Therry, notwithstanding his support of Robert Lowe's education policy, was ever the favourite subject for such satiric shafts. There was no malice in this whatever, but, to a man of the late Lord Sherbrooke's singular independence of character, all forms of flunkeyism appeared supremely ridiculous as well as contemptible. In the *Poems of a Life* there may be found a most ludicrous parody of the well-known song, ' Love Not,' the whole point of which was lost on the London critics, simply because they were not acquainted with the circumstances which called it forth and the men whom it so happily ridiculed.

It seems that through the influence of Mr. James Macarthur, of Camden (a mighty local magnate), Roger Therry

G.C.M.G. They were for the most part ambitious young men, who gladly enough enlisted under the banners of so dauntless a chieftain as Robert Lowe.

Sir Thomas Mitchell, the explorer, was likewise a contributor to the *Atlas*. Unlike most of its writers, he was a man past middle life, and in the very meridian of his fame. As far back as 1811 (the year of Robert Lowe's birth) he had fought in the Peninsula; already he had received the D.C.L. of Oxford, and had been knighted for his achievements as an Australian explorer. Sir Thomas Mitchell's connection with such a journalistic firebrand as the *Atlas* did not ingratiate him with Sir George Gipps, with whom, indeed, he had already come to an open rupture. He had been elected one of the members for the Port Phillip district in the Legislative Council, but as he held a Government appointment, Sir George Gipps intimated to him that he was expected to vote with the Crown officials. Sir Thomas Mitchell accordingly resigned his seat, and devoted some of his leisure to the expression of his disgust in the congenial columns of the *Atlas*. But his one ambition in life was to lead exploration parties into the trackless interior, and here Sir George Gipps was able to have more than ample revenge by refusing to furnish the money for such expeditions. This state of things supplied Mr. Lowe with the subject of a pleasing little ballad, which he entitled ' The Two Knights ' :—

> There was a knight in Paynim Land—
> Viceregal state had he ;
> And all the men that there did stand
> Must do him fealty.
> There came to him an errant knight—
> ' To the mountains let me go.'
> That there I might essay my might ;
> But the other knight said ' No.'

It was in the *Atlas* that Lord Sherbrooke originally published his ' Songs of the Squatters,' which give a graphic, but by no means enchanting, picture of the life of a pioneer settler. They deal, too, with all the points of dispute then raging between Sir George Gipps, the Council, and the Crown tenants, and it was this which made them so popular when they first appeared in Sydney, and so unintelligible to English readers when collected and published in a small volume a few years ago in London. As an evidence of their early popularity, it may be mentioned that in an admirable but long-since forgotten work by Samuel Sidney, entitled *The Three Colonies of Australia*, there is an entire chapter devoted to these 'Songs of the Squatters.' Several of those quoted—though the writer of the book was not aware of it—were from the pen of Mr. Lowe.

These light and amusing verses naturally lose much of their point in being detached from the columns of the newspaper to whose more serious articles they formed a sort of humorous commentary. The modern reader who turns them over is, as a rule, quite ignorant of the events to which they refer; he knows nothing of Sir George Gipps, or his District Councils, or Border Police; nor can he realise the dread powers of that terrible personage, the Commissioner of Crown Lands, who had the fate of the pioneer squatter very much in his hands. But the readers of the *Atlas* could thoroughly appreciate the point of such verses as these :—

> The Commissioner bet me a pony—I won ;
> So he cut off exactly two-thirds of my run ;
> For he said I was making a fortune too fast,
> And profit gained slower the longer would last.

> He remarked, as devouring my mutton he sat,
> That I suffered my sheep to grow sadly too fat ;
> That they wasted waste land, did prerogative brown,
> And rebelliously nibbled the droits of the Crown.

'The Squatter to his Bride' gives anything but an idyllic picture of early bush life. But to this day many of the old pioneer bushmen regard it as unrivalled in its fidelity,

and its grim humour has amused more than one genera·
tion :—

> Four hundred miles off
>   Is the goal of our way ;
> It is done in a week,
>   At but sixty a day ;
> The plains are all dusty,
>   The creeks are all dried,
> 'Tis the fairest of weather
>   To bring home my bride.
> The blue vault of heaven
>   Shall curtain thy form,
> One side of a gum tree
>   The moonbeam must warm ;
> The whizzing mosquito
>   Shall dance o'er thy head,
> And the guana shall squat
>   At the foot of thy bed ;
> The brave laughing jackass
>   Shall sing thee to sleep,
> And the snake o'er thy slumbers
>   His vigil shall keep.

In the same grimly playful strain he depicts the domestic
arrangements of the rude and primitive homestead, winding
up with this absolutely appalling statement to the truly
feminine mind :—

> So fear not, fair lady,
>   Your desolate way,
> Your clothes will arrive
>   In three months with my dray.

Mrs. Lowe naturally took a keen interest in the new
journalistic venture. In the following letter will be found a
reference to the _Atlas_, and also a minute and interesting
account of the daily life of the most distinguished of its
founders :—

                                        Sydney: Jan. 20, 1845.

. . . . We live much as at home. Robert and I never were,
nor ever will be, fond of early rising, so we get up about half-past
seven, or eight o'clock—unless we were to rise at five o'clock we
should gain little. The heat begins as soon as the sun has risen, and
continues great till ten o'clock, when the sea-breeze gets up, and in

the shade it is delicious. At ten o'clock Robert walks off to his chambers, which are at the end of this street; it is not above five minutes' walk. There Anthony Pope, his clerk, is waiting for him, and his labours begin. Anthony reads and writes law, and Robert sits in an American rocking-chair at his ease, dictating. Robert is getting more and more employment in the Courts, and is also very busy in politics. He has quite a *levée* of people. Between three and four he comes home, and we ride on horseback. Horses are cheap beyond all idea. You can buy a very nice one for 7*l.*, and their keep is also very reasonable. My horse runs in the pony-carriage, and I often drive myself. We ride frequently from 12 to 20 miles towards the Heads or Botany Bay. This exercise seems requisite here. I find I cannot walk far. I think at one time I walked too much, and brought on swelling and pains in my knees, which proceeded, they said, from the nerves in the back; so I took the warning, and have not walked much since. In summer the heat is so great the ground feels quite hot to the feet; but it is delicious to ride or drive. Everyone here has some sort of conveyance; the rich, nice carriages, and the poor, gigs and little pony-carriages. You would admire the wild, uncultivated plains and marshes towards Botany. Close to the sea the trees grow again and the shrubs are lovely. The sea is most wonderful in colour; under the horizon it is the deepest lilac purple, and fades towards you through every shade of blue into the loveliest sea-green with white breakers on a golden shore. The coast in parts rocky, in others with green grass down to the beach. After our ride we dine; at seven o'clock Anthony comes again and reads for Robert. When he leaves I read and write, and then we go to bed. We sometimes dine out, but refuse evening parties, except the large ones at the O'Connells'. We also have little dinner-parties at home; beef, mutton, wine, and poultry are so cheap that it makes very little difference having a few persons to dinner. We are now feasting on peaches and nectarines; I have an enormous plate of them before me, and stop every now and then to eat. I draw, and play on the harp, and sing as usual, but not so much as I used to do. I have more trouble with servants than at home. Poor little Mary and Bobby (the children of Mrs. Jamieson) are very good, and give no trouble. Bobby gave some symptoms of original sin the other day, and Robert whipped him, which had a most excellent effect. We intend, if possible, to find a house two or three miles from Sydney. Robert could ride backwards and forwards, and I think the change of air would be beneficial to him. As he gains health, his eyes always strengthen. They are much better, and I never hear him now complain of pain. He had a habit of putting his hands to his temple and pressing it, from feeling pain; I now never see him do this. But I do not tell him I think his eyes are stronger, for fear he

should read again to himself. He also often sits in an evening without his spectacles, unless I remind him ; formerly he never used to
forget them . . . .

I am forwarding the *Atlas* newspaper to you. Robert writes in
it, and you will see a series of Swiss poetical sketches,[1] which have
given great delight here. Sir Thomas Mitchell expresses himself
quite charmed with them. Some were written in Switzerland, some
here ; ' The Eagle' I think you know of old. . . . .

In a letter to her mother-in-law about the same time, Mrs.
Lowe excuses her remissness as a correspondent by saying that
her pen finds much employment in Robert's service. This arose
partly from his large access of business, and partly from his
contributions to the *Atlas*. In a postscript she adds : ' Pray
forward the *Atlas* to Mr. Biddulph, and tell me what he
thinks of it, as regards the talent it displays. The politics
are difficult to judge of unless on the spot.'

We can now picture Robert Lowe, barrister-at-law and
journalist, of Sydney, no longer a mere ' new chum,' but a
seasoned colonist, his professional income displaying an
agreeably rising tendency ; while his fame and importance as
a public man had increased rather than diminished by his
surrender of his seat as a nominee member of Council. Then,
as he tells us, he was regarded as a toady if he voted with the
Government, and as a traitor if he voted against it ; while
now, through the columns of the *Atlas*, he could express his
opinions freely on every subject under the sun, with the
delight and approval of the great mass of his fellow-colonists.

[1] See *Poems of a Life*, by Viscount Sherbrooke.

CHAPTER XVII

Sir George Gipps and the Legislative Council—District Councils—Quit-rents—
Lowe stands for St. Vincent and Auckland—Address to the Electors—
Returned unopposed—Speech from the Hustings—Schedules A, B, C—
Takes his Seat in the Council

THE rupture between the Governor and the Legislative Council
had daily increased since the evening when Mr. Lowe found
himself compelled to resign his seat as a Crown nominee. It
had become a case of war to the knife. Sir George Gipps
was an Engineer officer who had served in the Peninsula
with distinction ; he had been wounded at the siege of
Badajoz. Then he had acted as secretary to the Royal Commission appointed to deal with the grievances of the rebellious
Canadians (1835). Here it was he first displayed his rare
talent for drawing up official documents in terse, lucid, and
intelligible language. He was appointed Governor-General
of New South Wales at the most critical point of her history,
just as she was emerging from a penal dependency into a
self-governing colony.

In his new post Sir George Gipps revealed a singular
mingling of the military autocrat with the Radical *doctrinaire*.
He quickly made up his mind that all the ills of the colony
(including its bankruptcy) could be cured by means of
district councils. At his suggestion this scheme of district
councils had been embodied in the Imperial Act of Parliament
by which Lord Stanley conferred a semi-representative
Parliament on New South Wales. Briefly, the scheme
amounted to this : that the colony should be divided into

districts, and that each district should elect a council to decide on the amount of money required for public purposes for the year, half of which should be contributed from the colonial treasury, and the other half raised by a levy on the local property holders.

If any district declined to elect a council, the Governor had power to appoint one; and in default of a local treasurer, the Colonial Treasurer—who was the Governor's nominee—could, under his warrant, raise the amount by the forced sale of property in the district. In a sparsely populated pastoral country, possessing, it may be, countless flocks and herds, but with little or no ready money, it is easy to see how thoroughly unworkable this scheme of district councils must have been; and also, how it might be turned into an engine of oppression in the hands of an autocratic Governor whose power was practically unchecked. Mr. Sidney, in his *Three Colonies of Australia*, pertinently observes :—

When Sir George Gipps attempted to introduce his district councils, he found the colonists unprepared to travel for miles to elect a councillor, or pay five or ten pounds per annum for roads over which they never travelled, and bridges a hundred miles from their farms, and indignant at suddenly finding their property at the mercy of the Colonial Treasurer, the irresponsible officer of the Governor. The colonists determined to resist the district councils scheme. The Governor was determined to enforce it. It was his darling child; he had conceived it while looking out from his study on the dense population of a different state of society, and he was not the man to be beaten by circumstances.

Mr. Lowe, as usual, 'dropped into poetry' on the subject in the columns of the *Atlas*. He wrote a kind of irregular ballad with the title 'District Councils, or the Brazen Yoke.'

> A statesman made a yoke of brass,
>   A heavy yoke to bear,
> And said: 'I want some slavish ass
>   This brazen yoke to bear.'

It was not so much the scheme itself—though he thought it singularly unsuited to a primitive pastoral community—

but the arbitrary power with which it invested the Governor, that drove Robert Lowe into the camp of Wentworth and the squatters. In addition to the question of district councils, he also objected to Sir George Gipps's action in the matter of exacting ' quit-rents '—a tax long in abeyance. It had fallen into abeyance for years, partly by reason of the widespread bankruptcy of the pastoral settlers, and partly because the Government had been unable any longer to furnish them with ' assigned servants '—that is, convicts on ticket-of-leave, who were farmed out to the squatters and other employers. Now, on a sudden, Sir George Gipps demanded the whole of the arrears of quit-rents from these unfortunate pastoral tenants of the Crown. As most of these were in a state of insolvency, this meant that Sir George Gipps or his agent would step in and sell off the homesteads, cattle, sheep, and all improvements.

To make this demand for the arrears of such a tax was a most pedantic and impolitic course of action on the part of the Governor. He was a strictly honourable, and even a kindly man, but his object was to show the Home authorities that under his *régime* New South Wales could meet, out of its own revenue, most, if not all of the expenses of its civil and military establishments. This was not only impolitic, but the height of folly ; for as long as England chose to regard New South Wales as an Imperial penitentiary—a kind of huge Newgate-over-the-Sea—it was only just that she should pay all the expenses of its maintenance.

On this question of ' quit-rents ' Mr. Lowe wrote some verses in the *Atlas* of a much more serious character than are most of his ' Songs of the Squatters.' He thus depicts the feelings of one of these pioneer squatters on suddenly finding himself sold up :—

> .   .   .   .   .
> Oh ! kindly spoke the ruler then ;
> He gave me land, he gave me men ;
> And I was happy and content,

My heart unsealed, my brow unbent;
I loved the cot beneath the trees,
The glorious light, the healthy breeze,
And blest the hour and blest the hand
That pointed to that glorious land.
Another, and another came,
And then a man, his very name
Blisters my lips like burning flame;
True to his masters he might be,
But fatal was that man to me.

He told me that the land they gave
    Freely to give they never meant;
That I was but a wretched slave,
    That toiled to pay them yearly rent;
He said for twenty years 'twas due—
Alas! his cruel words were true,
And I, fond wretch, I never knew;
And I had braved the noontide ray,
    The red sirocco's sultry kiss,
The watchful night, the toilsome day—
    Had laboured, struggled, spared for this.

They sold my cattle, sold my farm,
And left me with this withered arm
And broken heart to stem the tide
Of woe, with none but God to guide;
I was a man of iron frame
When to this glorious land I came.
But now am bowed by toil and shame,
    And grown before my season old,
For he—I will not speak his name—
    Has sold me like a slave for gold.

These lines are very unsparing towards Sir George Gipps; but it was, as I have said, a time of war to the knife between the Governor on the one side, and the 'popular,' or representative members of the Council, backed up by almost the entire non-official community, on the other.

Under these circumstances, it was not likely that the popular party would be long content to see such a champion as Robert Lowe without a seat in the Council. There was some talk of finding him one of the Port Phillip constituencies, for which he would have been an ideal representative, if only on account of his views on the Separation question. Then it was rumoured in the inner political coteries that the mighty Macarthur, of Camden, would atone for his sins in having placed such a time-server as Therry in the Council by nominating the ultra-independent Mr. Lowe. On this subject the following characteristic letter appeared in the Press : —

In the speech of Dr. Sherwin at Berrima on Monday, the 24th ultimo, occurs the following passage : ' They (the Messrs. Macarthur) have cast a slur upon the county of Camden which it richly deserves ; they were ready to hunt through the county for a stranger in the person of Mr. Lowe, who would have accepted the patronage of the Messrs. Macarthur if they would elect him free of expense to himself.'

Whether the county deserves this slur or not, the Messrs. Macarthur have not cast it upon them ; they never offered me their patronage, and, had they done so, there is no conceivable conjunction of circumstances under which I would have accepted it.

I am, Sir, your obedient Servant,

ROBERT LOWE.

Horbury Terrace : March 1, 1845.

However, a vacancy was soon found in the resignation of the member for the Southern counties of St. Vincent and Auckland. Mr. Lowe's address to the electors gives such a terse statement of his views on the questions then agitating the colonial public mind (except the education question, which had been altogether shelved for the time being by the veto of the Governor), that it may very well find a place here :—

To the Electors of the Counties of St. Vincent and Auckland.

GENTLEMEN,—Captain Coghill having, before sailing for England, resigned his seat in the Legislative Council, I have been invited to offer myself as a candidate for the honour of representing you. I therefore beg to solicit your support.

My opinions on most of the subjects which at present agitate the public mind are pretty well known, and I will therefore recapitulate them very briefly. I am decidedly opposed to district councils, which appear to me un-English and oppressive, superfluous in those countries which can afford to pay for them, and ruinous in those which, like New South Wales, cannot.

I look upon the grinding exaction of quit-rents as a most discreditable perversion of the Royal Prerogative, and the high minimum price of land and exorbitant rent demanded for sections as founded on a mistaken policy, which loses all by grasping at too much. I am friendly to the squatters, considering that upon their success alone can the prosperity of the agricultural interest be securely based. When in Council I endeavoured to promote that prosperity by preparing an address to Parliament praying that the British market might be opened to the grain of this colony as it has been to that of Canada ; if this be done, a limit will be established, below which the price of agricultural produce cannot fall. I am most anxious to carry out the retrenchment commenced in the public expenditure, and to obviate, as far as it can be done by law, the difficulties of individuals. With this latter object, and also with a view of striking at a pernicious system of credit, I proposed the abolition of imprisonment for debt, by which I believe many persons have been saved from insolvency.

Should it be my fortune to represent you, I will take care to the best of my power that your district shall have its fair share of the very slender means of local improvement which an expensive Government and a falling revenue place at the disposal of the Council.

Before the day of election arrives I shall do myself the honour to solicit personally your suffrages.

Till then believe me, Gentlemen,

Your most obedient humble Servant,

ROBERT LOWE.

He was triumphantly returned, no one having the temerity to oppose him.

Accordingly, on April 15, 1845, at noon, Colonel Mackenzie, J.P., proposed Mr. Robert Lowe as a fit and proper person to represent the counties. Dr. Bell seconded the proposition. No other candidate appearing, the returning officer declared Mr. Lowe duly elected, and the announcement was received with the usual manifestations of popular approval. Mr. Lowe then came forward, and addressed his new constituents as follows :—

Gentlemen, Electors of the Counties of St. Vincent and Auckland,—I am so fully aware of the important business which requires your attention this day that I will study to be as brief as possible in returning you my cordial and heartfelt thanks for the honour which you have just done me. I am, as has been truly said by one of my calumniators, a stranger to this county, not possessing a foot of land or a head of stock within it. . . . . We are now arrived at a great crisis: two roads are before us; the one will lead us to a higher and more durable prosperity than we have ever enjoyed, the other to still increasing misery and calamity, till we are blotted out of the list of colonies, like the unhappy islands of New Zealand and Van Diemen's Land,[1] by the misgovernment of the Colonial Office. For myself, Gentlemen, I have nothing to hope from a seat in the Council—it will not add anything to the very moderate income which I derive from my profession ; but I desire it because I wish to save you, or at least to endeavour to do so, from the ruin with which you are threatened by the Executive Government. When I entered the Council as a nominee of the Crown I considered that I had undertaken a trust for the benefit of the people, for the faithful execution of which I was answerable to God and man, and I foolishly believed on so discharging it I should be carrying out the wishes of the Government which sent me there. Such a novice was I in colonial government, that I actually believed the interest of the Crown coincident with that of the people. The only apology which I can make for this error is the ignorance which then generally prevailed concerning most questions at issue between this colony and the mother-country. But, Gentlemen, when I found the Governor, by a stroke of his pen, in defiance of the unanimous remonstrances of the country and of the lessons of reason and experience, bent upon annihilating the pastoral interests of the country, I was undeceived—I could not support that Government.

When I saw a system of district taxation introduced, and persevered in after remonstrances from the Council, in which I had the honour to bear a part, both by speech and vote—and introduced, not, as I believe, for the sake of the mockery of self-government under which their destructive nature was concealed, but for the sake of fastening more firmly on the colony the enormous annual expenditure of ninety thousand a year for police and jails, and of taxing the land already sold—God knows how dearly !—for the purpose of making the remainder saleable by the erection of roads and bridges—I would not, I could not, support that Government. While they were playing this disgraceful thimble-rig, while they were shifting this imposition from the ordinary revenue to the local taxation, I would not play the part of a confederate, and wink and connive at this trickery. When I saw the Government, straining

---

[1] Let it be remembered this was spoken in 1845.

to the utmost that prerogative which is only entrusted to the Crown for the good of the people, living upon the grantees of land, much of which had been dearly earned by naval and military service, and upon the accumulated arrears of quit-rent, which it was well understood would never be demanded, every feeling of justice and humanity revolted at it, and I could not support that Government. When I found that an enormous expenditure, utterly disproportionate to the means and wants of the colony, instituted from bribing voters in England at our expense by sinecure or half-sinecure offices, denounced by the Council, denounced by the judges of the land, and defended by none but its recipients and their hangers-on, was to be perpetuated, I could not support that Government. It has been said of me, and repeated time after time with a disgraceful pertinacity, notwithstanding my repeated and public contradictions, that I entered the Council pledged to the Governor. Gentlemen, had I done so, had I been capable of accepting a trust for your benefit, and delegating the exercise of that trust to another, I should be unworthy to stand before you as your representative this day ; but it was not so, and when I resigned my seat, it was not because I was pledged, but because I would not give anyone the opportunity of taunting me with employing a power I derived from the Governor systematically to thwart his measures.

As to your local matters, Gentlemen, I will endeavour, by making the tour of the county before I return to Sydney, to make myself better acquainted with them. I shall be very grateful for any information which any of you may at any time communicate to me on the subject ; at the same time, great as the claims of your district are on the ground of former neglect, I can, I fear, do but little for you. It is a penalty which must be paid by those who return members to represent the *colony*, that they will receive little in the way of patronage from the *Government*. Hope nothing from this Governor ; his whole attention is taken up by scraping together, by every discreditable expedient, a revenue which, being emancipated from the control of the representatives of the people, may serve the purposes of the Colonial Office. For you he cares nothing, and will do nothing. Gentlemen, the sorrow which I feel on taking leave of you is considerably alleviated by the reflection that I shall probably very shortly come here again on the same errand. The differences between the Governor and the Council are concentrated, are brought to a point ; each party thoroughly understands where and why they disagree, and collision has become unavoidable, and even desirable. Fire and gunpowder, the moment before their meeting, do not more certainly portend an explosion than the day which shall once more place the Governor and the Council face to face. Whether he will shrink from the conflict,

and seek some other land which, though he cannot find as flourishing, he may render as wretched as this, or whether he will dissolve
the Council, and thus give the constituencies a chance of riveting
their own fetters, I do not know ; but in the meantime your eye
will be upon me, and if the latter event happens, as I rather think
it will, you will, I trust, see no reason to give me a reception less
cordial than that with which you have honoured me to-day.

There is but one further point in this trenchant speech
from the hustings calling for explanation. When Mr. Lowe
so strongly denounced the ' disgraceful thimble-rig ' in reference to the finances of the colony, he had in his mind
the reservation of the sum of 81,600*l.* a year which, by the
Imperial Act of Parliament conferring a *quasi*-free Constitution
on New South Wales, was withdrawn from the control of the
Legislative Council. This reservation was comprised under
three schedules, A, B, and C, by which the salaries of the
Governor and judges, the cost of gaols and judicial establishments, were fixed, as well as the endowment to the three State
Churches of 30,000*l.* a year.   I should say, four established
Churches, or sects, for the Wesleyan Methodists had by this time
contrived to get access to the public purse.   The following was
the Civil List removed from the control of the Council by
special Imperial Act—

A. Salaries of Civil Officers	. . .	£33,000
B. Treasurer's and other Departments	.	18,600
C. Support of Religion	. . .	30,000
		£81,600

' Schedules A, B, C ' hardly sounds like a theme for the
Muses ; but Robert Lowe contributed nothing to the *Atlas*
that more tickled the fancy of the early pioneer colonists.   It
went straight, as Bacon says, ' to their business and bosoms.'
As these playful rhymes are thoroughly intelligible to any
reader who takes an interest in early colonial affairs, they
are here reproduced in full.

Schedules A, B, C

Fair Sisterhood with sweet, alluring faces,
Third of the Muses—total of the Graces:
SCHEDULES—beloved alike of Gods and Men ;
Though Patriots cavil at you now and then,
As if your forms were hideous to behold,
And only loved, like ancient dames—for gold.
Who would not wish, secure from Fate's alarms,
To slumber sheltered in your circling arms ?
Blest by your love, and basking in your smile,
No other Schedule shall he ever file.
Nor shall Insolvency, relentless dame,
Daughter of Tick and Misery, shriek his name.
Learning hath charms, but what is like to thee,
Thou most delightful form of A B C !
Children of Stanley, hail in glory trine,
Where transport and security entwine ;
For not alone the claiming coin is sweet,
But knowing nothing can that claim defeat.
A drought may come—the land may retrograde—
The cattle die in thousands—still they're paid.
Wool may fall cent. per cent., a losing trade,
And 'whelm the land in ruin—still they're paid.
Embarrassed Banks refuse to give their aid
To sinking settlers—still the Schedule's paid.
The Governor and smugglers make a raid
Against the Customs' revenue—still they're paid.
The broken compact has the land betrayed,
But what of that ?—the Schedules must be paid.
And when Australia low in dust is laid,
This be her epitaph—it's all been paid !
If, 'mid a triad so divine, the Muse
Might just presume a favourite to choose,
I'd rather not be put in Schedule A—
In that the Council has too much to say :
And though it's safe beyond their greedy clutch,
It makes one nervous when they talk so much.
C has advantages, I'll not deny—
It's all so snug, so quiet, and so sly ;
And it would suit my fancy to a T
If Stanley's honour were but pledged to C.
The poet's burning wish were just to clear
Five hundred pounds in each and every year ;
But if with castle-building e'er I meddle,
I'll wish myself within the second Schedule ;

For it alone has got a copious margin,
And a good salary will bear enlarging.
Where'er I turn, whatever berth I see,
I'll stick to Riddell's [1] berth in Schedule B.
Others with labour more or less are troubled,
He'd still do nothing, if his work were doubled.

Robert Lowe was now once more a member of the Legislative Council. But there could be no longer any question of the complete independence of his position ; he had, in fact, secured his unopposed election, mainly by his avowed and uncompromising hostility to the interference of Downing Street in the domestic affairs of the colony, through its eminently active and efficient servant, Sir George Gipps.

The session did not open till July 29, 1845, when we read in the official records that Mr. Robert Lowe was introduced to the Speaker by Mr. Windeyer, member for Durham, and Mr. Benjamin Boyd and Dr. Nicholson, members for Port Phillip ; whereupon he took the oaths and his seat as member for St. Vincent and Auckland.

We may well suppose that Mrs. Lowe did not allow her English friends to remain in a state of ignorance with regard to these stirring events.

I am sure (she writes) you will be glad to hear that Robert has become a very prominent public character, and is said to be by far the best speaker in the Legislative Council. This is rather a stormy position in the present state of politics here ; party spirit is running tremendously high, and Robert is the leader on the popular side. The whole weight of the Government is opposed to him and his party ; there is nothing the Government would not do to put Robert down. From his power of speaking and his general knowledge, and also knowledge of constitutional law, they find him a dangerous opponent. Their hatred is great in proportion to their dread. The Government newspapers abuse him beyond measure, and you would suppose from them that he was the most fearful

---

[1] The Colonial Treasurer, of whom in the *Atlas*, in a satirical 'Defence of the Treasury Bench,' Mr. Lowe cruelly said : 'If he may not have all the reputation of the others, it is owing to his having so little to do, rather than to his not doing that little well. He is said, indeed, to sign his name with consummate skill and with considerable velocity.

We are finishing the house; it was sold by an unfortunate mortgagee in England, put up to public auction, and by a lucky chance fell to us; 4,000*l.* was refused for the land four years ago. I shall make some drawings of the views. The scenery resembles Jersey, but is far more beautiful—the vegetation is so lovely. We have a beautiful bay to ourselves—I may say it is our own—the trees line the shore with drives through them; we have a waterfall of sixty feet, and this runs through a fine valley: it is a most romantic spot and just suits my tastes.

These views of their favourite home in the New World always hung on the walls of Lord Sherbrooke's house in Lowndes Square; they were really beautiful, and gave his English friends, accustomed to the low, leaden skies and murky atmosphere of London, a most fascinating vision of the shores of the South Pacific.

There is a sequel to the story not quite so entrancing to those most nearly concerned. After returning to England, Lord Sherbrooke, by the advice of his agent and friends in the colony, was induced to dispose of this property for a sum which would represent but a very small fraction of its present value.

No doubt from the point of view of health this removal to Nelson Bay was a very excellent change. Mr. Lowe had now not only such an increase of practice that he was compelled to devote much time to it, but there was also the never-ending work of a popular leader in the Legislative Council; of one, too, who, having put his hand to the plough, was not likely to turn back. It is true that his general health was extremely good, and that his eyesight had perceptibly improved—an improvement which he declared began from the moment that he shook off his medical advisers. But to one conscious of such peculiarly delicate organs, there must have always been the dread of a catastrophe. He had himself found it essential to use his eyes only by means of those light-excluding goggles, which at this time he devised, and through which light was only admitted from the pin's point in the centre. He also thought it wise to devote some portion of each day to active out-of-door exercise. In the case of so busy a public man this desideratum could only be obtained by fixing on a place of residence which demanded a walk, or, better still, a ride on horseback to and from the city daily. Being very fond of horse exercise, Mr. Lowe chose that means of getting from Nelson Bay to his chambers and the Legislative Council.

Very soon their residence was completed, and although they were now cut off from all general society, their picturesquely situated sea-side home was a favourite resort of a select few. Mr. T. B. Boulton, the artist, formerly of Sydney, has sent a few notes, which give a pleasant picture of the select circle which gathered by

> The splendour and the speech
> Of thy lights and thunders, Coogee,
> Flying up thy gleaming beach.

. . . . . .

'I was a frequent visitor at their charming residence near Coogee Bay in view of the Pacific Ocean; and enjoyed the lively and brilliant conversations on all subjects, but particularly those on science and poetry. Many were their pleasant guests, but chief of all was the late W. Sharpe Macleay, whose descriptions and remarks charmed everyone. Indeed, I have heard Mr. Lowe say that he knew the best talkers in England, but not one of them was his equal in conversational power. Mr. Lowe I also met at Elizabeth Bay, the residence of Mr. Macleay, and on one occasion, at dinner, Mr. Lowe was speaking of an eclipse of the sun, and said the disc was very nearly obscured, but he could not distinguish the colours of the corona, when one of the guests at table, Mr. Stuart A. Donaldson, asked, "What is a disc?" to which Mr. Macleay, taking up a plate which he held before him, replied with great vehemence, "That is a disc," to the great amusement of all the other guests. . . . One day as I was reading under the shade of one of the beautiful honeycombed sandstone rocks, I observed Mr. L. and Mr. M. walking on the shore, when two hulking " larrikins " suddenly appeared on the scene, and they were at once warned that it was private property, and that they had no business there—to which they said they should go where they liked. Mr. Lowe at once picked up a bamboo which had been washed up by the lazy tide (being seconded by Mr. Macleay), and applied it with such effect on their backs that they roared out and soon " made tracks." . . . His memory was wonderful, and I well recollect meeting him when on the Bathurst circuit at Kirconnel (Dr. Palmer's), when he took one of the children on his knee and repeated some of his nursery rhymes. Some years after, on the same circuit, he stayed again at the Doctor's, and took the same child on his knee and asked her if she remembered the rhyme, but she had forgotten it, on which he repeated it, and half a dozen more ; but it did not signify if it was in his childhood or yesterday, everything seemed stereotyed on his brain. . . . One day as he was walking along Macquarie Street with Mr. Charles Cowper, the conversation turned on some political question, and he quoted a passage from Hallam's *Constitutional History*, which Cowper said he had quoted wrongly. He replied, " I know I am right." The other disputed the point, and said, " I only read it yesterday." Mr. Lowe said, " I don't care if you read it an hour ago, I know my quotation of the passage is correct, though I have not read it since I was at Oxford ; but to prove it, here is the Library, so let us go in and refer to the work." He asked for the volume, turned up the page, and was found to be right to the letter.

' Not only did Mr. Lowe ride from his seaside home to his office and back, but he usually travelled by the same means when on circuit ; Mrs. Lowe, who was an excellent horse- woman, very often accompanying him. On one occasion she rode in one day along the coast and through the bush—

for in those days there were no roads—from Woollongong to
Coogee.

'Mr. Lowe's own love of these excursions on horseback
once gave him that very unpleasant experience which every
Australian storyteller seems to have made the subject of a
tale. He was literally "lost in the bush." So lasting an
impression did this make on Mrs. Lowe's mind, that she often
described it as the most miserable experience of her life in
Australia.

'It seems that he went on circuit to Maitland and thought
he would ride to Sydney, through the most difficult country
in the colony, intersected by swamps, rocks, and the river
Hawkesbury. As might have been expected, he lost his track,
and, having got off to walk by the side of his horse, then lost
him also. As the expected hour of his return had long gone
by, Mrs. Lowe was in the utmost anxiety, which was not
lightened by the fact that the people by whom she was surrounded as workpeople were all convicts, some of whom she
despatched as a search party with no feeling of confidence.
Intelligence at length arrived that he was safe at a farmer's
on the Hawkesbury, but that he was in a sad plight and had
greatly suffered; indeed, he paid dearly for his temerity, for
it took at least a month to bring him to his ordinary condition.'

After the breach with Sir George Gipps, the Lowes wisely
determined to give themselves up to their few intimate friends,
avoiding mere social acquaintances and indiscriminate enter-
tainments. Neither of them entered Government House
again during Sir George Gipps's *régime* ; though the following
'item of intelligence' in the local press would seem to show
that the relations between Lowe and the Governor were not
wholly broken off :—

FASHIONABLE MOVEMENTS.—On the day of the prorogation of
the Legislative Council [November 13, 1845], the Governor visited

the grounds of Robert Lowe, Esq., M.C., at Nelson Bay, and inspected the cottage now building there.

In one of her letters to England Mrs. Lowe describes her new home with all the glow of genuine enthusiasm. She always enjoyed the climate of New South Wales, though after the first two years its sultry and languid summers seriously affected her health. But she writes thus in the year 1845 :—

You can form no idea of the beauty of this climate : our winters are delicious ; the finest October day you can recall to mind is only a faint resemblance of the weather here. I fear I shall look with horror on the leafless trees when I return home ; all the native trees are evergreens, and most beautiful ones. The flowers are splendid ; the only fault is, they are all on bushes, so the ground is never coloured by them.

It must be frankly admitted that Mrs. Lowe's letters of this period are not very complimentary to the society of Sydney. But she thoroughly appreciated the high qualities of the one or two intimate friends whom they saw frequently at Nelson Bay. Of these she specially mentions three : Sir Thomas Mitchell, W. S. Macleay, and Sir Alfred Stephen. ' Sir Thomas Mitchell ' (she writes), ' whose work on this country I dare say you have read, is a great friend of Robert's. We have also a very clever man here, Mr. William Macleay, who is a well-known naturalist, so that, though I am inclined at times to abuse the society of this place, there are still some very agreeable exceptions who would be considered an acquisition anywhere.'

The work of Sir Thomas Mitchell alluded to by Mrs. Lowe was *Australia Felix*, a book which, in a very special sense, may boast the rare distinction of having added a province to the Empire ; for it was its admirable descriptions of the rich pasture lands of Port Phillip which caused the influx of pioneer settlers into what is now the colony of Victoria. Apart from his fame and achievements as an explorer, Sir Thomas Mitchell had all the acquirements and tastes of a scholar; he was fond of literature, and had published a translation of Camoens's *Lusiad*. Mr. William Macleay, most welcome of guests at Nelson Bay, has already been mentioned more than once. With these Mrs. Lowe couples the name of Sir Alfred Stephen, who, at a very early stage of their intimacy, would seem to have formed the highest opinion of Lord Sherbrooke's capacity and character. He was already Chief Justice of the colony, a position he held for many years, and, though nine years Lord Sherbrooke's senior, Sir Alfred is still living in Sydney in his ninety-first year—' a beautiful old man, whom it was a delight to have seen,' writes Mr. Froude in his *Oceana*.

Sir Thomas Mitchell, Sir Alfred Stephen, William Sharpe Macleay, and the future Lord Sherbrooke, sitting together as they frequently did at Nelson Bay, all in the full vigour of their rare conversational powers, would have been considered a distinguished group in any city in the world. Lord Sherbrooke always declared, though in after years he was intimate with the cleverest and most cultured men in England, that he had met no one whose conversation was more varied and more charming than William Macleay's. With such companions, one could not be said to be out of the only world worth living in—the world of ideas—and the leisure hours which Robert Lowe enjoyed with these old colonial friends, within sight and sound of the ' wide Pacific,' were amongst the happiest of his life.

The following letter, written at this time, shows that he was then in friendly relations with his only possible political rival in Australia—the late William Charles Wentworth.

Robert Lowe to the Rev. R. Michell, B.D., Oxford.

Nelson Bay, Sydney : November 30, 1846.

My dear Michell,—Never a very good correspondent at any time, the absence of common topics and the weakness of my eyes have reduced my efforts in that line to almost nothing. I trust that you and yours are wending, on the quiet road of Oxford, your way of life with as few annoyances and as many pleasures as are consistent with the condition of humanity. My prospects are very good. I have as much practice as I can well get through, and am rapidly taking the lead at the Bar, which I assure you is no easy task in this colony. I have got a beautiful place on the shores of the Pacific, about five miles from Sydney ; am saving money and investing it at good interest, so that in a few years it will be within my option to return to England. My wife is quite well and happy in laying out her grounds. My eyes are indifferent, but certainly better than when I left England, and I am quite satisfied with the result of the expedition.

The object of this letter is to ask your assistance on behalf of a gentleman (Mr. Wentworth) well known as a writer, a lawyer, and a politician, to all who have any knowledge of New South Wales. He sent his eldest son, William Charles Wentworth, to Trinity College, Cambridge, but on my advice has decided to place him for a year with someone who is in the habit of taking charge of restive colts ; and I am now writing to you to beg you to find such a person. A Cambridge man would be preferred. Young Wentworth is intended for a barrister. I know no one to whom I could apply with so much confidence as yourself, from my long experience of your judgment and discretion in all matters relating to the management of young men. Any arrangement you may make will be ratified by Mr. Wentworth's agents, who will attend to the pecuniary part of the matter. Whatever you do, please to communicate to them.

I am very sorry to give you this trouble, but I am sure you will feel for a parent who is quite unable, from the immense distance and the pressure of business, to come to England himself, and has no one to whom to entrust a matter of so much difficulty.

With kind regards to your wife, in which mine begs to join, believe me, my dear Michell,

Your old friend,
ROBERT LOWE.

The rector of Bingham passed away in the year 1845 ; but the news of his death did not reach Nelson Bay for many months, as communication was then painfully slow between England and Australia. By the Rev. Robert Lowe's will, his lands in the town of Nottingham and in the county of Derby were devised in equal shares to his second son Robert, and his youngest son, Frederick Pyndar Lowe.

CHAPTER XIX

THE POPULAR LEADER

The Wentworth Banquet—Robert Lowe and Imperial Federation—Private
Friends and Public Funds—The Speakership and Bi-weekly Dinners—
Lowe on Economy—Hon. Francis Scott, M.P.—Land Legislation—Death of
Richard Windeyer—Death of Lady Mary Fitzroy—Caroline Chisholm

IN the letter to his old Oxford tutor, Robert Lowe makes not
the slightest reference to his activity as a popular leader in
the Legislative Council. If the reports of the proceedings of
the Council, however, be examined, it will be found that the
new member for St. Vincent and Auckland was one of the
most prominent public figures in the Colony. He went in
and out daily from Nelson Bay on horseback, attended the
Courts, where he was making an ever-increasing income, and
thence to the Council Chamber, where he spoke with brilliant
effect on almost every political question of the hour. Mrs.
Lowe does not omit to let their English relatives know how
steadily and rapidly he is mounting the ladder of success.
'All who hear Robert speak' (she writes), 'both in Court and
Council, say he is greatly gifted ; and men who have been in
the habit of hearing the best speaking in the House of
Commons and at the Bar say he would make his way rapidly
in England. The judges, Sir Alfred Stephen and Mr. Dick-
enson [afterwards Sir John Nodes Dickenson], tell Robert it
is folly for him to remain here. Robert wishes to return on
my account, but he never shall destroy his prospects for me.
He has struggled hard, and, considering his sight, the result
surprises even me.'

This is the first actual intimation of any intention of returning to England ; and it will be seen that the immediate cause was the failing health of Mrs. Lowe. She herself says in this letter : ' I now feel the value of my love for nature ; to me it supplies society, and as long as I am well enough to ride about our shore and above on the superb cliffs that overhang the coast, I want nothing more. But I have not been well, and my strength has failed me much at times ; then it is that I feel so wishful to see old friends again.'

' Robert (she continues) is much away ; the Bar and the Council engross so much of his time.'

The letter goes on to assure her English friends that the prospects of the colony are brightening, and that her husband, whose income has reached 1,000*l.* a year, is making wise and profitable investments. ' Is it not strange' (she adds with *naïveté*) ' that Robert, so unlike a money-making man, should be making a fortune ? '

There was a great public dinner given in honour of William Charles Wentworth in the hall of Sydney College (January 26, 1846), at which most of the leading men in Sydney, who were not Crown officials, were present. Chief among these were Robert Lowe, M.C., Richard Windeyer, M.C., Dr. Lang, M.C., Mr. Archibald Michie, barrister-at-law, Mr. Donald Larnach, and Mr. (afterwards Sir) James Martin. It was on this occasion, in reply to the toast, ' A speedy and thorough reform of the Colonial policy of Great Britain,' that Mr. Lowe delivered one of the most eloquent and effective of his Australian speeches, and, according to the local critics, entirely outshone Wentworth himself. The interest in the following passage is heightened by the palpable allusion to Gladstone, Cardwell, and others, with whom he had contended in debate at the Oxford Union :—

Many of my college contemporaries have been called on to fill offices of trust and importance to the State. . . . They have been placed in those offices by the voices of the people, and when they acted unwisely, they might be removed; but by coming out here, I have not only closed to myself that path of ambition, but have ceased to be a part of the governing body—have lost all control over the political destinies of the community to which I belonged, and have sunk into the slave of those who were once my equals. Even if it were an offence to join one's lot with that of the struggling colonists of Australia, political disfranchisement and degradation was too severe a punishment for it.

It is noticeable that in this remarkable after-dinner speech Mr. Lowe gave eloquent expression to strong Imperialist views. He was not one of those, he declared, who looked forward to separation from the mother country as inevitable. ' Were they not of the same language—of the same race? Had they not in common glorious recollections of the past, high and lofty interests of the present ? ' He then painted in the blackest colours the bungling and incompetence of Downing Street, and proceeded to lay down a line of policy by which he considered the tie between England and the colonies could be perpetuated, and the rights and liberties of both communities preserved. The political sentiment, no less than the eloquent expression of the following passage might have inspired the late deeply respected statesman, William Edward Forster, and will surely appeal to the mind and heart of Lord Rosebery :—

A line of demarcation should be drawn between Imperial and Colonial legislation, and all meddling interference in matters of a domestic nature should be utterly and for ever renounced. They were the best judges of their own wants, their own circumstances, and could legislate for their own welfare better than those who were totally ignorant of both; he claimed for the Colony the right to regulate her local affairs by her local Assembly, without the control of any power on earth. In Imperial matters also, a voice should be given to the Colonies—a share in the government of which they were made to feel the effect: for if the Colonies were to share in the results of Imperial policy, it was fit they should have a voice in its delibera-tions. If it was intended to carry out the principle, that colonies were integral parts of the British Empire, they had a right to be represented in the British Parliament; they would then be heard,

their interests would then be cared for. If the representative of
Middlesex claims a right to control the destinies of New South
Wales, the representative of New South Wales should have a
corresponding influence on the destinies of Middlesex. Statesmen
were yet to learn that the prosperity of the whole is best secured by
making every part prosperous; that there is no conflict between
the interests of the Colony and the Empire, and that the notion of
sacrificing the former to the latter always originates in the narrow
and selfish view of a part, and not in a comprehensive survey of the
whole. England herself is but a part of the Empire, and when she
treats us as if she were the whole, she is actuated by a narrow and
provincial spirit. If this were granted, then indeed would England
and her colonies be knit in an iron confederacy, supreme in her
strength; then might she be, as I hope she ever will be, triumphant
in arms, in arts, in literature and in freedom. But if this should
not be granted, then might she look for evil, for mourning, and
for woe.

It cannot be gainsaid that this is the doctrine—pure and
unadulterated—of Imperial Federation ; a doctrine which
Lord Sherbrooke, in later life, might not have felt altogether
able to endorse. But it should certainly stand as the expression of his opinions when he was a leading colonist and a
most popular public man in Sydney, engaged, too, in perpetual warfare with the officials in Downing Street, whom he
so vehemently opposed mainly because he considered their
course of action calculated to detach the Colonies from the
mother country.

This was almost the last occasion on which Lowe and
Wentworth appeared as political allies. After the recall of
Sir George Gipps, the squatter party, of which Wentworth
was the natural leader, was, under Earl Grey's policy,
'transformed' (to quote Lowe) 'from the suppliant into the
master.' He himself then, as we shall see, opposed the
squatters, who were led by his former ally, and became the
upholder of the rights of the great mass of the people.

In these lax days it is counted almost a virtue in a public
man to succour his friends at the public cost. Robert Lowe
had no friend in all Australia for whom he had so affectionate

a regard as for William Macleay; while for his friend's father, the venerable Speaker of the Legislative Council, he, like the rest of the community, had the very greatest respect. It was eminently characteristic that when Alexander Macleay resigned the Speakership, and Wentworth moved a resolution to compensate him for the loss of his English pension during the time that he had acted in that capacity, on the vote being taken, it was found there were fourteen ayes and two noes; the two latter being Lowe and Cowper.

The question of a successor to the Hon. Alexander Macleay was the cause of a most amusing debate in the Council. Wentworth—among whose defects bashfulness was not prominent—consented to be nominated as Speaker on condition that he should be allowed to take part in the debates, and that he should have a 'dinner salary,' and a residence provided for him. It was desirable, he told the members, ' that the Speaker should be placed in a position to extend hospitality, which would promote the despatch of business by softening the asperities so apt to spring up in the warmth of debate.' He pointed out that in England the charitable institutions would languish without the custom of public dinners. Amidst shouts of laughter he declared that the Speaker's dinner in the House of Commons had become ' an established part of the Constitution.' ' And,' he added, ' in this colony, where the members of the Legislature receive no wages for their labours, and are at a long distance from their abodes, it is only right and reasonable that the public should be at the expense of entertaining them once or twice a week.'

Sir Maurice O'Connell actually rose and warmly supported the proposition.

This was too much for Lowe, who had been fighting the battle of retrenchment side by side with Wentworth for years. At the same time no one perceived the ludicrous aspect of the whole matter more clearly. His speech, which even in those slow days found its way into at least one journal published in London, was a satirical masterpiece. Apologising for speaking before any member of the Government, Lowe said :—' I protest against this motion on behalf of the constituency I represent, on behalf of the principles which I have ever joined the hon. and learned member (Wentworth) in advocating, and, I feel almost constrained to add, on behalf of the hon. and learned member himself.'

He continued in a really high strain of eloquence to show that in an impoverished colony the dignity of the Council would not be maintained by increasing the salary of its chief officer in order that he might entertain the members at dinner. ' When ' (to use his own words) ' in a season of heavy and prevalent distress, the Council, in a spirit of sympathy which it was bound to feel, gave moderate salaries to its officers, it advanced its dignity in a far higher degree than it could have done by investing the Speaker with the most gorgeous panoply.'

Lowe said that he could not reconcile Wentworth's motion with his former persistent advocacy of a policy of retrenchment in accordance with which the House had cut down salaries and abolished offices because the expenditure was more than an oppressed and groaning community could bear.

Then he continued :—

I, for one, could never sit down to these bi-weekly feasts. To me, fancy would ever be conjuring up some bloody Banquo's ghost —shades of displaced police magistrates, and curtailed clerks, to push me from my seat; while the banquet would vanish like a fairy feast, leaving nothing but rock, and dust, and ashes behind. . . . Right and proper it is that the Speaker of the House of Commons should be invested with all the pomp and state of circumstance; but how different our position in New South Wales. Here it seems to me that free institutions have been hung up, as it were, in a pillory, deprived of all that renders them respectable and respected in other countries. In such a condition it becomes us rather to cast off all empty forms, all outward show and display, and to endeavour rather to assert our dignity by the ceaseless effort to retrieve our constitutional rights, than by investing this mockery of a Legislature with the forms and attributes of an entirely different Assembly.

In the same earnest and eloquent spirit, the orator proceeded to express his regret that Mr. Wentworth, whom, on ' so many occasions he had been proud to follow, and to whose judgment he had often paid the greatest deference,' should have made such a proposal, and for a reason, he added, that concerned the honourable and learned member himself. For he had entertained an opinion that the day might arrive when that gentleman, retiring from the contentious arena of debate, sated with the strife and applause of political discussion, might have sought for repose in the Chair.

After this motion, how could such an event take place? Mr. Lowe then mentioned the cost of ' this legislative establishment,' and pointed out that they had not been sparing in censure of subordinate bodies that had cost more than they were worth. If they carried this motion, the public would soon suspect that they had no toleration for any jobs except their own.

Then, as though suddenly struck by the humour of the whole thing, he drew a ludicrous picture of the two rival candidates for the Speakership :—

I feel sure that the House will reject the motion which, if carried, I should expect to see followed up by two gentlemen with two bills of fare as candidates, one coaxing a vote with champagne, whilst the other tapped them on the shoulder with Burgundy—one tempting them with turtle, whilst the other preferred some other *recherché* delicacy.

At this stage, Mr. Robinson, the Quaker member for Melbourne, who had become a mere squatter's nominee, and an abject worshipper of Wentworth, must have given some indication of his views and intentions, for Mr. Lowe suddenly turned round upon him and observed that ' he fancied from the cheers of the hon. member for Melbourne that he intended

to follow humbly in the wake of the hon. and learned member
for Sydney, and no doubt in the speech he would address to
the House he would be able to reconcile the pomp and display,
which the motion was intended to encourage, with his own
modest-coloured and plain habiliments—just as he had found
it easy on another occasion to reconcile the transporting troops
and munitions of war with the principles of universal peace.'

Mr. Robinson did support the motion on the extraordinary
ground that the Lord Mayor of London had 14,000*l.* a year
granted him for state alone. An illustration that must have
filled the lordly Wentworth with ineffable scorn. As might
be expected, Charles Cowper expressed his regret that one by
whose side, session after session, he had fought the battle of
retrenchment, should have brought forward such a motion.
Even the Colonial Secretary and Attorney General, in calmer
and more official phraseology, condemned it. But the Joseph
Hume of the Council, Richard Windeyer, who thoughout his
career was a most consistent reformer of abuses, was really
indignant, and pointed out ' that the object of the hon. member for Sydney, and the object of those who resisted any reduction in the salary of the Governor were precisely similar ;
they both wanted to increase the strength of the table-cloth
chains which are so binding in many instances—and as the
Governor had the power of giving good dinners, his learned
friend wanted to set up an opposition shop on the popular
side.'

In fact, almost every member was opposed to the proposal,
and Mr. Wentworth, without a blush, announced that as the
feeling of the House was so thoroughly against him, he should
not press the motion, but would withdraw it.

In many respects the entire proceeding was eminently
characteristic of the two chief actors in the scene. One can
well imagine what a merry meeting it must have been when
Robert Lowe's personal friends next assembled at Nelson Bay,
and heard the story of Wentworth and the Speakership.

Lowe's activity as the representative member for St. Vincent and Auckland was unbounded. He was in the very prime of life, just turned thirty-five, and the position of entire independence which he now held in the Council seems to have stimulated his active and powerful mind. There was not a political question in any way affecting the rights of the community or the liberty of the individual colonist which he was not prepared to discuss with point and settle with promptitude.

For some time Lowe had ceased to contribute to the *Atlas*, over which, indeed, he exercised no control whatever after the year 1846. He now devoted his energies entirely to the Council Chamber and the Bar. After the too early death of Windeyer, he seems to have taken up the *rôle* of 'Joseph Hume' himself, and to have subjected all items of public expenditure to a constant and most rigid scrutiny. One afternoon, August 5, 1847, he entered the Council rather late, having been detained in court, and, turning to Deas Thomson, the Colonial Secretary (for whom personally he had no small measure of respect), he made some amusingly characteristic remarks on the easy-going and rapid manner of voting away public money. 'Most easily,' he said, 'did the wheels of legislation seem to run under the guidance of his hon. friend the Colonial Secretary, and the tractable and guiding disposition of the representatives of the people in that House.' He would advise the constituencies, one and all, never again to return a lawyer to represent their interests in the Council, because he might be by chance detained in court half an hour, unable to get away owing to some delay about a paltry sum of five or ten shillings, and by such an accident the public interests might suffer. He himself had been forced to wait, sorely against his will, that very afternoon while a jury were in anxious discussion whether they would give a plaintiff damages to the amount of 1*l.* 15*s.* or 2*l.* It was just four o'clock when he entered the House, and although there was on the paper a previous order of the day, he found in one short hour the House had voted away 26,000*l*. of the public money, and if it had not been for the timely entrance of his friend, the hon. member for Cumberland (Cowper), they would have added to it the further sum of 6,195*l*.

In May 1847, he moved for leave to bring in a Bill for compensating the families of persons killed by accident—a transcript of the Act then recently passed in the Imperial Parliament. But the subject which engrossed most of his attention from this time until his departure from Sydney was the Land Question.

On May 11, 1847, he made an important speech in presenting a petition signed by 138 of his constituents of St. Vincent and Auckland in favour of the reduction of the minimum price of land from 1*l*. an acre to 5*s*. In this speech he even supported the plan of what is known in Australia as 'deferred payments,' by which the settler pays for his land in instalments. Only by these means, he urged, could the Government hope to settle the people on the lands of the Colony; only in this way could a genuine yeomanry be formed in Australia.

Daily the breach between Robert Lowe and the squatter party grew wider. It only needed the promulgation of Earl Grey's new Land Policy to make that breach irreparable. In order to render intelligible his public conduct when that Minister's famous Orders in Council were promulgated, it is necessary to explain the transformation that had taken place in the *status* and position of the squatters of New South Wales, since the time when they trembled before the arbitrary acts of Lord Stanley and Sir George Gipps.

Smarting under the aggressions of Downing Street and the agrarian experiments which Lord Stanley and Sir George Gipps had learnt from the too ingenious Gibbon Wakefield, the squatters, being shrewd men, saw that their only hope of rescue was to appoint and pay a vigilant agent in the House of Commons. Men like Charles Buller and Bulwer Lytton,

with whom they were in constant correspondence, were either
too philosophical or too literary to make efficient wire-pullers;
but they found in the Hon. Francis Scott, brother of Lord
Polwarth, an almost ideal representative of their interests at
Westminster. Mr. Scott was a barrister, a director of the
South Western Railway Company, a first-class business man, a
country gentleman highly connected, and a Conservative M.P.
He accepted the post, the salary of which was fixed at 500*l.*
a year. Mr. Scott's position with regard to the Australian
pastoralists was precisely the same as that held by Mr.
Roebuck for the Jamaica planters, and by Edmund Burke
for the colonists of what is now the State of New York.
Some of his Australian principals were as well connected
as himself, having relatives in both Houses of Parliament;
and Mr. Scott was soon able to organise a party in the House
of Commons [1] which very narrowly watched the proceedings
of Colonial Secretaries of State.

It would be absurd to blame the squatters for doing their
utmost ' by constitutional means,' as the phrase goes, to improve their lot. But it very soon became apparent to Robert
Lowe that the new Secretary of State, Earl Grey, had been
induced to surrender the entire rights of the Australian community in the public estate to the pastoral tenants of the
Crown. Up to this point he had in the main fought and
worked side by side with Wentworth; but as soon as Earl
Grey's despatches were laid on the table of the Legislative
Council—and even before, as their purport had leaked out—
they became the leaders of two fiercely opposing parties.
Lord Grey had, indeed, little as he probably suspected it,

---

[1] At a great banquet in Sydney, Mr. Archibald Boyd remarked that ' In
paying their (the squatters') just tribute to Mr. Scott, they should not be forgetful
of the claims of others. They had received the greatest assistance from Lord
Polwarth, from Mr. Mackinnon, M.P. for Leamington, and Mr. Pringle, M.P.
for Selkirkshire.' How many Victorians, I wonder, know why one of their
counties is named ' Polwarth '; or that so much of the colony was in these days
a sheep-run of the brothers Boyd.

surrendered the entire colony into the hands of some five hundred pastoral tenants of the Crown. For he had actually been induced to bestow upon them fixed leases for fourteen years of their runs in the ' unsettled districts ' (that is to say, the whole of what is now New South Wales, and Victoria, and the South of Queensland, with the exception of a certain radius round the few chief towns). At the same time he retained the high Wakefieldian price of land, thus practically prohibiting further settlement.

When Earl Grey's Orders in Council arrived, a select committee, with Lowe as chairman, was appointed; its report was laid on the table of the House in September 1847. It was a powerful ' document.' Lord Grey, he said, had divided the colony into the ' Confiscated ' and the ' Unconfiscated.'

To make confusion worse confounded, Earl Grey next attempted to revive the practice of criminal transportation, to the huge delight of the squatters, to whom he had given a practical monopoly of the land, and thus proposed to follow it up by the bestowal of free convict labour. By this means the former suppliants became indeed masters of the situation.

The series of philippics—for they were nothing short of that—which Robert Lowe delivered in the old Legislative Council of New South Wales on the Land Question, would of themselves form a volume. In the opinion of so good a critic as the late Sir James Martin, Chief Justice of New South Wales who as a young man listened with rapt attention to them, the speeches were never surpassed even by Lord Sherbrooke's greatest efforts in England—the famous series of Anti-Reform speeches.

It will be possible to glance, and no more, at one or two of these orations, towards the end of this volume; but it is worthy of note in passing that these Australian speeches were on the popular side of a burning question; by means of them, though he alienated most of his old squatter friends, he became nothing less than the popular idol. Working men and the honest poor emigrants who had voyaged to the other side of the world only to find themselves more vigorously cut off from their 'common mother the Earth' even than in England, were loud in his praises; finding their way into the gallery of the old Council-Chamber, and seeing him standing up almost alone against a phalanx of Crown officials and pastoralists, now in complete alliance, they were unable to restrain the expression of their admiration. How different was the effect of his more famous orations against Reform in England need not now be dwelt upon.

By the death of Richard Windeyer in 1847, at the comparatively early age of forty-two, Lowe lost the one henchman whose services he would have valued at this crisis. It is singular that Sir George Gipps and his most persistent opponent should have passed away, one in England, the other in Launceston, Tasmania, at about the same time, and, I believe, from the same cause—internal cancer. Richard Windeyer had devoted so much of his energies to public matters, that he died leaving his private affairs in a far from prosperous condition. 'After my father's death,' writes his distinguished son, Sir William Windeyer, Puisne Judge of New South Wales, Lord Sherbrooke proved himself a most generous friend, and to his kindness it was owing that my interrupted education was continued.' In the same letter, which will be found in the second volume of this work, Sir William remarks that the youth of Australia owe to Lord Sherbrooke the Act by which they are enabled to go to the Bar without, as before, having to enter themselves at one of the Inns of Court in London.

Before the new Orders in Council reached Sydney, and were laid on the table of the House, Robert Lowe sounded the note of warning :—

The squatters now look on me as their enemy; but certain am I that, if they would open their eyes and look to their own true interests beyond the little vista of selfishness to which they at present confine their gaze, they would not call me their enemy. In this cause—the cause of the colony—no selfish feeling shall deter me from what I feel to be my great and responsible duty, and it is with proud feelings instead of shame that I am able to assert that I represent the opinions of almost every colonist in New South Wales who is not a squatter.

In the same strongly personal vein, showing how greatly he was moved by the change in his relations to his former friends, he went on to declare that he ' was not opposed to the squatters—he would make the burden upon them as light as possible ' :—

I would give them every encouragement to go forth into the wilderness, to gather the wealth of the colony, and to bring it back in wool ; but to give them a permanency of occupation of those lands—those lands to which they had no better right than that of any other colonist—which were the inalienable possession of generations and generations yet unborn, I can never consent to. Its effect would be to lock up all the lands of the colony, to reduce the rest of the population to a state of vassalage and serfdom, to throw abroad in the land the torch of discord, jealousy, and dissension. It would be to leave succeeding generations an agrarian law as a legacy, to be a bone of contention through future ages, such as history told them it had ever been. It would be to create in the social and political structure of the colony an element of perpetual strife, violence, and anarchy, till, wearied out with ceaseless struggles, it ended in the abrupt and total subversion of the order of things. The prophecy which I had ventured to make when urging the land resolutions on the Council, is now about to be fearfully fulfilled. I then predicted that a system of conciliation in lieu of one of oppression towards the squatters would be adopted by the Home Government. The measure now proposed by the present Minister is far more dangerous, though not so harsh and insulting, as the policy pursued by Lord Stanley. For against regulations intended to oppress a class, all could unite—it *forced* them to unite, and kept them together ; but in the present circumstances, the bait of immediate selfish emolument is held out, and many would, in the greedy contemplation of that, lose sight altogether of the general good.

From the time of the delivery of this speech, Robert Lowe assumed the post which Wentworth had relinquished—that of the popular leader in the Legislative Council.

Although his political position was now one of singular isolation—for he had both the Crown officials and the squatter party against him—he renewed to some extent his social relations with Government House. Thus, on the Queen's birthday, May 24, 1847, we find 'R. Lowe, Esq.' amongst those presented to Sir Charles Fitzroy at the levée.

Mrs. Lowe about this time writes to Mrs. Sherbrooke of Oxton :—

I have seen more of Sir Charles and Lady Mary Fitzroy. They are most polite to us, and I like them very much. I have just been planting seeds that were collected on Dr. Leichhardt's expedition ; a gentleman who accompanied him gave me a few seeds of each new flower which they discovered. I intend to make drawings of our new place. I only fear you will think that I have exaggerated its beauties, but I assure you that it would be beyond my power to do so. I lead a very quiet life, and now seldom go into Sydney. Robert rides backwards and forwards every day, and I am sure the exercise is most beneficial to him. The horses of this country are as safe and sure-footed as the mules of Switzerland, and display a surprising degree of intelligence, which I attribute to the life they lead as colts in the bush. They have a most extraordinary facility in finding their road, and seem to be aware of the habitation of man miles before reaching the spot.

After giving a rather deplorable account of the social condition of Sydney, both as to its so-called higher and lower classes, Mrs. Lowe pays a special compliment to the female emigrants from the north of Ireland. In another letter to the same correspondent she refers to the two little charges who were part of the Nelson Bay household.

The two little children are very good. Polly is now sitting close to Robert reading Burke's works ; she reads beautifully, and is not yet quite nine ; she will have been with us three years next Christmas. Bobby, I think, is my favourite ; he is such a nice little boy, with a sweet temper, and is growing really quite pretty ; he has dark eyes, and a most faithful countenance. You would be quite amused to see him wait at dinner. Our new Governor, Sir Charles Fitzroy, is very popular, and Lady Mary Fitzroy is liked.

Lady Mary Fitzroy, indeed, became a greater favourite daily, but was unfortunately killed in a carriage accident toward the close of 1847 at Paramatta, to the great grief of Mrs. Lowe and all who were admitted to her intimacy.

A somewhat dramatic scene took place at this time between Mr. Lowe and Bishop Broughton, against whom, it must be admitted, he displayed at times his strong anti-clerical bias. Mr. Lowe introduced a Bill to give clergymen a freehold in their benefices; the Bishop begged to be heard against it at the Bar of the House. 'The scene,' writes Mr. Rusden, 'was striking. . . Throughout his address, of which Mr. Lowe admitted the eloquence, the Bishop was heard with respectful attention.' The Bill was withdrawn.

It was also about this time that Lord Sherbrooke was brought into relations with Caroline Chisholm, 'the emigrant's friend.' That lady, an English Roman Catholic, had first arrived in New South Wales in 1839 with her husband, Captain Archibald Chisholm, of the Indian Army, then on sick leave. What she saw of the misery of the poor emigrants determined her to return and devote her life to their cause. Naturally, Lord Sherbrooke had as great a horror of professional female philanthropists as had the creator of Mrs. Jellyby; but, like most of the leading colonists at that time in Sydney, he freely acknowledged that Caroline Chisholm was a clear-headed and practical woman, with plenty of self-reliance, and fully able to carry into practice her charitable schemes. There was something, too, in the courage with which she had, single-handed, fought the battle of the poor and helpless outcasts of the Old World, which appealed to his sense of chivalry.

When Mrs. Chisholm first arrived she was received with marks of favour by the Roman Catholic clergy; but, as Mr. Samuel Sidney observes: 'As soon as they found it was to be a universal, or, to use the Irish term, a "godless," scheme of practical philanthropy, and not sectarian and proselytising, they opposed it vehemently.' As the same writer points out, the Crown officials were not very enthusiastic about housing and looking

after shoals of immigrants, as it meant 'more work, some supervision, and no increase of pay.' The squatters—who were
the chief employers of labour—preferred single men 'without
encumbrances ; ' whereas Mrs. Chisholm's pet scheme was to
settle married couples and their families on the lands of the
colony. Dr. Lang, who was a host in himself, at first, on
account of Mrs. Chisholm's faith, raised the ' No Popery ' cry,
though afterwards he somewhat reluctantly acknowledged the
honesty of her motives. Thus, like most persons who do a
work in the world, Mrs. Chisholm had to do it alone. Eventually she won the hearts of the poor of all races and creeds,
and the admiration of all worthy colonists. In August 1847
a committee was formed, of which Robert Lowe was a prominent member, to raise a subscription to augment Mrs.
Chisholm's slender income in order to assist her in her emigration scheme. Among those who supported this movement
with their names and subscriptions were : Alexander Macleay,
W. C. Wentworth, Charles Cowper, Dr. Nicholson, J. B.
Darvall, S. A. Donaldson, J. P. Robinson, W. H. Suttor,
Francis Lord, W. H. Manning (Solicitor-General), William
Bland, Captain O'Connell, and Clarke Irving—all representative colonists. As well as supporting the movement by
pen and purse, Robert Lowe wrote some verses in honour of
Caroline Chisholm, which I transcribe, partly because their
authorship has lately been disputed in various Australian
journals.

TO MRS. CHISHOLM

The guardian angel of her helpless sex,
Whom no fatigue could daunt, no crosses vex,
With manly reason and with judgment sure,
Crowned with the blessings of the grateful poor ;
For them, with unrepining love, she bore
The boarded cottage and the earthen floor,
The sultry day in tedious labour spent,
The endless strain of whining discontent.
Bore noonday's burning sun and midnight's chill,
The scanty meal, the journey lengthening still ;

Lavished her scanty store on their distress,
And sought no other guerdon than success,
Say, ye who hold the balance and the sword—
Into your lap the wealth of nations poured—
What have ye done with all your hireling brood
Compared with her, the generous and the good ?
Much ye receive, and little ye dispense :
Your alms are paltry, and your debts immense ;
Your toil's reluctant, freely hers is given :
You toil for earth, she labours still for heaven.

CHAPTER XX

MR. GLADSTONE'S PROPOSED PENAL COLONY

Archbishop Whately and Charles Buller—Dr. Bland and the Australian
Patriots—Review of the Transportation Question—Mr. Gladstone's De-
spatches to Sir Charles Fitzroy—Wentworth's Select Committee—The
Penal Colony in North Australia—Robert Lowe in the *Atlas*—A Popular
Idol

IN order to complete the narrative of Lord Sherbrooke's
career in New South Wales, it will be necessary to lay special
stress on the two great colonial questions in the discussion of
which he took so large a share, namely, the settlement of a
genuine yeomanry on the public lands, and the stoppage of
the transportation of criminals from Great Britain and
Ireland.

But before entering into these matters, it may be well to
pause and note that the chief actors heretofore on our stage
had now disappeared. Sir George Gipps was succeeded by
Sir Charles Fitzroy as Governor of New South Wales, and
Lord Stanley, the Colonial Secretary, was succeeded, firstly
for a brief while by Mr. Gladstone, and then by Earl Grey.
During Mr. Gladstone's tenure of the office he attempted an
experiment in Northern Australia, so remarkable in itself and
so suggestive, in the light of his successor Earl Grey's
transportation policy, that it may be well to consider it with
some degree of care and fulness.

When Mr. Gladstone stepped into Lord Stanley's place, an
article appeared in the *Atlas* headed ' British Politics,' in which
the new Colonial Secretary was thus referred to : ' Whether Mr.

x 2

Gladstone will prove himself to be more conciliatory and more constitutional [than Lord Stanley] remains to be seen. He is, we believe, an amiable and kind-hearted man, whose only failing is stated to be a leaning towards the foolish doctrines of Puseyism. If he has a due respect for the civil liberty of his fellow-subjects in the colonies as well as in the mother country, and has good sense and independence enough to liberate himself from the trammels of his underlings, he may do some good—as much perhaps as the present system will admit of.'

Little did the writer imagine that the first act of Mr. Gladstone as Colonial Secretary would be to send out despatches to Sir Charles Fitzroy in favour of the resumption of criminal transportation. To realise the commotion that the publication of these despatches caused in the colony it will be necessary to explain the state of public feeling which had grown up both in England and in Australia on this question.

Mainly through the exertions of that wonderfully clear-headed and able man, Richard Whately, Archbishop of Dublin, Sir William Molesworth's Committee of the House of Commons (1838) had pronounced against transportation to Australia as the accepted form of what was called 'secondary' as distinguished from capital punishment. Before this committee Dr. Ullathorne, the Roman Catholic Vicar-General, gave some appalling personal testimony as to the social condition of the island of New Norfolk, whither were drafted all the worst and most incorrigible convicts from New South Wales. Nothing, however, even in the pamphlet which he subsequently published on this subject, is more horrible than the plain statement made to Sir William Burton by an intelligent convict when the judge visited New Norfolk for the purpose of trying a number of refractory prisoners in 1834. 'Let a man's heart,' he said, 'be what it will when he comes here, his Man's heart is taken from him, and there is given to him the heart of a Beast.' Of course, the colony of New South

Wales was by no means in the awful state of its wretched
insular satellite, which was entirely reserved as a receptacle
for incorrigible criminality. For all that, the evidence given
before the Select Committee of the House of Commons clearly
shows that it was in a condition that no civilised and self-
respecting community could much longer tolerate, while Van
Diemen's Land was only a shade better, if at all, than Norfolk
Island.

But it should be clearly stated that there is no greater
myth than the prevailing impression that shiploads of criminals were forced by hard-hearted English officials on unwilling
colonists. This statement, which may sound rather heterodox,
especially in the ears of ' Young Australia,' can be proved to
demonstration. Dr. William Bland, one of the leading colonists of New South Wales, who was then the colleague of
Wentworth in the representation of the city of Sydney, wrote
on behalf of the Australian Patriotic Association a series of
' Letters to Charles Buller, Jun., Esq., M.P.' These ' Letters '
were published, and dedicated to ' William Charles Wentworth, Esq., M.C., in Admiration of his Talents, and as a
Token of sincere Regard.' (Sydney, 1849.)

The purpose of this correspondence with Charles Buller
was to endeavour to convince him that the transportation of
criminals, and the assignment of convicts to private service,
were alike beneficial to England and to Australia. These
' Letters ' afford conclusive evidence that while leading Englishmen, notably such men as Archbishop Whately, Sir William
Molesworth, and Charles Buller, were on the broadest and
most disinterested grounds working for the cessation of
criminal transportation, many leading colonists, among whom
were the ' Australian patriot,' William Charles Wentworth, his
friend and colleague Dr. Bland, and Sir John Jamieson, the
most prominent of pastoralists, were moving heaven and
earth—or, rather, doing a vast amount of subterranean political
wire-pulling—to stock their country afresh with English and

Irish jail-birds.[1] In one of these letters to Charles Buller Dr. Bland unblushingly observes : ' *We are aware of the diffi-culties in our way—that the leaders of every party in the House of Commons are opposed to the continuance of those systems, par-ticularly to that of private assignment.*'

The patriotic doctor then goes on to explain to his correspon-dent that an ' assigned convict ' is, in respect to his ' assignee,' precisely in the same position ' as the free servant is to his master.'

It is startling, but perhaps wholesome, to compare such views with the notable utterance of Archbishop Whately, who wrought a revolution on the subject in the minds of thought-ful Englishmen.

The punishment (said Whately to Judge Denman) is one which causes more mischief than it does pain, and which is the more severe to each in proportion as he is less of such a character as to be deserving of it. . . . . When Shakespeare makes someone remark to Parolles : 'If you could find a country where but women were, who have undergone so much shame, you might *begin an impudent nation*,' he little thought, probably, that the experi-ment of beginning such a nation would be seriously tried, and from not having quite enough of shameless women, we should be sending out cargoes of girls to supply the deficiency.[2]

Charles Buller, in reply to Dr. Bland, pointed out to him and the other ' Australian Patriots,' that, as long as trans-portation existed, they could not hope to have responsible government. Buller knew well what he was talking about, and did not mince matters. ' I am fully convinced,' he wrote, ' that it is idle to make any effort for the establish-ment of representative institutions in New South Wales as long as transportation to it continues.'

For, as he pointed out, even the most liberal-minded Eng-lish statesman would hesitate to confer such institutions on a

[1] At no time were many Scottish criminals sent to Australia, which is a reason generally overlooked for the superior energy and *morale* which have made the Scotch so pre-eminently successful as colonist there.

[2] *Life and Correspondence of Archbishop Whately*, third edition, p. 96.

convict-ridden community. Free emigrants of a better class, too, would not choose a penal colony for their adopted home, and that of their wives and children. ' Nor will that prejudice,' he added, ' be removed while men of great influence like the Archbishop of Dublin, and periodical publications of no less influence, continue by denunciations of the state of the Penal Colonies to foster and augment the dislike to emigrate to them.' But Dr. Bland and the 'Australian Patriots' were quite unabashed, and even ventured to controvert the Archbishop's unanswerable arguments against transportation ; for which of us cannot find arguments in support of a profitable practice ?

The following brief letter from Bland to Charles Buller is quite an historical curiosity in its way :—

Sydney : November 22, 1840.

You state that all parties are agreed in withholding free institutions from New South Wales while it continues to be a penal colony. We regret the error on which this determination is founded, and not less the lateness of the receipt of information in this country in respect of that error, and which alone prevented its timely refutation on our part. This circumstance we attribute to the unfortunate interval in the representation of this country in Parliament between the years 1837 and 1839. For though on the retirement of Mr. Bulwer,[1] that office was nominally transferred to yourself, yet from your unavoidable absence in Canada we have been possessed of the benefit of your important services only from the opening of the session of 1839.

Despite these 'Australian patriots,' transportation practically ceased from 1840, and no criminals were sent to New South Wales during the governorship of Sir George Gipps. As often happens in the conduct of human affairs, this great moral reformation came at the very worst possible time. It came

---

[1] Lord Lytton, the novelist, who afterwards became Secretary of State for the Colonies. He had previously written to the Patriotic Association, advising them to appoint a Parliamentary agent in London ; they accordingly appointed him, and forwarded a cheque for 500*l.*, the amount of the annual honorarium, which, however, he declined to accept, and gave his services gratuitously.

at that time of terrible financial depression when the whole
colony seemed to be in a state of insolvency; and it increased
the commercial gloom and made the lot of the squatters and
other settlers still harder. For it must be remembered that as
long as the colony was an Imperial penal station, there were
thousands of convicts and hundreds of soldiers to be fed, and
consequently fortunes were made (chiefly by rascals) out of
Government contracts. Trade, especially in the sale of rum, was
brisk. Nor can it be denied that for some years the free emigration to New South Wales was very inadequate both in quality
and quantity, so much so that these ' Australian patriots ' and
their friends all over the country were able to make out a
case in favour of the resumption of transportation.

Still, any keen and impartial observer on the spot could have
discerned that New South Wales was steadily improving socially,
morally, and financially, and that, as a consequence, free and
untainted immigration would soon set in. Even before Sir
George Gipps left there was every sign of increased material prosperity, when suddenly, like a thunderbolt, came Mr.
Gladstone's ill-omened despatch to Sir Charles Fitzroy, in
which he threw amongst the colonists, like the apple of discord,
the renewal of criminal transportation, and, as a consequence,
' cheap labour.'

This despatch was dated Downing Street, April 30, 1846,
and began as follows :—

To Governor Sir C. A. Fitzroy, New South Wales.

Sir,—I am desirous that at the commencement of your administrative duties as Governor of New South Wales, you should be
possessed, in a form as definite as the state of the case admits, of the
views of Her Majesty's Government with regard to the introduction
of convicts into that colony.

You are aware that the practice has been for some years past to
exclude New South Wales from the sentences of transportation
passed in this country. . . . . Her Majesty's Government sym-
pathises with the impatience of the colonists of New South Wales
under the system which prevailed there some years ago. . . . .

But the question is essentially and entirely different, whether it might not be a measure favourable to the material fortunes of New South Wales and unattended with injury to its higher interests to introduce, either directly from England at the commencement of their sentences, or from Van Diemen's Land at some period during their course, a number of prisoners, small in comparison with the numbers that were carried to that colony under the former system of transportation.

It is not difficult to imagine the joy of Wentworth, Bland and the Australian Patriotic Association, when Sir Charles Fitzroy made this despatch public, as he did at once, with a view of eliciting colonial opinion. The present colony of Victoria, whose boast it is that it never directly received English criminals, was selected as a *corpus vile* for the experiment.

The labour of such persons [convicts] would be more liberally remunerated in Port Phillip than in Van Diemen's Land. They would be much more thinly dispersed among the population, would form a scarcely perceptible element in the composition of society, and would enjoy those favourable opportunities of improving habits and character, which transportation, according to its first theory, was designed to afford ; and if this disposal of them, during the latter portion of their respective terms, should follow upon a period of really efficient discipline in the probation gangs (which as yet I by no means despair of their being made to yield) during the earlier portion, in such cases I conceive, while the economical benefit to Port Phillip would be great, the hazard from which such an immigration can never perhaps entirely be set free, would be reduced to its minimum, and the hopes of the ultimate reformation of the convicts proportionally raised.

One can again picture the jubilation of the Messrs. Boyd and those other pastoral tenants who had made Port Phillip ' one vast squattage,' at this prospect of cheap convict labour. Mr. Gladstone did not even stop here, but threw out the suggestion that a limited number of convicts from England might be introduced into New South Wales itself for the execution of public works, such as the making and repair of roads, ' always presuming that they are neither destructive to health, nor essentially liable to moral objections.'

This is the gist of the despatch. Never did the happy Epicureanism of Sir Charles Fitzroy display its superiority over the severer sense of responsibility in Sir George Gipps than when, on receipt of this document, he at once published it, and so gave the colonists, as he said, an opportunity of deciding the matter for themselves.[1] Such a despatch would have given Sir George many a sleepless night, and, probably, have led to a fierce conflict with the Legislative Council in which (like the brave gentleman he was) he would have borne the brunt, and done his best to shelter his master in Downing Street.

This despatch threw the community into a state of wild commotion. Wentworth, who had now become the chief of the ' transportation party ' and the political leader of the ' squattocracy,' moved in the Council for a select committee to inquire into and report upon the entire subject of the transportation of criminals into New South Wales. It was duly appointed, with Mr. Wentworth himself as Chairman, and Robert Lowe as one of its members.

If anyone will take the trouble to read the evidence given before this transportation committee, he will be simply astonished to see how uncompromisingly the squatters gave their evidence in favour of again receiving English criminals. Mr. Benjamin Boyd, for instance, stated that ten thousand convicts could be taken ' beyond the boundaries,' and be profitably assigned to the squatters. He would land them at Portland Bay, Twofold Bay, and Moreton Bay, so as to avoid Sydney and Melbourne. Every employer preferred ticket-

[1] Sir Charles Fitzroy was in reality of that type of aristocratic viceroy, now almost universal in our great self-governing colonies. He was the third son of General Lord Charles Fitzroy, brother of the Duke of Grafton. His wife, Lady Mary, was daughter of the Duke of Richmond. A man with such connections was not likely to fear the powers of Downing Street, as did the class of ' official ' governors, whose pension and promotion depended entirely on the Secretary of State. On landing on the lovely shores of Port Jackson, Sir Charles is said to have observed : ' I cannot conceive how Sir George Gipps could permit himself to be bored by anything in this delicious climate.'

of-leave men to bounty emigrants. 'I have few immigrants,' he added, 'in my employ.' He maintained that the Americans had got control of the South Sea fisheries in the Pacific because of the scarcity of labour in the Australian colonies.[1] Mr. Lowe plied Mr. Boyd with many pertinent questions, to which he gave careful and guarded replies ; but there was evidently the happiest understanding between him and Mr. Wentworth, as the following questions and answers will show.

By the Chairman.—Do you not think the ticket-of-leave system one of the happiest devices possible for reforming these people ?— Yes : I have already mentioned that I believe I am one of the largest employers of labour in the colony, and I have always found the ticket-of-leave men the most efficient servants.

By Mr. Lowe.—Would there not be an outcry raised if you were to pay these people wages, that they were placed on the same footing as free men ?—Such has been the demand for labour, and the exorbitant rate of wages demanded by the bounty emigrants, that we have been obliged by necessity to hire expirees from Van Diemen's Land ; and until there is a fall of at least 50 per cent. in their demands, the emigrants will have no right to complain.

By Mr. Lowe.—Might not this state of things be a means of deterring free people from coming to this colony altogether ?—I do not think it would have that effect, as the prosperity of the colony, with an ample supply even of convict labour, would soon induce free immigrants to seek it as a field for employment.

Mr. Wentworth then proceeded to ask the witness some questions about 'systematic religious instruction ' for these ' exiles,' which Mr. Boyd answered in the most beautiful and becoming spirit.[2] The report of this select committee bears

[1] Mr. Boyd said Great Britain and her colonies had only fifty-nine vessels ; America 670 whalers in the Pacific, employing 20,000 men, consuming upwards of 200,000*l.* worth of provisions annually, and importing into American harbours 1,666,000*l.* ; yet these vessels came 16,000 miles to fish on our coasts.

[2] Mr. Benjamin Boyd actually indited and published a letter to Sir William Denison, then Governor of Van Diemen's Land, ' On the expediency of transferring the unemployed labour of that colony to N.S.W.' (1847), in which he observes : 'England formed penal colonies at the uttermost ends of the earth ; the capital and free labour which followed were not enticed hither under any provisions of abolishing the convict establishments ; capitalists and labourers

evident traces of Wentworth's masterly hand, though it is not difficult to perceive the restraining touch of Lowe, who was about to become the principal agitator against transportation in any shape to any part of Australia.

In this report there is a clause about a 'new penal settlement immediately to be formed on the very northern boundary of this colony.' This refers to a subsequent scheme propounded by Mr. Gladstone to Sir Charles Fitzroy. He required only a week after the sending off of the original despatch to concoct an entirely new plan for the revival of transportation to Australia. Writing from Downing Street on May 7, 1846, he proposed to found a convict colony in Northern Australia, northward of the 26th degree of south latitude, by letters patent under the Great Seal of the United Kingdom. Sir Charles Fitzroy, like most of the disciples of Epicurus, was not without a sense of humour; but it is difficult to say whether he sighed or smiled as he read this eminently characteristic despatch, and thought of the rising tide of popular indignation in Sydney when he should publish it in the newspapers. Mr. Gladstone thus began his discourse to Sir Charles :—

No truths can at once be more familiar, weighty, and indisputable, than that the first rudiments of every new colony should be selected from the most virtuous, intelligent, and hardy classes of the colonising State ; and should be composed of capitalists and manual labourers, bearing a due proportion to each other.

I sincerely and deeply regret the impossibility of taking those great principles for our guide in the present instance.

Public opinion has demanded, and Parliament has enacted, the abolition of the punishment of death in almost all cases except treason, murder, and the infliction of wounds or injuries with a murderous intention. Hence the importance of an effectual

eagerly flocked to shores where the large disbursements of the public treasury, and the sustained demand for labour, presented a standard of profit and remuneration unattainable in the mother country, and in the attractive rates of interest and the high scales of wages and rations, both the employer and the employed waived all reference to the " moral contagion " *which a few alarmists now profess to dread.'*

secondary punishment has become greater than ever.—[Hence—to cut Mr. Gladstone a little short—transportation to Australia to be revived.]

But here a difficulty presented itself. 'It has happened, either by the enactment of positive laws, or by pledges said to have been made by her Majesty's Government, that no place is left in Australia for the reception of transported convicts, except Van Diemen's Land and Norfolk Island.' Hence, Mr. Gladstone argued, the necessity for the erection of the new convict colony of Northern Australia under Colonel Barney.

The despatch concludes :—

I cannot but advert to the possible, though I do not doubt improbable, difficulty with which you may have to contend. I advert to the dissatisfaction with which the Legislature and the Colonists of New South Wales may contemplate this measure. I should much lament the manifestation or existence of such a feeling. It would be with sincere regret that I should learn that so important a body of Her Majesty's subjects were inclined to oppose themselves to the measures which I have thus attempted to explain. Any such opposition must be encountered by reminding those from whom it might proceed, in terms alike respectful and candid, that it is impossible that her Majesty should be advised to surrender what appears to be one of the vital interests of the British Empire—[i.e., to create a fresh Alsatia at the Antipodes].

Having practically relieved New South Wales, at no small inconvenience to ourselves (as soon as it became a burden), of receiving convicts from this country, we are acquitted of any obligations in that respect, which any colonist the most jealous for the interest of his native or adopted country could ascribe to us.

In a second despatch, covering two newspaper columns, dated May 8, he gives minute instructions as to the method of establishing the new convict colony of Northern Australia. Nor was this all. The *Lord Auckland* sailed early in January for Northern Australia, having on board : Lieutenant-Colonel Barney, superintendent of the projected colony, Mrs. Barney, and family; W. W. Billyard, Esq., chairman of quarter sessions; James S. Dowling, Esq., crown prosecutor ; E. C. Merewether,

Esq., acting colonial secretary; Mr. G. H. Barney, clerk;
Assistant Commissary-General Darling; Captain Day, 99th
Regiment, Mrs. Day, and family; Mr. W. A. Brown, deputy-
sheriff; Mr. Robertson, surgeon; Mr. George O. Allen; Mr.
W. K. Macknish, wife and family. These, with twenty
soldiers, and some labourers and servants, comprised the
nucleus of Mr. Gladstone's penal colony.

However, Mr. Gladstone retired from the Colonial Office
at this juncture, and his successor, Earl Grey, wrote promptly
to Sir Charles Fitzroy, on November 15, to this effect :—

> I cannot conceal from you that her Majesty's present con-
> fidential advisers dissent from the view taken of this subject by
> their immediate predecessors, even in reference to the state of facts
> under which they acted, and to the considerations by which they
> were guided. . . . Since the decision was taken there has been such
> a change in the state and circumstances of society in the Australian
> colonies as would, could it have been foreseen, have doubtless been
> regarded by the authors of the project as conclusive against it.
> . . . Her Majesty will, therefore, be advised to revoke the letters
> patent under which North Australia has been erected into a separate
> colony; and the establishment formed there must be immediately
> discontinued.

Mr. Lowe rose to the occasion. His pen now rarely found
journalistic employment, for, after re-entering the Council, he
soon ceased his connection with the *Atlas*; but such a subject
as Mr. Gladstone's proposed penal colony was altogether too
tempting. In the first instance, he dealt with it in a stirring
leading article, written in his most pungent style. Then,
when the expedition under Colonel Barney sailed out of Port
Jackson, he wooed the comic Muse:—

> How blest the land where Barney's gentle sway
> Spontaneous felons joyfully obey,
> Where twelve bright bayonets only can suffice
> To check the wild exuberance of vice —
> Where thieves shall work at trades with none to buy,
> And stores unguarded pass unrifled by,
> Strong in their new found rectitude of soul,
> Tamed without law and good without control.

Still more ludicrous was the subsequent wail over the fiasco, which appeared in the form of an inscription on the monument proposed to be erected on the spot where Colonel Barney landed at Port Curtis :—

> Here Barney landed—memorable spot
> Which Mitchell never from the map shall blot . . .
> For six long hours he did the search pursue,
> For six long hours—and then he thirsty grew ;
> Back to the rescued steamer did he steer,
> Drew the loud cork and quaffed the foaming beer ;
> Then ate his dinner with tremendous gust,
> And with champagne relieved his throat adust,
> Fished for his brother flat-fish from the stern,
> And thus victorious did to Sydney turn !

Passing from poetry to the hard facts of the cost of this futile experiment, I find, from an official memorandum, that it amounted to some 15,402*l*. 6*s*. 2*d*., all of which was simply thrown into the sea.

However little one may accept the absurd saying, *Vox populi vox Dei*, it is quite true that it was the bulk of the respectable labouring men and women of Australia who won the battle that cleared their shores of the taint of convictism. As will be shown in a succeeding chapter, they found in Robert Lowe a valiant and eloquent leader, who threw himself heart and soul into the question, and became—what he never was before or after—the idol of the masses.

CHAPTER XXI

NOTES OF A GREAT SPEECH

Legislative Council, Sydney : Oct. 9, 1846

BEFORE passing on to the stormy scenes, many of them enacted under the blue vault of heaven, when Robert Lowe, in
defiance of all his inborn traditions—his love of close reasoning, his keen but scholarly wit, his distaste for mere empty de-
clamation—found himself compelled to be the leading agitator
in the colony, let us take a glance at some notes of a fine and
thoughtful oration delivered by him in the Legislative Council
on his favourite subject of education.

This was on the evening of October 9, 1846, when he rose
to move :—

> That an Address be presented to his Excellency the Governor,
> praying that he will be pleased to place on the Estimates of
> Expenditure the sum of 2,000l. to meet the expenses of schools to
> be conducted on the principles of Lord Stanley's National System
> of Education ; and that his Excellency will be pleased to appoint
> a Board favourable to that system, and take all other steps necessary
> for bringing it into immediate and effective operation.

It will be remembered that almost from the time he
entered the Council as a Crown nominee, Mr. Lowe had
been the chief educational reformer in Australia. The question, moreover, had for the last two years been amply discussed both in the Council and on the public platform.
During this period the clergy had organised their forces,

while the leaders of the Roman Catholic church had made a complete *volte-face*. It was from that quarter that the reformers had most to fear ; for its flocks were both numerous and ignorant. Mr. Lowe began to see that the victory would not be won easily, and that, do what he might, it would in all likelihood take some years simply to ' educate his masters '— the voters in the community. But he remained undaunted ; and, on the evening referred to, set himself the task not only of explaining the advantages of a general system of education, but of meeting and controverting the position taken up by his opponents, who declared that he was advocating a ' godless ' system. His answer to this charge will furnish the first extract from his speech, which is given as nearly as possible in the words he used in addressing the Legislative Council.

A ' Godless ' System.

The objection urged to this system when it was first brought forward was that it was a godless and irreligious system. Now, I am ready to confess that I am an advocate for irreligious teaching— that I would have people made shoemakers or tailors without the aid of religion at all—that all mechanical arts should in fact be taught irreligiously. I am of opinion that religion should be mixed up with none of these things, on the principle that it is sufficient to teach one thing well at a time ; and if children are to be taught to read and write, their attention should be confined to reading and writing, and I repudiate the idea of teaching reading and writing according to any system of religion. So also I am for an irreligious system of arithmetic, for I can see nothing but evil from blending theology with simple addition, or cosmogony with subtraction. God forbid that I should wish children to be brought up irreligiously. I would have a child instructed in religion as in anything else, but what I want is that religion should not necessarily be mixed up with instruction in reading, writing, and arithmetic. The whole fallacy, indeed, turns on the word education ; if the word meant reading and writing, then ought religion to have nothing to do with the matter ; but if it embraced a wider scope—if it contemplated the entire training of man—the fitting for higher views and nobler purposes than those for which his original nature fitted him—if it was to raise and improve the whole faculties of his being, to make him a

enlightenment, or to encourage the splitting up of the community into sectarian parties? Apart from the selfishness, or cowardice, involved in submitting to the latter system for the sake of a little peace, could there be a doubt on such a question? Would that Council stop to calculate when such a chance was offered? I apprehend not. It will not be excusable if it does not by every means in its power seek to put a stop to the spirit of bigotry and sectarianism everywhere prevailing. Some there are too old to be instructed, from whom these pernicious principles cannot be extracted, people who have come out with all their burning prejudices deeply instilled into them, and who will bear them to the grave. But finite as its power is for good, and infinite for evil, it is within the sphere of that House to say that these prejudices shall wane, if not entirely perish with the present generation—it is within its sphere to prepare a happier soil in the minds of the rising generation, for those great principles of religion which are inherent in every shade and denomination of Christianity.

Common or Conjunct Schools.

The result was that those schools did enlighten the people—did free them from crime, the offspring of ignorance—did make them wiser, happier, better. What, on the contrary, had been the effects of the denominational system? It had been to keep the many in darkness, whilst for the sake of show it had educated the few; nor could there ever be any other result while the teaching of doctrinal points of religion was mixed up with the principles of ordinary education. I will now touch on another branch of the subject, or rather view the subject in another light. It would appear, whether they would or would not, that this colony was to receive convicts, that the Home Government had so willed it; and whether they received them direct, or as expirees, convictism was to be its destiny. If then we do not at once decide on some general plan of elementary instruction, even that Volume on which our religion is based, in which its precepts are to be read, and its promises made known, will be a sealed book to two thirds of the rising population of the country. And what must be the result? That the ignorant population will greedily receive the invitations to vice and crime, and the leaven of convictism will leaven the whole lump. Instead of rising upwards in the scale, for the reformation of the convicts, they must degrade down to a level with them. What elements, I would ask, are we not letting loose over the land if we shut our faces to the extension of education? If we refuse to give the power to read to the many, in order that the few may be instructed in accordance with religious prejudices—instead of becoming the seat of religion, of morality, of enlightenment and civilisation to which it might have been converted, the colony must sink down into the depths of degradation too dreadful to describe. Polluted and lost, her state would only be that which the poet had pictured, and which, except in the words of the poet, I will not attempt to picture.

Religion, blushing, veils her sacred fires,
And unawares Morality expires;
So thy dread empire, Chaos, is restored,
Light dies before the uncreating Word.
Thy hand, great Anarch, lets the curtain fall,
And universal darkness covers all.

That, I believe to be the destiny reserved for this colony if a more extended system of education be not immediately set on foot ; and whatever might be the opinion of those whose eyes are blinded in this matter, and who would reserve them for that fate with a dogged determination, I believe it to be the duty of this Council, its imperative duty, to take this matter into its own hands, regardless of clamour out of doors, and to legislate for the present and future enlightenment, the present and future welfare and happiness, of the people by adopting the system I have advocated.

Although the famous lines from the *Dunciad* may seem somewhat forced in the eyes of Australians and Englishmen of the present day, they were singularly appropriate at a time when English ministers and colonial capitalists had leagued together for the revival of criminal transportation.

With all his eloquence, Lowe only succeeded in carrying his Address by twelve votes to ten, and Sir Charles Fitzroy, following the precedent of his predecessor—prompted, it was said, by the same adviser, Bishop Broughton—refused to place the 2,000*l.* asked for on the estimates. But, as the subsequent history of Australia has shown, these statesmanlike, if at the time unsuccessful, efforts have borne good fruit. It is to the broad and philosophical teaching of Robert Lowe in these early years, more than to that of any other Australian public man, that our fellow subjects at the Antipodes owe their existing State school system.

CHAPTER XXII

MR. LOWE AND THE SQUATTERS

Earl Grey's Land Bill—Mr. Lowe on Downing Street solicitude—Wentworth
and the Waste Lands—Roman Nobles and Australian Squatters—Lowe's
appeal to the Squatters—To the Council—Lowe's Reply to Wentworth—His
Pamphlet—The Division—Review of the Land Question—Agrarian Gamblers
—Character of Wentworth—Lowe determines to return to England

On June 1, 1847, Earl Grey's despatches relative to his new
Australian Land Bill were laid on the table of the Legislative
Council. They had the effect of consolidating the squatters'
influence, and of winning over the dreaded Wentworth to the
side of the Government. The bribe was a tremendous one.
By the regulations of the Orders in Council, the whole of the
Crown lands of New South Wales—which, let it be borne in
mind, then included the present colony of Victoria—were
divided into three classes, the 'settled,' the 'intermediate,'
and the 'unsettled' districts. In the settled districts the
squatters' 'runs' were to be leased from year to year; in the
intermediate, eight years' leases were granted to the Crown
tenants, subject to two months' notice in the event of any part
of the run being required for sale; while, in the unsettled
districts, the occupying squatters were granted fourteen years'
lease with the right to a second term of fourteen years if the
lands were still unsold. Moreover, the squatters of the intermediate, as well as of the unsettled districts were to have
what were called 'pre-emptive rights,' by which, if they
themselves chose to become the purchasers at the upset price
of 1*l.* per acre, their runs were exempted altogether from

public auction. Consider for a moment the effect of this
portentous agrarian experiment for which Earl Grey was responsible.

The colony of Victoria, then the district of Port Phillip,
was, as Mr. Boyd said, at that time 'one vast squattage.'
Although so few years had elapsed since Sir Thomas Mitchell
had first gazed upon the rich pastures of what he called
'Australia Felix,' it was completely divided from the Murray
to the sea into sheep and cattle runs. An enterprising young
Englishman with capital, arriving about this time to 'take
up country,' went overland to Sydney and informed the
Governor that every acre in Port Phillip was already appropriated. Now, under Lord Grey's Orders in Council the whole
of the present colony of Victoria, with the exception of a small
area round three towns, Melbourne, Geelong, and Portland,
was to be practically handed over for what seems an indefinite
period in the life of a young community, to these squatters.
We have here the origin of the long and bitter agrarian strife
in that colony, as well as an explanation of the deep-rooted
feeling of hostility felt towards the squatters as a class by the
bulk of the community—a feeling which did not die out until,
by successive local Land Acts, the Crown lands were clumsily
'unlocked.'

It is a striking proof of the provincial spirit which is still
so prominent a characteristic in all the Australian colonies,
that the best informed writers in Victoria, in dealing with the
Land Question, always attribute their partial emancipation
from the squattocracy whom Earl Grey had made into a
privileged caste, purely to their own local efforts, to the Land
Convention of Melbourne, or to Mr. J. M. Grant's '42nd
clause,' in an amended Land Act. They entirely overlook, or,
rather, have quite forgotten, the magnificent stand which
Robert Lowe made in Sydney in 1847, before Victoria existed
as a colony, when it was merely a pastoral adjunct of New
South Wales, known as the Port Phillip district.

If, however, they investigate the matter, they will find that to Robert. Lowe, and to him alone, belongs the honour of upholding, almost single-handed, the rights of the whole community to the Crown lands of Australia; and they will also find, further, that it was he who first fought their battle against the combined forces of the English Government, the local Executive in Sydney, and the whole weight of the squatter party, led by the former champion of the people, William Charles Wentworth.

As soon as the Orders in Council were made public, this unequal battle began. Before they were promulgated, Mr. Lowe, on September 25, 1846, had moved and carried a resolution as to the reduction of the upset price of land. It is noteworthy that Wentworth and his party still supported this line of policy. On June 21, 1847, with Earl Grey's despatches on the table, he moved a resolution : ' That with reference to the proposed Orders in Council laid on the table of this House on June 1, 1847, this House reaffirms the resolution agreed to on September 25, 1856, that is to say, that while the minimum upset price of 1*l*. per acre is maintained, the squatting system can never be settled on a just and satisfactory basis.' On this occasion he failed, and the Council stultified itself by negativing its previous action. Robert Lowe, however, delivered a most memorable speech, which contains a fuller exposition of the Australian Land Question than any ever delivered. Seizing upon an admission of Lord Grey in his despatch ' that this squatting occupation is only to be temporary,' he exclaimed :—

Glad am I to find that the noble Secretary had not so far forgotten his own English feelings, had not so abandoned his duty as an adviser of his Sovereign, as to have contemplated the perpetuation, in this dependency of the Crown, of so pernicious, so degraded a system. That he looked forward to a period—if these orders were carried out I fear an imaginary period—when the broad wastes of New South Wales would cease to be wastes, but would become the abode of civilised men, and flourish with the arts of life. I say it is an imaginary period to which Earl Grey, through the ignorance or hallucination in which he is involved, looks forward—and if this dream of settling the squatters on the Crown lands, and at the same time maintaining the minimum price is acted on; it must remain for ever an imaginary period. The principle of the despatch was right, but the means of working out that principle were utterly wrong ; and this was one of the blessings which we owe to legislation 16,000 miles off. The intention of Earl Grey was evidently to correct an abuse. But were these leases the way to avoid the abuse of favouritism ? Did they not involve a more glaring, a more extended system of favouritism than was ever before displayed in the world ? What right had any particular class of a community to the grant of particular rights and privileges denied to others ? On what ground—I reiterate the challenge of the other night—on what ground did the squatters stand forth and claim these concessions extended to them in favouritism over the whole of the rest of the colony, who had an equal right and an equal claim ? Where were the great services they had rendered to the State ? Where were the records of their noble deeds, and high achievements, and their devoted services ? Where were these to be found ? The splendid estates conferred on a Wellington or a Marlborough were no marks of favouritism, were in no sense the abuse of patronage, but the just reward for distinguished services offered by a grateful people. But could the squatters put in any such claim as this ?

He then proceeded to argue with cutting irony that if this were Lord Grey's plan for averting favouritism, it would have been better to hand over the freehold instead of the fourteen years' leases to the squatters. Another argument that Earl Grey used for granting these leases, and at the same time maintaining the high upset price of land, was a favourite one with the disciples of Gibbon Wakefield, that it would prevent the dispersion of the people. This word dispersion seems to have had a most terrifying effect upon all the colonising theorists of that time. Wakefield had taught them that to encourage, or rather not to check, this tendency to seek ' fresh woods and pastures new,' which is surely the very essence of the colonising spirit, was to bring about a return to barbarism. So we find Earl Grey supporting this wholesale alienation of the public estate on the ground that it would act as a check ' to that tendency to an undue dispersion of the inhabitants,

which is found so strong in countries in progress of settlement, and where the population is still very small in proportion to the extent of territory.'

Lowe's reply to this form of Downing Street maternal
solicitude is worth preserving.

It is somewhat strange that such a doctrine as this should
be inculcated by Earl Grey, the strenuous, the uncompromising
advocate of Free-trade, the enthusiastic admirer and follower of
Cobden, and the consistent supporter of all the great measures
which have been passed of late years for ensuring the freedom of
the commerce of Great Britain. In England this statesman would
have the channels of trade to run free and uncontrolled, but he
disclaims this natural and social right when dealing with Australia.
In England, the butcher, the baker, the builder, the farmer—all
trades, all callings, are left unrestricted, and men follow their
own inclinations. But the rule is not to be applied to the colony,
where we are not able to judge what is best for our own interests.
Here, if left to themselves, men would disperse—and why should
they not disperse, if they thought it fit and profitable to do so?
Could not Earl Grey see that if men felt it to be their interest to
disperse, impelled by the hope of gain, or even the mere love of
adventure, they would do so in spite of all these absurd restrictions
intended to concentrate them? This policy of compulsory concentration, if it could be carried into effect, would operate with immense
power in checking those hopes and feelings of the human breast
which were the soil in which the spirit of enterprise had root and
growth. Concentration is the result of wealth, not the cause of
it. When men—when a community—grew wealthy, they would
always concentrate; it was the natural tendency of human nature.
But while wealth remained to be acquired, while that which gave
concentration its attraction and charm, while the comforts that
attached to it, and which the division of labour alone could afford,
were still wanted, men would follow the natural bent of their dis-
positions and disperse to seek for wealth where they thought they
would best find it.

By this line of argument he again demolished the Wakefieldian policy of keeping up a high or fancy price for the freehold of the Crown lands. Lord Grey, in fact, seems to have
eschewed that wise judicial law never to give a reason in
delivering judgment, for his despatch literally teems with

theories and generalisations as to the value and proper disposal of the waste lands in a dependency. Every sentence in these despatches seems to have been seized upon and controverted by Lowe. It would be tedious, and it is perhaps unnecessary, to attempt to reproduce this elaborate refutation of the policy of these Orders in Council. He showed that, with all the literary artifice employed by Edward Gibbon Wakefield, his pet theory, which had entangled and fascinated so many English public men, only amounted to dear land and cheap labour in a new land whither most of the people had come to avoid both. In this, as in all his speeches, it is difficult to condense Lord Sherbrooke's utterances and yet bring out all the points, because, as the bewildered sub-editor said, ' they are all points.' He deals with the question of immigration in a most fresh and suggestive manner; but at this time he never long kept away from his main theme—the iniquity of handing over so much of the public lands to the squatters.

Those who are familiar with the subsequent history of Australia will be the first to recognise the truth of the warnings which he uttered, as to the injustice and impolicy of favouring a class whose prosperity depended rather on the state of the home-market than on the social or material advancement of the colony. In eloquent words he predicted in this very speech that which actually took place by the creation of a favoured pastoral oligarchy, whose interests must be diametrically opposed to those of the rest of the community. All these evils, he declared, had fallen upon them because one or two men, high in office, had failed to understand the constitutional law that the public lands of the colony were vested in the Crown, as trustee for the whole people of the colony. He maintained that these Crown lands could not be bestowed on any individual or class of individuals, any more than a man's private estate could be made over without the consent of the proprietor.

At this novel doctrine the squatters in the Council became very restive, and the Quaker representative of the great pastoral interests controlled by Messrs. Boyd and Co. (Mr. Robinson) seems to have interjected something about these pastoral leases being a great boon to the community.

The hon. member for Melbourne (retorted Mr. Lowe) might like to have my coat, *if the colour suited him,* but it was not for that reason that anyone might give it to him; and it was equally true that he might, with respect to this land, wish to stand in the shoes of the colonists, but that gave no right to anyone else to give the shoes of the colonists to him. It was not the land of a class, but of a community, which was not prepared to make this great boon to the squatters for their exploits in vanquishing kangaroos and cutting down gum-trees.

Lowe then turned to his most redoubtable foe, and proceeded to reply to the assertions of Wentworth, who from this time forth had one most convenient argument—viz. that the waste lands of Australia were practically valueless for all purposes of settlement, and only suited to nomadic tribes.

'If they are so valueless,' retorted Mr. Lowe, 'then the hon. and learned member for Sydney can have no objection to returning these leases.' As to the claim of occupancy, that presupposed the abolition of all law and the return to the social condition favoured by Rob Roy—

That they should take who have the power,
And they should keep who can.

Then came the claim of discovery. Were those who set up this claim, asked the speaker, prepared to give to Dr. Leichardt the whole of the territory just discovered by him? Now, he was a genuine discoverer, a great explorer, and a man of scientific mind, who richly merited the tribute of thanks and admiration which that House had awarded to him. But Dr. Leichardt would be the last man to prefer such an absurd claim; and, if so, what claim had those who had obtained their runs from shepherds and insolvent people who had got jammed in the pressure of the times? 'If you advance this

claim of discovery,' said Lowe, 'as a reason why you
should have the people's lands, be honest and consistent, and
give to Dr. Leichardt a like title to every foot of ground over
which his horse's feet passed.'

Wentworth having challenged Lowe to cease criticising the schemes of others and to propound one of his
own, the latter said that his system was very simple : it was
merely to reduce the upset price of land to five shillings or
less an acre, and to leave the squatter in his present tenure
until the land was actually purchased by the *bonâ-fide* settler.
The speaker then said :—

I will call the attention of the House to the great similarity in
the Land Question in this remote and insignificant dependency to
that in which it stood on that far greater stage, and with those
infinitely greater actors of the forum, who were concerned in it ;
for I am not one of those flippant theorists who, because we have made
some discoveries—because we happen to have discovered gunpowder,
the art of printing, and other improvements, believe that we are at
present equal in intellect and power to the great men of old.   Let
the House carefully mark this resemblance, and ponder over what may
be coming.   Their Sylla, their Marius, might yet be unborn, but the
same causes would bring about the same effects ; the same system of
oppression and tyranny, if history were not a fable and experience a
liar, would in its own time bring forth these bitter fruits.   The
bones of those who were urging on this system might go down into
the dust ere the evil they had occasioned should be consummated.
Generation after generation might pass away, but let them beware,
for even now they were lighting the torch which, flung upon the
land, might smoulder for a time, but in the end would burst forth into
universal conflagration.

Lowe then read a passage from the history of the
Roman Republic describing the social and political condition
of Italy in the time of the Gracchi, and begged the Sydney
legislators to ponder over the picture, and the many analogies
it presented to their own condition.   He drew a close parallel
between the policy of the squatting party and those who had
wrought the ruin of Italian husbandry.   In Rome we read of
the increase of slaves ; was not the demand for labour at the

minimum rate on which beings could exist already loud in
Sydney ? Were they not having cannibals[1] poured upon them
in consequence of their aggression on the lands. Again, the
Roman nobles seized on vast tracts of land, as the squatters
are doing now.

There was one fine dramatic incident in this great and
impassioned speech. Turning away from men like the Boyds
and Robinson, who were mere speculating gamesters in land
and labour, Lowe made a direct and personal appeal to the
genuine pioneer squatters : —

I appeal to those only who are interested in the colony; to those
who think of, and have faith in, her future glory and after destiny ;
those whose names were, and would be, recorded in her future
history; those who in her critical conjunctures and times of need
had rendered her good service ; those who were cherished and
esteemed by her inhabitants, and whom I should be sorry to see go
down to the grave with the tarnished fame which an act like this
must involve. To these I may not inappropriately address such an
appeal ; but not to those mercenary speculators who, solely influenced
in all their actions by the sordid love of gain, those heartless, selfish
men who came out here, not to make it their abiding-place, not to
bring with them to it those high English feelings, that love of
liberty which alone could make a country great and good, but to
sell the colony into degradation that they might aggrandise themselves ; those deceitful men who made professions concerning
education which they never felt nor strove to carry out, of improvements which they never made, of capital which they never invested
— to these I would make no such appeal, but, with that contempt
they deserve, bid them take their pound of flesh and begone.

It would be possible to cull more than one such indignant
passage as this from this powerful speech, which constantly
soared into flights of lofty eloquence, and seems to palpitate
with passion, with noble invective, or with withering scorn.
We are often told of some favourite tragedian who, after
middle life, holds the most critical and fashionable audiences

[1] The kidnapping of the savages of the South Pacific for labourers and
shepherds was then in full force, and carried on openly by the Boyds, Robinson,
and others interested in squatting.

in London spellbound by his dramatic intensity, but who had acted the same part with the same fire to small provincial audiences twenty years before. Such seems to me to have been the experience of Lord Sherbrooke as a Parliamentary orator. In reading these impassioned sentences, laden, too, with thought and the fruits of a ripe scholarship, one cannot but feel that the stage was too small on which such talents were then being exhibited. But we should, perhaps, bear in mind— and I do not think that the thought was ever absent from Lord Sherbrooke whilst he dwelt in Australia—that this handful of men in the old Legislative Council of Sydney were laying the foundations of a great English-speaking commonwealth and of free institutions at the Antipodes.

At all events, on this question of the right to the waste lands of the colony there is no mistaking his terrible earnestness. He was evidently conscious, too, that his was the voice of the people of the colony, and he told the squatters in the House that he intended to leave no stone unturned to avert or overthrow Lord Grey's new Land Bill.

' I know,' he exclaimed, ' that you would gladly shun these discussions, and that you wish I should not speak above my breath on these matters ; that you would willingly hide from the English Government the intense desire you have to retain these lands.'

He then made a last appeal to their enlightened selfishness. Reduce, he said, the upset price of land, give over the dream of acquiring a monopoly of the colony, and let there be something left to attract the stream of healthy immigration, and you may yet reap the reward in a remunerative market for your stock at your very doors. Then, referring to the division of the colony into ' Settled ' and ' Unsettled ' districts, he drew a most gruesome picture of its inevitable effects :—

I would ask those who are possessed of this desperate avarice, and, like Alexander Selkirk, long to reign lords of all they survey,

what will they do for their children? The land under these
regulations will become a divided land; it will be like a human
being struck with paralysis, one side vigorous, and glowing with the
blessings of civilisation, and the busy hum of men; the other, dull
and cold and torpid. There must be a line drawn through the
land—the line between life and death. What would they do with
their children in this stunted region of shepherds and stillness,
from which all the liberal professions were shut out, and from
which wealth, the wealth of a community, must be excluded?
I believe there is something in population which in itself tends
to wealth. Look at Canada, with a barren soil, one paltry export—
of timber—with a climate that shuts the door against the energies
of the people for half the year, with a revenue contemptible as
compared with ours; yet even there the great establishments of
education for professional instruction are kept up, and flourish.
How different the desolate regions of the squatters! For, would
they come forward to bring population round them—would they
erect villages, and hamlets, and churches, and schools, on the
land on the faith of these fourteen-year leases, or do they even
pretend to say they would if they had the fee-simple? Carry
this measure into effect, and it could have but one of two issues—
either the leases must be withdrawn, or rebellion must ensue.
How long, when they had an all-powerful influence in the House,
would the squatters continue to pay their rents? How would they
get labour? Did they think the native population would be content to go back and live this degraded and inanimate life of a
shepherd? A great deal had been said about railways, but what
object could there be in making railways if all the land was to be
locked up in leases? Would that Council ever do so degraded an
act as to vote money for any such purpose, increasing the value
of lands thus leased away, and of which the lessees possessed the
pre-emptive right of purchase?

Mr. Lowe wound up this remarkable oration by an appeal
to the Legislative body itself which, he said, might be trite,
but was none the less worthy of their weighty consideration.

It was, that if popular representative institutions were
ever to take firm root in the soil of Australia, then 'the
deliberations of that Council ought to be as untinged, as
untainted by any suspicion, as the Courts of Judicature.' He
recognised his own solemn responsibility in bringing so
deliberately such a series of charges against an influential

section of the community, and he knew that, perhaps for the
first time, the outside public were keenly watching their
conduct and discussions. What they had to avoid at such a
crisis was giving occasion for the finger of shame and ridicule.
'It is this,' he concluded, 'that I fear: that they who ought
to give the tone to the public virtue and shape the political
education of the colony should give to sceptics in political
virtue a pretence to sneer at those institutions which it ought
to be our common glory to revere.'

Never had Lowe risen to such heights, never had he
or any other member confronted so powerful an opposition,
composed not only of the ordinary officials and Crown nominees,
but of the able band of political squatters now under the
leadership of Wentworth.

When the former popular tribune rose, it is true he spoke
of his successor with unfeigned admiration, as possessing
'an eloquence far greater than my own, or than that of any
other gentleman in this Council.' But he quickly descended
into mere scurrilities, and his one charge against Lowe
was that he was a theorist, without practical knowledge of
pastoral matters. There is only one point in Wentworth's
reply which need be specially commented upon, as showing
the bitterness of this political controversy, in which, it seems
to me, Robert Lowe was bearing so gallant and so disinterested
a part. In one portion of his speech Lowe had said, with
evident earnestness, that if these Orders in Council were
put into effect he should leave the country and return to
England, and he urged upon the Council to reject Earl
Grey's Land Bill altogether—a course which Wentworth
would have been the first to advocate in the days when he
was really the great 'Australian patriot.' The way in which
he now took up this challenge is worth relating :—

The hon. and learned member for Auckland (he exclaimed)
had told them that if these Orders were put into effect he would
leave the country. If the Council could be guilty of conduct so

disreputable, so unworthy, and so contemptible as to fling back
upon a Minister a Bill the offspring of their own resolutions, he,
Mr. Wentworth, would leave the House. He should feel that its
dignity, its influence, its self-respect, its honesty, were gone, and
henceforward the post of honour would be the private station.

Anyone familiar with the parliamentary history of New
South Wales can picture the same vehement orator using the
very same words if the Council did *not* fling back upon a
Minister a Bill of which he himself disapproved.

This tremendous discussion was adjourned from night to
night,[1] and on the evening of June 24th Lowe rose, and in a
speech of equal length and power to that with which he had
opened it answered his opponents on every side of the House.
But the finest and most effective passage was his dignified
reply to Wentworth :—

The hon. and learned member, in a strain which he had never
adopted before, proceeded to denounce the colony as a barren waste,
unfit for cultivation, unfit for the reception of civilised man. It
was with pain that I heard him deliver these denunciations. I
have always delighted to contemplate New South Wales as a great
and glorious country, and to picture the hon. and learned gentleman
as taking the first place among the native-born who have attained
honours and distinction in their own land. I had thought that it
would alike be his pride and his glory to shine the first in the annals
of the colony—as he had outstripped the comers from older Europe
in the march of intelligence and patriotism. It was, therefore, with
deep regret that I heard him from time to time speak so harshly of
the capabilities of his native land. Even I, a stranger, a cork
floating on the ocean, one who might be here to-day and away to-
morrow, cannot but feel some sentiments of gratitude to this
country—not, perhaps, like those which swell my bosom for my own
land ; but I have drunk her water and breathed her air, and, grateful

[1] Nothing will more clearly show how keen was the duel between Lowe and
Wentworth than a remark in the *Sydney Morning Herald* on one of these Land
debates :—' As member after member rose to make their observations, it was
evident that Mr. Lowe and Mr. Wentworth were watching the debate. A protracted debate was expected, but suddenly a long pause ensued, and the Speaker
put the question. . . . Mr. Wentworth was determined not to speak until Mr.
Lowe had addressed the House, in order that he might have the reply ; and
Mr. Lowe had adopted the same course with respect to Mr. Wentworth. The
question was put while the one was waiting for the other.'

for these benefits, I could not travel over the country and find all
barren from Dan to Beersheba. But to hear this dispraise from a
son of the soil, one born and bred in the land, was more than
displeasing. I hope it may not be so, but it looked as if the hon.
and learned member was depreciating the article he wanted to
secure. He (Mr. Wentworth) has accused me, perhaps rightly, of
ignorance of the physical state of the country. I have but little
judgment in such matters, so I do not entirely rely on my own
opinion. But I believe I give him no mean authority when I name
Sir Thomas Mitchell, the Surveyor-General of the Colony, who tells
me that the stations of the hon. and learned member for Sydney
are like paradises. Sir Thomas passed through them on his late
journey, and returned enchanted with the beautiful scenery and
pasturage which he had witnessed. These were the stations of the
hon. and learned member, but, perhaps, as they appertained more
nearly to him, his modesty would not permit him to praise them. Sir
Thomas, however, spoke of them as a man in raptures ; and perhaps even his hon. and learned friend would pause before he accused
the Surveyor-General of ignorance.

These (continued Mr. Lowe in the same vein of raillery, and
using his opponent's actual expressions)—these were the wastes,
the sterilities, the Saharas, the lands withered with the blast of the
desert, which had been so prominently dwelt on and so con-
temptuously depicted, although it must be admitted that the
occupant had evinced no ill-will towards having the possession of
them secured to him.

The modern reader, even if bred and born in Australia, and
to some extent familiar with the history of its Land Question,
can form no idea of the marvellous grasp and the knowledge of
every detail displayed by Mr. Lowe in this elaborate reply to
the squatters. It was a veritable *tour de force*. The future
historian, anxious to know the various stages in the evolution
from a purely pastoral and nomadic condition to the higher
and more complex social state to which Australia has now
attained, will find in these agrarian speeches of Mr. Lowe
most suggestive matter. Reference might also here be made
to the remarkable pamphlet which about this time he published in Sydney, under the title, *An Address to the Colonists
of New South Wales on the proposed Land Orders*. In this
pamphlet, in a highly condensed and purely argumentative

z 2

form, will be found the substance of his matured views on the
Land Question in Australia. If, as may be confidently predicted will be the case, a complete volume of Lord Sherbrooke's speeches, addresses, and pamphlets should one day
be given to the world, this address, though dealing with a
bygone controversy in a remote colony, should assuredly find
a place.

Mr. Lowe thus concluded his speech in the Council :—

The present motion would be defeated, not by the will, the
opinion, the sense of that House, but by the junction of a party
governed by self-interest with the unwilling, but fettered members
of an irresponsible Government. To say, after what they had seen
that night, that there was no danger to be apprehended from the
growing influence of the squatters was simply to close the ears
to the warnings of human experience. They saw an unwilling
Government dragged at the wheels of the chariot of the hon. and
learned member for Sydney—while they might have spread life and
vigour, and wealth and prosperity through the wide range of the
Colony. 'If they had done these things in the green tree, judge ye
what they will do in the dry.'

The division was then taken, and may be here recorded
as showing the names and opinions of the members of the
Legislative Council of 1847 :—

Ayes	Noes
Mr. Lowe	Mr. Dangar
,, Murray	,, Darvall
,, Lamb	,, Foster
,, Lord	,, Parker
,, Bowman	Capt. Dumaresq
,, Brewster	The Commander of the Forces
,, Bland	Mr. G. Macleay
,, Suttor	Capt. O'Connell
,, Icely	Mr. Wentworth
,, Cowper (teller)	,, Wild
	,, Allen
	The Attorney-General
	Mr. Robinson (teller)

The figures of the division, it will be seen, are close ; the names, for the most part, save to a very few surviving old colonists, will convey little or nothing. But to the people of New South Wales in 1847, those names conveyed a great deal, for, as Mr. Lowe said, the division list proved his assertion— that every member of the Council who was not a Crown official and therefore compelled to vote in favour of Earl Grey's measure, or else a squatter and therefore directly interested in its provisions, was on his side. This entirely disproves an assertion, frequently made by colonial writers even up to the present day, that Robert Lowe was an inconsistent, and to that extent untrustworthy, political leader in Australia, because he had first of all been the chief champion of the squatters, and afterwards their principal opponent. The answer is that he was their chief champion when they were fighting for their constitutional rights, and their principal opponent when they were grasping at the patrimony of the whole people. As he said himself, he may, perhaps, have made mistakes, and not even have been altogether consistent in the plans he had put forward during the years he had been in the colony, ' but his lips had ever been the organ of his heart.'

It was, indeed, the social conditions that had changed. Robert Lowe's land policy for Australia was, in brief, while treating the pastoral tenants of the Crown with strict fairness, and in no wise subjecting them to any arbitrary exactions, to make every effort to establish a genuine yeomanry. This was the meaning of his constant efforts to get Australian wheat into the English markets duty free ; it was for this that he devoted night after night to the discussion of the question of what were called the ' waste lands ' of the colony, which he maintained could never be permanently settled save by means of a minimum, and not, as Gibbon Wakefield held, by a maximum upset price. As already stated, Lowe was chairman of a special committee appointed by the Council on this subject of the price of land, and he himself prepared, with his own hand, the report of that committee, which agrarian reformers, even of the advanced school of Mr. Henry George, might do well to peruse. It greatly enhanced his reputation at the time, and the *Sydney Morning Herald*, in a leading article (Oct. 16, 1847) thus commented on it :—

We must not conclude without offering to the Committee, and especially to their gifted Chairman, our hearty thanks for their valuable services. . . . Of the report we can, with all sincerity, declare that we prize it as an ornament to our official literature, an honour to the colony, and an acquisition to the course of political science.

Wentworth and most of the squatter party supported Lowe at first in his strenuous endeavours to cheapen the price of land. But when Earl Grey offered them the fixed tenure of their ' runs,' with the proviso that the high price of Crown lands should be maintained, they speedily forgot all their former liberal professions. We can hardly wonder at it, for human nature is weak, and the Orders in Council converted them—a handful of men—from tenants at will into something very like proprietors of the enormous territory which now forms the two chief colonies of Australia, with a population of over two million souls.

It does not fall within the present narrative to relate how after all most of them profited very little by Earl Grey's ill-considered land legislation. Briefly, it may be added, that with the gold discoveries of 1852 there came an enormous influx of immigration, quickly followed by the granting of responsible government to New South Wales and the newly-created colony of Victoria. After violent public agitation, these newly-created colonial legislatures, in answer to the cry ' Unlock the lands,' wrested from the squatters the privileges which Earl Grey had conferred upon them by an Imperial Act, and, so far as they could, carried out the agrarian principles which Robert Lowe had laid down some years before in the Legislative Council of Sydney. Lord Sherbrooke, therefore, while baffled by the coalition of the Crown officials and squatters, may be most justly regarded as the true father of the yeoman class in New South Wales and Victoria, and as the first of Australian land reformers.

Before bringing this chapter to a close, a few words with reference to the *personnel* of the leading squatters of this time may throw light on this fierce controversy. It must not for a moment be supposed that they were in all cases utterly selfish, grasping, and unpatriotic. Many of them were, as Lord Sherbrooke himself declared, high-spirited and cultured men, and some of them of the best blood of England. In one of the most striking passages in the particular speech of the series of agrarian philippics, from which extracts have been reproduced in this chapter, he appeals personally to this class—the class of genuine pioneer squatter—those who in Australia's critical conjunctures and times of need had rendered her good service. At the same time he contrasts with these 'those mercenary speculators' who gave no thoughts to the welfare of their fellow-subjects or to the future of Australia, so long as they might aggrandise themselves. To these he says: 'I would make no such appeal, but, with that contempt they deserve, bid them take their pound of flesh and begone.'

It was really these latter—mere land jobbers and speculators carrying on vast undertakings with borrowed English capital—who, by their political machinations and influence in London, had managed to get control both over the Colonial Office and the local Legislative Council. The story of the two brothers, Archibald and Benjamin Boyd, and of their financial and political agent, the Quaker Robinson, would furnish the subject for a striking colonial romance. Benjamin Boyd had arrived in the colony in a yacht of the royal squadron some time in the early 'forties,' and, as he had a fine appearance, a glib tongue, and apparently unlimited money, dressed well and talked much of his aristo-

cratic connections, he was at once accepted in Sydney as a
great man whose resources and capital would revive the
drooping fortunes of the place. He began gambling in land
on the most gigantic scale, and projected a town, or rather
city, at Twofold Bay, the details of which make Dickens's
account of Eden in *Martin Chuzzlewit* seem quite matter
of fact. He and his brother had started a huge financial
institution, at the head of which he placed the unfortunate Mr.
Robinson. They owned whaling vessels, which they manned
chiefly with Maoris and South Sea Islanders. They beguiled
poor immigrants hundreds of miles from Sydney to one or
other of their innumerable runs; then offered them the
princely wages of 10*l.* a year, with beggarly rations. If they
refused, they were compelled to walk back, and an old colonial chronicler tells us that 'while a few strong men walked
back over the mountains, those who remained created such a
feeling in the country that Mr. Boyd could not venture to
visit his stations until the time of the year when the police
magistrate, with a guard of policemen, took his annual round.'
The extent of country which Archibald and Benjamin Boyd
at one time controlled was simply enormous. These Napo-
leonic operations were all carried on by borrowed money from
London, and so one day the crash came.

　　Then Benjamin Boyd, broken in fortune, started off in his
yacht for the South Sea Islands, where he was killed and
eaten. It was a horrible death, but there seemed a rude
justice in it, for he and his brother and their agent Robinson
had kidnapped hundreds of these unfortunate natives and
shipped them to New South Wales to work for little or
nothing on their stations, where they died in shoals. Mr.
Archibald Boyd, who was quite as dazzling a personage as
his brother during this brief champagne time of froth and
excitement, managed to get back to England, where he ended
his days in a garret in Bloomsbury, writing novels of the
Family Herald type. Had he but told the story of his own

brief career as a pastoral king, it must have been the most
fascinating of Australian narratives. The Quaker Robinson,
who seemed at first to have a really promising career before
him, became the dupe as well as the agent of the Boyds, and
after the crash died suddenly in Sydney—it was rumoured by
his own hand. It seems almost incredible that such men as
these could have affected the political history of a great
colony : yet nothing can be clearer than that it was through
their influence and astuteness that the Hon. Francis Scott
had been appointed the paid agent of the pastoralists in the
House of Commons, and that by this means the squatters had
been transformed from suppliants into masters.

Had Wentworth remained true to his former patriotic
convictions, these men would have been powerless. But this
remarkable man—the one truly great man of our race born in
this strange new world of Australia—proved deaf to the appeal
so eloquently made by Lowe to his nobler nature. The bribe
was too great; the Orders in Council made secure his position
and gave him the virtual mastery in the local legislature.
Mixed with the fine gold of his great spirit and masterful
personality, there was a strain of base alloy ; and, truth to
tell, the Wentworth of nearly sixty years of age, though he
could still rouse himself to great intellectual efforts, was no
longer the earnest vehement reformer and patriot of earlier
days.

Robert Lowe had publicly declared that if, by the un-
principled alliance of the Crown officials and the pastoralists,
this squatter oligarchy was to be set up, he would no longer
remain in the country. It was, indeed, after the division on
this memorable night had been taken in the old Legislative
Council, that he confided to his one intimate friend, William
Macleay, that as soon as he could arrange his affairs he would
return to England. There were evils, he said, in the system
of an old established aristocracy; but to have a brand-new,
overbearing, traditionless squatting oligarchy placed over you

was simply intolerable.   He had, however, still a work to do.
He was yet to stand forth as the champion of the rights of
the free immigrants—the untainted population of the colony
—against the further deplorable attempt of Earl Grey to
revive the practice of criminal transportation.   Moreover,
Robert Lowe was to become member for Sydney.

CHAPTER XXIII

A SLAVE-TRADE PHILIPPIC

The 'Orator' in *Heads of the People*—German and French Immigrants—
The Squatters and the South Sea Islanders

THE series of brilliant and impassioned speeches on the Land
Question had raised the fame of Robert Lowe as an orator to the
very highest pitch among the whole of the colonists, urban and
pastoral, of New South Wales.   This is shown by the fact that
an enterprising journalist of Sydney who had projected an
illustrated weekly newspaper called *Heads of the People* (a kind
of humble forerunner of *Vanity Fair*), singled him out for his
issue of Sept. 4, 1847, as the type of the 'Orator.'   It is rather
amusing to find that the editor was unable to induce 'Mr.
Robert Lowe, M.C.,' to sit for his portrait.   He, however,
managed to produce a caricature, representing the 'Orator'
in a frock-coat, and with his hands (very ill-drawn) spread out
on the table, over which he was leaning in the act of addressing
the House.   This rude portrait has been at times reproduced
in Australia; but it is absolutely worthless as a likeness, as,
indeed, the editor of this long-forgotten Australian journal
admitted in the accompanying letterpress.

The portion of the article, however, describing Robert
Lowe's qualities as an orator may still be read with some
interest :—

Mr. Lowe (observes his early colonial critic) has many advantages, with some disadvantages, as an orator.   His advantages—and
in this respect he leaves all competition far behind him—are a rapid
and fluent delivery ; a splendid command over figures of speech and

rhetorical ornaments, sometimes, indeed, verging on the turgid ; a perfect acquaintance with the classics, and with modern literature, and a good knowledge of the law.

The writer then goes on to state that the contest in the Legislative Council for leadership ' lies between Mr. Wentworth and Mr. Lowe.' For himself, he gives the palm to the former, though admitting that he has none of the ' wonderful command of well-chosen words possessed by his rival.' With these two the colonial editor links the name of a man who was then almost at the close of his short earthly career — Richard Windeyer.

' Mr. Windeyer's *forte*,' he says, ' is satire. His sarcasms are more unpleasant to bear than the most virulent abuse.' After Lowe, Wentworth, and Windeyer, this not altogether injudicious critic considered that in Deas Thomson, the Colonial Secretary, the old Legislative Council of Sydney possessed ' a plain, matter-of-fact, business-like orator,' whose speeches would win the confidence and attention of any parliamentary body.

Lowe had, of course, completely alienated the most influential section of the community—the squatters. This he knew perfectly well, and during the remaining couple of years of his public life in Sydney he fought them, so to speak, with his back to the wall. The handing over of the millions of broad acres of New South Wales and Port Phillip to the pastoral tenants and land-gamblers seemed to haunt him like a nightmare. There is no doubt that it was the selfishness displayed by the squatters in thus getting possession of the public patrimony which drove him, during his last year in Sydney, into the leadership of the anti-transportation party. This was after his election to the city of Sydney, when, as I shall show, he was for a brief while the leading agitator and the most popular tribune of the colonial democracy.

Before narrating the events following on the general election of 1848, there are still one or two stirring episodes to recall in connection with his public conduct as the member for the joint counties of St. Vincent and Auckland. On August 27, 1847, a petition was presented from a number of German residents in Sydney praying to be allowed the privileges and immunities of English subjects. The German element has always been strong in the colony of South Australia, and very law-abiding and prosperous in all the colonies. It is pleasant to find that Lowe seconded the motion on their behalf; there was, however, a difficulty in the way, as no general statute affecting the naturalisation of foreigners had been passed by the Imperial Parliament. The Quaker member, Mr. Robinson, who could be very liberal where the public lands were not concerned, urged that the sooner they got rid of all restrictions, the better; in his opinion, they should encourage all foreigners to come and settle. These innocent remarks aroused Lowe's sense of irony at once. He rejoiced, he said, to hear that the hon. member for Melbourne was disposed to offer every inducement to foreigners to come amongst them, but the 'very strongest inducement would be the offer of a little of the land of which he and his class had been kind enough to relieve the colony.'

If French emigrants should come hither, driven out of their own country by the abolition of the law of primogeniture and the consequent subdivision of the land, it would be highly refreshing to them to see in how few hands the lands are vested here. They would say, at all events, 'Whatever rock these New South Wales fellows have split upon, it is not on the subdivision of the land.' (Roars of laughter.)

On October 1st, 1847, two days before the Legislative Council adjourned, Robert Lowe made a much more serious attack on the enterprising Boyd Brothers and their man-of-all-work, the Quaker Robinson, for kidnapping South Sea islanders, and shipping them to New South Wales to supply on their stations the free convict labour which was no longer accessible. As just now the South Sea labour traffic is a

350 LIFE OF LORD SHERBROOKE

burning question between various religious philanthropists
and the Government of Queensland, it may be as well to point
out that the kidnapping system of the Boyds, which Lord
Sherbrooke so powerfully denounced, was totally different
to the proposed 'regulated' Kanaka labour. These selfish
and masterful men, who had gone out to Australia merely to
make money as fast as they could, and who had become
virtual masters of the colony for the time being, felt themselves under no restrictions, moral or legal, in their transactions
with the unfortunate savages of the South Sea Islands. This
system of employing, even under governmental restrictions,
the labour of these inferior races is by no means yet settled
in Australia ; but it is plain that there can be no analogy
between the social condition of New South Wales and Port
Phillip in 1847, and that of North Queensland in 1892. In the
former case the islanders were kidnapped and conveyed in many
cases to the high plateau and more mountainous portions of
these southern and colder regions. There was no Government
supervision whatever, and whether the unfortunate islanders
died on these vast sheep-runs, or were speared by the aborigines,
then comparatively numerous, seemed to be a matter that concerned no one. We shall never know the proportions to which
this Polynesian slave trade attained in these early years ; but
of the hundreds of South Sea islanders who were imported by
the Boyds and Robinson alone, it is hardly likely that any
ever again beheld their native shores.

It is evident that this illegal traffic must have attained
considerable proportions when Robert Lowe from his place
in the Legislative Council gave notice of the following
motion:—

That an Address be presented to his Excellency the Governor,
setting forth that this Council begs to call the serious attention of
the Executive Government to the incipient slave trade which is
so rapidly springing up between this colony and the islands of the
Pacific Ocean.

That this House desires to point the attention of his Excellency

to the third and ninth clauses of the Imperial Act 5 Geo. IV.
c. 113.

That the existing traffic in human creatures obviously unable to
contract for themselves, and who must, therefore, be brought from
their native land either by force or fraud, is clearly within the
spirit (perhaps the letter) of this enactment, and that it is the duty
of the Government to take immediate and vigorous steps for its
suppression.

His speech in proposing this resolution on October 1st,
1847, was one of the longest and most impassioned ever delivered by him in that Council. The public excitement that
it evoked is shown by the number of columns it occupies in the
somewhat clumsy report of the next day's *Sydney Morning
Herald*. It is much to be regretted that Lord Sherbrooke
in later life did not find time to revise this report, for the
subject is an important one, and after almost half a century
is still a question of Australian, if not of Imperial import and
significance.

In his indictment of this traffic in Polynesian labour Lowe
did not hesitate to characterise it as ' a new form of the slave
trade,' into the past history of which he entered with great
fulness. But he admitted that the materials on which he had
to build this charge were few and scanty ; it was but an
incipient slave trade, against which he wished to guard the
colony :—

I stand not in the same position that Wilberforce did when he
raised his voice against this trade. Then its supporters came unblushingly forward and avowed their acts, for they were not then
legally criminal. But a dark, mysterious veil is thrown over this
traffic : we hear of frays and bloodshed, of the cutting off crews of
boats, we hear of presents to chiefs ; but of detailed accounts of
this commerce we have none. We know nothing of the condition
of the people that are brought here : whether they were prisoners
of war, whether they were slaves at home, whether they came of
their own free will, or were at the disposal of the chiefs.

The speaker then proceeded to analyse the nature of the
alleged contract under which these South Sea islanders were

brought to work on the sheep-runs of New South Wales and
Port Phillip :—

The form of the precious contract was as follows :— 'I ——
[blank, to be filled up by some hard name], 'native of' [blank
again], 'in the Pacific Ocean, have this day agreed with' [here
follows the name of the captain of the vessel], 'on the part of Mr.
Benjamin Boyd, of the City of Sydney, N.S.W., to serve the said
Benjamin Boyd in the capacity of a seaman in any of his ships or as
a whaler, either on board or on shore, or as a shepherd or other
labourer, in any part of the colony of N.S.W., and to make myself generally useful for the term of five years.'

Now, what abstract idea could these savages have of Benjamin
Boyd, with whom they were contracting ? The Hindoos in India,
it was said, took the East India Company to be an old woman, and
the same sort of feeling in the present case was not unlikely. But
what could these savages know of Mr. Benjamin Boyd ? How could
they know whether he was a demon of good or evil order ? It was
not pretended that they could form an opinion. What abstract
idea of a shepherd could these natives have, when they had never
seen a sheep on their native island at all ? But there was a further
stipulation, that the servant thus introduced should make himself
generally useful. Now, the gentlemen who frequented the registry
offices knew very well what were the duties this term involved. But
was anybody foolish enough to believe that the savage did so ?
Then, again, it was stipulated that they should serve for a period of
five years ; and perhaps the hon. member for Melbourne (Robinson)
would inform them what powers of enumeration were possessed by
these savages to enable them to comprehend what the period of five
years was. Perhaps they might be similar to the Cherokees, who
were unable to reckon more than three, and when asked as to any
greater number, pointed to the hairs of their head to signify that they
were innumerable. Then followed the other part of the agreement,
in which this man-stealer, on the part of Mr. Benjamin Boyd, agreed
to pay these savages wages at the rate of 1l. 6s. per annum, with the
following weekly ration, viz. :—meat, ten pounds ; and he supposed,
although it was a matter of some difficulty among civilised people to
determine her Majesty's weights and measures, they, the savages, knew
what ten pounds was. Maize, wheat, or flour, seven pounds ; doubtless the savages have a knowledge of wheat, maize, meal, and a correct
abstract idea of a mill. Then, as to clothing, there was, first of all, one
pair of moleskin trousers, the savage being, doubtless, well acquainted
with the texture and manufacture of moleskins ; a pair of linen
trousers ; a woollen shirt, which he ought as a shepherd to know
something about ; a cotton shirt ; and next he came to an article of

peculiar interest, doubtless, to the savages –it was 'one Kilmarnock cap.' Now, though neither a cannibal nor a native of Tanna, I am myself utterly unacquainted with the meaning of a Kilmarnock cap. One blanket completed the outfit.

Thus, with one shirt and a blanket these poor wretches were to be sent from the burning heat of a tropical sun to Maneroo, which has a winter of almost European severity. Whether this was slave-trade or not, it was a piece of inhumanity which ought to call down the execration of the House, and of which I trust there are members who will not shrink from expressing their opinion.

The agreement then went on to say 'that the full meaning and terms of this agreement, as read in English, having been first truly and clearly explained to me by ——, who understands my native language, I affix my mark hereto in testimony of my concurrence in this present engagement.'

The date followed; but I am glad that the words *anno Domini* are left out, as it shows that even the most obdurate consciences shrank from the introduction of the name of Christ into this document.

Speaking in this strain of mingled irony and indignation for a couple of hours, Lowe moved the resolution, which was seconded by Charles Cowper. Robinson rose and defended himself and Benjamin Boyd. He stated that the importation of South Sea islanders into the colony arose in this way : Some five years ago the whaling industry, previously an important one, was abandoned ; the whaling boats were in consequence idle. They could get no seamen. At first New Zealanders were shipped to the extent of the third of a crew of a whaling vessel, and then increased to one-half. This proved success-ful, and was the foundation of 'savage' labour. They then went to the Pacific Islands. True, some of these islanders were cannibals ; so were the aborigines of Australia. Mr. Robinson then solemnly read Boyd's instructions to one of his station-managers as to these imported islanders, from which it would seem that it was necessary to keep them in bodies, as a safeguard against the attacks of the 'old hands' (meaning the convict shepherds). As for their rations, Mr. Robinson explained that they had no tea or sugar, but plenty of potatoes ; they were very intelligent, and could count.

Mr. Robinson further read the articles of agreement with the Chinese at one of the stations controlled by the Boyd syndicate. By article eleven three days were allowed in every year to the Chinaman for the performance of his religious rites.

In the subsequent debate the Colonial Secretary (Deas Thomson) avowed his intention of voting against the motion, but admitted that the importation of ' savage ' labour might ruin the colony. The Attorney-General (Plunkett)—the official whom the Boyds and Robinson most dreaded—was more outspoken than his colleague. He unhesitatingly condemned ' savage labour at sixpence a week and a shirt a year.'

Robert Lowe then rose and said the object he had had in view was completely achieved. He had called the attention of the House and the country to what he had designated an ' incipient slave trade ' ; and an incipient slave trade nine out of ten would now consider it. After the remarks of the Attorney-General he was quite willing to withdraw his motion and leave the matter in the hands of the Government, on whom he had not the slightest intention of casting any imputation. In answer to Wentworth's taunt that he had agitated this question of Polynesian labour merely out of ill-feeling towards the Boyds and Robinson, Lowe replied with great feeling and indignation :—

The hon. member for Sydney has condescended to charge me with being actuated by ill-feeling towards the hon. member for Melbourne and those with whom he is connected. I can assure the House that I wish to blast no man's character ; that I have no feeling against either of the persons named—but I have a feeling respecting the things which they do. I have a strong feeling respecting monopoly, against griping, over-reaching and tyrannous oppression ; and it is because I believe that they, and the hon. member for Sydney also, did these things, that I have any feeling of opposition towards them. What is it to me that they have inundated the country with cannibals; that by their grasping monopoly they made that which might be a garden into a wilderness? I am only a sojourner; I could cut the cable and leave the colony to them—some of them sons of the soil, who had accomplished its ruin—to the enjoyment of the fruits of their own work.

It is hardly necessary to repeat that the Labour problem has assumed quite a different phase in Australia in our day. In fairness one must admit that the proposal to introduce Kanaka labour into North Queensland has received the support of Sir Samuel Griffith, a Liberal statesman of distinction. Whether Lord Sherbrooke would have supported the policy of introducing, under strict governmental regulations, the labour of South Sea islanders on the sugar plantations of northern Queensland is perhaps doubtful. But that he would have felt very little sympathy with the tyrannical policy of the Australian Trade Unions is certain. Nothing stirred him so much as the sight of oppression and injustice, whether exercised by individuals or by classes.

CHAPTER XXIV

Lowe's Address to the Electors of St. Vincent—Action of Henry Parkes and Sydney Electors—Returned for Sydney without canvass or expense—His last Letter ' home '

THE General Election of 1848 was the most exciting and the most important that had ever been held in the colony. Mr. Lowe decided to stand again for his former constituency, and on July 1st issued the following Address to the electors of the united counties of St. Vincent and Auckland :—

Gentlemen,— When you did me the honour to elect me as your representative, I was earnestly desirous of carrying out three objects—the reduction of the minimum price of Crown lands to a reasonable sum ; the removing from us the impending danger of district councils ; and the applying a searching and systematic economy to the public expenditure.

On the first of these subjects, the reduction of the price of lands, a majority, consisting of officials who are obliged to vote according to the direction of the Government, and large squatters, who consider the maintenance of this price essential to their private interests, have, in the last session, declined to express any opinion, and I have thus the mortification of seeing that, while the Legislative Council is hesitating, the question is practically settled by the division of the most valuable and saleable lands of the colony among about one thousand colonists, who can neither sell, cultivate, nor improve them.

As to the question of district councils, we are threatened with a Constitution which not merely adopts them, but makes them the point upon which the whole system of government is to revolve. And yet upon this subject also the Legislative Council has felt itself unequal to express any opinion. The country has spoken, but its representatives have been silent.

As to the public expenditure, 1 have been one of a small minority usually outnumbered by the officials and Crown nominees in our efforts to stem the torrent of corruption. Our ill-success may be attributed to three causes—the unaccountable conduct of many representative members, who have absented themselves from the Council altogether; to the almost uniform support given on principle by the members from Port Phillip to any measure of the Government; and by the lamentable want of independence of some of the members of the middle district. From these causes, after all our boasted economy, we leave the expenditure of the country as large as we found it, and have given the sanction of a partly-elected assembly to abuses which we ought not to have tolerated for an instant.

It is under these discouraging circumstances, Gentlemen, I again offer my services to you as your representative. As far as depends on me, those services shall be rendered with the same zeal and independence; but the constituencies of the country must determine whether they shall be attended with better success.

I regret that the shortness of the period fixed for the return of the writs, and my indispensable professional duties, will render it impossible for me to attend personally at the election, and to give to you that account of the trust you have reposed in me which you are entitled to ask, and which I am willing, and I believe able, to render.

I am, Gentlemen,
Your obedient servant,
ROBERT LOWE.

It is clear that Lowe had created widespread popular enthusiasm on behalf of himself and his political convictions; for without his consent, or even knowledge, a number of the leading electors of Sydney met together and decided to requisition him to allow himself to be put in nomination for the metropolitan constituency. In the only daily journal that Sydney then boasted—the *Herald*—for July 5th, 1848, the following announcement appeared :—

CITY ELECTORS.

The friends of Robert Lowe, Esq., are requested to sign the requisition, copies of which are lying at the undermentioned places :—

Mr. H. Parkes's, Hunter Street; &c. &c.

The City of Sydney had two representatives in the Legislative Council, and both the old members were seeking re-election—William Charles Wentworth and Dr. William Bland. It is very clear that the object of Mr. (now Sir Henry) Parkes and his friends in bringing forward Robert Lowe was to challenge, and if possible conquer, the stronghold of Wentworth. However, at first the late member and candidate for St. Vincent and Auckland was clearly averse to so hazardous and apparently hopeless an enterprise.

On the same day that Mr. Henry Parkes's announcement appeared in the paper there was a report of a political meeting held on the previous evening in the Mechanics' School of Art, Pitt Street, on which occasion Robert Lowe had supported the candidature of Mr. John Lamb for the city in a remarkably able address. But the anti-Wentworthites—or, as the squatters called them, the Radicals—were determined that Lowe should himself stand. Accordingly, the following requisition was hastily prepared and signed by a number of his enthusiastic admirers :—

To Robert Lowe, Esq.

Sir,—We, the undersigned Electors of the City of Sydney beg you will allow yourself to be put in nomination as a candidate for the representation of our interests in the Legislative Council at the forthcoming General Election. In the event of your complying with our request, we pledge ourselves to use our utmost endeavours to secure your return.

J. R. WILSHIRE, Alderman.	S. SAMUEL.
W. S. MACLEAY.	P. N. RUSSELL.
ANTHONY HORDERN.	G. A. LLOYD.
HENRY PARKES.	W. W. BILLYARD.
JOHN ROBERTSON.	

The committee formed to collect signatures to the above requisition have determined to put Mr. Lowe in nomination at the approaching election and to poll the last vote.

By order of the Committee,

J. K. HEYDON, } *Joint Secretaries.*
HENRY PARKES, }

With the exception of the ex-Mayor and William Macleay, these electors of the City of Sydney were all young unknown men at the time.   But it is noteworthy that two of them afterwards filled more than once the office of Prime Minister, while two others became Treasurers and Postmaster-Generals of the colony ; and every one of the nine who thus requisitioned Lord Sherbrooke to stand for the metropolis became, in some way, a man of mark.

Robert Lowe at first held back, no doubt for the reason that he had already offered a renewal of his services to the 'joint counties.'   Mr. Parkes, however, as all who know him can testify, was never the man to be lightly put aside from his purpose.   He lost no time in using his persuasive powers, and to some effect, for on the following day, July 8th, this startling announcement appeared in the columns of the *Herald* :—

To the Electors of the City of Sydney.

Brother Electors,—We ask you to vote for Mr. Lowe because we believe he will strenuously endeavour to enlarge the elective franchise [surely a strange reason when we think of the great anti-reform speeches in the House of Commons].

We ask you (it continued) to vote for him because we believe he will be the successful advocate of an equitable alienation of the public lands and an economical expenditure of the public money. In short, we ask you to vote for Mr. Lowe because we in our hearts believe he will be the ablest defender and most incorruptible promoter of our common rights and liberties, not being bound by any predilections of self-interest.

Electors and Freemen,—You have been told that Mr. Lowe will not take his seat for Sydney if elected.   This is not true ; here are Mr. Lowe's own words :—

' In answer to a question from you, whether I would sit for the city if elected, I repeat, YES.

' I could not so far insult the citizens of Sydney as to refuse.

' Yours very truly,
' ROBERT LOWE.'

Mr. Lowe was thus placed somewhat in the tantalising position of Captain Macheath between the two charmers ; and although his enthusiastic admirers in Sydney offered to defray his expenses, he did not definitively consent to stand. But on July 13th a letter written by him appeared in the newspaper, apparently in reply to some hostile criticisms as to his indecision in the matter.

To the Editors of the ' Sydney Morning Herald.'

' Non fumum ex fulgore, sed ex fumo dare lucem.'

Gentlemen,—As it appears from your paper that there is some misconception abroad as to my position with respect to the Sydney election, I beg to make the following statement :—

When I was asked to become a candidate for the City of Sydney, I said No, because I was a supporter of Mr. Lamb, and because I had already addressed my former constituents. When I was asked whether I would sit for the City if elected, I said Yes, because to refuse would have been to insult the citizens and to forego the possibility of a triumph for those principles with which I am identified ; and because neither my duty to Mr. Lamb nor to my former constituents seemed to me to require such a denial. In this I can see neither coquetry nor contradiction. It is one thing to refuse to solicit an honour, it is another to refuse to accept it when obtained. I will not solicit the votes of the electors of Sydney, but if they return me unsolicited I will not refuse the seat. I know no words which can make this statement of my intentions more explicit ; if I did, I would use them.

I am, Gentlemen,
Your obedient servant,
ROBERT LOWE.

The election was fought out with the utmost determination on both sides. The nomination took place on July 27th, and dense crowds began to assemble at the hustings as early as ten in the morning. When Lowe put in an appearance on the platform he was greeted with tumultuous applause ; while Wentworth, now self-deposed from his position of popular idol, was hissed by the crowd, though cheered by his immediate friends. Wentworth was nominated first, and received with cries of ' Coolies !' ; but when Alderman Wilshire came forward to propose Robert Lowe, deafening cheers rent the air, which were renewed again and again when his proposer declaimed :—

' Mr. Lowe had been represented as the idol of the people.
. . . The people had formerly their political idols, but missionaries had come in among them, who had taught them the folly and wrong of such worship.'

This very palpable hit at Wentworth was of course mightily relished by the surging crowd. Mr. Weekes, Lowe's seconder, drove the wedge home :—

Who so fit (he asked) to represent them as Mr. Lowe? Had he not stood almost alone in the late Council? Would they allow such a man to be the representative of some fifty bark huts in a distant district? If they returned Mr. Wentworth, they should take care to send in Mr. Lowe to look after him. Mr. Lowe was the only man in the colony able to grapple with that intellectual giant.

As might naturally be supposed, these observations had a decidedly ruffling effect on Wentworth, and he proceeded to abuse the new popular idol in his most vigorous style. Nor did he fail to remind the electors of the splendid eulogy which Lowe had passed upon him, when they were political allies, on occasion of the Wentworth Banquet. ' Only two years ago this man,' he said bitterly, ' had heaped praises on me—had, in his flattering, eloquent way, designated me as the great son of the soil.'

When Lowe came forward he was received with rapturous applause, again and again renewed. Silence being at length obtained, he addressed the electors with the utmost animation and vigour. He began by saying that he stood before them in a very peculiar position. He was not a candidate for the representation of the city. He had not solicited a single vote. He had not either addressed or canvassed the electors. But a number of gentlemen who approved of the principles which actuated his conduct in the Legislative Council had thought fit to give their support to those principles, and had that day put him in nomination.

Then, point by point, he calmly reviewed his own public

career, and met the plausible taunts of Wentworth as to his inconsistency ; with emphasis he declared that it was the squatters who had lost sight of their political principles, not himself : —

I have been consistent in fighting for liberty ; the squatters have been consistent in fighting for money. I would remind Mr. Wentworth that, at the very meeting at which I praised him, he had said that he spurned ' fixity of tenure,' which he was now so anxious to retain. Mr. Wentworth had then declared that he sought no tenure beyond that of occupation until the land was wanted for sale. When Mr. Wentworth made that declaration I thought of him only as a patriotic and gifted son of the soil, and in the simplicity and folly of my heart praised him as an example to the rising generation.

Electioneering crowds in Australia are among the quickest in the world to seize a point or appreciate a palpable hit, and this sample of the ' retort courteous ' was loudly cheered. The battle thus begun was fought out to the bitter end. It was soon seen that though Wentworth's own seat was impregnable, that of his old friend and follower, Bland, was by no means secure. Wentworth, like a wise general, employed all his strategy to defend the weak spot in the citadel. ' Whatever your verdict may be with regard to myself' (he declared), ' if it be the last public service I am to render you, I charge you never to forget your tried, devoted, indefatigable friend, William Bland.' It was all of no avail. When the poll was declared it was found that the candidates had polled as follows : —

Mr. Wentworth	.	.	.	.	.	.	1,168
Mr. Lowe	.	.	.	.	.	.	1,012
Mr. Lamb	.	.	.	.	.	.	950
Dr. Bland	.	.	.	.	.	.	874

After the declaration of the poll Lowe returned thanks in a speech of great force and fervour, saying that if he were to live for a thousand years, and to employ the whole of the time in contesting elections, he could never again expect to achieve so signal a triumph. And what made it the more

valuable in his eyes was, that it was not a mere personal
triumph, but a triumph of the political principles which he had
stood almost alone in vindicating.   It is surely a singular
thing that the future English statesman, who in after years
showed the greatest distrust of the *vox populi*, should have
thus been returned by pure popular enthusiasm, without any
solicitation on his part, and at no expense to himself.[1]
Despite the fierce contest, he spoke in the highest terms of
his colleague's political capacity:—He knew of no man in
Australia, no man out of Australia, with whom he should be
more proud to act; nay, if Mr. Wentworth would but regard
public affairs from a national, and not a merely personal
standpoint, there was no one whose leadership he should be
more proud to follow.

Notwithstanding his deep distrust of the worth and stability
of the wealthier classes, Lowe advocated the immediate establishment of responsible government, or, as he expressed it, the
giving to the people ' the power of expending their own money
and making their own laws.' He despaired of the ' petty
aristocracy ' of the colony, which was banded together to
uphold a giant monopoly opposed to the public interest. And,
just as he had learnt to distrust the pastoral class, so he
could not look to the mercantile interest to support him in his
desire to promote the welfare of Australia—an interest, he
declared, that had long been rocking to and fro—now in the

---

[1] 'The committee who conducted the free election of Mr. Robert Lowe beg
to lay before the electors the following statement of their gross receipts and
expenditure, and to append acknowledgments of the appropriation of the surplus
to the funds of the Benevolent Asylum and the Sydney Infirmary :—

	£	s.	d.
Total amount of receipt . . .	118	10	9
Total amount of disbursements in the election . .	109	8	3
Half surplus to Benevolent Asylum	4	11	3
Ditto Sydney Infirmary	4	11	3
	£118	10	9

Aug. 23rd, 1848.   W. COLEMAN, *Treasurer.*'

insolvent court, now out of it—without stability, without consistency. He would as soon think of building a fortress on an earthquake as he would of depending on a class like that. To the pick of the working classes alone, the skilled artisans and the sober, vigorous, free immigrants, could he turn in his hope of a brighter future for the land of Australia.

Many, on reading this declaration, will rub their eyes, and doubt if this can indeed be a faithful echo of the warning voice that so eloquently denounced the widening of the franchise in England, and the admission of the working classes to a share in the government of this country. It was the same voice, the same man ; the essential difference lay in the circumstances. Robert Lowe at this period saw no salvation for Australia save in the worth and manhood of the free, untainted working-class immigrants—the honest, plodding toilers from English fields and cities ; above all, the shrewd Scotch artisans of skill and character, such as Dr. Lang was sending out. These were beginning to pour into Sydney ; and it was Robert Lowe's most earnest hope that they would overpower and eventually root out the 'rotten seed' with which the land had been so freely sown.

That his words about the working classes were no mere politic flattery of the mob is at least clear enough ; for he wound up by telling the working men of Sydney who had returned him that, while he promised to listen to their representations, he reserved to himself the right of exercising unfettered his own judgment. In the excitement of the hour his hearers may not have noticed the significance of these words ; but they were no idle utterance. However, the proceedings of the day terminated by the new member being dragged home in triumph by the people in Alderman Wilshire's carriage.

Robert Lowe keenly appreciated the honour conferred upon him, as the following letter—the last written by him from Australia—will sufficiently show :—

Robert Lowe to Mrs. Pyndar of Madresfield.

Nelson Bay, near Sydney: August 17, 1848.

My dear Grandmother,--I cannot allow anyone else to deprive me of the pleasure of telling you of a very great compliment which I have recently received, and which, in our little community, is quite as important, and looked upon as quite as great a distinction, as if I had been appointed a member of any provisional government. I was requested on the recent deposition of our little Colonial Parliament to become a candidate for the City of Sydney, which is a very considerable place, containing a population to the number of 50,000, or one quarter of the whole Colonies. I declined the honour, but the people would not be refused, and without my becoming a Candidate, returned me after a very severe contest, in which a great deal of money was spent, and immense exertions made against me. It is gratifying to me, and will, I hope, be so to you, to find that in this remote place I have been able to create for myself so strong a feeling in the minds of so many of my fellow-colonists, and to reflect that for this, and all else of good that I enjoy, I am indebted entirely to your generosity, which has saved me from an odious drudgery which, I am firmly convinced, would have ended in the loss of my health and sight. I hope most sincerely to hear by the next ship as good accounts of you as we had by the last. No one knows better than I do how great a misfortune it is to have the use of the inestimable organs of sight in any way impaired. But even this I find the mind may be schooled to bear, and I know no one to whom their eyes have been a source of such inestimable pleasure as to you.

How strange this new French Revolution must seem to you, like a dream of the past which you must so well remember. The historical parallel is very striking : the fixing the rate of wages and food, the intimidation by the mob under which all parties act, and under which the new Constituent Assembly will meet like the old National Convention.

My wife begs to join me in kindest love to yourself and your guests.

Believe me always
Your grateful and dutiful grandson,
ROBERT LOWE.

This was written to his mother's mother. She, too, it will be seen, had sympathised with him in his trials and struggles.

CHAPTER XXV

MEMBER FOR SYDNEY

Port Phillip declines to send Members—Lowe's Letter—Earl Grey elected for
Melbourne—Lowe and the Sydney Unemployed

DURING the progress of this Sydney election Lowe told the
electors that it appeared to him somewhat doubtful whether
the newly-elected members would ever take their seats in the
Legislative Council. The reason of this strange announcement was that certain leading residents in the then district of
Port Phillip (now the colony of Victoria) had openly expressed
their determination not to elect any members to the Sydney
Legislature. This caused great alarm in Sydney, and the
Herald of August 2, 1848, appeared with a startling leading
article headed, ' The Port Phillip Conspiracy to Strangle the
Legislative Council ' :—

'A set of hare-brained fellows having on the day of nomination at Melbourne determined that no members at all should
be returned from that part of the colony, and having thereby
caused the returning-officer to retire from the hustings without the means of endorsing a single name on the back of his
writ, the very grave question arises, Will it be competent for
the Legislative Council to sit ? '

It was on this grave constitutional question that Mr.
William Kerr, town-clerk of Melbourne, and founder of the
Argus newspaper, wrote to Mr. Lowe, and received the following reply, which is of historical interest so far as the present
colony of Victoria is concerned. It will be noted with pleasure,

by all Victorians worthy of the name, that there had actually
been a movement on foot to nominate Lowe as one of the
members of the province :—

Robert Lowe to the Town Clerk of Melbourne.

Sydney : July 29th, 1848.

Dear Sir,—I beg to acknowledge the receipt of your letter announcing to me the decision of the constituency of Port Phillip not
to elect any members at all, and the consequent abandonment of
the intention which you were so kind as to entertain of putting me
in nomination to represent the electoral district of Port Phillip.
You will have heard before this reaches you of the result of the
Sydney election, which has been equally gratifying to me and con-
firmatory of my principles.

I merely allude to it to show you that I am perfectly disinterested
in the suggestions which I take leave to offer to yourself and my
brother-colonists of Australia Felix. All who take the trouble to
read the proceedings in Council are well aware that I have always
endeavoured to give Port Phillip fair play, and have never joined in
the dead set which has been most injudiciously and improperly
made against it by men who ought to have had more enlightened
views, and to have treated with more deference and respect the
unanimous opinion of the province. I trust, therefore, you will
receive my advice as that of a friend anxious to serve you, not of
an enemy anxious to mislead you. My opinion is, that you are
acting unwisely in not filling up the seats of your six representatives.

I do not presume to give an opinion whether it is better for the
province that those seats should remain vacant than be filled up by
such persons as have hitherto been sent, and as a colonist of the
Middle District I must candidly say, that if Port Phillip sends us
nothing but gentlemen who confine their attention to inflating the
price of land and the amount of Government expenditure, we are
better without such gentlemen than with them. It is a mistake to
say that the absence of the Port Phillip members will throw us more
into the hands of the Government. For the last two or three years
the Port Phillip members have contributed much to the strength of
the Government—nearly as much as the nominees of the Crown ;
but what I am afraid you have done, or at any rate will do if you
persist in the same course, will be to prevent the Legislative Council
from being constituted, so as to proceed to the despatch of
business.

As regards the Squatting Question, this is much to be regretted.
The election seemed to incline against the squatters in the Middle

District, and I feel confident that the nominees of the Crown will be of the same way of thinking.

Thus, had the Council been allowed to meet, had Port Phillip merely elected five members who absented themselves from the sittings of the Council, I should have been able to have brought this struggle for the preservation of the lands of the colony to a successful issue ; but now every selfish and unworthy influence is left at liberty to be employed upon the Government, and the lips of those who would speak for the colony are sealed.   Every effort will be used to induce the Government to make intermediate districts as small and the unsettled as large as possible.   Whether it resists this pressure or no will mainly depend on the strength of the anti-squatting party in the Council.   That party you, in your zeal for separation, will not permit to act, and thus you hand over your beautiful district to the clutches of a despicable monopoly, from which ages of the most enlightened and patriotic exertion may not suffice to free you.

I would also beg to suggest that your contumacy—for such it will be regarded by the Home Government—though it will probably accelerate the period of your separation, will probably render that separation much less advantageous to you than it would otherwise be.   As a friend of freedom, I should much regret to see you handed over to a nominee Council, or, what is still worse, to a Council elected by local cliques, elected according to Lord Grey's nostrum.

I cannot believe that if you abdicate your franchise now you will get it back at the time of separation.   It appears to me, that in your natural desire to get rid of us you are abandoning your lands to the squatters and your franchise to the Crown.   I would, therefore, beg respectfully to recommend you to fill up the seats of your districts with five anti-squatters, which I apprehend you are well able to do ; but if you do not choose to be represented in the Legislative Council, at any rate fill up the vacancies; and thus give the Council an opportunity of meeting, and of fighting with the squatters on your behalf that battle which you seem unwilling to fight on your own.

If you think the publication of this letter will serve any good purpose, it is much at your service.

I am, dear Sir,

Your obedient, humble Servant,

ROBERT LOWE.

William Kerr, Esq., Melbourne.

Mr. Kerr published this letter in the *Argus* on August 11 ; but in the meantime the ' hare-brained fellows ' of Melbourne had disfranchised themselves, as the writ had been already returned without any name having been endorsed on the back of it. The Sydney Government, however, consented to re-issue the writ, but, to punish Melbourne, made Geelong the place of nomination. It was then that the enterprising residents of Port Phillip determined on a sensational *coup* in order to bring their great grievance home to the minds of the English authorities. To show the absurdity of the system by which the affairs of their province were conducted by half a dozen gentlemen in the remote city of Sydney, the separation party nominated (of course without asking consent) the Duke of Wellington, Lord Brougham, Lord Palmerston, Lord John Russell, and Sir Robert Peel. This farcical proceeding was intended to show Earl Grey how absurd the then existing system had become. They even went further, and actually elected Earl Grey himself as the member for Melbourne in the Legislative Council of Sydney.

The Colonial Secretary, little knowing what these irreverent Port Phillipians were capable of doing, was duly proposed and seconded in opposition to a widely-respected local squatter, Mr. John Fitzgerald Foster, a gentleman who subsequently became Acting-Governor of Victoria, and who, in compliance with the will of his uncle, Lord Fitzgerald and Vesey, assumed those names by which he is known to this generation. Mr. Vesey Fitzgerald still lives to tell the members of the Carlton Club how he contested Melbourne in 1848, and was beaten by the 'phantom Earl.'

The poll was declared on August 26 as follows :—

Earl Grey	295
Foster	202

It was a pure frolic, but it gave a great deal of trouble to the Sydney Government, and made the Sydney newspaper fairly frantic. 'An affair of treason against the majesty of common-sense'; 'its perpetrators deserve to be whipped';

'a forfeiture of the franchise': such were the journalistic comments.

We think (says the *Herald*) Earl Grey, when he comes to know of the Melbourne atrocity, insulting to the noble Lord's own person, as well as to the Imperial Legislature, will pronounce the people of Port Phillip unfit for the franchise, and will give them a Council of Crown nominees.

Earl Grey himself, however, took the matter in a much lighter spirit when chaffed in the House of Lords about being the new member for Melbourne. The proceeding, however, was not so purely farcical as it looks, and, as a matter of fact, Earl Grey had to plead formally a want of qualification as the reason for not taking his seat in the Sydney Legislative Council. The Crown law officers declared his election to be valid, but that, should he allow two sessions of the Council to elapse before going to the Antipodes and taking the oaths, then his seat as member for Melbourne would be legally vacant. It was, indeed, a thoroughly characteristic colonial device for forcing on the attention of the Secretary of State a specific grievance, and there can hardly be any doubt that Earl Grey's sham election expedited the creation of the colony of Victoria and the granting of Australian self-government.

Robert Lowe had not very long been member for Sydney before he exhibited to the working classes in a very characteristic way that independence of judgment of which he had forewarned them on the hustings. Sydney, from that day to this, has always been more notorious even than Melbourne for what are called 'meetings of the unemployed.' Like all cities, young or old, Sydney has always had what the late John Bright called a *residuum*; that is to say, a number of utterly unfit or miserably unfortunate persons who, especially in democratic communities, clamour for State assistance at all times of personal distress or public difficulty.

After the triumphant return of the 'popular idol' a

number of these men, who had called a public meeting to air their grievances, were thoroughly taken aback by the reply which they received from the new member for Sydney. Writing to a Mr. Cunninghame, who, it seems, was editor of a journal called the *People's Advocate*, and had organised the meeting of unemployed operatives, Mr. Lowe thus replied to the invitation to attend :—

Sir,—I must beg to decline to attend your meeting for the following reasons :—

Because the revenue (which is principally raised from the wages of the people) ought to be expended for the good of all, and not of a particular class.

Because it is just as improper to spend public money to keep up wages as to keep up rents or profits.

Because I do not think the mechanics of Sydney ought to put themselves in the position of paupers receiving charitable relief at the expense of their equally distressed fellow-colonists.

Because those who anticipated an immediate profit from the intended expenditure are the worst possible judges of its necessity.

Because the attempt to prevent labour finding its level must, in my opinion, be either useless or mischievous.

Because I will never be a party to spending public money in order artificially to raise the price which employers of mechanics in the interior must pay for their services, and thus to arrest the progress of improvement throughout the colony.

I have stated my reasons thus at large out of respect to the meeting, with whose wishes I regret it is not in my power to concur,

And I remain, Sir,
Your obedient servant,
ROBERT LOWE.

Sydney : December 19, 1848.

The meeting was fairly aghast. It is true that two other well-known members of the Legislative Council also wrote declining to attend; but their letters were of the vague and shuffling description. As soon as the assemblage could recover itself, a Mr. Lynch rose in a frenzy to his feet—and anyone familiar with such public meetings can hear the rich roll of the Irish brogue in these disjointed and indignant sentences :—

You have been termed paupers ! And that by the pet of the people ! For your pet, Robert Lowe, on the evening of the election, from his own verandah in Elizabeth Street, declared that the mechanics, the working men of Sydney, were the only real freemen in the colony. And now, by Heaven ! 700 to 1,000 mechanics are walking about Sydney idle. . . . We applied to two country members, who declined to attend, but did not write such an insulting document as our own city member. Every syllable of which (hissed out by Mr. Lynch) grated on the ear. [The audience demanded to hear Mr. Lowe's letter again, and it was read accordingly]. In the name of God! (yelled the exasperated Mr. Lynch) what does he mean ? If the money was given by the Council to the mechanics, would they keep it buttoned up in their pockets ? Would it not every Saturday be expended with a small shopkeeper, from whom it would travel on to the middleman and the merchant ?

A subsequent speaker, in a somewhat more connected and relevant manner, said that though he was one of Mr. Lowe's most enthusiastic admirers, he could scarcely believe his eyes when he first saw this letter. Mr. Lowe had declared himself the representative of the mechanics of Sydney, he had applauded their public spirit, and told them that they were the real people of the colony. Now he refused to support them, on the ground that they were a class.

This is quite enough of the oratory of these early leaders of the unemployed movement. It was inevitable that they should quickly fall to loggerheads with the new member for Sydney—a city which to this day so many of their kind have loved so well that no offer of regular work ' up-country ' can ever induce them to leave it. Robert Lowe had now a much weightier question on his hands, for Earl Grey had set about in earnest to re-introduce the evil system of transporting the criminals of the old country into Australia.

CHAPTER XXVI

ROBERT LOWE AND EARL GREY

EARL GREY was possessed by the laudable ambition of enrolling his name among those whom the late Walter Bagehot terms ' nation-builders.' In a remarkable despatch to Sir Charles Fitzroy, published in Sydney on December 25, 1847, the Colonial Secretary elaborated a new political Constitution for Australia. This scheme, to which he had evidently given a considerable amount of thought, proved so unpalatable to the colonists that even this masterful Minister was forced to abandon it when Sir Charles Fitzroy informed him that it had met with universal condemnation. Briefly, Earl Grey proposed that the district councils, those languishing and, indeed, all but non-existent bodies, should form ' electoral colleges' for the purpose of returning a representative assembly, while a second Upper Chamber was to be composed entirely of Crown nominees.

The immediate effect of the publication of this scheme was to reunite Lowe and Wentworth. In fact, all the leading colonial politicians and the whole body of the electors ranged themselves into one solid, overwhelming Opposition. A meeting was promptly held to consider Earl Grey's new Constitution, with the Mayor of Sydney in the chair, when resolutions were passed expressing astonishment and regret that a mere modification of the old close-borough system should originate with the son and representative of the noble earl to whom Britain was indebted for the Reform Bill.

It is unnecessary to quote the full text of these resolutions, although they bear evident traces of the handiwork both of Lowe and Wentworth, who were the two most prominent figures at this meeting. The resolutions were indeed withdrawn, and a committee appointed consisting of a number of leading and representative public men of that day in New South Wales, of whom Robert Lowe and W. C. Wentworth, from a political point of view, were decidedly the foremost.

This committee at once organised a great public meeting, which was held on January 21, 1848, in the Victoria Theatre. The pit and boxes, we are told, were densely thronged, while the stage was crowded with the 'most influential gentlemen of the colony of every shade of political opinion.' It was on this occasion that Mr. (afterwards Sir James) Martin made his first notable speech in Sydney; while among the other speakers were Mr. Archibald Michie, Mr. S. A. Donaldson, Mr. James Macarthur, and other leading colonists. But the two great guns were, of course, the members for Sydney —Wentworth and Lowe; now standing again side by side on the same platform. Next day the *Sydney Morning Herald* referred to 'that brilliant orator, Mr. Robert Lowe, whose eloquence on such a theme is the more impressive from being associated with a professional knowledge of the law.'

This unstinted praise is by no means too lavish. It is not possible to read even a summary of this speech without recognising its power and brilliancy; as stated with regard to some previous colonial speeches, it is probable that Mr. Lowe never rose to loftier flights in England. Indeed, it is evident that in one respect he was heard in these early days of the colony to greater advantage; for in Australia he took rank not only as a foremost speaker in Parliament, but as a most moving orator at mass meetings.

The burden of his discourse was that, instead of accepting

Earl Grey's pedantic constitutional experiment, it would be wiser for the colonists of New South Wales to transplant as far as possible the Constitution of the mother-land. This, indeed, was the burden of all the speeches, notably of Wentworth's. Such an enthusiastic and united expression of public feeling could not be ignored even in Downing Street ; and on receipt of Sir Charles Fitzroy's despatches this scheme of Earl Grey was promptly abandoned. The Colonial Minister, indeed, met with equally hostile criticism within, as without, the walls of the Legislative Council.

On May 2, 1848, Wentworth, in a speech of great argumentative power, brought forward in the Council a series of resolutions against this new Constitution of Earl Grey. His chief supporter was Robert Lowe, who spoke enthusiastically of Wentworth's 'clear and luminous speech, entitling him to the thanks of the country and the House.' He went on to say that he agreed with nearly every word uttered by his colleague ; but he would enter into a friendly discussion with him on the advantages of the bicameral system.

It was true they could not have a house of dukes and marquises like the House of Lords. Nor did he think, let it be composed of whom it might, that it would command much respect, but there were plenty of men fitted for it. As to a chamber entirely composed of nominees, he held that it would be unconstitutional for it to take part in money votes.

Wentworth, who had once again become filled with democratic ideas, wound up what was really a very great night's debate with unflagging ability. 'Give the Governor this shelter,' he declared in his denunciation of Upper Houses, ' and let what will arise, he might sit quietly in some snug parlour of his palace, where the gale of popular opinion or indignation could never reach him.'

It was to this speech that the late Lord Sherbrooke made special reference after he had returned to London, when he delivered his luminous address on the Australian Colonies Bill

before the members of the Society for the Reform of Colonial
Government in 1851, on which occasion Sir William Molesworth presided.[1]

Upon the withdrawal of Earl Grey's scheme, the English
Ministry handed over this constitutional problem to a committee of the Privy Council. But the usual delays, not to be
wondered at in the settlement of so grave a question, ensued,
and it was not until after endless discussions in the British
Parliament that the present system of responsible government
in Australia was established. By this time Robert Lowe had
left Australia and become once more a citizen of London, and
was indeed a member of the House of Commons.

Before his departure from New South Wales, Lowe was
called upon to take a yet more prominent part in opposition
to another and more dangerous innovation on the part of
Earl Grey. On this subject he had no longer the powerful
support of his colleague, but had to face instead the combined
forces of the Crown officials and those of the dominant
squatter party led by Wentworth himself.

This question was Earl Grey's attempt to renew criminal
transportation, the frustration of which may be regarded as
the turning-point in the history of Australia. To no part of
his colonial career did Lord Sherbrooke look back with greater
pride than to the decisive stand which he took against the
policy of Earl Grey on this question. And rightly so, for he
manfully assisted to make Australia what she is—an uncon-
taminated, self-respecting and self-governing English community—instead of what she was intended to be, and what so
many of her own sons would have liked her to remain—a
wealth-producing, but utterly degraded penal settlement.

In a previous chapter, the one entitled 'Mr. Gladstone's proposed Penal Colony,' some slight fore-glimpse has been given
of the state of public feeling in Australia about this time with

regard to the transportation of British criminals. In that
chapter it was pointed out how strongly popular feeling was
excited when Sir Charles Fitzroy published Mr. Gladstone's
despatches. This arose from the ever-increasing number of
free, untainted immigrants, who had made their home in this
new world at the Antipodes, relying on the express declaration
of Lord John Russell, that from 'August 1840 transportation
to New South Wales would cease for ever.' Earl Grey was
now the Colonial Minister, and several years had elapsed since
this fiat had gone forth. In the meantime, owing mainly to
the untiring efforts of Dr. Lang, numbers of sturdy Britons,
in the prime of life, full of energy, with good practical abilities,
and with unblemished characters, had made Australia their
adopted country. It was from this ever-increasing body of
genuine colonists that Earl Grey was to receive his most severe
rebuff and Australia to secure her freedom from imported
criminality.

It has been shown that the squatters as a class—and they
then formed the dominant class in New South Wales and Port
Phillip—were strongly in favour of the revival of transportation.
This is revealed in the most unmistakable manner by the
correspondence that passed between Dr. William Bland, representing the 'Australian Patriotic Association,' and Charles
Buller, the deeply lamented young English statesman, whose
death was in no ordinary sense a loss to the Empire. Earl
Grey, a man of the highest ability, who without doubt as
Colonial Minister gave more time and attention to the Colonies
than has any English Minister before or since, now made a
fatal blunder. He was unfortunately a man of the *doctrinaire*
type—one who was likely at a crisis to evolve a cut-and-dried
scheme without duly taking into consideration the temper of
the people upon whom he was prepared to experiment. I
have already stated that a new and ever-increasing class of
free immigrants had been for some years past pouring into
Australia, and that these men and not the few hundred

squatters, with their vassals the ' ticket-of-leave men,' would
now decide whether Australia was to become a free and worthy
English State, or to remain in great part a remote Imperial
penitentiary.

It was at this critical period that Earl Grey devised what
he doubtless considered to be a new and most innocuous system
of transportation. The cargoes of criminals were no longer
to be known as ' convicts,' but (such is the virtue in a name!)
as ' exiles.' It was, as Earl Grey explained in his despatch
of September 3, 1847, ' a scheme of reformatory discipline.'
These ' exiles ' were to be sent to the colonies only after they
had undergone a term of imprisonment in Great Britain, and
in all cases ' the wives and families of such exiles, together
with a number of free emigrants, equal to the number of such
exiles, shall be sent out at the cost of the British Treasury.'
Truly a nice-sounding scheme with a brand-new beautiful
name—but meaning in plain unofficial language that Australia
was to remain the ignoble receptacle of British rascality.

Mr. Lowe at first adopted a cautious and tentative attitude
with regard to this question of the revival of criminal transportation. There is an old saying, ' Once bitten, twice shy.'
He had already found that by throwing the weight of his great
eloquence and talents on the side of the squatters, he had not
so much helped them to assert their constitutional rights, as
he had unwittingly enabled them to secure a monopoly of
almost all the land of South-eastern Australia. This was
indeed a severe lesson, and the very hardest which, as a public
man, he was forced to learn in the strange school of colonial
experience. Absolutely independent, and then, as always,
beyond the reach of those personal ties and considerations
which warp the judgment and opinions of even honest men,
he now found, owing to his previous alliance with the squatters,
that he could not utter a syllable without being taunted with
inconsistency, if not with mere caprice.

Robert Lowe, under the circumstances, no doubt felt that

it behoved him to be wary. He saw—no man so clearly—that the squatters, having got possession of the public lands, now wanted as a further boon a supply of unpaid labour to work them. The eagerness of Wentworth and his henchman, Bland, in supporting Mr. Gladstone's crude experiments in transportation, and later on the more systematic scheme of Earl Grey, became daily more and more apparent. From the first, Wentworth, in the Legislative Council, warmly supported 'exileism' and proposed a series of Resolutions on the subject on April 10, 1848. In the course of the debate Lowe merely insisted that, if this new plan were put into operation, the colony should at once demand military protection at the expense of England, and Imperial loans for public improvements. It must be frankly admitted that up to this time Lowe had expressed no strong indignation against criminal transportation. On the contrary, he spoke with great caution and moderation, and apparently in the tone of a man not altogether averse to a somewhat perilous social experiment. Read between the lines, however, his speech on this occasion showed clearly enough the direction in which his mind was trending. Turning to the squatters, now, in conjunction with the Crown officials, the absolute masters of this primitive semi-representative Parliament, Lowe warned them that their visions as to what the effect of this measure might be were perhaps rose-coloured.

The results look brighter in the vista of anticipation than in reality. It reminds me of an elegant engraving in a recent number of the *Illustrated London News* of a thriving town in the remote parts of the colony, with houses erected, streets laid out and built on, and where a beautiful harbour, crowded with vessels and crowned by a magnificent lighthouse, appeared in most majestic picturesqueness.[1]

There was nothing yet, however, to show that Lowe meant to separate himself still more widely from his old

---

[1] Probably the city which Mr. Benjamin Boyd projected on these lines, on the shores of the still desolate Twofold Bay.

squatter friends and allies by directly opposing them on the transportation question. In fact, when he sat as a member of Wentworth's special committee, he did nothing to show any distinct divergence of view, save that he 'heckled' Mr. Benjamin Boyd rather vigorously. But when in the year 1848 Earl Grey thought fit to revoke Lord John Russell's policy of 1840,[1] and to revive criminal transportation throughout the whole of Australia, Robert Lowe ranged himself with the popular democratic party against the squatter and official aristocracy.

We shall have now to contemplate the late Lord Sherbrooke in a character that may well astonish those who knew him best. From the moment that Earl Grey attempted to revive criminal transportation, not only to the whole of Australia, but also to South Africa, in defiance of local public feeling and without any of the conditions as to sending out the wives and families of the 'exiles' and an equal number of free immigrants, Robert Lowe stood out in the streets and public places of Sydney as the leading 'agitator' of the day. It is not difficult to divine that it was the arbitrary methods of Earl Grey, as much as the evils of his transportation policy, which so aroused the fury and the indignation of this strange popular Tribune.

It is rather unfortunate that the only systematic work deserving the name of a history of Australia should have been written by a gentleman who was at this time engaged in

[1] Great credit is due to Earl Russell, but he was merely a bird of passage. It was his successor, Lord Stanley, the late Earl of Derby, who was head of the Colonial Office from 1841 to 1845, to whom Australia owes that long respite from imported convictism which enabled her free population eventually to get the upper hand. This wayward statesman, but great English noble, deserves, on this account alone, a statue in every capital city of the Antipodes. Had Lord Derby put in force, during these years, the transportation policy afterwards adopted by Lord Grey, he would have met with little or none of the strenuous opposition in the Colonies themselves, which proved too strong for that ill-fated minister; and it is difficult to see how Australia could ever have emerged from being an Imperial penitentiary.

pastoral pursuits in New South Wales, and was therefore a
supporter of 'exileism.' But though Mr. Rusden loses no
chance of sneering at the anti-transportation leaders, he is
compelled to confess that Earl Grey acted in a most wrong-
headed and impolitic fashion. Be that as it may, the Colonial
Minister acted promptly; he sent out his shiploads of convicts, first in the *Neptune* to the Cape of Good Hope, where
the colonists refused to allow them to land, much to the delight
of John Mitchell who was a prisoner on board, and of course
loved to behold the Saxon at strife with his kind. After a
weary delay, the captain had to sail away and land his criminals
in ill-fated Van Diemen's Land, now the fair island of Tasmania,
from which it will be remembered Mitchell subsequently made
his escape by in reality, if not technically, breaking his parole.

By the Order in Council of September 1848, Earl Grey, in
defiance of Australian sentiment, had, on his own initiative,
once more made Australia a penal settlement. It was now
1849, and during the last two years public feeling had intensi-
fied. The most prominent anti-transportation leader up to
this time was Mr. (afterwards Sir Charles) Cowper, who in after
years very fitly rose to be Prime Minister of New South Wales,
and later on its official representative in London. The people
in the then comparatively small township of Melbourne,
emulating the colonists at the Cape, refused to allow the 'exiles'
to land when the first convict ship sailed into the waters of
Port Phillip. Mr. Rusden's comment on this is simply that
'Melbourne, as usual, was demonstrative.' To my mind,
considering that Mr. Rusden for so many years filled the responsible post of Clerk of Parliaments in Victoria, and that he was
one of the most prominent and most favoured residents of
Melbourne, this bald comment in a voluminous history is unworthy of himself as well as of the occasion. There were men
quite as respectable and quite as law-abiding as Mr. Rusden
(for one, the Chief Justice of Victoria, Sir William Foster
Stawell) among those 'demonstrative' early colonists, who

marched down to Hobson's Bay with the view, if necessary, of
preventing by force the landing of this first batch of Earl
Grey's criminal hordes.

Mr. Rusden, who requires three bulky volumes to record
the more or less parochial affairs of Australia, dismisses the
historic action of the residents of Melbourne in preventing the
landing of these convicts by a short contemptuous phrase.
This seems to me a strange way of writing Australian history,
and I much prefer the allusion to this episode made by Sir
Archibald Michie in a popular lecture delivered some years ago
at St. George's Hall, Melbourne : ' Take the convict question,
for instance, on which public opinion here once showed itself
nearly to the point of rebellion, when a large body of spirited
colonists, amongst whom was the present Chief Justice (for
which I honour him), marched down to Sandridge, resolved
that a newly arrived cargo of convicts, per ship *Hashemy*,
should not land here.' [1]

The convict ship *Hashemy*, being unable to land her cargo
at Melbourne, sailed for Port Jackson with a view of deposit-
ing them in Sydney. It was then, on July 11, 1849, that
Robert Lowe appeared in his new *rôle* of Tribune of the People.
The vessel had been looked for from day to day by crowds
scanning the harbour from the quay-side. When, at last, the
convict-ship entered the far-famed Heads, and sailed up the
lovely expanse of blue waters, the leading merchants on the
wharves and the chief shopkeepers in the city closed their
establishments and quietly, but resolutely, proceeded with
hundreds of their fellow-citizens to the open space above the
Circular Quay. Here the only coign of vantage was a dis-
used public vehicle, from the top of which the speakers, in full
view alike of the convict-ship and the Governor's residence,
addressed the assembled thousands, standing in the pelting
rain. To make the scene still more dramatic, there lay at

[1] *A Lecture on the Westminster Reviewer's Version of Victorian History.*
By the Hon. Archibald Michie, Q.C. (Melbourne, 1868.)

anchor, almost alongside the *Hashemy* with her felons, a number of emigrant ships full of free untainted English men and women eager to become Australian colonists and settlers.

The crowd awaited patiently their accepted leader, the popular member for Sydney, but Mr. Lowe came not. At length Mr. Robert Campbell, a much respected merchant, was called on to preside. A loyal but strong protest was then read by Mr. Lamb against the re-introduction of British criminals, when suddenly Robert Lowe made his appearance amidst enthusiastic applause, and proceeded to second the adoption of this protest ' of the people of the colony of New South Wales against the outrage which had been so insultingly and offensively perpetrated upon them.'

The new Tribune was in excellent form ; and, after reading some of his fine denunciations we may well believe the story related by Mr. Rusden of the old woman in the crowd who, unable to restrain her enthusiasm, exclaimed, ' Ah ! bless his dear old white head ! '

The threat of degradation has been fulfilled. The stately presence of our city, the beautiful waters of our harbour, are this day again polluted with the presence of that floating hell—a convict ship. In the port lies a ship freighted, not with the comforts of life, not with the luxuries of civilised nations, not with the commodities of commerce in exchange for our produce, but with the moral degradation of a community—the picked and selected criminals of Great Britain—educated in her crowded streets, among her starving masses. New South Wales must be the university at which these scholars in vice and iniquity must finish their course of instruction. New South Wales must alone supply the college where these doctors in crime can take their last degrees.

Lowe then reviewed, in a series of short, pungent sentences, the action of Cowper and himself in the Legislative Council in opposition to Wentworth, who, it will be borne in mind, was his colleague in the representation of the city of Sydney. But even when, full of indignation against the high-handed methods of Earl Grey in forcing British criminals on the colony, Lowe was not able to speak for long without reverting to the question of the public lands. He viewed, he said, this attempt to inflict a degrading slavery on the colony only as a sequence to the recent confiscation of the public lands by the squatters. 'That class had felt their power—they were not content to get the lands alone; without labour they were worthless—and, therefore, they must enrich themselves with slaves.'

This was not a question of the injury which the 250 felons on board the *Hashemy* would do the colony. It was a question whether the inhabitants of this colony should be subjected to the contamination of trebly convicted felons, and whether they should submit to a measure to enhance the value of their confiscated lands. It was not the mere fear of competition amongst operatives which now united them on this question; it was not a mere breeches-pocket question with the labouring classes, though it might be with the employers. It was a struggle for liberty—a struggle against a system which had in every country where it prevailed been destructive of freedom.

Lowe closed with a most eloquent warning in reference to the loss of the American colonies; and the protest which he had seconded was put to the vast meeting and passed with acclamation.

Then uprose a young artisan who has for many years been the most celebrated public figure in Australia, but who on this occasion, as he declared, was the mouthpiece of the 'largest class in the colony—the working class.' It was in this vein, as a working class representative, that Mr. Henry Parkes spoke throughout with marked force and ability. Save as a working man, he said, it would have been unwise and presumptuous in him to detain the meeting longer; but this was pre-eminently a workman's question.

Did the 1,400 emigrants now afloat on the waters of Port Jackson believe when they left Great Britain that they would find a convict-ship in the midst of the vessels that brought them hither? Would they, had they dreamt of such a thing, have sacrificed all home ties and volunteered to degrade themselves? The only course consistent with justice to the colonists at large was that the convict-ship and cargo should be sent back.

After Mr. Parkes had finished, Mr. (now Sir Archibald) Michie moved that—

A deputation be appointed to wait immediately upon the Governor with a protest, to request him to forward it to the Queen, and that the deputation consist of the following gentlemen :—
The Chairman (Mr. Campbell), Mr. Robert Lowe, Mr. Lamb, Mr. Nicholls, Mr. Michie, Dr. Aaron, Mr. Parkes, Mr. R. Peek, Mr. Heydon, Mr. Coleman, Mr. Hawkesley, Mr. R. Curtayne, Mr. Knight, Mr. E. M'Encroe, Mr. Pembroke, Mr. Strong, Mr. Ham, Mr. Mullins, Mr. J. R. Wilshire, Mr. Simmons, Mr. Jennings, Mr. C. Kemp, and Mr. Gilbert Wright.

This somewhat formidable host at once proceeded to Government House, but Sir Charles Fitzroy, who appears to have discovered that worry and anxiety might beset a man even in that ' delicious climate,' would seem to have lost all his usual *sang froid*. In fact, what between Earl Grey, the convict-ship in the harbour within sight of his windows, and the deputation clamouring at his gates, Sir Charles, for an old soldier, had quite lost his head. He sent out to say that only six gentlemen could be admitted to his presence, and the gates were then promptly closed against the others. Lowe was of course one of the six. The private secretary, doubtless in the inimitable manner of his class, then proceeded to inform the favoured half-dozen that it would be necessary to forward a copy of the protest in writing to Sir Charles, who would appoint a time to receive the deputation and return an answer.

In due course this was done, and a request was at the same time forwarded to his Excellency asking him to appoint a time when he could meet them. And so, for the time being, the proceedings at the Circular Quay ended. ' The meeting ' (says the *Sydney Morning Herald*) ' dispersed without any noise or tumult, and the conduct of the people throughout was grave, decorous, and becoming.'

On the following Monday, June 18th, a public meeting, called by the ' Deputation Committee,' was held on the same spot.

Lowe, who was received with enthusiastic cheering, begged to read the resolution which was put into his hands—

That, considering the discourtesy shown by His Excellency the Governor to the former meeting and to its deputation, this meeting abstains from appointing a deputation to wait upon His Excellency with the preceding resolutions and address, but requests the Chairman to transmit them to him, with a written request that His Excellency will be pleased to forward them to Her Majesty the Queen for her gracious consideration.

He began by saying that he was rather at a loss to know why he had been pitched upon to move this resolution, unless it was that they had selected him ' to bell the cat '— and if such was the case, ' bell the cat he would.' This was, of course, taken as a preliminary attack on Sir Charles Fitzroy, and was lustily cheered accordingly ; but Lowe said that he was not inclined to deal harshly with the Governor, as he believed that that gentleman entertained a kind of languid sympathy with the colonists, and would even help them so long as by so doing he did not risk his reputation with his masters in Downing Street, or imperil his own situation. But Sir Charles Fitzroy had rescued Port Phillip from the infamy of receiving the criminal cargo, which he now wished to inflict on Port Jackson. Both harbours were in the same colony, and the Governor's conduct was, therefore, a direct insult to the people of Sydney. Lowe then proceeded to give a very graphic account of the precautions taken by Sir Charles Fitzroy to guard against the presumed violence of the previous meeting.

The gates of His Excellency's palace were closed, a double military guard with bayonets fixed, as if expecting an attack, was stationed there, the cavalry of the colony—the mounted police were quartered in the stables, and the kitchen of the house, filled with soldiers, was garrisoned as kitchen never was garrisoned before. All these precautionary measures against any attack on the person of the Governor took place for what?—because the people had met peaceably, calmly, but determinedly, to protest against the grossest outrage that had ever been perpetrated on any community.

What did the friends of Sir Charles Fitzroy say for him in excuse on this occasion? That he was afraid! He a 'soldier and afeard!' He, an old Waterloo hero, and afraid of a few people, shivering and hungry, and who would have been most glad to have got rid of the duty entrusted to them as quickly as possible! He knew well that the object of the people in meeting on the former day was to discuss this convict question, not to attack his palace; and, although the Governor might have been frightened, there was no intention to frighten him.

At least (added Mr. Lowe with great gravity), I did not intend to frighten him, and, if I have done so, I beg his pardon, and hope never to do so again.

But what had the Government to be frightened at? Did they take the deputation to be robbers and murderers? If Sir Charles Fitzroy wanted to look for such characters, better for him to go and seek them on board the convict-ship in the harbour. Great disrespect had been shown to the people, in that, out of a deputation of twenty-three gentlemen sent to Government House by the meeting held last Monday, only six were admitted. What was the reason of this? Was the Governor afraid of his silver spoons, or did he think the deputation would proceed to a general sack of the house, and drink all the claret in his cellars? Or was it thought sufficient that six pair of dirty shoes should be allowed to intrude upon the viceregal carpet? Surely in this matter the people had met with great insult. Then, again, the deputation had reason to complain of the manner of their reception when they were admitted to the viceregal presence. It was very natural that they should, beyond merely formally presenting the protest and resolutions to His Excellency, desire to have a little conversation with him. They endeavoured to do so, but they did not succeed.

For my own part, I can say that I behaved much more civilly than usual. I was unusually polite, and yet the deputation, instead of being allowed to address anything to His Excellency, were quietly and coolly bowed out of the room. The fact is that the Governor of a colony is necessarily surrounded by parasites and sycophants, who are always anxious to keep him from any presence save their own. There was also a certain class of paid officials, who, though their principles might be of a higher and better character, still were anxious to advise His Excellency to measures which would enable them to retain their own salaries. To these two classes only was the Governor generally accessible, and it was not, therefore, surprising that he should not be very well pleased to meet a deputation from the people.

Having disposed of the Governor, Robert Lowe took a higher flight, and proceeded to defend a resolution asking Her Majesty to dismiss Earl Grey from her Council.

He said that though this course might appear foolish and quixotic to many persons, it would have an appreciable effect on the English Government, and on English public opinion. It would be a most effective way of showing that New South Wales resented this policy of criminal transportation. He then proposed a resolution in favour of the establishment of responsible government. Lowe's principal argument was given in this form :—

There were forty-five dependencies of the British Crown ; of these, some few had responsible government ; these few were limited to Canada, New Brunswick, and Nova Scotia. Was this invitation to receive the convicts of Great Britain sent to those colonies ? Dare the Government have sent it ? No ! But here, mocked as the colony was with a wretched mongrel imitation of representative legislature —in the Cape of Good Hope, without any representative legislature at all—in South Australia, in Van Diemen's Land, and in New Zealand, with their wretched Nominee Council, the people were solicited to receive the convicts of Great Britain.

What stronger illustration could be advanced in favour of the necessity of responsible government ? How many hours, how many minutes would this question have been discussed had responsible government prevailed ? The very entertainment of such a question by any Government would have been sufficient for its decisive destruction.

He then declared that the existing government of New South Wales was a small second-hand bureaucracy. He went very far indeed in denouncing the lavish expenditure entailed on the colonies by the Imperial authorities, and even urged the policy which Lord Granville carried out many years afterwards, of the removal of British troops, which he declared were useless in Australia.

He said, and with truth, that it was far too much the habit of the men in office in England to regard the Colonies as intended, not for the benefit of the bulk of the English people, and as the great means for the expansion of our race, language, laws, and religion ; but merely as places where their sons and relatives could be provided for with light berths at heavy salaries. There is no one who has studied the history and development of colonies, from the late Sir George Cornewall Lewis down to the humblest scribe in a remote bush newspaper, who has not found out that this is one of the chief reasons why Crown dependencies have, as a rule, been utter failures compared with those colonial communities which have acquired the right of managing their own affairs.

Lowe illustrated the broad distinction between a love for, and loyalty to, the traditions and inheritances of the English race and a mere submission to Downing Street officialism, by the following apt allusion to the battle of Waterloo :—

To-day is the 18th of June ; thirty-four years ago a victory, the greatest, the most decisive, the most important, the most noble that had ever graced the annals of a civilised nation was achieved by the valour, the unconquerable energy, of British soldiers. Many amongst those who stood around him might be the descendants of the heroes that fought that day. Those heroes did not brave death on that occasion, they did not obtain that great and glorious victory, to provide for the sons and nephews of officials only. It was not for that that they fought and bled—it was for the rights of their country and their kind ; and base would the men of Australia be if they sat down contented with one shadow less of the rights which those soldiers, their ancestors, earned for them with the sword, and which they had bequeathed to them.

' The meeting dispersed quietly, and it is our duty,' writes the *Herald*, ' to say from our own experience of such assemblies in the home country, a more respectable, (in every sense) a more calm, peaceable, and well-conducted political meeting could not take place in any portion of the British dominions.'

These two monster open-air meetings, in which it will be

seen that the late Lord Sherbrooke was altogether the principal figure, did much towards the settlement of the question of the transportation of criminals into Australia. None of the convicts on board the *Hashemy*, says Mr. Rusden, were allowed to be employed in the metropolitan county of Cumberland; they were removed 'up country' at the expense of their employers, or sent on by sea to Moreton Bay. The convict ships that subsequently arrived at Port Jackson were compelled to carry their cargoes also to this northern settlement, now the flourishing colony of Queensland.

It was some years before transportation ceased throughout Australia. But by the refusal of the district of Port Phillip to receive the prisoners on board the *Hashemy* and the public protests headed by the late Lord Sherbrooke when that vessel appeared in Sydney Harbour, the transportation policy with which Earl Grey had so unfortunately linked his name received its death-blow. The subsequent resistance to this evil and ill-considered policy, which flourished for some time longer so rankly in Van Diemen's Land (Tasmania) and in Western Australia, led to the banding together of the various colonies in an anti-transportation league. This was the actual beginning of that policy of colonial co-operation, based on the feeling of colonial interdependence, which must eventually lead to Australian Confederation.

CHAPTER XXVII

THE CLOSING YEAR IN AUSTRALIA

Lowe's Attack on the Sydney Corporation— Proposed University for Sydney—
Challenged by Dr. Bland—Lowe's Offence to the ' Emancipist ' Class— Sails
for England - A Footnote on Stanley, Gladstone, and Grey

ROBERT LOWE'S colonial career was now drawing to a close.
He retained his seat in the Legislative Council as member for
Sydney until the last ; and he also continued to take an active
part in public affairs almost up to the very hour of his
departure. There were, indeed, two public questions in which
he took a most prominent part during his closing year in
Australia. One was the motion to abolish the Sydney Corporation ; the other was the Bill to establish the Sydney University.

On September 9, 1849, Lowe proposed the adoption of the
report of a select committee recommending that the Sydney
corporation should be abolished. His speech on this occasion
might well startle a generation dry-nursed on county councils.
But the select committee of which he had been chairman had
indeed drawn up a report in favour of the abolition of the
corporation—mayoral robes, aldermanic dinners, and all—and
it was in support of this dreadful thing that Lowe delivered
not the least remarkable of his colonial speeches.

Certainly his arguments for the abolition of municipal institutions generally, and the municipality of Sydney in particular,
will sound strange in the ears of most men whether ' Progres-
sives' or ' Moderates,' Liberals or Conservatives. But Robert
Lowe had the rare merit (if it be not rather a defect in a politician) of never being commonplace ; and consequently, whether

one agree with him or not, it is generally refreshing to follow the line of his arguments on any subject, enforced as they always were by a clear, pointed, and vigorous phraseology.

If we look to the origin of municipal institutions, he declared, we find that they were commenced in barbarous times in order to do in a bungling way that business which the Government could not do itself. They were the offspring of the Feudal system, and it was absurd to say that because they were then useful in protecting the many against the few, the weak against the strong, that such elective boards are specially fitted to look after the cleansing and lighting of modern cities.

It was mere cant to affirm, parrot-like, that the elective principle should always be upheld. No less an authority than Edmund Burke had asserted that popular election was in itself a great evil only to be endured because it sometimes obviated a greater. There was no inherent virtue in popular election; like all human contrivances it could only be tested by *results*.

If in any case the good did not exceed the evil, let them discard the elective principle altogether.

There had been elective monarchies, but I have yet to learn that I am guilty of anything unconstitutional when I say that I prefer hereditary monarchies. There have been elective judges, but I have yet to learn that I am guilty of anything unconstitutional in saying that I had rather see the judges of the land appointed. There were elective magistracies, and I know not why I should be deemed unconstitutional because I wish the magistrates to be appointed rather than elected. And by the same reasoning, it was not unconstitutional to seek to divest the Municipal Corporation of Sydney, and all other municipal corporations, of the elective principle. The question, therefore, narrowed itself to this, not whether the course proposed is constitutional, but whether the elective principle, as applied to corporations, is attended with beneficial results.

. . . .

In this age belief in municipal institutions will be exploded. Reverenced by antiquarians, they are condemned by economists; they have ceased to be bulwarks against oppression and sanctuaries of freedom; and they have proved themselves to be totally un-adapted for administrative functions.

This was the general line of argument which Lowe adopted; but when he went on to support the petition of 2,600 of the citizens of Sydney for the abolition of their corporation, he adduced some very startling local facts. He declared that the expense of working the corporation had been about 90 per cent. on the gross expenditure; and that instead of improving the city council was growing worse daily, ' until it had at last reached the lowest point of municipal pessimism.' Why should such an unsatisfactory and corrupt body be perpetuated? In this connection he even denounced what he called the ' pot-house argument,' that there should be no taxation without representation. In the face of its misdeeds the city council had approached the House to ask for greater powers and extended funds; but the House would not fulfil its duty if it lent any ear to such a request. Year after year, as mayoralty succeeded mayoralty, no one had taken the trouble to look into the city expenditure and receipts; the collectors had never been called on to give an account of their stewardship, until, almost by accident, defalcations to an unknown extent were discovered.

Becoming epigrammatic, as was his wont, Lowe alleged that municipal bodies ' combine the maximum of dilatoriness with the maximum of rashness.' He then dragged to light some of the evidence given before the select committee, which would seem to point to the fact that Sydney could boast a kind of infantile but thriving Tammany Ring in the year 1849. According to this evidence, the tenants of councillors' houses were invariably employed on the city works; and the ' houses of a councillor were always tenanted when the said councillor was on the Improvement Committee, and mostly untenanted when he was not.' The great thorough-fares of Sydney had been neglected, while roads on the very outskirts had been put in complete repair—roads in which there were no houses or traffic, but which skirted the private property of some enterprising city father.

Mr. Lowe went on to say that what he as a taxpayer wanted was to see the streets cleansed, drained, lighted, and paved in the most efficient and most economic way. In lieu of the idle frippery of mayors, aldermen, and councillors, he would appoint—not *elect*—a body of paid commissioners. These commissioners would have a plain, businesslike duty before them, which they could perform without any long speeches before or after dinner. He therefore moved—'That the Acts incorporating the city of Sydney ought to be repealed.'

A lively debate ensued, in which Wentworth and the Colonial Secretary bore the chief part against him and his select committee. Lowe replied at considerable length and with remarkable vigour. It had been urged by Wentworth that the great achievement of the Whig Government was the passing of the Municipal Reform Acts. This, Lowe admitted, was an achievement; not so much for what it did, as for what it undid. It served to sweep away the old rotten corporations; but since the passing of these Acts, into such great contempt had these institutions fallen, that it was with difficulty people could be found to accept office in them.

The motion on being put to the vote was lost; but, strange as it may seem, public feeling in Sydney was undoubtedly in favour of the proposal to abolish its own city council. Commenting on the debate and the division, the *Sydney Morning Herald* observed: 'Many of them would have preferred that the resolutions had been carried in their original integrity; but all must be pleased that the charge preferred by Mr. Lowe's committee has been declared proven, and that to this long-neglected and deeply-injured city something like justice is at length to be done.'

Three nights afterwards, Lowe rose to withdraw certain resolutions of which he had given notice in favour of the immediate establishment of responsible government. His reason for doing so, he said, was that Mr. Hawes, the Under-Secretary of State for the Colonies, had given a pledge in the House of Commons for the alteration of the Constitution of the Australian Colonies. His second reason for requesting to withdraw his motion was that his political friends and supporters considered the time inopportune owing to the disturbances in Canada. He himself had found nothing in what he read of the proceedings in Canada to justify any opposition to the granting of self-government to Australia ; but these circumstances weighed more heavily on the minds of his friends, and so he consented most reluctantly and most unwillingly to withdraw his resolutions.

The question, however, on which Lowe took the most prominent part during this closing year was Wentworth's Bill for the foundation and endowment of a University in Sydney. Lowe was, indeed, at first, Wentworth's warmest supporter in this matter, and was nominated as one of the original members of the Senate.[1]

This plan of Wentworth's in nominating the members of the Senate off-hand was resented : first by Mr. James Martin, who was not included in the list, and subsequently by Mr. Lowe, who was. Furthermore, Lowe objected to the manner in which Wentworth had attempted to rush the measure through the House, and to the presence on the proposed Senate of Wentworth's friend Bland, who, though a man of some education and of good standing in Sydney, had had the misfortune to have been transported in the earlier days to the colony for his share in a duelling transaction in India.

[1] The names of the Senate as proposed by Wentworth were as follows :—
Sir Alfred Stephen, Chief Justice ; Edward Deas Thomson, Colonial Secretary ; J. H. Plunkett, Attorney-General ; Charles Nicholson, Speaker ; W. C. Wentworth and Robert Lowe, Members for Sydney ; James Macarthur ; S. A. Donaldson ; Edward Hamilton ; William Macleay ; Hastings Elwin ; William Bland ; Francis Merewether ; E. Broadhurst ; A Denison ; Matthew Henry Marsh.

At the same time Wentworth had proposed to exclude the clergy altogether from the governing body of the University. This anomalous state of things caused Robert Lowe to make a characteristically pointed remark which led to some unpleasantness at the time. ' It would take much discussion,' he said, ' to convince that House that it was a good principle to exclude the clergy as a body, and to admit convicts into the government of such an institution.'

Bland was no longer a member of the Council, but at once applied to be enabled to present a petition in defence of his social fitness to take his place on the University Senate. But though in no sense of the word an ordinary criminal, for it was admitted that he had committed no offence that a man of the highest rank at that time would have blushed to own, still, he was an ' emancipist' ; and, under the circumstances, it was eminently injudicious on the part of Wentworth to place him in what was in reality a false position. The Legislative Council ruled that the petition of Bland was inadmissible ; and he then issued a challenge to his assailant couched in the most violent terms. Such matters as these should be lightly passed over, as things done in the heat of the moment ; certainly no friend of Bland (who it will be remembered had attended Lowe during the period when he was threatened with blindness, and who knew well that he was almost as disqualified for duelling as a man born blind) would repeat the charges he thought fit in his anger to make against the personal courage of one who, throughout life, was absolutely deficient in the sense of fear. Mr. Archibald Michie obtained a rule *nisi* on behalf of Mr. Robert Lowe calling on William Bland to show cause why a criminal information should not be filed against him for attempting to provoke a breach of the peace.

It is noteworthy that the Chief Justice, Sir Alfred Stephen, and his two colleagues, in their very impartial judgments, deliberately declared that Bland had no just cause of offence whatever.

The debate (said Sir Alfred Stephen) turned upon a principle of
vital importance to this colony, and to the proposed University, viz.
whether persons who had been transported to this colony were
eligible to be on the Senate. That question was fairly debated, it
was argued, by Mr. Lowe as a question of principle, and no particular
reference was made to Mr. Bland, nor was his name mentioned.

Sir Alfred added that—

From the bench he could only recognise Mr. Bland, for the
purpose of the debate, as one of those who came to the colony as a
convict. Off the bench, he had the highest esteem for him, for his
very good qualities ; he knew that his case was a peculiar one, and
had been distinguished from others by society here.

This affair passed over harmlessly. But the ' emancipist '
class was then numerous and influential enough to make its
resentment felt. This was a consideration, however, that would
never have made Lowe hesitate to express his views with the
greatest force and freedom. His attitude in regard to this
question of the Senate was regarded not only as a personal
attack on an individual, but as a clear denunciation of an
entire class, and from the point of view of his own ease and
comfort it was most injudicious. The profound hostility of
many old colonial settlers to Lowe may be attributed to the
stand which he took in trying to exclude the ' emancipists '
from the University Senate.

The constitution of the original Senate, however, was not
the only point on which Lowe widely differed from Wentworth.
In Wentworth's scheme of a University it was provided that
when the number of graduates amounted to fifty, they should
elect their own Senate. According to Lowe's forecast this
meant that at the end of six years the management and
government of the University would be in the hands of these
local graduates ; and as certain of these would hail from the
other colonies,[1] it meant that the University would be placed
' in the hands of some twenty or thirty Sydney youths who had

[1] The totally different social conditions of Australia in 1892 to some extent
nullifies this criticism ; but the provincial spirit is still strong.

never been out of the colony, and knew nothing of University matters whatever.'

This fact should be noted, he said, by the scholars from the home Universities who might be invited to Sydney to fill professorships. It was in discussing this part of Wentworth's University scheme that Robert Lowe, as far as I have been able to glean, showed for the first time his deep dislike to that narrow provincial spirit which, it must be confessed, is so sadly prevalent in all colonial communities. His words, spoken almost five and forty years ago, are true to this day, and could be pondered with advantage not only in the city in which they were delivered, but in every city and township of Australasia.

When that collegiate Millennium should have arrived, in which age should give way to youth, experience to inexperience, in which, in all probability, the narrowest local and provincial sentiment should take the place of a broad, general, and catholic spirit, then perhaps might flourish the principles so much in fashion among the native youth with their favourite maxim, ' Australia for the Australians!' Then might the new senate, with its handful of local youthful graduates, appropriate the ample salaries provided for the professors to appointments of their own making of men chosen from amongst themselves. Those who knew anything at all of University manners —those who had mingled in a world wider than this scattered community - would be the first to admit the danger and to dread all such inducements to the fostering, especially in a seat of learning, of a narrow and provincial standard of excellence.

Without any allusion, open or covert, to Bland's case, Lowe, in this really excellent speech, in which he scattered so much good counsel as to the lines on which the first university in Australia should have been laid down, thus referred to his own Oxford experiences ; in doing so, he boldly grasped that dangerous and unpleasant ' emancipist' question, which most of the members found it so much more convenient to ignore.

I was for eleven years at the University of Oxford, I have taught in that University, and can say that out of the hundreds of high-minded young men with whom I became associated as their tutor there was barely one who would have consented, for the largest sum of money, to sit as a professor under a direction in which any person who had been transported for crime could form a member. If the Council wished to ruin their infant University, let them ignore this warning; then must they fall back on the native talent before alluded to. They might command a kind of talent from England, but a talent without honour and without character; an importation that would do but little for the fame and stability of their University.

Wentworth was, however, determined to rush his University Bill through the Council and to nominate whom he chose for the Senate. With all his great qualities, his superb energy, and his naturally broad imperial views, by long domination over inferior men in a small isolated community Wentworth had himself degenerated into an overweening provincial. He was, moreover, the accredited leader of the old squatter oligarchy, which was unfortunately closely associated with so much that was evil as well as so much that was good in the social condition of early New South Wales; and thus, as Goldsmith so happily says, he

Narrowed his mind,
And to party gave up what was meant for mankind.

The consequence of Lowe's opposition to these provisions in the University Bill was that the measure was rejected. In a very fair and impartial leading article entitled ' The Fate of the University Bill ' (*Sydney Morning Herald*, October 12, 1849), Wentworth is entirely blamed for this misadventure. That remarkable man, however, in October of the following year, succeeded in passing the measure, and so he may justly be regarded as the founder of the first University established in Australia. By this time Robert Lowe had returned to England, and for a brief while Wentworth held undisputed sway in the Legislative Council of New South Wales. Under the new Constitution, however, he was to find himself entirely overthrown by the new democratic forces of the time. In September 1851, when Sydney sent three members to the new Legislative

Council, Wentworth was the lowest on the poll of those returned; while his chief opponent, Dr. Lang, triumphantly headed it. Wentworth felt the blow acutely, and the rest of his life was chiefly spent in retirement in England, where he died, in his eighty-first year, at Marleigh House, Wimborne, Dorsetshire, in 1872.

By this time the late Lord Sherbrooke had attained to his highest distinction in the Imperial Parliament; but there is no record to show that he and Wentworth ever met during the last sixteen years of the life of the latter in this country.

To revert to the closing year of Robert Lowe's sojourn in Sydney, it is worth pointing out that almost up to the very last hour he took an active part in public matters which he thought likely to advance the interests of the community. As late as January 8, 1850, we find him attending a meeting of the Sydney Railway Company, of which the late Sir Charles Cowper was in the first instance president and afterwards manager. On this occasion Lowe made a most sensible and businesslike speech, showing the great importance he attached to the development of the country by means of railway communication. It will be borne in mind that what are now the large and flourishing capital cities of Australia, connected by an enormous trans-continental railway system, were then, with the exception of Sydney, mere isolated bush townships. In his opening remarks at this meeting, Lowe announced that he should not be much longer in the colony to ' watch the progress of this great national work ; ' but none, he said, took a deeper interest in it than himself. He was a large shareholder—indeed, he believed the second person to take shares in the Sydney Railway Company—

The first being the late respected Mr. James Simmons, a gentleman whose public spirit, and whose zeal and confidence in the establishment of railways in this colony, made his death a severe loss. Had Mr. Simmons been present that day, I am sure we should have found him ready to support, with his sound judgment and calm common sense, not the interests of any man or of any party, but the interests of the great object we have in view in the establishment of railways. I for one trust that the result of this meeting will be the healing of all our differences and the concentration of all our energies to that one great end. I shall be proud to go home and be able to proclaim that no other British colony had yet dared to attempt the establishment of railroads out of her own resources, except the depressed and trampled-on dependency of New South Wales.

Lowe then delivered a very warm eulogium on the tact and business-like abilities of Mr. Cowper, who was forthwith appointed manager by the meeting.

Cowper subsequently devoted himself exclusively to the affairs of the Sydney Railway Company, until it was absorbed by the government, when he returned to public life, and afterwards became Prime Minister of New South Wales.

Robert Lowe had for some time made up his mind to resign his seat in the Legislative Council, and return to England. He would not in all probability have taken the step when he did, but would have preferred to remain in order to bear his part in the first Colonial Legislature under responsible government ; but Mrs. Lowe's health had become seriously impaired, and for some time past her one desire had been to return to her friends and her native land.

Accordingly, on January 27, 1850, Mr. and Mrs. Robert Lowe, with their young charges, the orphan Jamieson children, sailed from Sydney in a small vessel for England.

To the deep disgust of his most active constituent, the present Sir Henry Parkes, Robert Lowe was permitted to leave the colony without that 'farewell banquet' which now marks the departure of every pushing politician or popular player, who looks upon it as a necessary advertisement in his precarious calling.

In closing this record of the brief but brilliant colonial career of the late Lord Sherbrooke, it may not be amiss to

add a few sentences by way of a footnote on the three remarkable English statesmen who filled the office of Secretary of
State for the Colonies during his sojourn in New South Wales.
These were : Lord Stanley (the late Earl of Derby), who was
Colonial Secretary from 1841–5 ; Mr. Gladstone, who held the
office for less than a year; and Earl Grey, whose tenure
lasted from June, 1846, to February, 1852. Readers of these
pages cannot fail to have noticed that Lord Sherbrooke
denounced the official actions of each of these three remarkable men with absolute impartiality. He was, however, always
careful to point out to his fellow-colonists that the evil was
in the system, and not in the particular politician who might
happen to represent the Colonies in the English Cabinet and
Parliament. Still, to many English readers, Lowe's words
and actions towards Lord Grey may seem too harsh, especially
when it is borne in mind that this high-minded and assiduous
nobleman sacrificed his political career in the cause of colonial
self-government. It was this self-sacrifice which made so
kindly and impartial a critic as Mr. R. H. Hutton, declare,
' Earl Grey is one of the wasted forces of politics.' To Lord
Derby, and still more to Mr. Gladstone, the tenure of the
Colonial Office was but a brief and passing episode in a great
and successful public career, terminating in each case in the
Premiership of England. But Earl Grey will only be
remembered as the Colonial Secretary. He probably gave
more time and attention to the Colonies than any half-dozen
other Secretaries of State. To him undoubtedly belongs the
credit of establishing the system of responsible government,
though Lord Stanley had initiated the parliamentary system
in Australia. But Lord Grey well nigh destroyed his boon
by saddling it with unworkable conditions. Moreover, he irretrievably ruined his reputation in the Colonial communities,
for which he had sacrificed so much and laboured so diligently,
by his determination to revive the evil practice of criminal
transportation.

ENVOI

In his latter years, Lord Sherbrooke frequently reverted to these early times in New South Wales. Often he would express a desire to revisit the once so familiar scenes—his old home at Nelson Bay; the beautiful gardens of his friend, William Macleay, at Elizabeth Bay; his favourite township of Goulburn, and the fair and fertile region of Illawarra.

'But I might not recognise them,' he would say; 'all will be changed.' He, however, always declared that he would be able to find his way in the well-remembered streets of Sydney, and to recognise almost every stone in the older portions of that still picturesque city. If at any time he chanced to refer to the fierce political battles of those days, he invariably added, 'no doubt I made many mistakes!'

It must be admitted that he had excited considerable personal antagonism, but at the same time he enjoyed a far greater measure of popularity than, to his own regret and to the misfortune of his country, ever fell to his share in England. I do not think, however, that he could have remained for long the Tribune of the People even in Sydney; there were indeed signs that his popularity would have inevitably waned. He was, with all his great gifts, his high courage, his earnest convictions, his skill in debate, and his frequent flights of genuine and most moving eloquence, a man not made to woo the general ear. He was constitutionally unable to condescend either to platitude or cant, which are absolutely essential to win, or at least to retain, popular favour; and he would always have felt it a personal degradation to secure the votes and voices of the crowd by pandering to prevailing prejudice or popular ignorance.

Such a man can be known only to intimate friends or kindred spirits —and these will ever be few. At every turn he is sure to have his motives, his words, his actions misrepresented or misunderstood. The great mass of mankind are, in one sense, not so much to blame ; for it is a distorted image, and not the man himself, that is presented to their dim vision. It is always this image which they passionately reject or passionately acclaim.

I have often speculated on Lord Sherbrooke's actual reflections and feelings as he sailed out of Sydney harbour in 1850. In later life he saw it all through the softening haze of years, and would merely express his regret that he had never found time to revisit Australia. On the eve of his departure he in all probability regarded things differently, and was perhaps not sorry to quit the place and close his colonial career.

But had he been a man consumed with self-complacency and prone to keen appreciation of his own merits and abilities, he might have reviewed the eight years of his colonial life with no little personal gratification as he gazed on the quickly receding shores of that country in which they had been passed. He was still in the prime of life, with his brave wife by his side confident as ever of his coming greatness. With his own fine brain and resolute will, unaided by friends or favour, he had achieved success, and even a measure of fame. At all events, in Sydney, as at Winchester, he had ' effectually shown by a most crucial experiment that he was not too soft for the business of life.' He had now secured, so to speak, a firm foothold in the world ; it was quite open to him to try what fortune awaited him in his native land. And he had laid the foundations of his fortune purely by hard work in defiance of difficulties and by honourable means that knew no deviation.

He had taken from no man his due, nor had he turned his public trusts to private ends.

It would be untrue to say that Lowe either liked the social life of Sydney or respected the tone of public morality in the colony. Popular as he became with the masses, there were things that deepened rather than destroyed his innate distrust of the unreasoning passions and prejudices of the 'many'; while, with regard to the 'few,' he saw much that must have made him almost despair of the future of Australia.

To Robert Lowe remained the one supreme consolation—he had fought the good fight. His eight years had been indeed one long battle against Colonial Secretaries, Governors, Society, Squatters, Emancipists—one unceasing battle. But, with absolute truth he could have declared that he had drawn the sword only for the well-being of the people to whom he would become little more than a passing stranger, and for the future greatness of the country that he was never again to behold.

INDEX

TO

THE FIRST VOLUME

—◆◇◆—

END OF THE FIRST VOLUME

PRINTED BY
SPOTTISWOODE AND CO., NEW-STREET SQUARE
LONDON